PATHFINDING WOMEN

WAXWOOD SERIES: BOOK 3

TAM MAY

Pathfinding Women
Waxwood Series: Book 3
Tam May

Quotes in the text are as follows:

Thoreau, Henry David. *Walden*. Pandora's Box Classics.Original publication date 1854. Kindle digital file.

Luke 6:37, New International Version

DEDICATION

To Aila and Becky for their encouragement and support of my work.

CHAPTER 1

Want more feisty Gilded Age heriones who go against conventions? Love intricate mysteries with humor and a fun cast of characters? Then you'll love my free offer at the end of this book! So don't forget to check that out when you get to the end. Happy reading!

The inhabitants of Washington Street, the bluest of the Nob Hill blue bloods, engaged in the most malicious gossip when one of their own got married or died, and Emma Miller's wedding in the spring of 1899 was no exception. As Vivian leaned against the tree in Mrs. Bilton's lavish garden, shaking away the hornets from the nest hidden among the overgrown vegetation, she marveled at how their words poisoned the sweet April morning. She was still recovering from the venomous talk at her grandmother's funeral seven years earlier.

The current tongue-lashing was not toward any hitch in the wedding ceremony itself, for Mrs. Bilton helped Beatrice Miller to arrange everything, including the reception. Larissa, Vivian's mother, had been eager to host the breakfast at Alderdice Hall where she had had the gazebo repainted that fall, and the flowers were just merging their delightful scents with the pleasant breeze of the early morning spring. It would have been, her mother said, a step toward reinstating themselves into the good graces of Washington Street society after what her mother had called "that fiasco with your brother last year."

But Beatrice declined Larissa's offer with a chilly apology, informing her Mrs. Bilton had agreed to set up the breakfast in her garden. Vivian wondered whether Mrs. Bilton did it deliberately so Beatrice could have the prerogative of refusing Larissa whom, Vivian had to admit, had always treated her distant cousin as if she were offering crumbs off her table.

Since the Washington Street magpies could not very well speak ill of a wedding reception arranged by one of their own shining socialites, they had chosen a more formidable target, the newly completed City Hall. The group near the gazebo comprised the original socialites and their daughters headed by Amber Griffith and Coleen Wingham, ladies still young, though not as young as the most recent wave of debutantes.

"The plaza faces the entrance," Amber was saying. "We need not bother with Market Street at all now."

"Just as it should have been in the first place," Coleen said with a nod. She married Ezra Wingham only two years before but was already speaking as if she were native-born by latching herself on to Amber's skirts. "A city hall ought not to be part of the city landscape when it is so close to the downtown, as it's in San Francisco."

"That Gothic dome is very impressive," Mrs. Marsden, a timid woman, ventured.

"Baroque, dear." Mrs. Breen corrected her as she corrected every affront to social grace that she deemed worthy of her attention.

"Yes, yes, of course," the woman muttered.

"After twenty-seven years, I think we deserved a new city

hall." Mrs. Wingham helped herself to two lumps of sugar in her coffee. "The old one was quite fine, but the new city hall—"

"Quite fine?" Though Vivian had promised herself to remain silent, she couldn't help but speak up now. "It was a monument to this city's blundering politicians!"

All the ladies glared at her as if to remind her she and her mother had been asked to the wedding primarily because of their family ties to the Millers.

"I'm sorry." She slunk back against the tree.

"Rather blasphemous words coming from the lips of a young woman," grumbled Mrs. Breen. "Your mother oughtn't to allow you to read about politics and such."

All the ladies turned as if one body to gaze at the corner not far away. Larissa had placed herself at the disposal of Mrs. Moodie, the groom's rather elderly and deaf mother, whose age excused her lack of discretion.

"My mother has given up trying to tame my tongue," said Vivian with a sweet smile. "I don't doubt my peers' words are as blasphemous as mine, though they don't speak about politics."

"We at least don't meddle with radical reforms, Vivian," Amber said in her ice queen way. "Miss Moore's opinions are not welcome here."

Mrs. Griffith, Amber's mother, who had joined the group just in time to hear the conversation, agreed, adding, "She has become too liberal with them as of late."

"The blue-stocking of Washington Street has an ally now, Mother," Amber said.

Vivian's head throbbed as it always did when something stirred the rage inside her like a hurricane. But she remembered her mother's admonition before they left the house: *We must tread with them as if they were eggshells about to break.* So she continued to smile, saying nothing.

Beatrice came then, her bright yellow dress sending a streak of blinding light against the dark green hues of that overgrown corner of the garden. Her cheeks were like two cherries, and she had been out of breath all day, though her step was, as usual, slow. "Doesn't Emma look lovely?" she gasped.

"I told you the cream would suit her better than the white, dear, didn't I?" Mrs. Breen smiled, patting her arm.

"And Mr. Moodie is so — so—"

"Refined," Lona Marsden Lenville, Mrs. Marsden's daughter, supplied with a bashfulness equal to her mother's.

"Yes, yes." Beatrice grabbed her wrist. "Thank you." She twittered away.

All eyes turned toward the bride, a rather scarecrow figure in her loose lace dress, the veil sitting a little tilted back on her head. Mr. Moodie, the groom, was, in contrast, a rather rotund fellow whose balding head shone like crystal under the morning sun, as he had taken off his top hat, holding it as if he were unsure of what to do with it.

Amber spoke first. "They make a rather awkward couple, don't they?"

"I've always been of the opinion one's husband should look as if one belonged in his company," Coleen stated, not without a little pride in her voice. She and Ezra looked more like brother and sister than man and wife.

"You mustn't fault her, dear," said Mrs. Breen. "After all, considering the circumstances—"

"Well, Emma turned twenty-eight last May, didn't she?" Mrs. Griffith asked.

"She went about it rather cleverly," said Mrs. Breen. "She got Mr. Moodie to stay in town after the New Year, just when Mrs. Lawrence insisted that he had to go back to see to his mother in Boston, and completely turned his head. Who would have thought?"

"When a woman is determined not to be a spinster—" Amber's eyes were like a fly's.

"Yes, she was rather keen on that," said Lona. "Well, she *was* the last of us without a husband and surely every set must have its old maid."

Here, Vivian felt they were all looking at her, although none of the heads turned in her direction. She bit her lip hard to keep from speaking out and, putting her hands behind her, began the ladder game where she counted from the thumb up to the last finger and down again. It did not have the soothing effect that it did when she was a child.

The tongue-lashing ceased, and the conversation switched to summer plans.

"The Lawrences are going to Catalina Island." Mrs. Griffith pulled the lace jacket around her ample bosom. "They say the fishing there is excellent."

"It's so hot down in the southern part of the state," said Mrs. Bilton.

"Mrs. Lawrence," said Mrs. Griffith with authority, "was telling me just the other day there are far too many tourists invading the city in the last few years."

"Well, that *is* a blessing for some, Leila," Mrs. Wingham pointed out.

"Fieldstone has those salt baths," offered Mrs. Breen. "Matthew has such a bad back from working at that bank all day, I think I ought to persuade him to take a few weeks off in August and join us there."

"We're going to Fieldstone," Mrs. Marsden said with a quivering chin. "There will be such a mad rush to the Cardinal. It's the best hotel in town, you know."

"We know," said Mrs. Breen, glaring at her. Then, she turned to Mrs. Griffith, who was the leader of their society. "What about you, Leila?"

"We'll be going to Waxwood this summer." The woman picked up her teacup.

The mention of Waxwood made Vivian grab the rough edge of the tree, the wood splintering her hands inside her lace gloves.

Mrs. Griffith cast an eye toward Vivian. "We had quite a lovely time there last year, didn't we, Vivian?"

"A lovely time," she murmured.

"The Tishers will be there again," said Mrs. Griffith. "Fern has become quite the belle of the season in New York, so I'm told."

"A shame your brother is away just now, or he might have caught her interest." Mrs. Bilton had now joined the party. "Jacob is a good-looking young man, as I recall." She eyed her. "He won't be back this summer, I gather?"

Vivian's hand raked against the tree to keep from bursting into tears, but her answer was short and composed. "No, ma'am."

"I forgot you know the place well," Mrs. Breen perked up.

"Not very well." She glanced at the corner where Larissa was still with Mrs. Moodie. As her mother reached toward the old woman with a fresh cup of coffee, Vivian realized her mother's hand was a little unsteady.

"Didn't your grandmother have quite an adventure there a long time ago?" Amber asked.

"Why, dear, that must have been forty-odd years ago!" Mrs. Breen laughed.

"Forty-five," Vivian said in a quiet voice.

"Oh, how clever of you to remember." The woman grimaced.

"It's changed so, of course," said Mrs. Griffith. "They've been making quite a showing in that little town in the last five or six years."

"Yes, I've heard Waxwood isn't merely a drab summer hamlet," Mrs. Bilton said. "They've made it into a rather succulent little resort place. Some businessmen got wind of it. That lovely little bay and the mountains and those too-ancient trees, what do they call them?"

"Wax wood trees." Vivian cleared her throat. "They named the town after them."

"Fancy you knowing that," Coleen remarked.

"I enjoy knowing about places," Vivian snapped.

"I'm sure you do." The young woman gave her a haughty look, as if knowing such things were beneath her.

"It's become highly cultivated," said Mrs. Marsden. "Clyde and I are seriously considering it for next year. If we hadn't planned to go to Fieldstone this year—" She sighed, clicking her tongue.

"I'm sure we shall not lack for amusement," said Mrs. Griffith. "I don't believe we were bored for a moment last year."

"They say the town has attracted quite a following in the arts," Mrs. Bilton chimed in.

"Oh, certainly, there are at least a dozen galleries there now." Mrs. Breen said. "It's developing quite a reputation for exhibits and art shows."

"Perhaps you ought to write to Jacob and tell him, Vivian." Amber's eyes were as sly as a fox.

Vivian eyed her back. "Jake wouldn't even think of returning to America until he finished his studies."

"Rather a shame," said Mrs. Griffith. "We had quite a little coterie there, didn't we?" She did not wait for an answer. "This year promises to be even better."

Vivian noted her mother had left Mrs. Moodie's side and had been silently looming near the group for some time. Her eyes were elsewhere, but Vivian knew her ears were keen on the conversation, for the muscles of her neck were strained.

"That sounds rather mysterious, Leila," Mrs. Breen said as she put down her cup. As if by instinct, all the ladies, young and old, leaned a little forward.

"Mother only means because our cousin, the Canadian buccaneer, will be there to look for a wife," Amber said in a confidential tone.

The ladies all rumbled in the uncomfortable garden chairs as her mother chided her, "Monte Leblanc is *not* a buccaneer, dear. He came by his fortune ruffling no feathers."

Mrs. Breen said in a mild voice, "I heard they're a little wild in Canada."

"Nonsense," Mrs. Griffith scoffed. "Monte and his father have traveled all over the world. And I'm hoping to persuade them to build a house on that vacant lot at the end of the street." Then she said, "He and I were inseparable as children." It was a surprising revelation, considering everyone on Washington Street knew Mrs. Griffith was rather self-conscious about the fact that she had spent part of her childhood away from San Francisco society.

"I heard he's frightfully rich," Hannah Breen, Mrs. Breen's daughter, who had been attacking the fruit bowl, spoke up for the first time.

"And frightfully old," Coreen said under her breath, too far away for Mrs. Griffith to hear, but close enough to earn a giggle among the younger set.

But Vivian had to wonder if Mrs. Griffith hadn't heard her, as she now admitted, "Monte isn't so young, of course. Two years shy of fifty."

"And widowed twice," her daughter added.

"Oh, I remember now!" Mrs. Marsden exclaimed. "We met them at the Baroness Ozelthorpe's villa several years ago, didn't we, Lona? As I recall, he was quite taken by you, but you were engaged to dear Gus by then." She stole a glance at her daughter, who, with her silvery blond head tossed with curls over her forehead and blue eyes cut into her delicate face, always grabbed any man's attention. Vivian glanced at her too, remembering how Lona had always used those tossed curls and eyes to ensure all male eyes were on her when they were both debutantes. That she had married Gus Lenville, a rather frumpy young man with a bobbing Adam's apple who hovered around her, did not surprise Vivian.

Mrs. Griffith said in her confidential way, "He and his father want to get into society here in the city."

Larissa had now come closer to Mrs. Breen and Mrs. Marsden. "Mr. Leblanc has had a roaring success with lumber mills out in Canada, hasn't he?"

"Indeed," Mrs. Griffith said with the same air of authority. "He retired from business some years ago. Monte just *adores* travel."

"The well-traveled man is a blessing in any society," Mrs. Marsden ventured.

"Both his wives died young, poor man." Mrs. Griffith sighed. "This is the first time he's thought about taking another."

"I should think so," Coleen said with indignation.

"If he's looking to get into society," Mrs. Breen said, "he couldn't do better than Sophie Barnsdale or India Dunstan."

Vivian thought about the two young ladies she had seen only once at a recent ball. They reminded her of cranes, the way their long necks stretched over the crowd of dancers, their eyes popping, their gazes so calculating, she knew they were both engaged in guessing which of the young men would ask them to dance next. She had been introduced to both of them, and they had curtsied to her as they would to a woman twice her age, then turned their backs and began speaking in low voices in the broken French of girls taught the language by a governess only for gossip. Vivian had moved away, stung in spite of herself, as she had understood a word here and there and knew that they were speaking of her and her mother.

"Older men do marry ladies young enough to be their daughters," Mrs. Marsden lamented.

"I don't think Monte is looking for a young woman necessarily," said Mrs. Griffith. "Not *so* young, anyway."

"Then if he wants our society, he really has only one option, doesn't he?" Amber remarked.

Again, though heads did not turn and eyes did not fall upon her, Vivian felt as if she were trapped under a disguised gaze of intention. She turned sideways, staring into the wrinkles of the bush near the fence, its blank green glowing a little with hues of small red fruit.

Amber's voice rose again with its raucous note. "He may suit you admirably, Vivian, if you care to show any interest."

Vivian turned back around and said in a jaunty voice, "If he's a buccaneer, as you say, why wouldn't I? My grandfather was such a man, wasn't he? It did him no harm to marry my grandmother, did it?"

This shut Amber down, but Vivian realized her mother was giving her a snappy look. She met Larissa's eyes. The blue that had been more shaded like the sea in the past year now held again their fine sparkle.

She and her mother left the wedding breakfast early because Larissa claimed a headache. As they made their way to the street, Vivian glanced back and saw blurred impressions of the silk and lace skirts, the button top of one man's hat, and the cream train following the bride around like an incessant puppy. It was as if they had stepped out of a painting.

"At least they're no longer gossiping about us the moment they think our backs are turned," Vivian remarked as they began the short walk from Mrs. Bilton's house to Alderdice Hall.

"Yes, they're starting to lose interest in us as fodder for their talk," her mother said, relieved. "Mrs. Griffith even said to me, 'We hope you'll consider coming to Waxwood again this summer' before we left."

"I'm rather surprised at her being so generous," Vivian remarked. "We haven't had many invitations this season, have we?"

"Mrs. Griffith has never behaved in the appalling manner of the others," Larissa insisted. "She was with us last year, remember. She knows what a trying time we had with your brother."

Vivian grasped the edge of her parasol, feeling the heaviness of the wooden handle hard against her hand. "Mother, you're not thinking of going?"

"Going where?"

"To Waxwood, of course." She watched as one of the new automobiles whizzed past them on the other side of the street, leaving clouds of dust in the air.

"Seven years ago, you went there willingly, against my wishes, even," said Larissa. "Then, last year, you practically refused to go, and now you sound horrified even at the idea."

"Seven years ago, I was looking for something," Vivian said quietly.

"Yes, and you found it." Her mother gave her a shrewd look.

"Which is precisely why I don't want to go now!" Vivian stopped and looked at her mother. "That place is evil for us, Mother."

"Don't be ridiculous," said Larissa.

"It ruined our social standing," Vivian pointed out.

Her mother began walking again. "I'll admit our position is a little precarious at the moment—"

"Waxwood ruined Jake's life!" Vivian felt herself choking.

Larissa looked straight ahead, her eyes a stinging blue. "I told you never to mention that."

"Put it away and don't think about it?" Vivian mocked, fighting back the tears.

They reached the gate of Alderdice Hall, and her mother glanced over her shoulder as she entered. "I don't think it's wise for us to remain in the city this summer when no one else will."

"Since our position is so precarious?" Vivian growled

"Precisely."

They entered the front hall, and Vivian watched as her mother laid out her accessories on the table as she always did when she returned from a party. Vivian gazed down at the velvet bag, the pince-nez her mother had carried with her since last winter, though she hardly needed them, and her fan. She suddenly saw how much Larissa had aged in the past year. She still had that regal pose that made the most of her unusually tall figure, but the lines showed around her eyes and lips, and there was a hardness set in her jaw now, as if she were perpetually preparing for tragedy.

Vivian gently laid a hand on her mother's wrist. "Perhaps you're right, Mother. We can't let them reject us over what they don't know."

"That's right. They don't know, do they?" Larissa's voice echoed in the dim hallway.

Pan, Vivian's Scottish terrier, pranced in, bobbing his head in greeting and giving a deep roar of a bark, despite his small stature.

"I hardly relished secreting myself in this dismal house for the entire summer, anyway." Vivian peeled off her gloves.

Larissa glanced at her as she lingered on the stairway. "Your grandfather spent two years and quite a lot of money building this 'dismal' house."

"And Grandmother hated it," Vivian reminded her. "She said we would one day be buried alive in it. And she wasn't far wrong, was she, Mother, considering what we've been through this year? That's a burning of a sort, isn't it?"

"You're talking in circles, as usual." Her mother ascended the stairs.

"I mean the way we've buried ourselves here since Jake went away."

Her mother's eyes wandered to windows facing the front of the house. The curtains were open because of the temperate morning sun, but Vivian could not see the features of her face. There was a catch in her voice, as she said, "You'd better take that dog of yours out into the garden before lunch." Pan whimpered, his head tilted back. He was always looking at Larissa with attentive eyes, as if trying to offer her a sympathy she didn't want. Larissa looked at the dog for a moment, then continued up the stairs.

The abelia had blossomed all at once, and they gave the place the scent of spring in a more congenial way than Mrs. Bilton's overpowering roses. Vivian sat on the grass, though she could imagine the disapproving glance that Mollie, her maid, would cast upon the green stains on her skirt later that evening. Pan was wagging his spear-like tail and looking at her with his sensitive eyes. She found a stick and threw it toward the lantana bushes on the other side of the garden, watching as he ran to retrieve it.

Her mind wandered to the wedding and the satisfaction she had seen on her cousin's face as she walked down the aisle. She recognized that look of achievement, as when one held a winning hand of cards. Even if the hand one played was just barely won, the fact that one had gained a perspective above the others at the table was enough of a victory. Emma, with her large hands and feet, her crooked smile, and her plain features, had once confided in Vivian as they watched the debutantes who had come out the same time they had, taking their vows one at a time that she feared the dye was cast upon her. "They're like dominos falling in succession," she had remarked. "Once one steps forward, the others follow to keep in line. I don't want to be the one standing at the end of the line."

She couldn't help but frown at the sun. Emma was the last, or almost the last. It was now she, Vivian, who was the last domino, the one that remained standing.

Pan returned with the stick in his mouth and dropped it in front of her on the grass, tilting his head with his affectionate, wise eyes, as if soaking in her contemplation. She nuzzled the dog's head. Sometimes in the past year, especially when they returned from Waxwood in the fall, and the house echoed with their hard heels, a reminder that only she and Larissa were left of the Alderdice family, when Pan had been her only comfort. What an irony that the man who caused the most harm to her brother was responsible for this one solace!

Despite her determination that past year to forget Harland Stevens, the memory of the man assailed her at the oddest moments. She could see the outline of the towering figure, his head raised above all others, his flaming red hair and his burning coal eyes. She had imagined that calm smile, that charming, mild voice that hid something more vicious and frightening. She loathed him as one loathed Lucifer and, indeed, in her eyes, there was no difference.

Pan struggled to get away from the embrace that had become too stifling. He paddled around the lawn, sniffing at various flowers, drawing away from the lavender as if it were on fire. She recalled the stalks of lavender at the church, the way they had given off their tangy scent, sending a wave of perfume over everyone's heads. Until Vivian smelled the lavender, she had not realized she was sitting with both her hands wringing her hand-kerchief. Watching Emma standing at the altar, she wanted to be her. Despite her escape into books since her husband Miles had died, aching in the back of her mind had been the idea imposed upon her since she came out at eighteen: she had duties to fulfill, expectations from both the Alderdice specters and Washington Street blue bloods. The thought of those duties at the wedding had filled her with determination, but now they frightened her as much as the day of her debutante ball, when she had held her grandmother's pink pearls in her hand, when the weight of them had reminded her of the weight of those expectations.

The door to the yard opened and Missy, the scullery maid, toddled out, carrying a tin of refuse from the lunch preparations. She gave a respectful bow to Vivian and, as she did so, Pan flew into the house through the door she had left open. Vivian rushed in after him amidst Missy's hasty apologies.

Vivian could hear Pan's scruffy barks in another wing of the house. She called to him, but he only barked in return. She reached the stairs and went up to the second floor, where Pan's roar echoed down the hall. Vivian passed through the corridor, catching sight of Annie, the housemaid, with the dust rag in her hand. Reaching the end, she found Pan there, his neck craning to look up at two large double doors that led into the east wing.

She realized the dog had not been idly rushing through the house. He had been following the same sense of ghostliness that had been filling her with apprehension as they neared the summer. Those doors led through a wood-paneled wing and onto a marbled floor where Ancestor Hall lay.

The place that had meant so much to Jake, with those lamb-faced portraits, had done as much damage to him as Mr. Stevens had. More so, perhaps, because they still hung in Alderdice Hall. She had pleaded with Larissa to take them down when they returned from Waxwood, all but Great-Grandfather Merton and Grandfather and Grandmother.

"You can't possibly want to maintain the façade now, Mother," she had said, her eyes burning with tears.

But her mother remained adamant. "We need something to hold on to, Vivian. Now, perhaps, more than ever."

Pan scraped at one of the doors. Vivian tried the handle, but it remained firmly in its place. She tried the other one, but it would not yield. She could almost hear the echo of the specters tapping on the marble floor beyond.

She picked up the dog and began walking back to the major part of the house. So, Larissa insisted on holding on to those Alderdice martyrs, but she had locked the door. A pain in Vivian's chest eased. The specters were locked in now, and perhaps they could begin again in the same place where she and her mother had ended last summer.

~

The dining room at lunchtime looked twice the size it had been when Vivian was a child. She had once read that rooms grew smaller through adult eyes. But as Basset served the soup, she looked at the cupboard that took up the entire wall, noticing how the ferns hovered with their delicate leaves near the window, and the candelabra glowed at the center of the table. It was then she realized why the room looked so large. It was because the dining room table was so empty, emptier than it had been all year. Larissa had come into the room for lunch and taken the place where Grandfather had sat at the end nearest to the window, the chair elevated slightly. Vivian, without realizing it, had taken her place at the other end facing her. She was staring at her mother as if at a doll, and she didn't wonder that Larissa saw her in the same way.

"Mother, I'd like to move to my old chair, if that's all right with you," she said. She had a sudden fear her mother could not hear her, so far off.

Larissa answered, "If you wish, dear."

Vivian slid the chair away and took the one on Larissa's left side. Pan, who had wandered into the dining room, though he was forbidden to sample the meal, settled under the table near her feet. Her mother sat upright, her ankles crossed, the spoon clanking against the rings on her fingers when she lifted it to her lips.

"I think we ought to go to Waxwood, just as Mrs. Griffith suggested," Vivian began.

Larissa peered at her. "You mean you've changed your mind?"

"Don't you remember Grandfather's wish for me as he lay dying?" As she said this, it was almost as if the croaking words echoed in the massive room: *Rissa, see that she marries again.*

"I didn't think you remembered," Larissa said softly.

"He wanted no more running off in the family," said Vivian. "This Mr. Leblanc wouldn't run off, if he's so eager to get into Washington Street."

"You're willing to entertain the idea of marrying again?" The idea struck a note of hope in her mother's voice as some lines from the last year disappeared from her face.

"It's been five years since Miles had his accident," Vivian said. "I don't even take a widow's name. You insisted on that, remember?"

"Only because I thought Miss Alderdice would be much more enticing to an eligible young man than Mrs. Caulfield," Larissa said. "Not that it seems to have done much good."

"Well, I think five years is ample time to recover from the sudden death of one's husband of ten months, don't you?"

"Is that what you've been doing burying yourself in books?" Her mother raised her eyebrow. "Trying to recover?"

Vivian grimaced. "The problem with being locked in a house with only one other person for so long is that you get to know them too well. You're right, Mother. I never really had time to know Miles, so how could I be the grieving widow?"

Larissa wiped her lips and motioned for Basset to take away the empty soup plate.

"Aren't you pleased?" Vivian observed her.

"Naturally," she said. "But you've always had a strong sense of allegiance to your family. I knew you would come around once you realized your place."

"My place as a socialite, you mean?" Vivian glanced at her.

"I mean your place as an heiress."

"Not entirely," Vivian said. "That rather depends on Jake, doesn't it?"

"Your brother has made his choice." Her mother's voice was wispy.

"There's always a hope he might change his mind, isn't there?"

"We're not discussing that," said Larissa. "We're discussing the future of this family."

"I thought that's just what I was discussing!"

They both remained silent as Basset slid in and served the Cornish hens and rice and Brussel sprouts. When he withdrew, her mother patted her hand. Vivian could feel the cold bands of her rings tapping against her skin. "I'm glad to hear you intend to get serious about your future. And I think you've chosen your suitor wisely."

"You say that without knowing him," she said.

"He's a relative of Mrs. Griffith's, however distant," said Larissa. "That's enough for me. And I've seen a few things in the paper about the Leblancs. Enough to know we needn't be ashamed to cast our lot with theirs."

"He's not yet my suitor," said Vivian with a little laugh. "With all the younger girls flittering about the way they have this season, I'm not at all certain I have a chance."

"You come from more original stock than they are, dear," Larissa insisted. "I've no doubt Monte Leblanc will see that."

Vivian shrank back, playing with the Brussels sprout at the end of her fork. Pan whimpered near her feet. "You make me sound like a prize cow," she muttered.

"You have everything the man could look for," said Larissa. "Mrs. Moodie was telling me quite a lot about the Leblancs. She and her son met them in Antwerp some time ago."

"I wondered why you were so intent on speaking to her again before we left." Vivian eyed her.

"She said he's not one to cultivate a woman with a frivolous manner," her mother continued.

"Well, if he is looking for graveness, he could find no one better than I."

"Vivian." Her mother looked at her. "If you marry this man, you realize we shall no longer be social pariahs?"

"I wouldn't exactly call us that," Vivian said. "If we were, Mrs. Griffith would never have invited us to Waxwood."

"Perhaps I'm exaggerating," Larissa admitted. "But you can't deny our footing has been none too steady here this past year. We're still on shaky ground."

"Our precarious position," Vivian said dryly, slicing into the Cornish hen, which now looked more like an entire turkey in the room's amplification.

Her mother continued in a lower voice, "They never believed for a moment your brother is in Europe, you know."

Vivian drew her eyes away. "Yes, Mother, I know."

"Mrs. Griffith was trying to send us a message," said Larissa. The afternoon sun had moved and made her face appear in a shadow. "She was trying to tell us we can right the whole matter, if you do what's expected of you."

"What's expected of me." Vivian sighed. "The jade necklace that chokes."

Her mother gave her an odd look, but went on. "If you marry Mr. Leblanc, they will look upon us as their allies, not their adversaries."

Vivian gave a dry laugh. "Malcolm Alderdice, the Flesa buccaneer, shall be no more if Monte Leblanc, the Canadian buccaneer, takes the place of his ghost?"

"No more ghosts, Vivian." Her mother insisted.

A pang of sorrow touched Vivian's heart as she put down her knife and fork. She saw her mother now even more clearly than she had seen her in the hallway: worn and tired, fighting still to become the socialite Grandmother had been thirty years ago. How much had she been through during the past years? Grandfather, whom she had loved more than anyone, had died. Jake had done that awful thing and gone away. The glacier of anger that had formed inside of Vivian against Larissa since her brother went away now melted with the warmth of pity.

She put her arms around her mother, something she hadn't done in a long time. "Poor Mother."

The figure remained unyielding, but Larissa did not pull away. "You can win Mr. Leblanc's heart. I know you can."

"I won't go making myself silly chasing after a man like all the others," Vivian warned.

Larissa smiled, a genuine amusing smile for the first time in a long time. "I should be very disappointed if you did."

Vivian picked up Pan and smoothed down a lock of his fur that had fallen into his eyes. The dog looked wistfully at her, his face set in sympathy.

CHAPTER 2

When they set out for Waxwood a few weeks later, Larissa agreed it would be prudent to take the Alderdice private car. "It's best for us to remain inconspicuous a little while longer until we re-establish ourselves."

"Grandfather would be ashamed of you," Vivian remarked as she arranged her books on the sofa at one end of the salon. "He would want you to flaunt those icy blue eyes of your at that little gathering of well-wishers who were seeing Mrs. Griffith and Mrs. Breen off."

"Your grandfather knew when it was time to withdraw," her mother insisted.

"He certainly did," Vivian said, not without a little irony. Even from life, Grandfather had known when to withdraw. "I wish Marvina was going to be in Waxwood this summer."

"Your association with her hardly helps our position," Larissa threw out. "The last thing we need is to spend a summer in her company."

"She's not a poisonous snake, Mother."

"Those who count frown upon her ideas," her mother said. "And with Mr. Leblanc, it counts."

"Marvina hasn't exposed my mind to her suffragist ideas more than I've exposed myself." Vivian leaned back against the cushions.

"You made that obvious," her mother said in an icy tone, "when you dragged me to that hideous play this winter."

Vivian sat up. "I found the character of Hedda refreshing."

"Refreshing!" Larissa scoffed. "An ambitious, conniving, evil woman, and you call that liberation!"

"I thought you would appreciate her," said Vivian dryly. "She was as obsessed with snobbery as you are."

"I am not a snob." Her mother arranged her lace work in her lap. "I have high standards, just like your grandfather did. I would hope you inherited that."

"My inheritance is of a more mulish nature." Vivian couldn't help but grin. Her mother was fond of saying she had Grandmother's obstinate nature.

Larissa glanced at her across the car, her pince-nez perched on her nose. "Your grandmother could tame that obstinacy for her duty."

"Duty," Vivian breathed. "That word again. You've been branding the words *duty* and *expectation* into me since I was a child."

Her mother smoothed down the edges of the lace. "Women like ourselves have obligations, dear, not only to our families, but to society."

"*Noblesse oblige?*" Vivian asked archly.

"If our position is to mean anything," Larissa said, her eyes trailing to the passing scenery out the window, "we must accept our fate."

Vivian looked out the windows too. The words were chillingly familiar. She remembered her grandmother's last letter from Waxwood: *I am resigned to my fate. I have come to see this year that it is not only what we expect of ourselves but also life's expectations of us.*

She tried to read, but she could not concentrate on the words. She slipped a deck of cards out of her reticule and began to play solitaire. A three of spades. The jack of diamonds. And then, she turned over the card on the pile and came face to face with the king of hearts.

Her mind flashed back to an odd newspaper column she had read soon after her husband went on the expedition that would prove fatal to him. Worried and nervous, she had frequented the Mechanics Institute, and every day, she would trek down the Nob Hill inclines that led into the downtown with air pressing through her chest, and by the time she reached the Institute, she was breathless but eager. She had discovered the small place near the back of the building with newspapers, and it had sparked her fascination. These were not the daily papers businessmen read on the cable cars that gave the sort of news people spoke of at dinner parties. The Institute subscribed to some of the most abstract and progressive periodicals she had heard about but never seen in newsstands around the city.

One of her favorites at the time had been a journalist who called himself "The Gentleman." He sought strange, sedate corners of the city, describing them in a rather flowing manner so that his column read more like ornate poetry than news. But the sincerity of his love for the wayward city comforted her.

One especially foggy morning, she read about an odd roof garden atop one of the more obscure buildings in the downtown which had, as The Gentleman described, "its own watchman." He described this watchman as an evergreen tree in a marble basin that stood in the center of the garden, greeting everyone with "its disregard for the smallness of human life." She had read:

In the winter, a net of Christmas holly and poinsettia surround it, looking upon their giant benefactor as if humbled by its massive grace. The tree itself is not without the charming decorations of the season, all sparkling eyes and lights. With the majesty of the King of Hearts, it peers at guests who come to amble within its reaches. Amber lights fall upon the silver balls flashing with adroit arrogance upon the ladies in particular, as if the King of Hearts were hinting at the reason for his puzzlingly tragic appearance at last.

In the summer, continued The Gentleman, the garden adopted nautical themes of rippling waves and painted fish:

Pale blues replace winter greens and reds, blinding glitter and sparkle for silk and gritty sand. The King of Hearts dons glass starfish and seahorses and shells, collected from the bowels of Ocean Beach, no doubt. But he is no longer a king, as it is natural the king should disappear, for summer is a woman. Who should take his place but the queen of spades, the queen without a king? And is there no one more befitting the gilded-eyed glare than the majestic lady who receives her inspiration from Pallas herself?

Vivian went home that day and pulled out the old deck of cards her great-grandparents used to play, sitting in its mahogany box as if waiting for her to open them. That night, as she sat with her mother and brother in the upstairs parlor, she drew out the cards mentioned in the column. The queen of spades had a doubtful look, grasping the flower in her left hand as preciously as she grasped the spear in her right. The old cards appeared to have taken on a diluted vision of Athena. Then she studied the king of hearts. With his left hand, he plunged a sword into the side of his head, a grim smile welcoming death on his lips.

The next morning, her friend Marvina came to call and found Vivian sitting in her room, both cards laid out in front of her, gazing at them with perplexity. When she told the widow of the column, Marvina laughed and threw aside her hat and gloves, sitting right on the rug beside Vivian. "I know the writer. He comes often to the San Francisco Arts Club. He has a rather fanciful way of turning a pin into a golden beetle, doesn't he?"

"Why do you think the king killed himself?" Vivian looked at the tragic figure.

Marvina shrugged. "I believe he takes after King Charles VII of France. They say the man became ill and went mad. He thought there were traitors all around him, including his own son. So perhaps madness made him plunge the sword into his head, not a broken heart, the way The Gentleman implies."

"Perhaps it was the queen of spades." Vivian placed her card beside the king. "A woman who holds a spear in one hand and flowers in the other may have contradictory intentions."

Marvina laughed. "You mean she persuaded the melancholy king to take the sword to his head? Many women have done worse."

After Marvina had gone, Vivian spent a long time studying the two cards. The desperate way the king plunged the sword into his head made her pity him, and for a while, she carried that card around with her, feeling protective of him as to a mangy dog. Over time, the animated colors scratched off the card so the sword looked more like a twisted cross. It made Vivian imagine the king had been forgiven and his sword turned into a cross.

It wasn't long after Miles' letters stopped coming that her mother discovered the card. They were about to leave for a ball, and Larissa rushed into her room, lamenting about a mislaid fan and, in her frantic search, knocked Vivian's pouch off the bed. Everything, including the king of hearts, tumbled out. As her mother was putting things back inside, she picked up the card. "What on earth is this? Another one of your strange ideas about specters?"

"No, Mother," she said. "Only a madman I pitied and wanted to comfort."

But Larissa's eyes had suddenly become mesmerized by the picture. The shine of excitement that always accompanied her mother's visage when they were going to one of the more prominent events of their set faded to almost a harried look of puzzlement.

"It's the suicide king," said Vivian. "Marvina thinks he killed himself out of lunacy."

Larissa's brilliant blue eyes turned granite, and her smooth skin that always showed such control dipped into crevices and lines. She took the card with both hands now and, for a moment, Vivian thought she was going to tear it to shreds. But then the lines disappeared, and her face became composed again, as if she had changed her mind. She put the card on the bed. "Put it back in the deck, dear. You know how your grandfather likes to play with those cards."

Now, as the train rambled on the tracks, shuffling along bright fields on either side, Vivian looked again into the face of the king of hearts. Seeing her own face in place of the dowdy king, the knife plunged into the side of her head, she dropped the card. Then, she dug out of the deck the queen of spades. Unlike the queen from the ancient cards, this queen was more modern and looked smug, as if she knew all along that she had forced the king to do away with himself.

She suddenly saw her grandmother's face on the queen. In fact, the two cards in this modern deck she had bought from a vendor at the station resembled Grandmother in different ways. Penelope Alderdice was the queen who had done away with the plucky artist named Grace Carlyle. *I am resigned to my fate.* Vivian suddenly wondered if she would end up like the king of hearts, plunging the sword into her head, numbing its intelligence and insights as she went about the duty of a Washington Street wife, mother, and socialite. Would it be Monte Leblanc who would be the queen, smiling devilishly in the face of his deed? Or would she be the one who would be the queen without a king?

The bobbing of the car had given her a headache. She rose. "I think I'll take a walk, Mother."

Larissa looked up from her lace work. "On a train?"

"Perhaps there are people in the parlor car," Vivian observed. "I feel rather restless."

"Do you think that's wise, dear?"

"We can't hide completely," Vivian said.

"We're not hiding," her mother insisted. "But we must be careful."

"I will be careful. But if I stay here another moment, I shall go crazy!" She slid open the car door, slipping into the connecting passenger car.

It was a relief to see other people. Something in their guarded silence as they gazed out the windows or read their books or clicked their knitting as if engaged in the most absorbing work in the world comforted her. These were not Washington Street blue bloods whose lives revolved in a merry-go-round of apathy and leisure.

She found the parlor car disappointingly sparse with only a few gentlemen who, having observed there were no ladies present, had turned it into their own private smoking car. They immediately rose with a bow and an apology when she entered, proceeding to grind out their cigarettes. One fiddled with his pipe.

"Don't on my account," she said. "I don't mind the smoke, if you permit me to open a window."

A man with sandy hair and a triangular mustache jumped up and opened one window just enough so the breeze would not upset her hat. She nodded her thanks and sat a little distance away from the men, intending to show discretion while avoiding the heady smoke, and looked out at the passing scenery.

The fair-haired man resumed speaking to his companion, an elderly gentleman in a rather dapper suit who held on to his stick as if ready to use it as a weapon at any moment. "I found it a rather grouse place when I was a boy," said the blond man.

"Grouse?" the older man inquired.

"Every time Aunt Leona sent me to town on an errand, all I

would hear was the grumble and mumble of the merchants. But I expect the business they were doing dissatisfied them. Back then, Waxwood was a lonely little place."

"Why did you bother to come, then?"

"Oh, I didn't exactly bother." The man grinned. "I was always sent there in the summer. Aunt Leona was, well, rather a fidgety person. Spinster and all that. I think she found life rather desolate after my grandparents died." He added, "Not that she should have. Ours was a large family. I had three uncles and two aunts besides Mother. I would have had three aunts, but poor Loretta died of fever well before I was born."

Vivian's entire body went rigid. *Loretta*. The name rang through her ears like the rolling of the train wheels.

"Still, I have fond memories of the place," the blond man continued. "The city park is pleasant. So is the bay. It's been rather overshadowed by all those resorts in the past years, though. I remember when you could look across the water and see only those wax wood trees."

"Odd phenomena, I've heard," the other man remarked.

"Yes, but the town is taking a better view of them," said the younger man, laughing. "I remember all the stories Mama used to tell me about the place. All sorts of demons and phantoms roaming among the trees. Mama had a rather fertile imagination," he added. "They used to call her Fanciful Flossie in the family."

The joints of Vivian's fingers hurt, and she looked down, realizing she was clawing the arm of the chair. *Loretta. Flossie.* There could be no mistake now.

"I'm rather looking forward to it," the older man sighed. "My nerves, you know. I'm hoping a few weeks on the beach will help."

"I'm sure you'll find it rather soothing," said the younger man. "Despite the grouses, I always do."

The elderly man finished his cigarette, then rose and,

excusing himself, left the car. The blond man remained facing the window so his back was turned toward Vivian. She moved to the chair the elderly man had vacated. "Forgive me for being inquisitive—"

The young man turned, smiling at her. "I've always found inquisitive women to be most interesting." His blue eyes flashed in approval.

"I'm not being as bold as you think." Vivian hid a smile. "We're almost acquaintances, you see."

"Oh?"

"I heard you mention your mother's name is Flossie, and you had an aunt named Loretta who died of fever."

"You've a keen ear, miss," he said.

"May I infer your name is Potter?"

The man blinked. "David Potter. How did you know?"

Vivian fiddled with the tassel on the bag hanging around her wrist. "My grandmother and Loretta were great friends. A good forty-five years ago, of course," she added quickly.

"Yes, those were old times," Mr. Potter said. "Who was your grandmother, if *I* may be bold and ask?"

"Penelope Alderdice." She added quickly, "She was Carlyle then."

He squinted at the sunlight bursting through the open window. "I don't recall — yes, I do! Mama told me once of the elegant lady who came to visit one summer, the one with the fiery red hair."

"Yes, that was my grandmother," said Vivian. Her hand instinctively flew to the back of her head, knowing that the strawberry blond glimmered in the harsh light of the train car with an identical fierce red shade. Only since her grandmother had died, her hair had reddened from the blonder pallor that had been so much like her mother's when she was a child.

Mr. Potter smiled. "I gathered she was a rather enchanting young woman. My mother was only a child, but she always remembered Miss Carlyle as terribly nice. She said to me once, 'I was frightened one night, and she soothed me.'"

"Yes." Vivian smiled. "The Pookah."

"The what?"

Vivian laughed. "Flossie was afraid of a monster called the Pookah one Halloween, and my grandmother convinced her it was just a story."

"How do you know that?"

"My grandmother told me," Vivian said. "In a letter."

David's voice lowered. "They were all sorry when she left, you know. I rather think they hoped she would make her home in Waxwood."

"She had obligations." The word still burned against her tongue. "She had to go back to San Francisco to marry my grandfather."

"Malcolm Alderdice, I take it." He nodded. "I remember reading about him in the paper. Quite a titan of industry."

"In his own way," Vivian said briefly.

"Mama said she was always afraid of him," he said with a laugh. "I gathered he was quite an intimidating man."

"In his own way," Vivian repeated, but a shiver went through her.

"Yes, men like that usually are." He leaned back, crossing his long legs.

They sat for a moment in silence. Then, Vivian asked, "Did my grandmother ever write your mother or Loretta from the city?"

"Only the first year or two," he said. "By then she had a baby, and I expect she was busy. Babies are a handful, aren't they?" He grinned.

They were both quiet for a little while in the way of strangers trying to think of something to say. Mr. Potter pressed his hands together, peering out the window. "Everyone thought it rather odd."

"Odd for a woman to have a baby?" Vivian asked with amusement.

"It was, apparently, when the news came from the mouth of Bertha Ross!" He laughed. "I take it you know about Bertha."

Vivian nodded. "I met her."

"I rather liked the way she was always fluttering about, going from one thought to another with no genuine connection," Mr. Potter said. "I remember as a child sitting on the kitchen table while she and Miss Ross did their chores. Bertha would sneak cookies to me when Miss Ross was in another room, talking a mile a minute the entire time. It was like a game trying to keep up with everything she said."

Vivian smiled, then grew serious. "I'm puzzled, though. If my grandmother was writing to your family, they ought to have known. A baby is not the sort of news one keeps to oneself."

"That's part of what was so odd about it," he said. "Aunt Leona told me when Bertha burst out with the news, they were all abuzz. Not a mention of anything of the sort in any of her letters."

Vivian felt uneasy then, staring out at the scenery, where the shades of green suddenly took on a murky gray. "When was this?"

"September 1855." He uncrossed and crossed his legs in the other direction in the fidgeting way of men too tall for their chairs. "I remember exactly because Aunt Leona said it was just before Aunt Loretta's funeral."

"September?" She was startled. "My mother was born in November."

"Well." Mr. Potter was aghast. "Well, Mr. Henderson must have made a mistake, then."

"Who's Mr. Henderson?"

"He was courting one of the belles," he said. "A fisherman now. But he gets confused when he reminisces sometimes."

"It's alright, Mr. Potter," said Vivian with a smile. "I'm not offended. I was merely curious." She leaned back again. "People do like to gossip about such things, especially the swells, when they're sitting at their dinner parties and have nothing else to talk about."

He laughed. "I'm not really a 'swell,' Miss Alderdice. A man may be born of means, but others judge him by how well he can make his fortune outside of what he already has."

"Yes." She felt her face become warm as she thought of her brother. "I know that." She gathered her pouch in her lap.

"I'm sure Mr. Henderson was wrong. As I said, these old folks have such blurred memories." He played with an unlit cigarette.

"But with old gossip, they remember those sorts of details," she remarked.

"They were all rather upset because she didn't come to Aunt Loretta's funeral," he admitted. "Oh, I'm talking poppycock. Forgive me, Miss Alderdice." He leaned forward with an exaggerated bow from the waist, making his tall figure looked doubled over.

She laughed and rose. "On the contrary. You made my breath of fresh air most intriguing. It's always amusing to untangle these little details when one hears different interpretations of the past. I thank you for speaking with me, Mr. Potter." She held out her hand.

He took it with a gentle grip. "If we're already being brazen, may I ask you to call me David? I feel as if we're old friends. Perhaps we are, in a way."

"David." She smiled. "And you call me Vivian."

"Shall I see you back to your car?" he asked.

"Don't bother," she said. "I'm sorry if my probing annoyed you. My mother used to call me Dagger Girl when I was a child. I was always 'twisting the dagger' with my questions." She gave a short laugh.

"Not at all," he said. "As I told you, I find inquisitive women most interesting."

"You ought to smoke that cigarette before you break it in half," she said, nodding toward the roll of paper still in his hand. It was, in fact, rather bent, like a crooked man.

She made her way back through the passenger car, feeling her steps uneven on the floor. The swaying of the car at that point on the tracks made her grab at the edge of the seats as she went through. A woman in a simple cotton dress flinched back, and Vivian, realizing she had touched her shoulder, apologized.

When she entered their private car, she found her mother had fallen asleep in the chair, her lace work still in her lap. She looked down at the serene face, not exactly a baby's, as the books claimed happened to a person in slumber, but younger-looking than her forty-four years. Forty-four years…

Vivian carefully extracted the lace work from her mother's lap, putting it back into the basket. She found an afghan thrown onto one of the beds in the stateroom and gently laid it across her mother's knees. Then, she went to the edge of their car and opened the door. The narrow observation deck was just big enough so she could lean against the iron rail and feel the wind whipping across her face like airy slaps. They were just crossing a bridge of what looked like a narrow river, but it was only a bed of rocks now with peeks of vegetation as evidence of its former glory. She read in the newspaper this summer promised to be a drier one than usual, but the vacant river surprised her, as it was still early in the season. She wondered if she were to take this same train in the fall whether the river would be at least trickling with water. October, perhaps; November, certainly; September, not likely.

September. The Waxwood belles and beaus had all thought her grandmother could not go to Loretta's funeral because she had just had a baby — the baby that was the woman with only a youngish pallor lying across the chair with such an elegant pose, as if she knew, even in sleep, someone might observe her at any moment.

But her mother's birthday was November seventeenth, "the day that Mr. Livingstone was in all the papers because he set eyes on Africa," her grandfather had always boasted, as if her mother's birth signaled some new exploratory territory as well.

She shook her head as the ribbons on her hat untied in the wind and waved in her face, flinching at the ticklish feeling. September, November — the months blurred in the minds of the old.

~

It took them a full hour to check in. The Waxwoodian was more crowded than it had been the previous year, and though none of the faces were the same, Vivian still had the sense she had seen many of them before. It was the same feeling she had when they traveled abroad and encountered other wealthy patrons languishing in the sunshine or lingering over their meal in the dining room.

"Now I know what they mean by 'birds of a feather.'" She swung her small bag over her other arm.

Her mother's blue eyes were watchful. "What, dear?"

"Did you ever consider, Mother, that we ought to see a new breed of people?" Vivian asked. "Ones who wear dirty shirtwaists and ill-fitted hats, and whose poorly made shoes scrape the ground and leave a mark?"

"Don't talk in circles," her mother said, sounding almost like a puppet.

"I don't talk in circles, Mother," said Vivian. "I speak the truth."

"I thought truth seekers were plain-speaking." Larissa gave her a wry smile.

"I only wished we weren't so alone." Vivian pressed her hands together.

"We're hardly alone," Larissa remarked, throwing her glance around the crowded room.

"Now you're being obtuse." Vivian gave her a look. "If there's one thing I've always been proud of, Mother, it's that you're more intelligent than the common lady swell."

"I can't understand why I can't find the Griffiths," Larissa muttered. "They left the same time we did."

"There's Mrs. Breen." Vivian caught sight of the woman whose hourglass figure matched the bell shape of her hat.

"And the Tishers will be here too," her mother reminded her.

"Heavens, how could I forget that?" Vivian said. "And with the Canadian buccaneer in tow. Fancy Mrs. Griffith's relatives staying with the Tishers in Boston last spring."

"It's unfortunate," Larissa agreed. "It means Fern is already ahead of you in her acquaintance with Monte Leblanc."

"I wasn't referring to them when I said I wish we weren't alone," Vivian said.

Her mother answered in a soft voice, "I know to whom you were referring."

She glanced at Larissa and saw her lips quiver. She knew her mother was thinking of Jake too.

Young male voices suddenly rousted above the twittering tones of females in the lobby. Their laughter pricked through the room and, although they walked with a firm gait, their step slid a little here and there with the recklessness of their entitled position as youths and as men. Vivian could hear the sniffing and whispering around them: *indecent, tactless, insolent.*

"I see Mr. Howe's friends are back this summer," she remarked, glancing at her mother. "But, where, I wonder, is Mr. Howe?"

"I suppose they have as much right to be here as anyone else," said Larissa in an even voice. "Let us hope they have improved their manners a little since last year."

"And where," Vivian continued, "is Mr. Howe's more infamous cousin?"

Her mother was silent. Vivian knew she was searching for the familiar figure, the tall and broad-shouldered man with the freckled face and the stormy eyes named Harland Stevens.

"They ought to graduate soon," Vivian said. "Perhaps they no longer need their chaperone." She cast her eyes at the young men, who had now taken their place at the back of the line. "At least they have their cigars in their pockets this time."

Larissa gave her a keen look. "I found Mr. Howe to be a very polite young man, Vivian."

"He almost led Jake to a nasty accident," she snarled. "Or have you forgotten?"

"I haven't forgotten," said her mother. "I have forgotten nothing."

Vivian glanced at the net of young men. "I've a feeling we will not be seeing Mr. Harland Stevens here this year."

"First specters, and now presentiments," Larissa said dryly. "I wish you would confine yourself to what one can see with one's own eyes, Vivian."

"I wish I could, Mother." Vivian couldn't look at Larissa as she thought of what her mother jokingly called her "presentiments": about her grandmother, her brother, even her grandfather. She had never wanted to be right, and yet, it was as if those presentiments unfolded despite her hope they never would. Perhaps she had earned the title of Dagger Girl.

Just then, a bustle of lace and feathers ruffled through the line, and Mrs. Breen appeared. Her lips matched the bell shape of her figure, with the upper lip raised a little too much over her protruding front teeth. "Why, Larissa! I didn't think we would see you here this summer."

"Mrs. Griffith invited us, and Vivian insisted." Her mother gave her measured smile as she pulled her suitcase forward.

"I imagine she did," said the woman, giving her a glassy eye.

"I'm rather interested, Mrs. Breen," said Vivian. "There ought to be quite a race to the finish amongst the bright-eyed young ladies when the Tishers arrive."

"Well, you can't blame them, dear," said the woman. "It is *their* season, after all."

"And mine has passed like the memory of a fine youth," Vivian said with mocking wistfulness. "You're so right. Twenty-six is positively ancient."

"Well, no, I didn't mean it quite that way."

"Vivian is only teasing you, Lenna." Larissa gave a light laugh. "You know how she is."

"Yes," said the woman shortly. "I know how she is." She turned and wandered back toward her place in line where Mr. Breen, her son, and her daughter and son-in-law were waiting.

"I wish you would be a little less acidic, Vivian," her mother hissed. "You know they don't find it amusing."

"Neither was I amused at the insinuation that I'm an old maid at twenty-six," Vivian hissed back. "I'm not a spinster or a bluestocking."

"Yet," her mother added without holding back a smile.

Vivian peered at her. "I never said I wanted to be either one, Mother."

Larissa's eyes softened. "You won't be, dear."

"At least you believe in me, Mother." She pressed Larissa's hand.

~

They did not see the Griffiths or the Tishers as they made their way through the crowds to the elevators, a hotel porter lagging behind with their suitcases. As they entered, she stole a glance at her mother. The hardness of one who had seen more than her share of burdens embossed the bony structure that had always stood out as aristocratic.

"Are you all right, Mother?" she asked in a tender voice.

Larissa sighed. "I suppose I'm a little tired." She patted Vivian's hand. "We'll rest before dinner, and I'll be all right." They squeezed past people as they got out at their floor.

From the stairwell, two figures appeared. Both were men dressed in plaid suits with slightly ruffled shirt fronts, and both had broad foreheads and square features that stood out distinctly on their faces. One was older than the other, so they clearly stood out as father and son, the father looking to be in his sixties and the son twenty years younger. They spoke in hushed voices, but their somewhat twangy tones carried down the long hallway.

As they came toward her and Larissa, Vivian caught the lingering bright eyes regarding them with an open stare that was not quite lurid but not as discreet as it might be. The men gave a slight bow in their direction and, without waiting for her and Larissa to return it, continued down to the other end of the hall, silent now.

"Well, that was fresh, wasn't it?" Vivian said with a laugh.

Her mother pulled her to the suite where their luggage was already waiting for them outside their suite. "Your observations are rather dim in some quarters, Vivian."

"I don't understand." She fished into her bag for the extra room key the hotel clerk had given her.

"I believe we have just had our first encounter with the Leblancs."

Vivian eyed her. "How do you know?"

"I don't," her mother confessed. "I only have a feeling."

She played with the key in her hand. "So that's the catch of the season, is it? He looked more like a dragoon than a buccaneer."

"He looked like neither one nor the other," said her mother sternly. "I thought they looked quite cultured."

"Is the father looking for a wife too?" Vivian grinned. "He took as much interest in us as his son when they passed."

"Vivian, don't be vulgar!"

They entered the suite just as the porter appeared with apologies for abandoning the baggage and brought each piece into the rooms under Larissa's firm guidance.

After he left, Vivian inspected the suite. Her heart turned cold. "Mother, we can't stay here!"

"Why ever not?" Her mother unpinned her hat and straightened her hair.

Her tongue felt dry. "Don't you see?" Her voice came out in a croak.

It was clear her mother did not see. She didn't see the silver panels careless past inhabitants had chipped now painted over. She didn't see that the painting on the wall was a John Singer-Sargent, looking just as faded as it had the year before.

"We were here last year!" she burst out. "Exactly in this room."

"Vivian, you have got to stop feeling that everything points toward the past." Her mother's voice was firm. "We're looking to the future now."

Vivian thought about the two men they had just passed. They looked amiable, and despite the lingering eyes, cultured, as her mother had said. The open face of the younger one, even though she had seen it for only a moment, appealed to her, and even their freshness had a bold honesty to it. And yet, she felt afraid. It was as if a man in a portrait had come to life and now, she would be forced to speak to him, take his arm, perhaps more. And then he would take her back into the portrait with him, and she would be trapped inside the gilded frame, the box folding over her like those knitted faces in Alderdice Hall. Only she would still be alive.

t five o'clock, Vivian and her mother emerged from their rooms where they had been shut in since the afternoon, refreshed, dressed in dotted rose and burgundy evening dresses, slipping on their gloves. Vivian imagined the suite next to theirs, the ladies engaging in the same adjustments, the men, if there were any, straightening their ties and pulling the edges of their dinner jackets around their bulky middles. A wave of sadness entered the room as she thought of the previous summer, when Jake had been with them. He would always be the first one ready, lingering in the parlor when they came out, his hands shoved in his pockets, his dinner jacket hanging on his lanky frame. His presence, though usually silent and still, was comforting to Vivian, as comforting as it had been when they were children in the playroom with only the glass circus in the cupboard as their companion, imagining the ribbon music and the dancing bears and prancing elephants.

She turned to her mother, wanting, in that sentimental moment, to tell her how much she missed her brother. But Larissa, as always, was so regal in the way she pulled the glove over \her fingers, making them fit their bony structure perfectly, that Vivian's tongue froze. And yet, she saw her mother had paused for a moment too, her eyes raised a little, with something in the arched brow, some feeling not quite in control.

But when she spoke to her daughter, her voice was quietly composed as usual. "I'm glad we bought that dress at Worth's. It suits you admirably."

"Salmon pink and black," Vivian remarked. "Rather at odds, aren't they?"

Larissa glanced at her. "I don't think so, dear."

"The pink of infant innocence, the black of the shroud," Vivian said. "Black is the color of specters, isn't it?"

She saw her mother's shoulders draw back. "I thought we agreed you were going to give up that nonsense."

"How can I, Mother?" she asked. "The Alderdices have a family legacy of specters."

"Yes, well, we shall dispense with morbid talk tonight," her mother said briskly.

Vivian slid the velvet reticule bag up her arm. "Aren't you going to say Jake is not a specter?"

"I don't want to talk about your brother." Larissa opened the door and stepped back to let Vivian exit.

Despite the exacting hour of the cuckoo clock, they were late for courtyard cocktails. The place was already milling with men and women in evening dress, some sitting on the iron chairs, others lingering over the shoulders of others. Larissa chose a table near the hedges facing away from the sea.

Vivian smiled bitterly as a waiter pulled back the chair for her. "You ought to have been in the Navy, Mother."

"I care little for boats," Larissa said absently as she was studying the crowd. "What, dear?"

Vivian laughed. "I was remarking upon the fact that you perfectly positioned us so we may have an overview of who's here and who comes in, and yet, should we be snubbed by the

Griffiths or the Tishers or other such blue bloods, no one need be the wiser."

Larissa said, "We're here precisely not to be snubbed any longer. And I don't believe Mrs. Griffith would ever snub us. She's been very understanding."

"Very." Vivian waved her handkerchief. "Especially considering she has no idea what she need be understanding about, since we've been telling lies about Jake all year."

They were silent as the waiter set down the cocktails in front of them. When he left, her mother continued, "You ought to be grateful she's looking out for your interests."

"My marriage prospects, you mean." Vivian sighed and glanced at the faded blue line of sea. "I used to think we were the most dignified family on Washington Street when I was a child. Rather arrogant of me, don't you think?"

"We *are* dignified," Larissa insisted.

"Oh, we put up a good pretense," said Vivian. "But ever since my debutante ball, I've realized we're like dolls inside a toy street scene. We maneuver ourselves from corner to corner, but we've never really inhabited the spirit of Washington Street."

"Your grandfather worked very hard to give us a place in society," her mother said. "I should be very disappointed if they cast us out now."

Vivian leaned forward. "Do you really think they would cast us out?"

"Oh, not overtly," said Larissa. "But each year would bring fewer invitations and fewer people would come to call on us. The message would be clear." Her voice shook a little as she spoke. "You remember what they did to the Fornhams when they allowed their daughter to marry that scoundrel? And your Mrs. Moore would have been more acceptable to them, even with her progressive ideas, if she had married again."

"I don't know that I would really care," said Vivian. She laid her hand on her mother's. "But you would. And the children are responsible for the parents, aren't they?"

"Well, I don't intend to be a burden to you," said Larissa in a wry voice.

Vivian smiled. "Perhaps we'll get lucky in the new century, and there will be no need for high society at all. Washington Street will retire like the old fossil it is."

"Well, I can't say I like being thought of as an antique," Larissa said with another wry smile as she raised her head a little to peer into the crowd. "I don't think Mrs. Griffith or her cousin would appreciate it either."

"Mrs. Griffith isn't an antique, Mother." Vivian lifted her glass. "She's part of the woodwork."

This made her mother laugh. Vivian marveled how, now that Jake was not with them, she and her mother had developed a language between them that, despite the veneer of etiquette, underlined the insights they both possessed about the world around them.

"Mother," Vivian ventured. "Mother, when were you born?"

Larissa slowly set down her glass. "What a silly thing to ask!"

"Not so silly, maybe," Vivian murmured.

"You know when I was born!"

"Yes," said Vivian. "I met someone on the train who confused me, that's all."

"Who in the world would be interested in when I was born?" Larissa brushed away the hanging ribbon from her hat the wind had blown in her face.

"He wasn't exactly interested in you," Vivian said with a grimace. "His name is David Potter, and he's the nephew of the late Loretta Potter."

Her mother's eyes had gone back to the crowd. "We know no Potters."

"*We* don't," said Vivian. "But Grandmother did when she was in Waxwood."

Her mother glanced at her. "Oh, I see."

"He was telling me some things about Waxwood after Grandmother left," she continued.

"You didn't take a fancy to him, did you?" Her mother's eyes were acute.

"Heavens no," said Vivian with a laugh. "We're more like old friends."

"Well, I don't want you to forget why we're here, dear," said Larissa.

Vivian tensed. "I've never been one to toss my head about and hide my face behind my fan at every eligible bachelor, have I?"

A large party emerged through the French doors. Among the fussy flounces of tulle and the parasols raised even as the sun faded to pose no threat to delicate skin, Vivian saw the three Tisher girls followed by their mother, whom she always thought of as a taller and more American version of Queen Victoria. Following them were the two men she and her mother had encountered in the hallway.

"It looks as if you were right, Mother," Vivian said. "It was the Leblancs we met in the hallway."

The younger of the two men helped Fern, the eldest of the Tisher trio, to her chair. The young woman threw her head over her shoulder with a gleaming smile that resembled the Cheshire Cat in the story of Alice. The middle sister, Cecily, generally considered the prettiest of the three only because her features resembled her mother's in their regality, took this as a challenge and stood stoically near her chair, waving aside a young man Vivian had never seen who was eager to accommodate her. Mr. Leblanc flitted away from her older sister, mumbling apologies as he held out the chair for her. Cecily rewarded him by taking out her handkerchief and waving it at him with an even more winning smile than her sister's.

"He'll have his hands full," Vivian chuckled. "As if one Tisher girl isn't enough to contend with!"

"Mrs. Griffith hinted all three of them are interested in Monte Leblanc," her mother remarked.

"Three!" Vivian glanced at her. "Bethel isn't even of age!"

"She's sixteen, dear. Old enough to begin looking for prospects."

"I see Mrs. Tisher had no objection to Bethel putting her hair up," Vivian observed. The girl had swept up her rather thin hair beneath her hat, exposing the collar of her blouse. "Grandmother would have had a fit if I had put my hair up like that at sixteen."

"Young girls are so much more brazen nowadays," sighed her mother.

Vivian could tell Bethel had mildly enchanted Mr. Leblanc, or at least he pretended to be enchanted. Bethel was leaning toward him across the table, her lips moving quickly.

"I can't imagine the Tishers would consent to let any of their daughters out of Boston society," Vivian said. "They think the Far West so inferior."

"I'm sure their prejudices would suddenly ease if one of their daughters married one of us," Larissa said with a little haughtiness.

"Mrs. Griffith said Mr. Leblanc was looking for an entrance with Washington Street,"

Vivian reminded her. "He wouldn't exactly be a native, would he?"

"If he's related to the Griffiths," said her mother with a pointed look, "that would hardly matter."

"But he might settle his wife in Canada after all." Vivian heart suddenly filled with terror. "Mother, we can't!"

"Can't what?" Her mother blinked.

"We can't live in Canada."

"What on earth are you talking about?"

"If Monte Leblanc decided not to build a house on Washington Street," Vivian continued, trying to steady her voice. "We couldn't leave California."

"We wouldn't be in Canada the entire year," her mother reasoned. "Only now and then, I imagine, enough to make an appearance."

"They would forget about us if we were no longer lived on Washington Street year-round," Vivian insisted. "I thought you didn't want them to shun us."

Her mother cast a shrewd eye upon her. "That's not the reason you're alarmed, is it, Vivian?"

"I don't want to leave friends." Her voice was steely. "Or family."

"We have no more family here," said Larissa in a hard voice. "Not now."

Vivian's eyes filled with tears. "You can't mean that, Mother."

"You're always speaking of the truth, aren't you?" Larissa asked. "I'm telling you the truth."

"He's your son!"

"Lower your voice," her mother hissed.

Vivian held her handkerchief to her eyes in the discreet way her mother and grandmother had taught her since she came of age. They sat in silence for a while, and she felt the tranquility of the sea again. "You know you can't will him away, Mother."

A crumbled look appeared on her mother's face. "You think I'm unfeeling because I didn't help him, don't you?"

Vivian looked down at her hands. "It wasn't your fault Jake refused to defend himself."

"I never told you this, Vivian," Larissa's voice softened, "but I went to Mr. Elsmere."

Vivian snorted at the mention of the family lawyer. "That old goat!"

"That old goat has friends in the right places," her mother insisted. "I thought he might pull some strings—"

Vivian sat up. "Mother! You did that for Jake?"

"Mr. Elsmere said your brother refused that too."

Vivian reached over and covered her mother's hand. "I'm sorry if I've been unjust to you."

"One cannot help a stubborn young man if he won't help himself." There was a catch in Larissa's voice.

The courtyard was in a lull now, all eyes on the sea. She covered Larissa's other hand so her mother could not escape her gaze. "Why don't we ask Mr. Elsmere to find out where Jake is?"

"Why would we want to do that?"

Vivian paused for a moment, feeling the withdrawal of the breeze. "So we can visit him."

The blood drained from Larissa's face. "I don't want you to ask me that ever again, Vivian."

"You don't think he needs us?"

"He's a man now, not a boy," said Larissa. "He did what he thought was his duty toward the family."

"Duty, expectation," Vivian snarled. "The shackles of *noblesse oblige*."

Larissa glanced up. "I believe Mrs. Tisher is waving to us, dear."

Vivian sighed and looked toward the center tables pushed together to make an impenetrable square. The woman in question, presiding with her stately manner, was indeed glancing in their direction. But her leaning head and acknowledging smile could hardly be mistaken for a warm greeting.

"You and she were as thick as thieves last summer," Vivian remarked.

"That was last summer," Larissa said in a rigid voice.

"She won't exactly be thrilled when she sees that you've put your dachshund in the race against her greyhounds."

"Why, dear, what a thing to say!" Larissa's smile was overtly pleasant as she said this, giving back the same tilted nod Mrs. Tisher had given her. "It's not a question of speed but suitability. Mrs. Tisher, more than anyone, would acquiesce gracefully to a young woman more suitable for Monte Leblanc than one of her daughters."

"All's fair in love and war?" Vivian eyed her mother.

"We shall be as gracious to her as she is to us." Her mother drained the last of her cocktail.

"You really think she'll be gracious to us?"

"Mrs. Griffith will see to it that she is," said Larissa, not without a little slyness. "She wants her cousin to meet as many people as possible this summer."

Vivian leaned forward. "Why should she want that?"

"Because, dear, she's built the Leblancs up so that now everyone is eager to meet them," said her mother. "She won't miss a chance to introduce them to everyone she knows."

Vivian couldn't help but smile. "What a crafty woman you are, Mother."

"Not at all," said Larissa in a mild voice. "I only know Washington Street."

"We've already had an introduction to the Leblancs," Vivian said wryly as she glanced at the two men. She noted they had exchanged their frumpy plaid suits for plain, darker ones, though their shirt collars were still more ruffled than starched and their bow ties hung a little loose from their necks.

"That was merely in passing," said Larissa. "That was not a *proper* introduction." She sighed, glancing at her daughter. "I fear your precarious associations lately have led you away from the path of social graces, Vivian."

"If you mean my friendship with Marvina Moore—"

"I don't wish to call it a 'friendship.'" Her mother lowered her voice. "You know I've always tried to allow you the utmost freedom."

"Freedom!" Vivian sniffed. "You've been standing over me with family and social obligation since I was old enough to understand what the word 'obligations' meant."

"Freedom in your leisure time." Larissa's voice was steel.

"Yes, I suppose you have," said Vivian. "I have no complaints against you, Mother. Nor against Grandmother. You were both indoctrinated into a rather condemning life, and it's only natural you should expect the same of me."

"You're very ungrateful, Vivian," her mother barked.

She played with the napkin on the table. "Women whose expectations exceed their wishes usually are."

"And what are your wishes, if I may ask?" Her mother put her chin in her hand, a note of sincere curiosity in her voice.

"I don't know," said Vivian. "That's just the trouble. I only know that when I marry, if my husband denies me the will to find it, I shall die."

She thought of the endless round of picnics, parties, boating trips, anything that exposed young people to one another in the company of their elders in the proper manner. She recalled from her debutante days the exhaustion, the constant appeasement, how the mothers of the young men had examined her and her fellow debutantes with gawking eyes for their marriage potential. These women of society made note of anything that might make the girls the least desirable horse in the stable like too much innocence, too much pluck, or too little initiative, and filed it away in their otherwise empty minds. And now it was to begin all over again. No gawking mothers, but she was still a horse waiting to prance onto the field to show her worth.

She glanced at the center table. Mr. Leblanc had pushed his chair a little back, and she could see him more clearly than she had earlier in the hallway. His physique was admirable for a man not far off fifty, with well-shaped muscles and a face that held hardly a wrinkle. With his hands on his knees, his lips pressed into a closed smile, and his eyes wandering from one Tisher girl to another as he listened to their chatter, he was both amiable and accessible. His father had a more stoic way to him, his face hardly moving a muscle as he drank one cocktail after another.

"The Tisher girls have certainly dominated the attentions of the buccaneer," she remarked.

"I wish you would stop calling him that," Larissa said. "I find it most offensive, and so would Mrs. Griffith."

"You shouldn't," said Vivian dryly. "Your own father was one, remember?"

"He was not," Larissa insisted. "Just because a man comes from humble beginnings and rises in society doesn't mean he did it in unsavory ways. Many people find it admirable nowadays."

"The Tisher girls must," Vivian said as she watched the table.

The Tisher trio were now swarming around Mr. Leblanc. Fern had somehow maneuvered her chair to his right and sat at the edge with her knees together, bending toward him as if she were going to drop her head in his lap at any moment. Cecily sat at his left, ready to cut into the conversation when her sister closed her lips and Vivian observed that the moment Fern took a breath, Cecily moved quickly, dominating the conversation. Even Bethel took her cue from her older sisters and moved her chair a little behind Cecily, facing the man's ear. Vivian could see she could get a word in edgewise here and there.

"They make quite a spectacle, don't they?" Larissa asked, also watching them.

"I would think Mrs. Tisher, with her queenly mannerisms, would have taught them more restraint."

Her mother sniffed. "And they think we Westerners are vulgar!" Her daughter rewarded her arch comment with a burst of laughter from her daughter. "I can't imagine why that delights you."

"Because you said it, and you meant it," said Vivian. "You ought to say what you mean more often, Mother."

"I was merely making an observation, dear," said Larissa. But Vivian could see she was pleased. "One must not be an ostrich to social convention."

"I suppose you'd like me to go over and teach those girls a little social convention?"

"Heaven forbid!" Her mother dabbed at her face with her handkerchief.

"Why not?" Vivian half rose.

"Vivian, sit down." The growl that escaped her mother's lips bore a resemblance to a lioness, alarming her enough to take her seat.

"I was only joking."

"This is not a situation for levity," said Larissa in a stiff voice. "We must approach it cautiously."

"How terribly scheming you are," Vivian teased. "You're very determined, I see." Her throat felt dry, as if it were closing up, and she signaled the waiter to bring her a fresh cocktail.

"I thought you were as well."

"Oh, I am," Vivian insisted, though she knew it sounded far from convincing.

Her mother leaned forward, lowering her voice. "Are you worried that youth is not on your side?"

Vivian glared at her. "Why does everyone speak of me as if I'm an old maid?"

"Because an unmarried woman past the age of twenty has always that to consider," said Larissa. "Vivian, I've told you repeatedly, you're as good as any of them. Better, even. I can't deny all those books and a certain amount of — well—"

"Mutiny?" Vivian raised her eyebrow, remembering how last summer her mother had accused her of possessing, like her grandmother, a "mutinous streak."

"Intelligence," her mother pronounced. "You are not the average young woman with the rather limited capabilities of the younger set. And Mr. Leblanc has more than once expressed his appreciation for ladies who know their own minds."

"How do you know that?"

"I read about him in the society columns in every paper I

could find before we left." Larissa patted her hand. "And Mrs. Griffith was only too happy to supply the missing pieces."

"So that's why you invited her to tea!"

"Mr. Leblanc is out to make a suitable match with a woman who knows San Francisco society," declared her mother. "He can hardly do that with the Tisher girls, can he?"

Vivian's eyes swept toward the Tisher party. She thought the buccaneer looked a little like a lost duck, his beak-like lips standing out a little under the handlebar mustache as his head turned slightly right and left and a little backward, depending on which Tisher girl was speaking. The picture struck Vivian as amusing. The bewildered gaze reminded her of a picture she had once seen of a man sitting on a porch with flies buzzing around his head, his hand raised, trying to determine which was the most tiresome one that should meet its death first.

Fern then dropped her handkerchief on the grass. It was a trick Vivian had seen her fellow debutantes perform before she married Miles. The obtrusive item must always look as if it had just slipped from the girl's fingers, her wrist poised so as not to let on she had in fact dropped it on purpose. Few men, her mother had once told her, could resist picking up a dropped handkerchief.

But the Canadian gentleman was too dense or too clever to fall for such a trick. For, even though the handkerchief lay near Mr. Leblanc's feet, he did not notice it. He had been listening to Bethel, her hands molding and illustrating as she leaned over the back of Cecily's chair toward the man. Vivian chuckled at the cross look on Fern's face. Her humor increased when she saw Fern's elegantly pointed toe slid the handkerchief closer to Mr. Leblanc's feet. Mr. Leblanc, however, was mesmerized by Bethel's story-telling and gestures. Vivian suddenly realized by the movement of her hands that she was showing a galloping motion, and she remembered the youngest Tisher girl had a passion for horses.

"Perhaps the buccaneer was never a dragoon," she observed, "but it wouldn't surprise me in the least if he rides like one."

"The man is quite athletic," Larissa agreed.

"If that's so," said Vivian. "I should imagine the child has more of a chance to win his heart than her older sisters."

"Oh, really, Vivian." Her mother sniffed.

Bethel finished her story and sat back, a triumphant grin on her face. Mr. Leblanc's lips twitched a little from the closed smile. Cecily lost no time and began some story of her own while Fern reached her elegant toe toward her handkerchief to slide it closer to the front of Mr. Leblanc's chair. As he turned to give the middle sister his full attention, he stretched his leg out, covering the handkerchief with his foot.

Vivian was aware she was laughing in an unsuitable, unladylike manner. Conversations again hushed in favor of the sea, so all she could hear was the echo of her own laughter. Tears filled her eyes, and she dabbed at them with her handkerchief.

When she had calmed herself, she turned to her mother to apologize, expecting one of her mother's knifing looks. But Larissa was smiling.

"Perhaps athletic men are fond of women who laugh outright," she remarked.

Vivian's head whirled around. Mr. Leblanc was staring right at her, his eyes reaching above the tuft of mustache with an almost glittering delight. His lips were still smiling, but they were parted now.

Vivian looked quickly away, feeling the warm flags in her cheeks. There was no flattery in her blush, merely anger at her own forgetfulness. She had not laughed like that in a year.

Just then, the waiter rang the dinner gong solemnly, as if it were a calling to church, and as everyone rose, fumbling with their things to go into the dining room, Vivian caught sight of Mr. Leblanc darting toward Mrs. Griffith and leaning to whisper something in her ear. The woman gave him a congenial smile and a nod.

"I wonder what little secret he told her," she muttered.

"We must hurry, dear," said Larissa. "We don't want to be the last ones."

"But it's fashionable to be the last ones," said Vivian with mock petulance. "One can make an entrance."

"That's exactly what we don't want to do," her mother said.

"I see. We blend in, like the salamander."

A sweep of tea-colored skirts appeared among the swing of bright trains, and Mrs. Griffith was there, taking Larissa's hand and leaning toward Vivian as she spoke in a buoyant voice, "So glad you've joined us in Waxwood!"

"Well, in a manner of speaking." Larissa glanced discreetly at the party in the middle of the courtyard, then back to Mrs. Griffith with an intent look.

"Well, naturally, dear, if we had known you were coming—" Vivian did not miss the raised eyebrows that signaled the woman's promise to get them invited into the Tisher circle but made no definite promises. "You've seen the Tishers, of course?"

"And they saw us," Vivian added.

"They meant to come and say hello, I know, but this courtyard is so crowded," said the woman. Vivian stifled a giggle.

"They're preoccupied with all their guests, naturally." Larissa nodded.

"Especially the young ladies." Vivian said.

"Oh, Emile and Monte have been with the Tishers for months now, and they got to know those girls quite well." The woman's tone dropped. "The reason I came, Larissa, is to invite you and Vivian to join us in the hotel parlor after dinner."

"That's very generous of you," Larissa said.

"We'll all be refreshed from the trip by then," continued Mrs. Griffith. "One ought to get to know one's fellow vacationers as quickly as possible." Her hooked eyes regarded Vivian with a meaningful look.

"We would be delighted to join you," said Larissa. "It will be good to see the Tishers again, won't it, Vivian?"

"I suppose so, Mother," Vivian sighed. "I had hoped to go straight to the suite after dinner and retiring with a good book."

"I really think you ought to come." Her mother's firm voice took on a warning tone.

"Yes, do, Vivian." Mrs. Griffith put her hand on the back of a chair as she leaned toward her, lowering her voice even further. "You see, the invitation didn't come from Mrs. Tisher."

"No, I didn't think it did," Vivian said with a wry smile.

"Monte himself asked me to ask you," the woman continued. "Shall I tell you his exact words?"

"Please do." Vivian tilted her head.

"He said, 'Leila, won't you introduce me to that jolly girl with the pretty face and the sweeping red hair?'"

"I prefer strawberry blond," Vivian said in mock haughtiness, patting the back of her head.

"You mustn't be flippant this time, Vivian," said Mrs. Griffith, a little put out. "When a man as worldly as he asks to make a woman's acquaintance—"

"Because I laughed at the absurd coquetry of the Tisher girl?" Vivian raised her eyebrows.

"Yes, they are rather absurd, between you and me," said the woman. "They seem to think it necessary to play such games in the East. Thank goodness we're more tastefully direct about such things."

"You won't refuse, will you, dear?" Her mother was still looking at her. "It would be rude not to come."

"Yes, it would," Vivian said. She felt a heaviness in her head, as if someone had put a pile of bricks on it. "I would even say it's impossible for me to refuse now."

"You make it sound like a dentist appointment," said Mrs. Griffith a little roughly.

Vivian straightened her spine. She had no fear of Mrs. Griffith becoming nasty, but her daughter Amber was another matter. And she had made a promise to herself and her mother to at least meet Mr. Leblanc. "I didn't mean to," she said. "Mother and I will be glad to come. I'm very flattered your cousin asked to make my acquaintance."

The change took Mrs. Griffith in, and she patted Vivian's hand with an "I knew you would come to your senses" look on her face as she swept through the crowd back to the Tisher party.

lthough the Waxwoodian parlor room was meant for all guests, it was almost an unwritten law that, after dinner, it belonged to those staying in the penthouse suites and whoever they wished to invite. So it was no surprise to Vivian that, as she and Larissa entered with the usual blasé manner of upper class-ladies, the scene resembled the teas and parties she had attended her entire life on Washington Street, with only the Indian patterned rug and blue velvet chairs to distinguish it.

"Only the background changes," she remarked to her mother.

Larissa gave her one of her usual annoyed looks as when she felt her daughter was speaking "in circles."

"We may as well be at one of Mrs. Griffith's soirees," she continued.

"You say that as if it were a punishment," said her mother with amusement.

"I'm not at all sure it isn't." Vivian smiled back.

Mrs. Tisher was playing the host, as if it were her own parlor to which she had invited only the very best. She darted forward, looking, as always, as if she were floating over the rug rather than walking on it. Vivian almost wished those thin heels of hers would stumble over a diamond in the pattern. "So good to see you again, Larissa. Vivian, you've grown more attractive since last year."

"I can't think why," Vivian replied. "When my prospects seem to shrivel up with every passing year." She endured a discreet pinch of silence from her mother.

"We were afraid you wouldn't be joining us," the woman continued. "We had heard your son was away."

"He's in Europe now," said Larissa in a smooth voice, as Vivian felt a gnawing in her stomach.

"Studying painting, I'm told," the woman smiled like an eel.

"He's very devoted to his art."

"Yes," the woman replied. "I remember."

Vivian marveled at how well her mother could lie. Larissa's features never lost their balance, and her pleasantly grated voice never wavered. The blue eyes struck one as having the essence of composure.

"You had company with you this spring, Mrs. Griffith told us," she said.

"Yes, we met Mr. Leblanc and his son in Paris," said Mrs. Tisher. "We had no idea they were relatives of Mrs. Griffith. Well-traveled gentlemen. They've been all over Europe and the Far East. Monte's second wife died ten years ago, poor man." This, she said with a lowered tone as her fan rose halfway to her lips. "Come take coffee, and I shall seat you near the windows. I know how much you like the sea air, Larissa."

A look of annoyance crossed Larissa's face, and Vivian saw why. The windows were against the far wall, and when Mrs. Tisher had seated them near Amber Griffith Stewart and Hannah Green, another daughter of a Washington Street family, Vivian caught sight of Monte Leblanc accosted by the Tisher girls some distance away. Potted plants padded the fireplace so she could barely see more than the edge of his beard and curved mustache.

Both Amber and Hannah, whose husbands were absent from

Waxwood, had been engaging in babble pertinent to young married women — Worth's latest models, hard-working husbands who canceled engagements to the theater at the last moment, and obstinate servants. But they both ceased and sat straight in their chairs as Larissa and Vivian sat down. Both cast their self-serving eyes on Vivian with the pitied look of women who knew the comfort of marriage on one who did not.

"Good to see you here, Vivian," Amber said. "You've been isolating yourself a little too much in the last year for my taste. A friend of George's was staying with us this spring, and we wanted so much for you to meet him."

"It's a shame you didn't invite me to tea," Vivian mumbled.

"Oh, we would have, but you're always so busy," mused Hannah.

"Yes, Vivian has been very busy," Larissa remarked. She lifted the coffee cup to her lips, but her eyes were on the fireplace.

Amber said, "I remember you once tried to get me to read — who was it now?"

"Charlotte Brontë," Vivian said in a dry voice.

"Oh, and she was so wicked!" Amber touched her chin with her fingertips. "That Jane Eyre with the married man."

"She had no idea he was married until the wedding, did she?" Vivian eyed her.

"I don't find such stories appealing." Amber's haughtiness was so pronounced now, it made her features flare up like a horse. "I prefer more congenial tales."

"Such as tales of shepherds and maidens" Vivian asked. Her eyes also wandered toward the fireplace.

"They *are* making a spectacle of themselves, aren't they?" Hannah glanced at the Tisher girls. "They haven't let that poor man alone for a moment since we arrived."

"One must establish one's position, mustn't one?" Amber pointed out.

" I find ladies vying for the attention of one man unappealing," said Vivian. "If he can't make clear his choice, he can very well find himself a horse or a dog." Both the young ladies giggled.

"That would hardly serve womankind, would it, dear?" Larissa remarked, still distracted.

"On the contrary, Mother," said Vivian. "It would serve us very well. One less pompous man in this world is always welcome."

"My, but your daughter has such progressive ideas, Larissa," said Amber. "I shouldn't wonder if she won't be joining Mrs. Moore and Mrs. Fowler next."

"They do excellent work," Vivian said stubbornly. "Marvina stayed behind in the city this summer for just that purpose. I've never met Albina Fowler, though I should like to. I've heard her talks are always enlightening."

"I read a piece from her in the *San Francisco Slogan* just last week," Hannah piped up. "She was talking about bloomers."

"Bloomers!" Amber scoffed.

"She thinks women ought to wear them all the time," Hannah said. "Not just for bicycling and the beach."

"I never approved of bicycles." Amber spoke with her flared features.

"It's all right for girls, perhaps," Larissa remarked. "But grown women ought to keep their two feet on the ground."

"How right you are, Larissa." Amber nodded with approval.

"I think they're rather splendid," said Vivian.

"Oh, really!" Two scarlet dots appeared on Hannah's cheeks.

By now, the small party near the fireplace had distracted Vivian. The Tisher girls, who had arranged themselves much as they had in the courtyard, with Fern on one side of Mr. Leblanc, Cecily on the other, and Bethel hovering behind over his shoulder, had been conversing, using their fans now instead of their hands. Mr. Leblanc, Vivian observed, was growing tired of them, as his sleepy gaze sagged even more so he looked almost shifty-eyed. He seemed to catch her look, and in the open, impertinent way of a stranger to American ways, held it while Cecily dared to put her hand on his arm as she chatted away, as if sensing his waning attention. Suddenly, he turned his head to Fern and spoke to her. The general ballyhoo of tables being shifted for bridge masked his words. However, Vivian observed Fern's serene smile as she stepped away from the fireplace. Mr. Leblanc nodded at the other girls, excused himself, and followed her.

"It looks as if he's made his choice," Amber remarked.

"There was no mystery in that," Vivian said. "Fern is, after all, the Tisher heiress."

Larissa rose. "I see the bridge tables are out. I shall leave you ladies to chat amongst yourselves." She threw her head back with a meaningful look at Vivian, though Vivian was unclear what message she was trying to convey.

All three ladies remained silent as they observed the new young couple. Even Vivian couldn't help being amused as she watched how carefully Fern maneuvered her lace fan. First in the right hand, then twirling it in her left hand, and then shifting it to her right hand again.

"She uses that fan like a weapon," Vivian remarked.

"Perhaps to her, it is," Amber said. "She is nineteen."

"And there is not much time for a ceremony?" Vivian eyed her.

"We women have little time, Mama always says," Hannah recited. "For — oh, that sort of thing."

"Some of us have all the time in the world," Vivian said.

"Perhaps, but only some of us." Amber looked almost like a ferret as she glanced at Vivian.

Mr. Leblanc had, to his credit, taken Fern's rather bold fan play with good humor, smiling and nodding. Then, touching upon the edge of his mustache, his eyes slid toward the window. Vivian caught the look of momentary displeasure on Fern's face, but she redeemed her composure quickly and, taking Mr. Leblanc's arm, sidled over to them.

"We're happy to see you in Waxwood again, Vivian." Her voice had a touch of ice in it. "May I introduce you to Mr. Monte Leblanc?"

Vivian recognized the man's eager countenance and too-quick bow, as if trying to contain his enthusiasm. She wondered if he asked Fern to make the introduction. Vivian was not immune to such flattery, and she felt warmed by it.

"Delighted to meet you, Mr. Leblanc." She pulled from all of her breeding to present herself as one who was worthy of justifying the introduction.

"Charmed." His voice was, unlike his physique, disappointingly thin. "May I?" Before waiting for an answer, he took the seat next to her that Larissa had vacated, leaving Fern to plop down next to Hannah.

"Please do," said Vivian, smiling,

At that moment, the younger Tisher girls flocked toward them, each carrying a stool, and perched themselves in front of Mr. Leblanc. Vivian couldn't help but notice the way the man's eyes darted away from annoyance, even as his lips remained in the closed, congenial smile.

Bethel, whose gregariousness Vivian always found refreshing, if a little buzzing, was the first to speak. "We've just been discussing the Drysdells."

"Odie and Eileen?" Amber leaned forward, pressing her knees with her hands. "We met them in Switzerland last winter." Her eyes slid toward Vivian. "You must have met Jessica when she was here two years ago, Vivian."

"Two years ago, I could have hardly met anyone," Vivian answered. "I was in mourning for my grandfather, remember?"

"So you were," Amber mumbled.

"It's a sad state when pretty women bury themselves in weeds and veils too long," said Mr. Leblanc, shaking his head.

"Yes, isn't it?" Vivian answered, though she thought the comment a little imprudent. "I met her the year before that, though. What about the Drysdells?"

"One learns a great deal by listening to stories about other people," Mr. Leblanc mused. "Especially those from other countries."

"Perhaps you'll tell us some of your stories from your travels sometime, Mr. Leblanc," said Fern, opening her fan wide.

"I would rather you tell me your stories," he said with a laugh. "American girls tell such charming stories."

"I'm sure Miss Tisher's story about the Drysdells will fulfill that promise," said Vivian.

The acrid tone slid by Mr. Leblanc, but not Bethel. The girl looked ashamed as her face cradling in her hand and the remnants of her childhood in the pout on her lips. Her sister Cecily eagerly took over.

"My sister only mentioned it because we thought it should interest you, Mr. Leblanc, since you know Jessica so well," she said. "She is engaged to the Duke of Farthington."

"That is interesting," said the man. Vivian could tell that he was struggling to remember who either of them were. "It is a brilliant match, to be sure."

"It's so important that a woman and man be made for one another, don't you think, Mr. Leblanc?" Fern tilted her head forward.

"But the Duke is such a gambler!" Bethel blurted out. "They say he has fallen in with the horses, and Jessica *is* an heiress." She sighed. "Heiresses are certainly lucky!"

"My dear, all the noblemen are like that," said Amber in a bored tone. "It is an exchange of gifts, really — an American girl's wealth for his family title."

"I shouldn't want to be a duchess under those terms," sniffed Bethel.

"If the horses are his only vice," said Mr. Leblanc with a chuckle, "I should say Miss Drysdell is very lucky indeed."

"But it isn't." Cecily's eyes widened. "Elizabeth Cornwall told me it's all over England that his grandfather and great-great-grandfather both went mad of the drink. It was like poison to them."

"Well, my dear, all families have their skeletons," said Mr. Leblanc.

"Oh, that's all fine when they are ancient ones," said Fern. "It's the skeletons still rattling in the closets that one must be careful of." Her eyes slid toward Vivian.

Vivian's hands grew stiff, even though the coffee Mrs. Tisher had given her was still warm. "Perhaps there would be no need for the skeletons to rattle if families told the truth from generation to generation."

"Yes, you are a great believer in the truth, aren't you, Vivian?" Amber asked. "No matter what the consequences."

"'Rather than love, than money, than fame, give me truth.'" Vivian quoted.

"You made that up right now?" Bethel's voice was sour.

"I didn't," said Vivian, smiling. "Henry David Thoreau did."

"You enjoy reading, I'm told." Mr. Leblanc turned to her.

"You don't sound as if you approve," Vivian remarked.

"Yes, Mr. Leblanc," Fern intervened. "Tell us your opinion of the blue-stocking." She shifted her fan to her right hand.

"I don't know that I would take the liberty of forming an opinion of any woman's stockings," the man laughed.

"Miss Tisher is referring to literary women," Vivian said.

"I was in jest, naturally," he said, a little too condescendingly. "I believe education can shape one's morals and successes, but so can one's life experiences. More so, perhaps"

"We were talking specifically about women." Vivian eyed him.

"A woman oughtn't to be so bookish," Bethel declared. "It's so unwomanly!"

"I don't disapprove of bookishness, Miss Bethel, as long as the woman leaves time for other things," he said.

"I think it's fine that women can read all the books they chose," Fern said. The care in her words made Vivian realize she was saying this more to appease Mr. Leblanc than out of her own conviction. "Until they are wives, of course. Then they have no time for books."

"Perhaps that's why Vivian reads so much," said Amber with her fox-like gaze. "She has all the time in the world. Isn't that what you said, Vivian?"

"And what would you consider time well spent?" Vivian eyed her. "Gossiping about other people's skeletons?"

"Skeletons need not be in closets to rattle," Amber shot back.

"Ladies, please." Mr. Leblanc looked away with a quick smile.

"You're perfectly right, Mr. Leblanc," said Fern. "It's hardly pleasant to be witness to a girlish quarrel." She lifted the fan to her face.

Vivian rose, her voice shaking. "I'd like to know what you mean by that, Amber."

There was silence and all the ladies — the Tisher girls, Hannah — shifted as if settling in for a good quarrel.

But Amber's haughtiness overcame her viciousness. "I meant nothing, Vivian. Nothing at all." She smiled a pleasant smile at Mr. Leblanc. "Vivian and I have always squabbled like two hens about nothing, Mr. Leblanc, ever since we were children. Don't pay any attention to us." She gave Vivian a tolerant glance.

"Well, I wouldn't want to cause a squabble over nothing," Vivian said archly. "So I shall get some air."

Mr. Leblanc jumped up. "An excellent idea, Miss Alderdice." His eyes and cheeks were glistening.

But the company of a man who was looking for a flirtation was the last thing on her mind. "I prefer to go alone, Mr. Leblanc."

"Walking alone at night?" This came from Fern, but all three Tisher girls leaned back as if they were witnessing a terrible tragedy.

"I didn't think even ladies in America do that," Mr. Leblanc remarked, returning her rebuff.

"You're wrong, sir." Vivian gave him a wry smile. "Even the simple and confined ladies in America enjoy a solitary constitution now and again."

"It's a woman's prerogative to do anything she wishes," said the man, his tongue stumbling a little with embarrassment. "I didn't mean to insinuate otherwise. But you will agree, Miss Alderdice, it's a man's prerogative to wish to protect her."

"I appreciate your offer, sir," said Vivian, her voice softening. "But I've been looking after myself for quite some time."

"As you wish." He shrugged and took his place next to Fern again, deliberately, Vivian thought.

As she strolled toward the door, she felt a hand clawing her arm. She turned and saw it was Amber. "It may be your prerogative, Vivian," she spoke in a whisper, "but it's not wise to reject Mr. Leblanc's offer."

"Are you so impatient to see me wed, Amber?" Vivian asked. "Does marital bliss prevail for you so much that your only wish in life is to see every woman achieve it?"

The young lady colored, as Washington Street gossips said under their breaths that her husband spent more time with his comrades at the Hercules Club than he did at the dinner table.

"I'm sure your mother would not approve," she said in an icy voice.

"My mother has rarely approved of much of what I do with my free time," Vivian said. "I've never let it disturb me."

"Perhaps you ought to," Amber said in a tart voice. "Your social position has been rather compromised as of late."

"Compromised?"

Amber was fanning herself vigorously, staring at the wall opposite with her haughty eyes. "You don't want to endanger it any further, do you?"

Now it was Vivian's turn to color, feeling her cheeks coloring. She turned her back on Amber and stalked out, her heels digging into the thick rug, but not before she had caught her mother's fierce look.

⁓

She went out to the front of the hotel, knowing the boardwalk would be crowded with people eager to get a glimpse at the sea as they took a pleasant stroll their first night of resort life. The night was pleasant, as the rash winds of the early evening had subsided into a restful breeze. The bay looked like a shadow of the sea behind it, but its waters were still and its cup-shaped shores on the other side peered across with moonlight catching corners of rocks, flinging a shining light back at her. She could see a distant vision of town across the way, the pier skirting the main vein of Waxwood's more practical side where the inhabitants made their living every day.

She couldn't help but lament how it was only seven years ago that she had stepped off the train to face a sleepy, lopping town where the bay spilled into a marshland with the wax wood trees dug into quiet peaks. She had walked down the main road and amiable eyes had watched her with pity because she wore mourning clothes. But they had not thought it peculiar that a woman in weeds was walking alone on their street, and they had not judged her with the ferret eyes of Amber Griffith Stewart.

The ferry was bobbing near the edge of the hotel, and the man who steered it lingered on the dock, smoking his pipe. The ferry to and from the new resort section ran well into the night, and the man looked tired. Vivian smiled at him and tied the shawl around her shoulders. She had not brought her hat out, so she fished into her bag for a handkerchief and tied it around her head.

The man helped her onto the ferry. "Kind of late, ain't you, miss?"

"I expect I won't be the only one," she said as she sat down on one of the wooden benches.

"No miss," he said, laughing and showing a few missing molars. "Young people here gettin' over to the town all the time, now that them saloons are open 'til midnight." He leaned toward her with a wink. "And the more wicked of 'em takin' the special wagon to Goldspur."

"Special wagon?"

"Oh, that's Mr. Shelley's idea," he said. "Down at the livery. He's got a regular taxi service with that wagon of his." He chuckled as a group of youths, three men and three women, dressed as fine as Vivian, boarded the ferry. One of the young men, who paid for himself and the young lady on his arm, caught her eye and gave her an interested look, but she turned around and leaned her arms against the bannister as the ferry headed slowly across the bay.

She had no idea what it was she wanted of the town, but by the time the man with the pipe helped her off the ferry, she knew exactly where she was going. She walked down the main street much as she had those years before. The town was livelier now, and not only from the young people who crowded around the doorway of the livery stable as she passed. Shops were still open, and saloon doors let out mists of smoke and laughter. Some emptier buildings, she noted, had become hotels, and people lingered on the porches in rocking chairs or leaning against the bannister. Though they dressed in country clothes, their mannerisms mimicked those she had witnessed earlier in the hotel parlor. Several young women used their fans to their advantage while the young men with whom they flirted either responded to the signals they wished to cultivate or ignored those they did not.

She passed the gazebo in the city park, and, for a moment, she felt a pinch in her breast as she remembered the turn up the road led toward the Ross house. She stepped into the street in that direction, but then retreated, realizing it was far too late to see

Bertha and Ruth that night. But she *would* see them. Even if her mother disapproved, she would see them.

She continued down the main street where the more commercial side of town turned into lonely streets. Here, there were no saloons, and many doorways were dark. Few people lurked about, and those who did ducked their heads as if they had something to hide. It was not an unpleasant place, merely more isolated and less illuminated with streetlights further apart than those near the pier. A little curve in the road revealed a light burning at the end of the street drew Vivian.

She stepped in under the swinging sign that read *Nettie's Drugstore*. Scents of vanilla and antiseptic told of the shop's strange combination of wares. A few small tables with iron chairs gathered close to one front window, while the other window showed displays of glass bottles with powders and liquids and faded labels. The small shop was filled with things, in fact, shelves stacked to the ceiling with whatever odds and ends anyone could need behind counters, on the sides and in the back.

On one other side of the store stood a narrow soda fountain with a polished marble counter, swiveling stools, and a mirror in the back. Behind it was a woman about Vivian's age, perhaps a little older, dressed in black crepe with a lace white collar and cuffs. She had a dust rag in her hands and was intent on polishing one particular spot on the marble counter. Her entire figure dipped into it, and her pointed elbows shot out as she dug into the rag with both hands. Strands of dark hair had edged out of her pompadour, swinging back and forth with her vigorous movements.

Vivian sat on a stool. "You're being rather violent on that poor counter, aren't you?"

The woman's arms released as and she glanced up at Vivian. "My mother used to say a woman has better luck taking her rage out on a rag or a broom than she has on any living thing." She wiped her hands on her apron and attempted to put the stray curls back in their place. "What will you have?"

"Strawberry soda." said Vivian placed her bag and shawl on the stool beside her. "You're Nettie, aren't you?"

"Your face looks familiar too." The woman raised her eyelashes as she tackled the soda machine in much the same fashion as she had the spot on the counter.

"We met last year at the BAWSPR meeting," Vivian said. The name seemed to bring a fresh anger into the woman's countenance. The pleasant features gathered with a savage look as she plucked a few strawberries into the glass. "I'm Vivian," she continued, trying not to notice.

The woman laid the soda in front of her with a straw daintily on a napkin. "Nettie Grace." She shook her hand. "I remember now. Marvina brought you."

"Yes," said Vivian.

"She's a decent woman," said Miss Grace. "I haven't seen her much lately."

"She decided to remain in San Francisco this summer," said Vivian. "The BAWSPR there is organizing some event with petitions."

Nettie cast a caustic eye toward the door. "Didn't do much good three years ago when they petitioned."

She had a sense Miss Grace's earlier attack upon the marble had to do with the organization she had only briefly seen the year before. Marvina had told her Miss Grace "could get the best of the devil in a temper." She decided it was better not to stir up this woman's wrath. "Marvina told me about your store, and I had to come see it for myself."

This made Nettie smile. "Call me Nettie, then."

"And you call me Vivian."

"Marvina calls it a little pandemonium," Nettie remarked, glancing over Vivian's shoulder.

Vivian smiled. "It does look a little chaotic."

"A little something for whatever ails you," said the woman, laughing. "I have no education. Difficult to manage those things on a washerwoman's salary." Here, her dull brown eyes took on a sheen of pain that turned them almost black. "So, I suppose I compensate for that with a broad selection of wares and my readiness to nurse you through your troubles."

"I didn't come here to have my troubles nursed."

"I'm sure you'll tell me now you have no troubles, and everything in your life is cream and peaches," said the woman with a wry smile.

Vivian shrugged. "You would think my troubles rather petty compared to yours."

"What troubles could I have?" The woman's eyes turned even blacker.

"You're in weeds," Vivian said. "That's trouble enough, I'd say."

Nettie sat down on the stool next to her, a little shaky. "My mother died."

"I'm sorry," Vivian said. They were silent for a time.

Then, Nettie said, "And how is *your* mother? I remember Marvina telling me she was like a gold statue — all yellow and ice."

Vivian chuckled, the woman had described her mother's blond hair and pale countenance always shimmering with elegance perfectly. "Very desirous I should marry again."

"Again?" Nettie said with a smirk. "You are a poor wretch indeed!"

"To a buccaneer, no less." Vivian grimaced. "Oh, he's friendly enough. A little unpolished, perhaps. He came from the Canadian backwoods."

"But he has a lot of money," Nettie supplied with a laugh. "Aren't mothers always like that?"

"Was yours?" Vivian challenged.

The eyes darkened. "My mother knew no one with means,"

she said. "Perhaps if she had, life after her absence would be easier for me."

They sat for a time in silence through the cool air inside the room as the overhead fans turned vigorously over their head. Nettie extracted a black handkerchief from behind her sleeve and began wiping her hands with it. "If you've come to town to catch a Canadian millionaire, shouldn't you be there with him instead of here with me?"

Vivian's hands felt damp inside her the gloves. She began to yank off the left one. "I was there. I came here to talk to a genuine person."

"And what did they talk about that annoyed you enough to want to speak to a 'genuine person'?" Nettie asked.

"Rattling skeletons!"

Nettie took her hand and gently pulled the glove off. "You're going to rip your own fingers off next."

Vivian grimaced. "I thought I was taking my rage out on a non-living thing."

Nettie inspected the glove. "You've stretched it out of shape. I'll wash and dry it against the stove."

"You needn't do that," said Vivian, touched.

"Perhaps I have more respect for fine things because I haven't had the pleasure," Nettie remarked. As she washed the glove in the sink, she asked, "What rattling skeletons are you referring to?"

"Family skeletons," Vivian said.

The woman peered at her. "I shouldn't think there would be room for discussion about such unpleasant things in your set."

"When they get bored with themselves, they move to other people," said Vivian with a growl.

Nettie shrugged as she hung the glove on a rod and returned to the counter. "I don't see there is much to discuss. Every family has them."

"That's what Mr. Leblanc said."

"Who's he?"

Vivian grinned. "The Canadian buccaneer."

"Well, he has sense, at least," said Nettie. "I take it the skeletons they referred to belonged to you specifically?"

Vivian stared down at the marble pattern of the counter. "You are astute."

"Then there is one solution," said the woman. "Put it back in the closet."

"I will, if I can," said Vivian. "If they'll let me." She removed her other glove, more gently this time, and tried not to think about the conversation with David on the train.

CHAPTER 5

Those first days in Waxwood passed by quickly, and Vivian felt as if a mist had wrapped around her as she settled into the mad rush of resort life. She was no different than those around her who stopped in the lobby or the courtyard, their faces distorted as if they had forgotten what it was they intended to do, then turned around, wandered back, and began again. Those who frequented the beachfronts and mountain hotels every summer and winter, like the Tishers, were unruffled by the hours that sped by during the first days of summer.

Mrs. Tisher was like a bull with her notepad and pencil, ambling about, raising her hand to this or that person, and bending her head together with Mrs. Griffith and Mrs. Breen, as they organized the summer activities of their set. Vivian knew it was only a matter of time before Larissa was asked to join them, just as she had the previous summer, and the four women would be seen after breakfast every morning in the lobby, standing in the most conspicuous spot where everyone had to walk around them. Four of the nine Muses, she had once remarked to her brother. They had laughed over which of the muses belonged to which lady: Mrs. Tisher was Calliope with her judicious manner;

Mrs. Griffith was Erato, as she was always trying to pair unwed young ladies with unwed young gentlemen; Mrs. Breen was Polymnia, since she was always correcting people's social manners and grammar; and their mother was Melpomene for no other reason than they both saw her as the tragic figure of the quartet, remaining a confirming voice in the background.

For the first few days, Vivian declined to join the activities and was left in peace to adjust herself to the pace of resort life. Meals divided the day, but in between, Vivian could not have said exactly what she had done, had anyone asked her. She had vague impressions of her eyes absorbing words on pages of books, of the clear blue-green sea feeling cold on her bare feet as she went walking, and of the roughness of the rocks on which she sat trying to decipher whether the little white line in the distance was a ship or a barge. Vivian had cultivated, like many young ladies her age, an independence of mind and Larissa, to be fair, never asked where she went or what she had done. There was, at least, that trust between them.

On Friday, Vivian awakened and, as usual, slipped quietly out of the suite before her mother stirred. She went downstairs to the courtyard where the mild breeze combed the surface of the sea, leaving a field of dark blue meshing with the sky. She had begun to keep a diary after Jake left and now unlocked it with the little key that hung on a chain around her neck. Her hand flashed across the page:

Mother still angry at me for leaving the parlor so abruptly that first night. How could I tell her about Amber's insinuations? Woke up this morning thinking of David Potter. I haven't thought about our little talk since we got off the train. What was he really trying to tell me? Will he end up being like Hermes, the messenger of truth and the soul guide? But Hermes was also the god of boundaries, so perhaps he shall bring a warning to abandon the journey, for I feel I am about to embark on one. I don't know if I have the strength for yet another one.

She locked her diary, and slipping it under her arm, strolled into the lobby. She expected to be empty in the early hour, but it surprised her to find the place in a furious uproar. People were already flouncing about, some of them with baskets, others with sheets of newspapers under their arms. Wide-eyed looks and laughter eased her alarm.

She joined her mother, calm and fully dressed in a morning suit, standing next to Mrs. Griffith near the windows watching the throng with some amusement. "It's like the Tower of Babel!" she remarked.

"Worse than that." Mrs. Griffith regarded the crowd with a critical eye through her pince-nez. "It's fish market day."

"Fish market?" Larissa sniffed. "I don't recall it from last year."

"A rather ghastly practice the new chef here began this spring," said Mrs. Griffith. "He allows guests to choose a fish at the market on Fridays, collects them, and at dinner, voila! One has a sumptuous meal of the fish one has chosen."

"It's a touch of genius, you must admit," Vivian remarked. "Who can resist being the mistress of her own dinner when on vacation?"

"That was not what Mrs. Griffith meant, Vivian," said her mother.

The woman gave a sprinkling laugh. "Oh, it's vulgar, to be sure, but I suppose it passes the time as quickly as any amusement here."

"You mean they all go?" Vivian asked.

"Certainly not," she said with a sniff. "I shall go only because Amber *insists* upon it. She has some idea we shall see the sort of people there that we would never see otherwise."

"Like humans staring at animals in the zoo," Vivian muttered. "Yes, Amber would feel that way."

"I assume Mrs. Tisher has something else planned," her mother eyed the woman.

"Naturally," said Mrs. Griffith. "The casino in Emsworth is open for the season, and she believes she can arrange a morning dance in their ballroom." She regarded Vivian with a glance. "But if I were you, Vivian, I would accompany us to the market."

"Oh?" Larissa was immediately alert.

"Monte expressed rather an eagerness to go last night," she said, her voice coming down to the confiding notch. "He has some reputation as an expert angler." She added with a smirk, "His father will no doubt try to talk him out of it, convinced by Mrs. Tisher that it's a disgusting practice and one in which no civilized person ought to take part. But I don't think he will succeed."

"I'd like to go, Mother." Vivian turned to Larissa. "I think it might be fun."

"Well, dear, I would hardly call it fun." Mrs. Griffith dropped her pince-nez.

"I think Vivian is only teasing you, Leila," said Larissa in a breezy voice.

"It's only a shame that the first outing into town has to be so plebeian." The woman sighed.

"And so disagreeably fragrant." Vivian could not hold back her smile. "I imagine Mr. Leblanc won't mind that much."

"I'm surprised Emile Leblanc is so keen to talk his son out of it," Larissa said. "I understood last night from Mrs. Breen that they're quite attached to one another."

"Oh, yes," Mrs. Griffith said. "Very much so."

"Rather too much, perhaps?" Larissa observed.

"We can hardly throw stones at them, Mother," said Vivian. "You and I have been inseparable ourselves."

"But we're women, dear," said her mother. "Men are more—"

"Independent?" Vivian asked archly.

"Autonomous," her mother emphasized.

"Oh, Monte spent many years away from his family in Ottawa when he was making his fortune," said Mrs. Griffith. "But they became attached to one another when—" her voice lowered again, "—Monte's first wife died. And his son." The last word dropped like a wooden nickel on the floor.

"Poor man," Larissa sighed.

Vivian gave an appropriate solemn nod as she headed for the elevator to put her diary in the suite before coming down again to breakfast.

Mrs. Griffith had, as usual, overestimated the propriety of her compatriots. For when they stepped on the ferry, it was fairly teetering with men, women and children, all dressed as if for church. Silk and lace parasols shifted against the wind on the bay, and men held their gloved hands on their hats. There was much laughter and talk. Vivian sat in a corner away from the Griffiths and her mother, folding her jacket close around her. She was not cold, but she felt more secure as the bay opened its mouth, inviting her to dive in.

The man who usually minded the ferry wheel caught sight of her and sauntered over. "Good t'see you again, miss."

"You're not at the wheel?"

"Breakin' in a new man," he said, glancing toward the front of the ferry.

"You have a full house this time," she said, smiling.

"I reckon it's the same young people, only they got their day clothes on 'stead of their nightclothes," he chuckled. "I ain't grumblin', though. Only right to laugh and carouse when you're young."

"I know some serious-minded young people," Vivian said.

"T'be sure, miss. I ain't sayin'. But, well, we're almost done with our times, ain't we? And we're goin' into what they call 'the modern age.' Don't rightly expect it to be different from the old age, but I suppose we won't know 'till we get there."

"You don't believe the 1900s will be any different from the 1800s?" She peered at him.

"One century's the same as the next." He stifled a yawn. "People live, people die, and babies come into the world. Maybe we got more steel and iron and newfangled gadgets. But people, miss, they never change. My granddaddy worked the boats down in San Francisco, and my daddy was a sailor. We all got the breath of the sea in our lungs. And my son, he's already third mate on a cruiser. See what I mean?"

Vivian blinked, shielding her eyes from the sun. But she could not see the man's face. "It's a legacy, I suppose."

"You can call it that." He chuckled. "Folks like us, we're too poor to leave somethin' worth pawning when times get tough. So I guess the breath of the sea's as good a legacy as any."

The whistle blew, and as the man turned around, Vivian suddenly sat up. "What's your name, sir?"

"Bless you, miss, ain't no one asked me my name in, oh, I don't know how long." But he bent down and held out his hand, his grin wide behind the whiskery face. "Ezra Blaine. Pleased to meet you."

She shook his hand. He had a surprisingly feeble touch, as she had imagined his hands would be strong after steering the ferry wheel.

Halfway across the bay toward the pier, Vivian could already see the fish market, which transformed the place from something that resembled a peaceful promenade on other days into a busy, flourishing camp. Large umbrellas threw brilliant colors from the distance, and she caught a glimpse of the tables underneath when the wind flicked them to one side. The merchants, mostly fishermen and their wives, grabbed the rods and pulled them back over the tables. She expected the scent to be overpowering as the ferry pulled up not far off, but the salty sea air still filled her lungs instead.

"Well, Vivian," Mrs. Griffith remarked, "your prediction of the market's disagreeable odors doesn't appear to be true."

"Oh, it's all very civilized here." Amber opened her parasol. She was in a more amiable mood than she had been in the past week, as her husband George had come down for the weekend from the city. She held on to his arm now as if it were her own private property.

As they entered the market, silvery flashes of color awakened Vivian's senses more than the scent: the orange, blue, and violet skins of the fish, their wide rainbow eyes, the bright red stains on the tablecloths and aprons, the gray rubber gloves with which the fishermen and their wives handled the fish. Snatches of words lent their own fresh color, as she heard argumentative tones of "Caught this mornin', sir, so it ain't hardly had time—" "Sturgeon, that one, can't get any better in these parts—" "What d'you mean, ten cents is too much? I assure you—"

"Rather like a sea carnival," she remarked.

"Not many people we know." Her mother strained her neck as she looked around.

"Perhaps the buccaneer has cast his own fishing rod into the bay," Vivian said. "He is, after all, an expert."

She felt a tap on her shoulder and saw her mother's face change to her hostess expression. Vivian turned and looked into the sleepy eyes of Mr. Leblanc. Two women lingered close behind him.

"Good morning!" His voice was buoyant, as if he had discovered a rare creature of the sea lying scattered on a table.

"Good morning, Mr. Leblanc," Larissa answered for her.

Mrs. Griffith held out her hand. "Monte, what do you think of our little frenzy here?"

"I think it's very charming," he said. "We have a market like this in Peterborough, of course."

"You do quite a lot of fishing there, I'm told," Amber said with a tilt of her head. "George once tried to teach me, but I ended up hooking on to a bush!"

"I'm afraid your skills lie elsewhere, my love," said George, giving a nervous laugh.

Mr. Leblanc bowed, but he had been drifting toward Vivian's side. "You have met Mrs. Sowberry and Miss Sowberry?"

"I don't believe we've had the pleasure," said Vivian. As Mr. Leblanc made the introductions, she held out her hand to Miss Sowberry. The young woman's mother accepted it from both her and Larissa, giving each a short, vigorous shake.

"Mrs. and Miss Sowberry were gracious enough to make what would have been a very boring week in Saratoga a very pleasant one," Mr. Leblanc added.

Mrs. Sowberry giggled like a delighted little girl. Then she said in a high-pitched voice, "Alderdice, did you say? I don't believe I know the name."

Vivian hid a smile as her mother pulled up to her full height, which looked considerably vast next to Mrs. Sowberry's rather stout and small figure, and pushed her foot out a little so the hem of her skirt swung back to reveal the shape of her ankle. It was a move she always made when she wanted to intimidate or show authority. "You're not from San Francisco, then?"

"We're from Nevada," said Mrs. Sowberry, attempting to raise her chin a little to mimic the majestic hold of the head that came so easily to dedicated blue bloods like Larissa.

Larissa continued, "My father built the Alderdice Shipping and Alderdice Luxury—"

"Ah, yes," the woman interrupted. "I recall some friends told me of the elegant Alderdice cruise ships. We hope one day to take one, naturally." She gave a quick laugh that sounded more like a reprimand.

"Naturally," Larissa echoed.

"Oh, San Francisco is a dream!" This explosion came from Miss Sowberry. The young woman could not have been more than Fern's age, but her skin was so pale that it looked almost transparent, and her reedy figure made her look like a statue. Yet Vivian liked the sweet, open face of one who would always be harmless.

"Indeed! Oh, indeed." Mr. Leblanc's voice rose with enthusiasm. "I am eager to see the California salmon, and I was told there is a man here named Rugworn who has the best." His sleep eyes searched the market. "You'll help us find him, Miss Alderdice?" His gaze was on Vivian. "Oh, you must join us! The chef promised he shall make *Ukha*."

"What is that?" Mrs. Griffith asked.

"A delightful fish soup I tasted when I was in Russia several years ago," said Mr. Leblanc. "Very rich but also very delicate. But we must find the best fish for it."

Vivian felt her hand being placed under his arm, and the party proceeded down the walkway. She realized Mr. Leblanc was ambling, allowing the pairs (Amber and George, Larissa and Mrs. Griffith, and the Sowberrys) to get a little ahead of them, leaving the two of them to trail behind.

He spoke in a low tone, "You're not angry with me anymore?"

"Why should I be angry?"

"Our last meeting was not a very auspicious one," he remarked.

"Last meeting?"

"We spoke of family skeletons."

Vivian smiled. "I was never angry at you. I shouldn't have gotten angry with Amber either. I know her scorpion tongue well enough by now." She changed the subject. "Mrs. Griffith said you're quite a fisherman yourself."

Here, he brightened and began telling her about the Otonabee River and the many varieties of bass he had seen there. "Bass has none of the richness of your salmon," he said. "That's why it will go so well with the *Ukha*."

He talked about Russia and, in particular, St. Petersburg, with its domes and majestic river and its wide city streets. "It's no wonder all the great Russian writers prefer it over any other place," he said.

"I thought you didn't approve of women who read books," Vivian remarked.

"I've changed my mind." A flush appeared on his rough skin. "I find American women so well-read."

Vivian smiled. She was taken in by the way the man spoke with deliberation, clearly trying to weigh every word he said so it would meet with her approval. "I imagine you've met many women during your travels."

"Oh, Mr. Leblanc has been everywhere!" This burst of fluttery words came from Miss Sowberry who, Vivian realized, was walking alongside her. She imagined her mother had deliberately forced her to fall behind.

"Not everywhere," he said with a laugh.

"A great many places, I imagine," said Vivian.

"You are fond of traveling, Miss Alderdice?" A little apprehension appeared in the hooded eyes.

"Not really." There was a small gasp from Miss Sowberry. "I've always been attached to my home," she explained. "And I have reasons for wanting to stay in San Francisco at the moment."

"It's not a very pleasant thing for women to travel," he said, then added, "Oh, to certain places with stately accommodations and plenty of culture. Paris, London, Venice. But there are places where women are not comfortable."

"Where men are not comfortable with them," Vivian said with a sly smile.

"I seem to be always offending you without meaning to," he mumbled.

"Not at all, Mr. Leblanc," she said. "You speak plainly, and I like that. I'm sure Miss Sowberry appreciates it as well."

"Oh, yes!" the girl exclaimed.

"Sometimes women are a burden to men." Vivian cast her eyes across a table with the silver-gilled carp. "Just as sometimes men are a burden to women."

The same high-pitched gasp came from Miss Sowberry, but Mr. Leblanc laughed outright and tipped his hat to her. Larissa glanced back with a satisfied smile while Mrs. Sowberry's eyes moved closer together with annoyance.

"You have modern opinions about marriage, then?" he asked.

"Some," Vivian admitted. "Like Mrs. Stone, I believe women should keep their maiden names after marriage, if they wish. That's one reason I went back to being Miss Alderdice when my husband died."

"A girl ought to make a home for her husband, wherever it is," said Miss Sowberry, but she sounded as if her opinion were being dictated by someone else.

"Whether or not she should," said Vivian, smiling, "I'm sure yours shall make a most pleasant one, Miss Sowberry." She said it sincerely and the girl blushed with joy.

They were near the end of the pier, her mother standing with Mrs. Griffith, looking out at the bay and talking. Just as she turned to Mr. Leblanc to suggest they join them, she saw David Potter at a table in the corner. He was rolling a cigarette, but the moment he saw her, he put it in his pocket and waved.

"Will you excuse me?" she asked. "I see a friend, and I must say hello."

"Friend?" The man glanced around.

She felt a prickle of annoyance. "There's a lovely view from the edge of the pier. Why don't you take Miss Sowberry? She's looking rather lost without her mother, poor thing." The young woman had wandered back toward the walkway, looking around.

"Delighted to see you again, Miss Alderdice," David said when she reached him.

"Vivian," she reminded him with a smile.

"Vivian, of course." He threw a glance across the bay where the gates of the Waxwoodian shone with their gilded lions in the front. "I was just telling Lucas there was probably some tennis match or something going on, and none of the swells would be here."

Vivian smiled. "There is a morning dance, I think."

"Ha!" The man beside him, dressed in a slick yellow coat and hat, let out a snort.

"Miss Vivian Alderdice, Mr. Lucas Henderson," David said. "You mind your manners, old man."

"That I never done in sixty-seven years, son." He grinned, his jovial smile matching those of the fish lying on his table. "I can talk all swellish when I got to, but I don't like it!"

"Lucas has the great fortune to be a member of the Potter clan by marriage," said David with mock loftiness. "He somehow won the heart of Miss Sallie Potter, my second cousin, twice removed, or thereabouts."

The man grunted. "The boy makes it sound as if Sallie and I were the black sheep of the family." He winked. "I was just a fisherman when Sallie took pity on me. Never dreamed I'd marry a woman what had more money than I had. Why, I didn't even know she was an heiress at the time!" He laughed. "But she was, bless her, and not much soiled by it either. I still got my boat and my eye for the trout, though. Sometimes the darling Sallie comes along, but she's a little poorly this Friday." He sighed. "When one reaches a certain age, miss, one must keep the bones from cracking, if you know what I mean."

"I know what you mean." Vivian sighed, thinking back to her grandparents and their last days.

David pushed a stool toward her, and Vivian settled herself, lifting her skirt from the dirty ground as much as she could.

"Vivian is interested in the years her grandmother, Penelope Alderdice, was in Waxwood," said David.

"Don't recall the name."

"You might have known her as Penelope Carlyle," Vivian said. "Or even Grace Carlyle."

The man wrinkled his nose. "No miss, can't say I did."

"Bosh, old man," said David. "You told me all about Penelope Carlyle and the man she married."

"Did I now?" He regarded the young man with jolly amusement. "And what, youngster, did I say?"

"You told me they married right after she left Waxwood."

"That was the summer of 1853," Vivi said.

"Was it now?" The man looked far away.

"And you also told David it surprised everyone when my grandmother didn't come to Loretta's funeral two years later," Vivian added.

"Well, now, that's strange," he said. "Don't go in much for dates."

"Numbers can sometimes matter," said David, turning to Vivian. "I'm an accountant by trade, you see, and numbers often have a significance to me that they don't have for others."

Mr. Henderson regarded her with one eye while he closed the other. "I wouldn't think a little thing like Miss Alderdice would have much interest in what happened fifty years ago."

"I haven't," Vivian insisted. "That is, I did once, but—"

"Miss Penelope Carlyle, oh, yes, now I remember her!" The man's face lit up.

Vivian hands folded in her lap. "Yes, she made quite an impression on Waxwood."

"Oh, I don't mean me personally, miss," said the man. "My Sallie met her once or twice. Summer of Fifty-Three, she was here, you said?"

"From the summer of fifty-two to the summer of fifty-three," Vivian said.

"And thereafter," said Mr. Henderson with a chuckle.

Vivian's hands felt icy and damp inside her gloves. "You don't mean she came back to Waxwood?"

"Oh, not in that way, miss," said the old man. He propped his foot up on a crate lying near the edge of the pier. "But you know, sometimes people, they just sort of stay 'round a while, like you never forget them."

"They become specters," Vivian murmured.

"That's a rather gruesome thought." David flinched. "Tell Miss Alderdice what she wants to know, Lucas, and don't shilly-shally."

"Young 'un, don't have no patience," said the man with a laugh.

"I don't want to know anything, really." Her voice carried out with the wind on the bay.

"Well, I recall now I was staying with Sallie and her family in 1855 — we were to be married that winter — and we was having a little birthday celebration for Sallie's mother when Mrs. Grant came rushing in, all a-flutter, like a chicken who just got its feathers plucked."

"I don't think I know Mrs. Grant," Vivian said.

"I mean Mrs. Bertha Grant," said the man.

Vivian's bag, which had been balancing precariously on her wrist, fell to the ground. David swooped down to retrieve it, brushing off the dust and grime with his handkerchief before he gave it back to her. Vivian thanked him, hoping he hadn't seen her hands trembling. "Bertha Ross?"

"The others always thought of her that way. I suppose that's why she took to it when her husband died. But I don't think it's right to refer to a lady by her maiden name just 'cause you knew her that way." His thick eyebrows knitted together.

"Please go on," said Vivian.

"Well, as I said, Mrs. Grant — Miss Ross, if you prefer — came in all a-flutter and we had to give her some wine to settle her. Then, she burst out, 'Penelope won't come to the funeral because of the baby!' Well, I didn't see nothin' wrong with that. Ladies gotta stay put when they have babies, don't they?"

"This was in 1855, you say?" Vivian asked. "When, exactly?"

"Well, it was the last of summer, I remember, 'cause David's mama Flossie had one of them summer colds, and she threw a tantrum when we Sallie tried to give her a mustard plaster."

"Mama always had a will of her own." David grinned.

"We were all worried about her," said Mr. Henderson. "In fact, we was going to see her, Sallie and I, after the birthday cake and all. But Miss Ross kinda spoiled it."

"I imagine it did," Vivian murmured.

"Oh, she meant no harm," said Mr. Henderson. "We were all just kinda surprised."

"Lucas, you've spent so much time with those fish of yours, your mind is as muddy as the bottom of the sea." David was clearly annoyed. "Stop bungling about."

"What I mean is," the man said patiently, "Mrs. Alderdice and Loretta, they were such good friends at one time, and we didn't figure on Mrs. Alderdice not trying at least to get to the funeral."

"I can see that," Vivian said. "But my mother was born in November." She didn't know why, but a coolness entered her chest.

Mr. Henderson shrugged. "It was all confusing."

"I don't see what's so confusing." David shrugged. "Aunt Loretta died in September, and Mrs. Alderdice couldn't come to the funeral because she was going to have a baby in November."

"You don't think so good with pretty ladies about!" the man snapped good-naturedly. The blond man reddened and peered out at the bay, his hands shoving into his pockets.

Mr. Henderson continued in a more congenial tone, "It was just the way she said it, miss. Miss Ross, I mean. Like there was something wrong."

"How did Miss Ross know about my grandmother?" Vivian asked. "David told me Grandmother stopped writing to people in Waxwood."

"Why, child, she'd just come back from there."

"From where?"

"Well, now, miss, that I'm uncertain of." The man rubbed his stubbled chin. "She went to visit her in the city 'cause Miss Carlyle — pardon me, Mrs. Alderdice — asked her to. But as far as I recollect, she weren't there all the time. She and Mrs. Alderdice, that is."

"Why, where were they?"

"Well, I suppose where ladies go when they're sickly and with child."

Vivian grasped her reticule. "I never heard my grandmother was confined before my mother was born."

Mr. Henderson was stunned for a moment. A couple who clearly had come from one of the resort hotels inspected the row of fish on his table and requested two of the plumpest ones. He absentmindedly wrapped them in newspaper and took their coins.

When they had gone, Vivian said in a gentle voice, "I'm sorry, Mr. Henderson. I didn't mean I doubted your word."

"Well, miss, I'm telling you what we were told," he said. "And it came from Miss Ross."

"Who is hardly a reliable source of information," David said briskly.

"Now, don't you go putting down Miss Ross, youngster," said the man in a savage voice. "She weren't no beauty and no intelligent girl, maybe, but she was a kind woman, good-hearted. I've known Ruth Ross since she was a child, and I won't have you saying nasty things 'bout her mother."

"I'm sorry, sir," said David.

"All I can remember is Mrs. Alderdice asked Miss Ross to come with her somewheres where she could rest and have her baby," he said. "That's what Miss Ross told us. Said the city was getting Mrs. Alderdice all in a fuddle, so she wanted to get away somewheres in the mountains. Didn't say where."

Vivian gazed at the water. Now so close, she could see there was a swirl of gray, and they were not so clear. "Thank you, Mr. Henderson. I must go back to my party." She saw both Mrs. Griffith and her mother glancing in her direction. Mr. Leblanc was, thankfully, preoccupied with the Sowberrys on the other side of the pier.

She struggled to rise, and David took her arm to help her. "I hope we haven't upset you, Vivian."

"Not in the least." She knew that her voice sounded less than sincere.

"I hope we shall see one another again sometime," the young man said. Mr. Henderson snorted behind him.

She replied with words to that effect and hurried to join Larissa and Mrs. Griffith, at which time Mr. Leblanc noticed her and, smiling, took her hand firmly in his arm again.

~

That night at dinner, Mrs. Tisher invited her and Larissa to join her party at the center table, and there was much merriment when the *Ukha* was served. Despite Mr. Leblanc's insistence on it being a rich soup, she found it light, its broth with the stinging flavors of peppercorns and parsley tickling her tongue, the salmon tender, and the leeks and carrots still with the bite that made the soup flavorful. It suited her palate, and, apparently, Miss Sowberry's, who could not stop raving about it in her breathless way. Fern Tisher, Vivian noticed, was less pleased with the simple dish, preferring the heavy creamed chicken and broccoli.

After dinner, she and Larissa joined the other ladies in gathering in the hotel parlor for cards. Fern and Cecily were taking turns playing lively tunes on the piano. But Vivian could hardly concentrate on the music or the game of solitaire she set up in the quiet corner by the window. The things Mr. Henderson told her kept running in her mind. Bertha in San Francisco. Grandmother ill. The year 1855. What did it all mean?

She looked around at the pale faces of the young ladies with their brightly colored dresses and fans, the older ladies at the card tables, sitting upright as if their corsets were too tight for them. Suddenly she felt as if she didn't belong there. It was a feeling she had had when her coming out season had transformed her from a quiet, bookish child with a single braid down her back to a woman with her hair pinned up, thrust into one dinner party and ball and picnic after another, so they all blurred together like the scenery from a merry-go-round. The more approving glances she had received from Grandfather, the more commandments and suggestions from the lips of her mother and grandmother, the less alive she had felt.

The men were filtering into the parlor, finished with their brandy and cigars. Vivian could see Monte Leblanc and his father standing in the hallway. She threw her cards aside and, pushing back the glass on the window, slipped out before anyone could see her.

She took the ferry into town and followed the main commercial road to Nettie's store. She sensed more than saw the people rushing around doing last minute Friday errands, the ladies with their hats tied under their chins and their baskets in hand, the men sauntering past in their work boots. But something about their industry and their hurriedness comforted her.

Unlike the night before, the drugstore was crawling with people, many of them in shabby clothes and torn hats. They formed a long line between the two counters, waiting patiently and speaking quietly. They moved aside to let her pass.

The back counter had been turned into a soup kitchen. Two cast iron gas burners stood in a line, one holding a large caldron and another with a coffeepot that looked more like a barrel. Thick glass plates and cups, most of them chipped, sat clean on one side, dirty on the other. Nettie's back was to the crowd, her rough hands scooping soup from the caldron, then shoving a few thick slices of bread on the edge of the plate. She looked as determined as she had the first time Vivian saw her, the darkness of black crepe broken only by the white apron she wore. Turning around, she caught sight of Vivian. The plate balancing precariously in her hands. "I need help," was all she said.

Vivian immediately put the conversation with Mr. Henderson out of her mind. She laid down her parasol and pouch, took off her hat and gloves, and rolled up her sleeves. Nettie directed her toward the small sink stacked with dirty dishes. Vivian had done dishes only a few times in her life, more of an experiment to help Missy, the Alderdice scullery maid, who sometimes had coughing fits and could hardly hold a dish in her hand. The scalding water turned her hands red. But the soup, with its clear broth and stark fish and vegetables, made the dishes not very difficult to wash. Nettie took them out of the clean tub herself and dried them as fast as Vivian washed them. The two women did not speak, but she could see a smile curving at the edge of Nettie's mouth, as if she hadn't expected Vivian to perform her task with such speed.

A tiny woman with a shawl covering her head and engulfing almost her entire head and face, said in a craggy voice, "Miss Nettie, Ezra's down again, got the pain in his back—"

"Take a few of those packets from the shelf, Mrs. Totter," said Nettie, flicking her head toward the left side of the store without stopping her task of ladling soup. "Pay me when you can."

"Bless you, Miss Nettie!" The woman bowed. Then turning to Vivian, she added, "Bless you too, miss."

She looked into the opening of the shawl at the woman's face. The lines in her skin wove into chaotic patterns, the face showing an endurance of life's beatings. The little lips peeked through the shawl into a smile, and the eyes pitted with circles. And yet, the woman was beautiful to her, more beautiful than the most polished Washington Street belle at her debutante ball.

The line dwindled, and Nettie ran out of soup before the last few. She rushed up a narrow staircase off to the side of the store and came down with a chunk of cheese. "I've no butter!" she exclaimed, as if this were a tragedy. But the hungry people thanked her profusely and found a place near the display windows. Quiet people slurped their soup and scraped their spoons at the bottom of their bowls. Nettie sighed and wiped her hands on her dirty apron.

"It seems like that line grows every Friday," she remarked, dabbing at her damp forehead. "I might need an assistant, if this keeps up."

"You do this every Friday?" Vivian's hands pressed at her lower back, as the strain of standing even on her low-heeled shoes had pinched their nerves.

"My mother started it a long time ago," she said. "She would go to the market just before dusk on Fridays and bring fish for dinner from the scraps they had left for pennies." She gave her a twisted smile. "They didn't want to give it to her, but no one could say no to Mama."

Vivian smiled. "She must have been a headstrong woman."

"She was," said Nettie. "She saw many of our neighbors were never there. They couldn't even afford the scraps. So she bought up all she could and make a big soup out of them and feed the neighbors. It went on from there."

"Very kind of her," Vivian said. "And very kind of you."

"I've known most of these people all my life." Her eyes swept across the crowded little store.

"But isn't it — apart from all the work — doesn't it cost quite a bit?"

"Have you really any idea how much food costs or doesn't cost?" Nettie glanced at her.

Vivian felt her face flush, and she turned away from the woman.

"I shouldn't have said that," said Nettie. "I get up early on Fridays, before the greengrocer has lifted his shutters. His son and I went to school together, so I'm like one of the family. He gives me enough of the riper vegetables for the stew. I go to the fish market early, as some of those fishermen are also old family friends and they don't mind selling to me at a cheaper price as long as no one sees. I baked the bread early this morning. It's quite edible. You ought to try it."

"The bread or the baking?" Vivian asked with a wry smile.

The woman laughed, leaning back a little. "Both. But I meant the bread." She took up the bread knife, but Vivian shook her head.

"I've had my dinner," she said. "A bowl of *Ukha*." At Nettie's set gaze, she laughed. "A Russian fish soup. We were at the fish market today too."

"Not buying the scraps, I'm sure." She eyed her.

"No, buying the choicest California salmon."

Nettie eyed her. "I take it you didn't like it much."

Vivian realized her agitation had again gotten the best of her. "It wasn't that. I heard some stories about my grandmother from an old fisherman."

"And the old man upset you?"

"I didn't think you saw anything but your caldron," Vivian said lightly, crossing her arms, as there was a small chill in the place. "Like a witch."

Nettie untied her apron and folded it. "I know we haven't known one another for very long, Vivian, but there are some people who have a keen sense of people's moods. I knew something unsettled you the moment you entered."

"Perhaps I am." Vivian leaned over the glass counter, staring down at the assortment of silver and porcelain pill boxes. "I'm not sure yet."

"When one hears what one doesn't wish to hear—"

"I never said that," Vivian insisted. "He told me things I didn't know, and they surprised me."

"He?"

"The fisherman, Mr. Henderson," she said. "He knew my grandmother forty-odd years ago when she was Penelope Carlyle. He told me things that make little sense to me." She began knocking on the glass.

"Whenever something makes no sense to me, I take care to turn it upside down and right side up until it does," said Nettie.

"And I take a journey," Vivian murmured.

"Follow the path until you reach the end." Nettie nodded.

"That's what frightens me, Nettie." She felt the pain of the woman's gaze. "I was pulled on that path once, and it wasn't pleasant. I don't know that I can stand to be pulled onto it again."

"What path?"

Vivian placed her hand flat on the glass. "The path into the past."

Nettie cocked her head. "You don't strike me as one who shies away from an arduous task. Look at how you threw yourself right into my soup kitchen." She laid a hand on her arm. "Don't think I'm ungrateful, even if I haven't had the good manners to say 'thank you.'"

A woman with a sunburned face and twitching eyes approached Nettie. "Have you any of that rose-scented soap left, Miss Grace?"

"I've a shipment I haven't unpacked yet." Nettie disappeared in the back of the store.

Vivian smiled at the woman, then went back to the display case. The woman ventured in a thin, tentative voice, "You spoke of Penelope Carlyle just now, miss?"

"She was my grandmother."

"Oh, a lovely lady, miss. So refined!"

Vivian stared. "You knew her?"

"Only to look at," said the woman. "I was, in my younger days, a parlor maid in the house of Mr. and Mrs. Leland Ross."

"But you wouldn't be — Tillie?" Vivian blinked.

"Why, miss, I can't think how you know my name." The woman smiled. "Must be the will of God."

Vivian smiled a little. "My grandmother mentioned you a few times in letters she wrote to my great-grandmother while she was in Waxwood."

"Oh, that was a grand summer for the young misses and gentlemen," said the woman with a sigh. "Many engagements were set between the beaus and the belles. I daresay some weren't as serious as they should have been." She gave a chuckle, then quickly blushed, as if she had allowed herself an indiscretion. "We were all sorry downstairs when Miss Carlyle went back to the city."

"Very considerate of you to say so," Vivian breathed.

"She was sick, poor thing." Tillie sighed. "Such a hot summer it was!"

"Yes," Vivian said. "Hot as coals."

"Her exact words!" The eyes widened so that the woman, whom Vivian judged to be now in her sixties, looked almost as if she were the parlor maid in a grand house again. "And that other time too, poor thing."

"Other time?"

"When Miss Ross went to San Francisco, miss," said the old woman. "She stayed an awful long time because Miss Carlyle — only she was Mrs. Alderdice by then — was sick with the child and had to rest all the time. And she was ever so nervous and frightened, but what woman wouldn't be, in her condition and feeling so poorly?" She then gave a vague smile. "Ah, but I'm sure Mr. Alderdice was a great comfort to her."

"I'm sure he was," Vivian muttered.

"He used to spend most of the day with her when she was sick that first time. The others, they would ask him to come out with them, but he always said 'no.'"

"My grandfather was never one for a crowd," said Vivian.

"Oh!" The woman's eyes widened again. "Why he's your grandfather, isn't he? I ought to have realized!"

Vivian mumbled, "He *was* my grandfather. He died three years ago."

"Oh!"

Nettie came back then, handing the woman a small package wrapped in rose paper and ribbon with a perfumed rose scent.

"It's too fine for the likes of me," the woman remarked. "But Cassie — she's my daughter-in-law — she's in confinement and, well, such little fineries cheer her ever so much." She dug into the worn pouch.

"Let me." Vivian insisted, drawing out a dollar and giving it to Nettie. "Give Mrs. — I'm sorry, I don't know your last name."

"It's Stout now, miss, Tillie Stout."

"Give Mrs. Stout the change."

"You're awfully kind," said the woman. "I ought to refuse but —" Here, two touches of red flared her cheeks. "We're short this week, and what with Cassie being so poorly—"

Vivian pressed the woman's hand. "It's nothing compared to the kindness you showed my grandmother."

"She was a noble lady," Mrs. Stout declared. "And I know you shall be too." The woman left with a lighter tread than she had entered.

When she was gone, Vivian couldn't help but grimace. "A noble lady. I've never done one useful thing in my life."

"You were useful to me tonight," Nettie insisted.

"You would have managed without me." Vivian slipped on her gloves. "I'm sure you have often enough."

"I've managed without anybody's help." The woman moved aside some dark strands still hanging on her face, though she had attempted to tidy herself up while she had been out of the store. "And people have gotten cold stew out of it."

Vivian chuckled as she pressed Nettie's hand. "You may call upon me anytime you need help. I'm at the Waxwoodian."

"I thought you might be," remarked Nettie. She then peered at Vivian with two almond eyes. "What do you intend to do now?"

"Do?" Vivian echoed.

"Are you going to tame this unsettling feeling of yours?" asked Nettie. "Walk down the path into the past?"

Vivian held on to her bag with both hands, thoughtful. "I don't know, Nettie."

"You speak as if it were a matter of life or death."

"Maybe it is," Vivian said. "A life or death of a family. Or maybe that family died some time ago."

A light summer rain had endeared itself upon the resorts of Waxwood during the night, so when Vivian woke up in the morning, the air felt a little cooler and cleaner than it had been the past week. Dampness brushed against her face from the open window, as if the rain had floated in during the night. But when she touched her cheeks, they were dry.

She lay in bed, looking around the bright room. The illuminating peaches and whites blazed out at her, in contrast with the more sedate violet and blue trimmings of her room at Alderdice Hall. She once asked her grandmother why the house Grandfather had built for her was so dark with stained wood and opaque curtains. She was thirteen and would never forget the way the usual mild look ingrained on her grandmother's face had hardened into a grim smile and how her pale skin had gone almost gray.

"He wanted to torment me."

"But he built the house for you!"

"That's not true!" The cry rang almost as crows passed above their heads, for they were out in the garden lounging in the gazebo. In a more sedate tone, her grandmother had continued,

"My mother had just died. He said, 'We have nothing left here on Rincon Hill. All the new houses are being built on Nob Hill.' I never wanted to leave my parents' house. He knew that. But he insisted I deserved the biggest and grandest place, now that I was an heiress."

"So, he built this house for you."

"He built it for himself," said her grandmother grimly. "To show up the others. He was making millions with the new national obsession with travel, and if he could not get the Flesa soot off his skin, he could at least show he had the money and the gumption to build a grander house than any of them could imagine."

"Why did he want it to be dark?" Vivian asked.

"He wanted to hide me from the world," Grandmother had answered shortly.

As Vivian rose and prepared for breakfast, her eyes burned from the room's brightness. Alderdice Hall was perhaps too dark, but the façade of pastel colors and light fabrics made the hotel equally unendurable.

She went down to the courtyard and wrote in her diary:

Bertha Ross. "Poor Bertha!" Such a sweet, harmless little bird, and yet, it always comes back to her. I must see her. Mother will not be pleased. But I must know if Grandmother was really ill that year in 1855, or whether it was just Bertha's imagination or confusion. The pieces must fit together.

She met her mother in the dining room for breakfast at their table, which now looked dismal compared to the lavish party headed by the Tishers in the center of the room. As Vivian took her seat, she glanced at them. "I thought we were initiated as one of the privileged last night."

"That was an exception," said Larissa. "Monte Leblanc insisted he promised you a dinner and wanted to join our table instead. Mrs. Tisher had no choice but to invite us to hers."

"You mean she didn't want us there?"

Her mother lowered her voice. "I believe it was the rivalry Fern who didn't want with you at the table as a rival for Mr. Leblanc's attentions."

"Oh, it's all so absurd!" Vivian spread her napkin on her lap.

"You didn't help matters any last night when you disappeared from the parlor." Her mother's face showed annoyance. "And through the window, no less!"

"Oh, you saw me?" Vivian couldn't help but smile. "You have the eyes of a falcon, Mother."

"Be thankful Mr. Leblanc didn't," Larissa snapped. "He would have been very offended."

Vivian eyed her. "I imagine he didn't lack for company."

"Indeed, he did not!" Her mother said. "Between Fern and Cecily, they must have played the entire collection of sheet music in Waxwood for him."

Vivian nearly choked on her scrambled eggs. "You really are too much, Mother."

"I was watching him closely," Larissa continued. "I don't think he's one of those older men who is looking for his third wife to be a child."

"I don't know that I would call Fern a child," Vivian said. "She's of age."

"I meant a child in the mind," her mother said.

"Mrs. Sowberry may not agree with you." Vivian speared a strip of bacon. "I'm sure she thinks her daughter has one of the most refined minds in the country."

"The daughter of a Comstock miner has hardly an inkling of what refinement means." She gave Vivian a meaningful look as she poured herself more coffee. "You were born with it."

"Because I'm an Alderdice?" Vivian glanced at her.

"Because you're an Alderdice."

"Mr. Leblanc doesn't seem bothered by Mrs. Sowberry's lack of refinement," Vivian pointed out.

"He will be, once he gets into Washington Street," Larissa

assured her. "He won't want to associate with such people, when he realizes we don't."

"No, we're very selective, aren't we?" Vivian lingered over her coffee for a moment. "Perhaps it was time we weren't."

"What do you mean?" Her mother stared at her.

"I'm going to see the Rosses while I'm here, remember, Mother?"

"Forget about the Rosses!" This came with a sudden leap away from Larissa's composed voice, the one that closed itself off to all dispute. Her mother was almost shrieking, though it was quiet enough to remain low above the clatter of china and silverware. "They are not our friends, dear."

"They're my friends," Vivian insisted.

"You were contented not to see them last year," Larissa reminded her.

"And it was rude of me," Vivian said. "You taught me to always drop in and see people when invited, didn't you?"

"Were you invited?" Her mother looked at her.

"I was," Vivian said softly. "Seven years ago."

"Well, then, it can't matter much now, can it?"

"It matters to me." Vivian put her cup down. "Are you forbidding me to see them?"

Larissa toyed with the spoon, as if she were contemplating putting more cream in her coffee. Then she laid it on the side. "You know I've never forbidden you anything."

"I shall make it up to Mr. Leblanc today," Vivian promised. "I will use all my coyest tricks to lure him away from the snapping jaws of the Tisher tigresses and the wobbling hands of Miss Sowberry and suggest a walk in the woods at the picnic."

"You ought not to joke about such things, Vivian," said her mother. But she could tell Larissa was pleased.

~

*A*s they all set out on foot toward the wax woods, Monte Leblanc fell into step with Vivian. She observed how the Tisher girls still kept watch over him, but the two younger girls withdrew a little more while their older sister was in constant attendance of the man. She wondered with amusement whether there had been a family council where Cecily and Bethel had been ordered to retreat from their sister's new prospect. Perhaps the family council had included a lesson in flirtation etiquette, as Vivian noticed that, despite Fern's attentiveness, she was less overbearing in her attentions to Mr. Leblanc, as if weighing every gesture.

"You enjoyed the *Ukha*, I hope?" he asked her in a low voice

"It was very good," Vivian said. "And very generous of you to invite us to your table to try it."

"I looked for you after dinner too, but you were gone." There was a slight note of reproach in his voice.

"I had a friend in town I had to see."

"Your mother told us you have quite a few friends in town."

"Did she?" Vivian looked ahead of her where her mother was walking with the elder Leblanc.

"They're not her friends, I gather." He chuckled. "My father, too, has people he would rather I not associate with."

"There's nothing wrong with the people I associate with," Vivian snapped, thinking of Nettie.

"I meant people not to his taste socially," he added hastily.

Vivian smiled. "Yes, I suppose you're right. Just because some people aren't in one's class doesn't mean they aren't good people."

He nodded, putting his hands behind his back as they walked. She noticed they were broad hands, more than she would have expected from a man whose figure was less imposing than his strength. "I have friends who are loggers," he said. "Some I've taken on as managers in my mills, but some preferred to remain with the trees."

"Not everyone wants a house of gold," Vivian pointed out.

Mr. Leblanc smiled and bent down to pick up a sprig of mint from the side of the path. "Have you ever been to Greece?"

"No," Vivian said.

"The streets are full of this." He shook the peppermint so that its crisp scent burst up in the air. "It clears the senses, they say."

"The myth of how it came to be isn't so clean," Vivian said. "A woman turned into a plant because of Persephone's jealousy."

"I know little about their myths." He shrugged. "I only remember the scents of the country and the blue seas. Green and blue, that's all I see when I think of Greece. I went there soon after my wife died."

Vivian's voice softened. "I'm sorry you lost your wife."

"Papa thought it was a mistake," the man continued, his voice almost a whisper, as they were near the wax wood trees. "It was too soon, he said. But one must live, mustn't one?"

"Yes, one must live," she said.

"I've been told you, too, have lost a husband." He glanced at her. "Widowhood harder on a woman than on a man."

"Why do you think so?" Vivian asked.

"Because a man can find so many other things to fill his time, but a woman—"

"Is confined to the lives of others?" Vivian gave him a prickly smile. "So, when the love of her life is gone, she has nothing."

"Don't misunderstand me, Miss Alderdice—"

"I don't think I misunderstood you," she said. "I don't blame you, either. Why shouldn't you think so, when everyone else does?" She pulled her shawl around her. "It may surprise you to know, Mr. Leblanc, that my husband and I knew one another for only three months. Then Miles went off on his excursion. He never came back."

She was breathless, realizing they were ascending the hill toward the point where the wax wood trees dominated their kingdom. The others were ahead of them, feeling around for the perfect place to lie down their blankets and baskets.

"Maybe it was better that way," he said gently. "You were very young, I take it?"

"Twenty."

"So young, you could begin all over again."

Vivian nodded, feeling small in the green kingdom of the wax woods. The trees had become more luscious, weighed down by the growth of those footprint leaves. The sun was dazing her as it sifted through the dancing branches. The bark looked as if it had grown thicker too, and Vivian knew if she touched even one tree, she would leave the mark of her fingerprints, as in softened wax.

She cocked her head toward Mr. Leblanc, who was waiting for her in his staunch, polite way. "What do you think of them, sir?"

"Eh?" The man blinked.

"The wax wood trees." Vivian smiled. "The infamous wax wood trees."

"Infamous?"

"The tree melts in the sun," she explained.

"There are odd things in the forests of Europe." He leaned against his walking stick. "We once took a trip into the Hoia Baciu Forest."

"Where is that?"

"Romania," he said. "It is said one may enter and never come out."

"I wasn't speaking of hauntings," Vivian said, feeling impatient. "The trees are a strange phenomenon."

"Those in the Hoia Baciu are as well," he insisted. "They flounder and twist all about like no other trees in the world."

She looked at him, the usual sleepy eyes gathering in a shifty look, his muscular limbs posing with the certainty of his place in the natural setting. She held out her hand, which he graciously took.

They reached the place where the others had settled, less populated by the wax wood trees and more elegant with soft tuffs of grass and wild flowers. The elder Mr. Leblanc sat next to Larissa with a glass of wine in his hand.

"Your father has consented to join us, Mr. Leblanc," Larissa said with her hostess smile.

"A pleasure, a pleasure." The elder man's voice was gravelly. "If it's not too forward, that is."

"We're very free here in California." Vivian seated herself next to her mother. "We don't stand on ceremony."

"We're a little roughshod ourselves," said the younger Mr. Leblanc with a laugh. This remark earned a stern look from his father, and he added, more humored still, "Papa's had an old-world education, you know. It was only through his own vim and adventurous spirit that he became a backwoodsman."

"We're no longer backwoods, I'll thank you to remember," his father hissed.

There was a moment of discomfort, and then Larissa broke in with her calm tone, "My father lived by those old-world customs too."

"It would be wise for young people to put their faith in such customs," said the elder Mr. Leblanc, shooting a glance at his son.

"I put all my faith in it, Papa," his son insisted. "If I didn't, I wouldn't be here."

Mrs. Tisher and Fern, who were stepping daintily through the grass around the clustered people, smiled and nodded at them. They did not speak, but in the smile was a knowing look from Mrs. Tisher toward Larissa which, Vivian knew, was a silent message of some sort, while narrowing eyes punctuated Fern's smile. Her mother's countenance relaxed with a satisfied smile. She couldn't help but feel a certain superiority, understanding that she and her mother had coveted the most sought-after men in Waxwood at that moment. She felt lighter and more whimsical than she had since she arrived in Waxwood, and said to Monte

Leblanc, "It doesn't sound as if you father has much hope for us in the new century."

"You misunderstand me, my dear." The older man's graying mustache, longer at the sides than his son's, stiffened. "I have every hope for those like you and my son. You're of a more sensible generation, if I may be so bold as to say."

"You may, sir," she said, though she was amused at the idea that he clearly thought her older than she really was. "But we're all moving in the same direction, no matter how many years we have behind us."

"Mr. Leblanc spoke of hope, dear," said Larissa. "You speak of progress. They're not the same."

"Indeed not," said the senior Mr. Leblanc with a sniff. "Hope is to embrace the traditions, perhaps add to them in the same manner. Progress can blind us to those traditions."

"It can even make us loath them," the younger Mr. Leblanc murmured.

Vivian watched as he took up a bottle of wine and struggled to open it. She had seen the way he handled the sheet music while Fern played the piano, those enormous hands turning each page with a delicacy that matched only a doctor pulling the sheet over a dead man's head. And yet, here in front of her was the man who had come from the backwoods of Canada, who had probably dragged logs through feels of snow and sawed trees down with an admirable swiftness. He leaned toward the jacket he had asked permission to lie on the blanket and slipped a folding knife out of the pocket with which he loosened the cork with one push.

"You don't believe we must break traditions sometimes?" she asked in a loud voice.

"I do not!" The older man gave her a stubborn look.

"It's as Mr. Leblanc said," Larissa took firm hold of the conversation, "one does not break traditions, at least not ours. One adds their own to them, and even then, only when they are worthy to stand with the old ones."

"But isn't it possible to break the old traditions while adding worthy new ones in their place?" Vivian asked.

"For example?" The elderly Mr. Leblanc persevered with his stubbornness.

"You're being too inquisitive, Papa," his son snapped.

"You don't object to giving us an example, do you, Miss Alderdice?" the older man asked.

Vivian met that gaze boldly. "Not at all, sir. An example: A young woman might marry a man and still be free."

"Free?"

"Vivian—" Her mother's gaze had taken on the warning look.

But she continued, "Free to have ideas of her own that even her husband might not altogether agree with."

"I care little for such ideas," the old man mumbled. "It makes people forget their place."

"You mean it makes women forget their place," Vivian eyed him.

"I'm sure Mr. Leblanc meant nothing of the sort," Larissa said.

"Your mother is right, Miss Alderdice," said the younger Mr. Leblanc. "Papa was only speaking in theories." He shot his father a look that was more severe than the one his father had given him.

The old man smiled. "I have nothing against ideas." But he was a looking at Vivian with piercing eyes, and she knew he was reconsidering whether his son's preferred company amongst all the ladies that flocked around him was deserving of the Leblanc name. He ventured, "Since we are not standing on ceremony, as you called it, may I ask you a rather personal question?"

"Of course," said Vivian.

"Do you like children?"

There was an unpleasant silence as Bethel and a young man closer to her age ran past them, their flying feet pounding against the ground, heightened by Bethel's giggles. Then, the younger Mr. Leblanc gave a laugh that sounded a little too hearty and said, "Papa, it's hardly a question for you to ask, since you have only one child."

"We would have had more had it not been for the hard winters and fever," the man sighed.

Vivian recovered from her initial heated moment. "I don't mind answering. I am very fond of children, and I hope any man I marry will be as fond of them as I am."

There was an almost audible exhale among their small group, floating with the fresh scent of the peppermint. "Every family in the best position ought to be rich with heirs," the elder Mr. Leblanc declared.

"Very sensible during these volatile times," Larissa agreed. "One never knows what we may leave, but children insure the future." A note of melancholy touched her usual grated voice. Vivian felt an ache in her heart, as she knew of whom her mother was thinking.

Cecily and Bethel were now going around giving each group a large plate with watermelon wedges. They ate in silence, though Vivian had lost her appetite. The other parties were in high spirits, laughter expanding in between scraping and clicking. She noticed Fern had seated herself alongside Huey Griffith, Amber's brother, whose engagement to a young lady in Boston did not keep him from flirting with the young woman, and Vivian caught Fern nodding with a coquettish air and wondered to what she was agreeing.

Watching them, she thought about the promise she had made to herself and her mother before they boarded the train. She glanced at Mr. Leblanc, whose hooded eyes were now more alert, and she realized he had also seen Fern and Huey. But there was no jealousy in his gaze. There was, in fact, a shadow of regret, as when an older man looks upon youthful flirtations as if he were remembering his own and wondering whether there would ever be such moments for him again. She suddenly saw Monte Leblanc as weighed down by the Leblanc family traditions as she was with the Alderdice ones. His past might be clean, but his future was still as murky as hers.

She rose. "I think I'll take a walk. I haven't seen these woods in so long, I'm curious to see if they've changed." She picked up her shawl and added, in the charmed voice she had once been so fond of imitating from her grandmother when she was a child, "I would be very pleased if you would come with me, Mr. Leblanc."

As they entered the thicket of trees, Vivian was aware of how much wilder the forest had grown. Vegetation that had not been there before stressed various shades of green and brown, and tufts of flowers appeared around the trees. They came upon what looked like the tail end of a stream showing a bed of silvery rocks at its bottom. This part of the forest was more alive with little creatures, but the salamanders and frogs only gazed at them as they strolled by.

"Why, it's as fierce here as the lowland forest in Ontario!" Mr. Leblanc declared, looking around in wonder.

"Is that bad?" Vivian stepped over a branch. She could see the toe-shaped leaves that had come from the wax wood trees brushing the ground.

"No, indeed!" said the man "My father took me out there to hunt moose for the first time. We saw a mother and its calf among the trees, and my father told me never to shoot a mother with a child. And I never have to this day."

Vivian smiled. "That sounds like a charming memory."

"And do you have a charming memory of this place, Miss Alderdice?" he asked with a smile.

She opened her parasol, though it was hardly necessary with the bushy trees hiding the sun above them. "I was once Diana with her crown of thorns here."

Trees pressed on all sides. The ground was dry, and she recognized the exact spot where her brother had posed her for his painting the year before. She surveyed the ground, her shoes meshing with clover. She stopped near a cluster of what she thought were daisies, but these were stranger flowers. Their centers spread yellow, as if they wanted to split in half. She picked one of them, feeling as if it were vibrating in her hand, and dropped it, shirking back.

Mr. Leblanc's eyes rested on her. She rose. "I'm sorry. This place—"

"Haunted with memories?" he guessed. "I know what you mean. There are places like that for me too." He looked through the parting of the trees.

"This entire forest is haunted for me now," she said. "And not just the woods either. I mean the town. People I've known through letters but never saw before — relatives of ghosts—" She shivered again.

Mr. Leblanc's voice came faintly behind her. "Are you feeling well, Miss Alderdice?"

She clutched at his arm. "Take me out of this place!"

"Certainly!" He led her toward the direction of the picnic. But she stopped him in a pleasant place with only a few trees, most of them redwoods.

"Forgive me," she begged. "I acted like a fool."

"Not at all," he said. "I take it you didn't enjoy being — what was it you said — Diana with her crown of thorns?"

"Diana, the Greek goddess of the hunt," she said.

"Ah, yes! The Greek myths." He sighed. "I'm rather glad I don't know them."

Vivian could not help but smile. "I liked being Diana. She was a powerful woman, though not always sympathetic." Vivian sat on the grass. "My brother asked me to pose for him. He was — is — a painter."

"And he painted you as Diana?"

"He painted a child, and someone else said it was Diana."

"Who would say such a thing?" the man growled.

She almost liked the anger in his voice. "A man with no scruples. He never thinks about the moral consequences of what he says or does."

He snorted. "Think no more about it, Miss Alderdice. Such a man is hardly fit to walk in the shadow of your footsteps."

She looked up at him, his figure erect, his face showing a determined expression. "You very gracious, Mr. Leblanc."

He leaned on his stick, made of mahogany and silver and a little too fine for the rough ground. "Was your brother a talented painter?"

"I thought so," she said with a small smile. Then she felt her cheeks flaring up. "What did they tell you about him, Mr. Leblanc?"

"They?"

"You know who I mean," she said. "Please, I want to know."

"It doesn't matter."

"It does to me."

He began drawing a circle with the edge of his stick in the dark brown dirt patch near him. "They gossip about him disappearing rather abruptly."

"My brother didn't disappear," she insisted. "He's in Europe studying painting. They know that."

"Yes, yes," he said. "Naturally."

"Mother and I know they don't really believe that," Vivian lamented. "So, what do they believe, Mr. Leblanc?"

He glanced at her. "You value honesty, don't you, Miss Alderdice?"

"Do you?"

"Very much."

"Then you'll tell me what they said, won't you?"

"Before I do," he said in a firm voice, "please remember I never believe in gossip and neither does my father."

"I'm pleased to hear it," she mumbled.

He kneeled down. "They think he went away because of nervous exhaustion."

To hear these words was almost a sick relief to Vivian. She sank against the grass. "I see."

"Did you know Mr. and Mrs. Stewart just returned from Europe before they came here?"

"No, I didn't know that." Vivian's breath drew in.

"Mr. Stewart had some business he had to attend to in Paris, and Mrs. Stewart accompanied him along with her brother Huey," he continued. "At least, that was how Huey told it to me."

"Go on."

"Huey knows a collector who knows some artists there." He began again to draw on the ground with the edge of his stick.

"Yes?" She sat very straight with her knees together.

"None of them had ever heard of a Jacob Alderdice."

They were silent as the surrounding woods heaved with the brush of feathers, buzzing flies, and a deep-throated call from some animal far away.

The stick scraped harder on the ground. "They didn't recall any American in the studios or cafes or art schools."

Vivian felt her breath coming out quickly. She rose, brushing her dress from the dirt flung on her from the wind. "Thank you for telling me, Mr. Leblanc. Now I know. One cannot fight a blind enemy."

"You don't have to fight anyone," he insisted. "I've seen dogs who hold their tongues better."

She graciously took his arm as they headed back toward the picnic. She gave one glance over her shoulder, seeing the patch of yellow in the distance where the parting of the trees gave way to the clover carpet. But she knew she was far from turning her back on it completely.

～

he party returned to the hotel in the early evening. The walk had tired Vivian, and she felt her arms heavy at her sides as they entered the lobby. She saw David Potter's slender figure pacing near a pair of couches where a few men sat with the evening paper, giving him a sour look because he looked like a buzzard circling its prey.

He saw Vivian and smiled, though he seemed hesitant to approach her. With an arch of his brows, he veered off of the lobby and into the hallway.

Vivian was alert and slipped her hat over her eye. "Will you excuse me?" she said to Mr. Leblanc, who had walked her into the lobby.

His gaze became shifty, and his voice was a little too polite when he said, "I see your friend has arrived."

"Friend?"

"I saw you speaking with him at the market."

"I won't be a moment." She hurried away before her mother, who had just turned toward Mrs. Tisher, noticed her gone.

David's good-natured smile looked almost out of place in the formal setting. "I've been waiting for you. I ought to have known you would be at some merry event. A college chum once brought me home to Nob Hill for the summer, and it was just the same."

"Sometimes I would rather hide away with a book," she said with a laugh.

"Or good company." His eyes swept behind her where the crowd was still visible. "I can't imagine there is much peace with those birds."

"I assume there's a reason you've come, David?"

"A perfectly sound one," he promised. "Good company. At least, that's my view, though I'm rather prejudice." He leaned on one foot. "Aunt Leona insisted I come here and told me not to return until I had dragged you by the arm to her humble little abode. She wants you to join us for dinner."

"It's rather sudden, isn't it?"

"I told her that, but my aunt, you see—" His face became almost grave.

"Your aunt is the kind who won't take 'no' for an answer?" Vivian guessed.

"It's not that," he said. "Aunt Leona, she's not been well, and at her age, I suppose she feels as if the minutes are slipping by."

"Yes, I can see how she would think such a thing." Vivian sighed, remembering how the minutes slipped away when her grandmother was ill.

"I told her it would be inconvenient, as I'm sure you have plans tonight."

"I don't have any plans," she said. "I'd like to meet your aunt."

"Won't your friends miss you?" He glanced uneasily toward the lobby.

"They're not my friends," she said truthfully.

He was thoughtful for a moment, then held out his arm. "Will you allow this friend to escort you to dinner, then? Henderson gave me his boat, and Aunt Leona's house is just at the other side of the bay."

"I would be delighted."

"You wouldn't rather — freshen up?" He glanced down at her.

She realized the back of her hair had released a few stands, and the sash on her dress was untied. She would have preferred a bath, but she feared if she were to go to the suite now, her mother would be there with her icy eyes and prying questions.

"There's a lady's lounge around the corner," she said. "If you'll give me a few moments."

"I didn't mean that you needed to," he blurted. "Aunt Leona wouldn't care if you came in a dressing gown, and neither do I. I thought for you—"

"A few moments," she repeated and rushed into the lounge, now nearly empty because many of the guests had gone up to dress for dinner. She tamed her strawberry locks and tied her sash, brushing off the back of her dress from any dirt left over from her stroll in the woods. She washed her face and felt instantly better. She emerged from the lounge and caught sight of some of her party still lingering in the lobby, Mr. Leblanc among them. She approached the desk and wrote a hurried note explaining she had been suddenly invited to dine with a friend for both the Leblanc and the Alderdice pigeon holes.

By the time she returned to David, she felt more herself, walking in the way her mother taught her when she was a debutante which, Larissa said, always brought a lady back to being a lady.

David directed the boat with more skill than she thought a young man for whom office work was more to his liking would possess. As he steered the craft, he talked about his aunt.

"I suppose she's what you would call a spitfire," he said. "But with her, it's more literal. She spits out her words tartly when she's riled up. So don't be alarmed."

Vivian smiled. "I've been among complacent ladies most of my life. The only thing that riles them up is when a bee dares to make its way near their teacup."

He laughed. "I saw many such ladies during my summer on Nob Hill."

"I'm very curious to know how your aunt knows about me."

"Oh, I didn't tell her," he said. "I mentioned meeting someone who knew someone who might have known Aunt Loretta, but that was all. It was Henderson." He grimaced. "He's always delighted to meet anyone who reminds him of those 'good ole days,' and he blabs to anyone alive during those times. Few left in Waxwood, sadly. Only my aunt and a few others, though none of them would remember Penelope. They were only children."

"I was being nosey," Vivian admitted. "It was only — that day on the train — I didn't expect to have to face my specter again."

"It's the way of ghosts, isn't it?" He sighed. "They disappear and then appear again to remind us they are still shadows lurking about."

"I used to have a remedy for such shadows," Vivian said, looking ahead to where the line of fading blue sky met the still brilliant line of blue-green sea.

"And what was that?"

"I would twist a dagger into their backs."

He laughed. "But you don't now?"

She wrapped her shawl around her shoulders. "I try to ignore them instead."

He shrugged. "One remedy is as good as the other."

"I don't know," she lamented. "I don't know."

It turned out Miss Potter really had a place just at the edge of the bay. Vivian liked the look of the modest, lemon-painted house as David pulled the boat up and tied it to the dock. It even had a modest garden with the violets bobbing in the wind, little dots of purple glaring off the front porch.

A woman with a rather stern countenance sat in a creaking rocking chair on the porch. As they climbed the steps, she rose slowly with the help of a twisted cane. The woman looked rather old and tired, and her knees shook a bit as she stood with one hand on the post, watching them ascend. But as they came closer, Vivian saw the cotton white hair and wrinkled skin betrayed a set mouth and sharp green eyes that surveyed her as if she were a cat about to be skinned.

"This is the young lady, David?" she asked in a curdling tone.

"Now, don't be intimidating, Aunt Leona." David gave her a quick kiss on her cheek.

"I am not the least intimidating," said the woman, indignant. "I am always a lady." She looked at Vivian from above a pair of small, wire spectacles that looked as if they were hardly good for their purpose. "Are *you* a lady?"

Vivian liked her rather bald question. "I should hope so, ma'am."

"Don't 'ma'am' me," snapped the woman, her lip curling. "Call me Leona, if you must call me anything at all."

"It's generally accepted that people call one another something when they meet," David mumbled, giving a wink to a middle-aged woman who stood at the doorway. A housekeeper, Vivian guessed. The woman winked back.

"I'm well aware of that, David." Leona held out her arm to Vivian. "As my nephew has seen fit to bestow upon me the *rudest* jest, you, as a lady, shall take me, as a lady, into dinner. It's on the table, Mrs. Shore?" She threw a glance back at the woman in the doorway.

"Has been for five minutes," the woman answered in a deep, wary tone.

"Splendid." Leona hobbled a little, her slight weight against Vivian's arm. "I so hate to wait for the roast to cool, don't you?"

"I never thought about it much," said Vivian.

"I gather you have had what one may call, with no violation of delicacy, 'advantages.'" The woman's nimble eyes gazed at Vivian's silk waistcoat, making her cheeks grow red. She wished her jacket had more buttons under which she could hide it.

"One must make do with what one is born," Vivian said simply.

"True, true," said Leona with half-closed eyes. "Though one may not stay in that position after one has kicked one's feet out of the crib."

"Aunt Leona used to write poetry for the *Waxwood Review* when she was young," David said in what passed for a low voice as they sat around a small, round table.

"So did your sister Loretta, didn't she?" Vivian asked.

The old woman regarded her with such vacant eyes that Vivian thought she had lost her sight for a moment. "How in heaven did you know that?"

"Bertha told me," she said. "Bertha Ross, that is."

"And how did you meet Bertha?" The woman tapped lightly at the soup that Mrs. Shore had put in front of her.

Vivian looked down into the clear, yellowish broth that had a rich chicken flavor that soothed her after the salty, tasteless consommé the chef at the Waxwoodian favored. "That's rather a long story."

"It always is," said Leona.

"What does it matter, Auntie?" David said. "You didn't ask Vivian here to interrogate her, did you?"

"I shall do my own questioning, young man. You eat your soup!"

He bent down to the bowl with half-smiling lips.

"She attended my grandmother's funeral," Vivian said.

"I see." She patted Vivian's hand. "Penelope Carlyle was your grandmother, wasn't she?" Vivian nodded. "Lively woman, I recall. Of course, I didn't know her very well. But my sister Loretta was devoted to her, and so was Bertha."

"Yes, they were good friends," said Vivian. "For a time at least."

"For a time?"

"The year Grandmother was in Waxwood," Vivian explained. "Then she married my grandfather, and — well, she didn't have much time for friends."

"She had time for Bertha." Leona's voice was indignant. "Bertha visited her for quite some time in that filthy city."

Vivian froze, a slice of bread in her hand. "Quite some time?"

"Certainly." Leona cocked her head at Mrs. Shore, who quickly took her cue and slipped the half-eaten soup bowl into her hands. "She was there for, oh, a long time, as I recall."

"You told me you remembered nothing about that year." David eyed her.

"My memory, Nephew, comes and goes like the wind." She eyed him back. "It does not appear to your liking. Nor mine, for that matter."

"Did your sister go with Bertha to the city to see Grandmother?" Vivian asked.

"I'm afraid not, child. Loretta was ill for ages." The woman's lips set in a thin line. "Poor, dear Loretta. Married not three months to a preacher, and then—"

"He was a fine man," David interrupted. "Mama says so."

"Your mother has a goose's way of looking at people," snapped his aunt. "As I was saying," she looked at Vivian, "Loretta died, poor dear, some short months after that, and we thought Penelope would come to the funeral. Then we got Malcolm's letter."

"My grandfather sent a letter?" Vivian asked.

"He did indeed." The woman's mouth was set. "All prim and proper."

"What did the letter say?"

"My, but you're a curious one, child."

Vivian blushed and looked down at the plate Mrs. Shore had put in front of her. "I'm sorry. I don't know why I should ask. It can hardly matter now."

"You want to know about your family, don't you?" David asked.

She felt again the pull of the light down the path in her mind, a walkway with a pair of eyes leering at her, daring her to follow.

"It was all crisp politeness." Leona said this in a tone that made Vivian know just exactly what she thought of it. "Malcolm was always polite."

"Vivian asked you what the letter said, Auntie." David picked up his wineglass.

"Don't you go drinking too much, Nephew," snapped his aunt. "You get mighty bumbling when you do."

He gave her a sniff, but set down the glass and picked up his water tumbler instead.

"'Course I don't remember the exact wording." Her eyes narrowed. "But I recall his profuse apologies that Mrs. Alderdice couldn't be at the funeral because she would have a child soon.

He also said they wouldn't be coming to console, as they had plans to go abroad right away."

"Abroad?" Vivian's fork slipped from her hand. "But that's impossible!"

"Well, that's what he said. I can't say if I believed him at the time. Those cultured people say a lot of things for the sake of decorum." She pushed aside Mrs. Shore's hand as she tried to put more green beans on the plate. "Bring the salad, Edna. Can't think what you were waiting for." The housekeeper gave her an even smile and withdrew.

"Auntie, Vivian is one of those cultured people." Her nephew was indignant.

"Well, sakes, you know what I mean!" She put her hand on Vivian's shoulder. "Malcolm was never one to get straight to the point. Always in a flurry about everything. Took me and Claire several times reading it over to understand what he was saying."

"And Bertha didn't go with them because of your sister's funeral?" Vivian asked.

"Well, now, I tell you, it was all crazy, the goings on with Bertha."

"How do you mean, Auntie?" David helped himself to more potatoes.

"Oh, Bertha was Bertha, but more ruffled about than usual." Leona put her chin in her hand. "Always pulling at her handkerchief, insisting it wasn't right, it wasn't right."

"What wasn't right?" Vivian asked.

"Everything, I gathered," said the woman. "Her not being with Penelope abroad, for one thing. I don't believe I ever saw her get angry at anybody in her life, but, land's sake, she was sure fuming at Malcolm that fall!"

"I wonder why she wasn't invited," Vivian said.

"According to her, Malcolm wanted a professional nurse with Penelope," said Leona. "Now, I'm not against that sort of thing, if you got the money. But Bertha did well enough in that mountain place — Lica, Lico, I think was the name of it?"

"There's a Lico in the southern part of the state," said David. "Up in the mountains."

"That's the place. Well, she was there for months with Penelope, so why she should suddenly be — what's the fancy word for it?" She gazed at her nephew.

"Inadequate," he supplied.

She sniffed. "Why she should suddenly be inadequate, I don't know."

"And why my grandmother should suddenly have the strength to go abroad when she had to be confined for months is strange," Vivian said. "And why could she go abroad but not to Loretta's funeral?"

"Now you're being a little too mysterious." David grinned.

"Let the girl ask her questions, young man." The woman curled her lip. "I like a young lady who asks questions rather than giggles all the time." She turned to Vivian with congenial eyes. "Malcolm said something about the grief being too much for her. I expect he was right." Her eyes grew heavy and dark.

The dinner ended, and they retired to the parlor for the coffee. The carefully placed gaslights and china angels and maidens gave the room a pleasant air. Vivian felt more at ease there than with the more stoic wood and pointed corners of the dining room.

"Bertha must have been with my grandmother for a long time to feel so hurt they didn't ask her to go abroad," Vivian remarked.

"Oh, all told, I'd say she and Penelope were together about a year."

"A year!"

"It wasn't so out of the ordinary in those days for a young woman to have a companion with her when her husband went abroad," said Leona, pouring the coffee. As she handed Vivian her cup, the aromatic scent made Vivian's stomach churn.

"Grandfather was away?"

"Some important business or other," said the woman with a sniff.

"Yes, I remember now. My mother told me something about that once," Vivian said.

"It was good of Bertha to come all the way to the city to be with her," David said, smiling. "I suppose she wasn't such a bad old biddy."

"Mr. Henderson said she was in a state when she came back," Vivian remarked.

"Why do you think she was so alarmed, Auntie?" David asked.

"I haven't the faintest idea." Leona shrugged. "Bertha and I weren't really friends, you know. I always thought her rather a goose."

"You think everyone who is the least childlike a goose," David retorted. Vivian glanced at him, surprised, as, unlike the banter she had heard between them all evening, this one had a note of resentment.

"And so they are," his aunt answered, obviously unaware of the change in mood.

"Do you think Mr. Henderson was right?" Vivian asked. "Bertha was fretful about something?"

There was silence for a moment with only a distant clatter of glass and water, which Vivian took to be Mrs. Shore washing the dishes. Leona leaned back against the pillows, her eyes half closed and her face wary. In a tired voice, she said, "Bring us some sherry, will you, David, dear?" Her glance went to her nephew, and her voice was almost mild.

"Certainly, Auntie." He gave Vivian a look that showed his worry as he went to the maple cabinet and produced an ornate bottle and three small glasses.

"I'm sorry," said Vivian, crossing her hands on her knees. "I won't ask any more questions. What can it matter now?"

Leona turned her head, regarding her with a biting look.

"You've been saying that all evening, child. Are you trying to convince me or yourself?"

Vivian glanced at the sherry glass David had put into her hand. She suddenly remembered that day at her grandmother's funeral, with Bertha and her pealing laugh, her sweet, wrinkled face, and dancing gray eyes. Bertha, who had held the sherry glass in her hand but never drank it because she had been starving for heaven knows how long. And now Vivian could not pick up her glass because she was also starving. Her hunger was not for food, but for the drug of the past.

"I don't need your apology," Leona was saying. "I told you before, I like young ladies to ask questions."

Vivian couldn't help but smile. "So does David."

"Our reasons are entirely different." She scowled as her nephew handed her the glass. Vivian saw him blush a little as he returned to the couch. "As you have put a direct question to me, I shall give you a direct answer. Yes. She said Penelope didn't miss Malcolm in the least."

"Why would that make biddy-bird Bertha so anxious?" David asked with a wry smile.

"I don't read people's minds, Nephew," said the woman.

Vivian picked up the sherry and drank it. It had a slight cherry flavor that burned her throat. "Grandmother was used to being alone. Grandfather was away much of the time back then. He was eager to help my great-grandfather grow the shipping company."

"Businessmen are like that," David mumbled.

"And, too, she was a society woman." Vivian felt her throat still burning. "She had so much to occupy her time."

"Indeed," said Leona. "Bertha jabbered on about the dinners and the parties. But Bertha said Penelope was more interested in sitting on the grass at the park, 'making those clever pictures of hers.'"

It was as if the light in the room had suddenly become

dazzling, even though the sky had fallen a darker shade of blue. "Are you sure she said 'pictures'?" Leona sniffed.

"She was drawing again, then."

"Again?"

"We thought she stopped when she left Waxwood."

"Perhaps her friend encouraged her to take it up." The woman held out her empty glass, and David, openly surprised, refilled it with sherry.

"I wouldn't imagine Bertha was the type to encourage anything out of anybody except exasperation," he remarked with a smile.

"Now don't be foolish, Nephew," his aunt snapped. "Bertha may have been a scatterbrain, but she had a good heart. But I wasn't referring to her."

"Who then?" he asked.

"A rather scruffy young man living in San Francisco. He used to live in that artist colony. What was it called, David?" She peered at her nephew.

Vivian felt her heart jump. "You mean Brandywine?"

"Oh, Penelope told you about it."

"Not exactly," Vivian said, though she had always felt the letters she read to be almost like Grandmother confiding in her.

"Now *you're* being evasive," said David with a grin.

"Don't be a little silly." His aunt shot him a warning look.

Vivian felt her eyes grow heavy. "I'm afraid I'm the one who's been silly."

The old woman put a wrinkled hand on Vivian's. "I expect Vivian will want to go back to her hotel now, David. You shall take her back in Henderson's boat and see her to the door of her room or whatever monstrosity passes for a room in that abode."

Vivian smiled and pressed the woman's hand back. "I'm sorry to have brought up so many painful memories."

"It does well for an old person to remember." She gave a little curve of her set lips for what Vivian imagined passed for a smile in her eyes. "You'll see that when you're my age."

She was silent on the boat, feeling the easy wind shaking through her, as if it were rattling her bones. The lamps that graced the boat's edges and sides, plentiful like fireflies, swayed back and forth with the current of the waters. The reflection of the glowing lines showed through the pliant ground. She knew they marked her path, the path she could no longer avoid.

CHAPTER 7

The next few weeks carried Vivian through the first month of their Waxwood stay. The lethargy she had felt the past year, receiving so few invitations from the Washington Street swells, vanished into a whirlwind of endless picnics, morning dances, excursions, boating parties, and tennis matches. She remarked to her mother one morning as she was dressing, "I don't think I've been so breathless since I was a debutante."

"It's what we needed, dear." Her mother, holding her hat in her hands, leaned against the bureau. "You've been very agreeable to everyone, and that helps tremendously."

"In other words, you expect me to be a little less independent in future." Vivian snatched the shirtwaist from her bed.

"Not necessarily," said Larissa. "We just don't want to give anyone the wrong impression."

"You know, I've been watching Mr. Leblanc, and I don't think he really has a serious interest in Fern or even Miss Sowberry," Vivian said thoughtfully.

"Oh?" Her mother's eyebrow went up.

She slipped on the shirtwaist and adjusted the tie around her neck. "And I don't know that he thinks much of our society now."

Larissa approached the bed, grasping at the post. "What makes you say that?"

"He told me what they're saying about Jake," Vivian said. "What they're *really* saying."

A heavy silence followed. "Who brought up the subject, him or you?"

She snapped the last button in back of the shirtwaist and straightened it out over her chest. "We broached the subject among a discussion of forest ghosts."

"Don't speak to me of specters," her mother snapped. "Not anymore."

Vivian sat on the bed. "He brought it up, but I wanted to know."

Larissa ran her finger along the brass frame of the bed. "You didn't tell him anything?"

"I told him what we've been telling everyone else."

"But he didn't believe it?"

"I don't think he much cares what the truth is." Vivian shrugged as she rose and slipped on the jacket that had been lying on the bed. "He told me they all think Jake is in a lunatic asylum."

"And how did they come to that conclusion I wonder?"

"Amber and Huey were in Paris, and no one there ever heard of Jacob Alderdice."

Her mother turned to the mirror above the bureau and pinned on her hat. "You said Mr. Leblanc doesn't care."

"He doesn't."

"Then they can gossip all they like, can't they?" She turned to her with a smile. "You're managing it all beautifully, dear."

"Am I?" Vivian couldn't help but snicker. "Perhaps I'm more like you than Grandmother after all. Grandmother wouldn't chase after a man, would she? She let Grandfather chase her."

"It's not a question of chasing," said Larissa. "But sometimes, a young woman must do what she loathes for her duty to her family and to society."

"Must she?" Vivian thought about that night with Leona, about looking at the sherry glass and the reflection of memory in the slightly yellowish crystal.

"Of course she must!" The answer came with a heavy insistence.

Vivian followed her mother out to the suite parlor. Larissa attacked the accessories lying on the couch, stretching her gloves delicately over her fingers, checking her beaded bag, shaking out her parasol. Vivian remembered how much she used to love to watch both her mother and grandmother preparing for an outing as they arranged themselves in perfect feminine garb. "There comes a time when she has to choose whether to go on twisting the dagger or wear the necklace of expectations, even if it chokes her," she said almost to herself.

Throughout breakfast, she had that dagger and necklace on her mind. She saw them sitting on a scale with Lady Justice balancing them on her shoulders, one leaning down more than the other, each in danger of precariously flinging the other away. She half listened to her mother talk about the casino in Emsworth, some thirty miles from Waxwood.

"Mrs. Tisher says they've hired a rather modern band that plays music out in the courtyard," said Larissa. "Music and dancing and even champagne!"

"At ten o'clock in the morning?"

"Why not?" Larissa smiled. "It makes the rest of the day jolly, as long as one is careful."

Vivian toyed with the edge of her coffee spoon. "I can't go today, Mother. I'm going to see the Rosses." The name slipped into a pocket of quiet space with a quick lull in the room.

Larissa's mouth set in a line. "I thought we agreed to forget about the Rosses."

"I told you I intended to see them. Now, I must."

"Why must you?" her mother shot out.

"Because it's polite," Vivian answered quickly.

"They've brought nothing but strife and sadness to our lives," her mother insisted.

"To me, Bertha Ross brought truth and foresight."

"Truth and foresight?" Her mother's cup clattered inside the saucer. "She told lies!"

"They weren't lies," Vivian insisted. "I know you wish they had been. Maybe sometimes I do too."

Larissa's keen eyes gazed at her with such force, Vivian had to look down to avoid them. "Last time, you agreed with me it was best to forget them."

"I merely want to go calling, as friends do."

"Friends!" Larissa lowered her voice. "I don't think your grandmother considered Bertha Ross much of a friend either. She was merely like a devoted puppy whose affections flattered her for a time."

"That's not true," Vivian snapped. "They were close friends."

"Oh, I know *she* said so," Larissa said. "But your grandmother never did."

"How could she?" Vivian felt her voice rising despite her inbred acumen. "She was dead before we even knew of Bertha Ross's existence."

"Vivian." Larissa folded her napkin on the table. "You know I don't dictate to you, but I think it would be very unwise of you to disappear on Mr. Leblanc now."

"I don't intend to," Vivian said, rising. "I will write him a very sweet and apologetic note about why I must be gone for the day, and, this evening, I will invite him to take a stroll with me on the boardwalk and listen to him rattle on about fox hunting or dog racing or whatever he likes."

Her mother was looking unblinkingly at her. "Why do I have the feeling there is more to this visit than just politeness?"

Vivian said quickly, "I'm merely making a friendly social call."

Larissa raised her eyes a little unevenly. "And that's really all there is to it?"

"That's all there is to it." Vivian knew she wasn't as firm as she needed to be.

But her mother accepted this as she rose and slid the chair against the table. "I think it's a mistake."

"Don't let Fern or that Sowberry girl get the best of Mr. Leblanc," Vivian said. "Not that I'm afraid of my standing with him, but the poor man might wilt under all that sugar water."

The idea made her mother smile.

~

*V*ivian followed the boardwalk to the end of the row of majestic hotels and resorts where it spilled into a shopping area especially made for the swells, establishments of upper-class leisure displayed with a crisp, clean veneer, the windows etched with goods working people had no use for. She reached the center of the exclusive street, what even the Waxwood inhabitants now called "Gallery Row." The line of curved windows displayed art that gave away the taste of its owner.

Further down, jilting out of the straight line as if it had privileges, was a silver sign scripted with the words *Culver's Gallery*. Vivian felt a stir as she thought with acid amusement of the role its owner, one Mr. Culver, whom she had never met, had played in the drama that marked her brother's descent into Hades.

Just then, a small man in a rather tight suit and spectacles, his head noticeably egg-shaped under his tight little hat, emerged from the gallery. Vivian, sensing this was Mr. Culver himself, quickly scurried down one of the bright alleyways that led into a courtyard where more shops sat quietly waiting for people to notice them.

She found a small place wedged in the corner and bought a

rosewood tea caddy shaped like a chest. The young sales lady helped her lay the chest in a basket. Vivian watched as her delicate hands laid it on the straw bed with the care of a builder laying the foundations for a mansion.

"You do that very well," she said, smiling.

The woman did not look at her, nor did she acknowledge the complement.

"You enjoy your work?" she continued.

"Better than a factory or office," the woman said with distraction. "Women like me have little choice nowadays, if they want to keep their virtue." She stole a glance at Vivian, her eyes prickling like stars.

"I suppose you must be very careful," Vivian muttered.

The woman gave her a salty look. "My honor is as important to me as yours is to you." Then, she added in a slightly vicious tone, "more so, even."

Vivian stiffened. "I never meant to imply that it wasn't."

The lady closed the lid of the basket and handed it to Vivian, "Three dollars, please."

Vivian counted out the bills. Her face warm with annoyance as she added, "We're not all parasites. Some of us do wonderful work in our own way."

The woman put the bills in the cash register, then leaned against the counter, gazing at the fine silk tie of her shirtwaist, the green silk of her suit. "It ain't what you do for others. It's what you do for yourself."

Vivian felt a wave of fury at the woman's snappy remark and judging eyes. She flounced out of the shop, her heart pounding.

Mr. Blaine was not there, and the younger man taking his place inclined toward curt answers without looking up from his duty and preferred silence from his passengers. So the ride was a rather windy and lonely one.

It took her some time to find the Ross house again. As she neared the gate, she heard a faint cry of a piano coming from inside, which surprised her, as she did not remember seeing a piano in the Ross parlor. But the house itself was just the same, with blue and gray fixtures, boards nailed into crosses across the walls, and shutters that had earned it the nickname of the "criss-cross house." Vivian felt a surge of warmth as she recalled Bertha's lively eyes and sweet voice. Even Ruth, though guarded and a little cold, had thawed and invited her to return. She now regretted it had taken her seven years to do so.

The piano was louder as she knocked on the door, though it was more noise than music. It stopped for a moment, then went on. Vivian knocked again, a little harder. This time, the piano stopped, and she heard footsteps. As the door creaked open, she suddenly felt the slight panic of seeing someone for the first time in a long time.

There was no mistaking Ruth. Gray peppered in with the light brown hair, and she looked even taller and thinner than she had the last time, but those small, dark eyes regarded her with more bewilderment than malice.

"Hello, Ruth." Vivian felt suddenly uncertain. Just then, a girl's head appeared from behind the screen door, her eyes popping through her round face. "I'm disturbing you."

"Mary was just finishing." Ruth recovered from her astonishment and now conducted herself as a teacher to a pupil. "You may go, Mary, but don't forget to practice the Ravel. I'll see you next week."

The child already had her things in hand and, casting a grateful glance at Vivian, slipped past her, bounding down the street.

Ruth opened the door all the way. "I see you didn't come empty-handed once again." She looked at the basket.

Vivian entered the small house, shabbier than she remembered, but comforting in its lightness and simplicity. "I've no picnic this time."

Ruth pulled her shawl around her. "Some of us aren't too proud to accept gifts."

Vivian felt a slight pinch from the reprimand but set the basket down. "You weren't playing the piano just now, then?"

"I take pupils," said Ruth. "One must earn a living when one is alone."

"Alone?"

A gray shadow appeared over her face. "Mama died eight months ago."

Vivian felt as if someone had given her a blow in the head. She eased herself into a chair, thankful for its hard, rigid back, as it helped to compose her. "I'm sorry."

"Perhaps I would believe you more if you had come to the funeral," said Ruth in a quiet voice.

Vivian blinked. "I would have if I had known."

The archness on her face eased. "That explains it, then."

Vivian pressed her hand. "I was speaking to Tillie the other day—"

"I know no Tillie."

"She was the kitchen maid in your mother's house when she was a young woman."

"I never met a lot of the people from Mama's youth." Ruth examined the caddy before putting it on the table. "I never even met my grandparents. They died before I was born."

"Tillie has fond memories of your mother," Vivian said. "She told me something I didn't know. About the time my grandmother was here." She observed the woman.

Ruth's features became like stone. "Is that why you're here? To open Pandora's box of woes? I believe you referred to it that way the last time?"

"I came to see you," Vivian insisted. "You invited me, remember?"

"I don't recall I did."

Vivian looked at her. "Perhaps you didn't."

This made Ruth smile. It was a strained smile to go with the lines on her face. "I'll put tea on, and we'll go into the parlor like proper ladies."

Vivian had only glanced into the parlor doorway the last time she was in the house, but now she could see it fully. It was a pleasant room, larger than the parlor at Leona's place, though it didn't look as if the criss-cross house was any bigger than the one on the bay. But the parlor was roomy with just the right amount of furniture, inviting but not crowded. Vivian could tell that, in earlier years, the fussiness popular forty years ago had graced the room, as white squares appeared where pictures had been taken down from the walls, and shelves were a little scant, as if bric-à-brac had once stood there. Small, knobby indentations appeared on the modest brown carpet, giving the impression that furniture had been removed.

"A very pleasant room," she remarked.

"For sitting, perhaps," said Ruth. "Not for playing the piano. The keys sound like hammers banging against the wall."

"Maybe that's due more to the heavy fingers of your students," Vivian suggested.

Ruth gave a little laugh. "You were always so polite, Vivian." Her face grew serious as her voice softened. "My mother never forgot how gracious you were to her, and how you made her remember her girlhood. I thank you for that."

"I hope I didn't trouble her," Vivian said, feeling a sadness rise in her throat.

"It was yourself you troubled, I fear," said the woman. "Tell me, have you finally exorcised your specter?"

"I thought I had." Vivian played with the fringe on the cushion. "Now, I don't know."

"Then you *have* come to open Pandora's box." Ruth ogled her with an uncomfortable silence. Then she excused herself to make the tea, and Vivian heard the soft clatter of china from the kitchen.

She wandered to the piano, a tall, boxy instrument. She sat on the little stool and plucked the keys. The sound was more delicate and high-pitched than she had imagined as her fingers went softly across with the tune of Strauss's "Roses from the South" that her grandmother had taught her. As the music waltzed through the small parlor, Vivian could see herself as a child of eight or nine, her grandmother sitting beside her, watching how her fingers moved across the keys, stopping to show her where she made a mistake and making her do it again. Grandmother had been a patient teacher, the measured patience that, Vivian now knew, came with the upbringing of "the proper lady" in Washington Street society. Her mother and grandmother had tried to teach the same to her, but Vivian's nature was such that, if patience was a virtue, hers was downright naughty.

Ruth came in carrying the tea tray, her hands shaking a little, as if it were too heavy for her. Vivian rushed to help her. "You play well," the woman remarked.

"I play well enough so that one may not be ashamed of me," Vivian said. "That was all that was ever required of me."

"That's better than I can do," Ruth said. "I have a knack for the technique but not the melody."

"Then why do you teach it?"

Ruth shrugged, pouring the tea. Again, her hand shook a little. "It was the only thing I knew how to do."

"It's been hard for you, Ruth," Vivian said, her eyes growing misty.

"When Mama was alive, we had an annuity," said the woman. "But when she died, even that negligible amount was gone." Ruth leaned back. "I don't mind it, really. Having pupils keeps me from being alone all the time." She was watching Vivian, her hands resting on either side of her on the couch. "Why a sudden interest in all this again, Vivian?"

"I was pulled into it," Vivian admitted.

"By whom?"

"Leona Potter."

Ruth gave a brief smile. "She always thought Mama was rather silly, but I suspect she had the greatest affection for her."

Vivian leaned forward. "Leona told me some things about my grandmother and your mother that disturbed me."

"It must have, for you to come see me."

"I would have come anyway, Ruth," Vivian said.

"What was it she said that disturbed you?"

"Did you know Bertha spent quite a long time with my grandmother in the city?"

Ruth nodded. "Penelope sent for her."

"I wonder why."

"I suppose it's natural for a new bride to be a little uneasy." She put butter and jam on a slice of toast and handed it to her. "Not that I would know about that." She said this with a glance into the mirror that hung on the opposite wall, as if she were appraising herself.

"Is that what your mother said or what you say?"

"Mama said nothing." Ruth's tone was stoic. "She didn't worship your grandmother as much as you think. She didn't talk about her day and night."

"Perhaps not, but she did like to talk about the past," Vivian retorted. "She told me that herself. And especially about her youth."

The woman blinked a moment, looking at a vase of daisies placed near the window. "Penelope's father was ill, and her mother stayed with him night and day."

"I remember my mother telling me something about my great-grandfather being ill," Vivian said. "And my grandfather was away at the time too."

"Mama said Malcolm wasn't there when she arrived," said Ruth.

"When exactly was that?"

Ruth glanced at her. "I'm surprised no one told you."

"Why should they?" Vivian felt Ruth's reluctance giving the room an icy chill.

"Exactly," said the woman, placing her hands in her lap. "And why should you be so interested in such mundane details now?"

"It's piqued my curiosity." Vivian held on to the handle of her teacup. "Leona said she thought Bertha stayed about a year."

"I wouldn't know."

"Come now, Ruth." She frowned at her. "Bertha had a splendid memory for dates."

The woman did not answer. She took a slice of toast, but it slipped from her hands and fell to the rug. She snatched it up and put it aside on the tray. Everything she did suddenly made Vivian alert.

"How long was she there?"

"I don't like these interrogations, Vivian," Ruth snapped. "You haven't come on a cordial call, like you claim."

"I don't mean to interrogate," Vivian said. "I only want to *know*."

"Well, I'm afraid I can't help you." The woman's tone was final.

They sat in silence for a time. Vivian knew enough about Ruth to know the woman had as much loathing for probing into the past as Larissa. She set down her teacup and rose, approaching a crochet picture hanging on the wall. "This is rather good."

"Mama made it," she said. "She used to do quite a lot of that when she was younger."

"She had a deft hand," Vivian said. Then, returning to the couch, she said, "If you won't tell me anything, can you at least confirm what I already know?"

"If I can," said Ruth.

"Mr. Henderson — do you know him?" Ruth nodded. "He told me your mother had been with my grandmother when she returned to Waxwood for Loretta's funeral, but not in San Francisco. My grandparents had gone to Lico."

"I don't know where that is," the woman snapped.

Vivian took a breath. "You've never heard of the place?"

"I'm not so well-traveled as you are."

"A small town — tiny — in the mountains somewhere near Santa Barbara."

Ruth sat with the teacup on her knee. "There's nothing surprising in that, is there?"

"It wasn't a leisure trip," said Vivian. "My grandmother was going to have my mother."

"She was a young bride, wasn't she? Brides get nervous when they have their first child. Or so I'm told," she added in a caustic tone.

"Mr. Henderson said your mother was rather upset when she came back to Waxwood."

"Oh, you saw how Mama could be," Ruth said, a little off-handedly.

"You don't think she had a reason?" Vivian pressed her hands into her knees.

"What are you suggesting?"

"I'm suggesting nothing," she insisted.

Ruth looked at the daisies near the window again. "Maybe Penelope was ill."

"Mr. Henderson told me she was sickly," said Vivian. "So did Leona."

"But you don't believe it?" Ruth was eyeing her.

Vivian picked up her cup again, but it was cold, as cold as her own hands. "Leona also told me my grandmother began drawing again around that time."

"Again?"

Vivian grimaced. "You remember little from our chat at my grandmother's funeral, do you?"

"I often forget what I don't care to remember," said Ruth shortly.

"Leona thought Grandmother was 'encouraged by a friend' to

take it up again. She described the person as a 'scruffy young man.' She thought he came from Brandywine." Vivian paused, glancing at the woman. "We both know whom she meant, don't we, Ruth?"

The woman was still for a moment, then collected the empty plates and cups, putting them on the tray. "Thank you for bringing the tea caddy. I'm not used to such luxuries, as you can imagine."

"Did Bertha ever mention Evan or what happened to him after my grandmother left?" Vivian's voice echoed in the scantly furnished parlor. "And don't tell me she said nothing about him!"

"She sometimes lamented over him," said Ruth. "'Poor lamb, poor lamb,' she'd say. But that was because of his sister."

"Yes, I know," said Vivian. "Verina told me."

"Ebba went away," said Ruth. "Not long after Penelope left."

"To Glockpool." Vivian nodded.

"I heard something about him leaving the colony for a time," Ruth said. "But I don't know where he went, and I don't think Mama did either. That's the truth, Vivian."

Vivian blinked, then gave a small smile. "Let me carry the tray."

They made their way to the kitchen. Ruth put on an apron and washed the dishes. The way she handled the china, with a cold delicacy, made Vivian realize her mind was elsewhere.

"You once said you don't have the right to deny someone else the knowledge you don't want yourself." Vivian leaned against the counter.

Ruth's hands lingered over the lid of the teapot. "That's true."

"What about knowledge you have and might be important to another?" asked Vivian. "Do you have the right to deny that knowledge?"

Ruth turned off the water and wiped her hands on a towel. "Not if I had it."

"Perhaps you have more than you realize." Vivian glanced at her.

The woman did not answer. She put the caddy on the counter almost lovingly.

"Where is Verina now?" Vivian asked.

"You're not going to—" The woman's face grew pale.

"I only want to make a social call," said Vivian. "I want to see all my friends from Waxwood."

"And if they don't wish to see you?"

Vivian was quiet for a moment. "Where is she?"

The woman gave her a crooked smile. "I once said you were far too perceptive." She sighed. "She lives in Goldspur now. She's working as a shop girl for some general store there. But don't be surprised if she doesn't want to see you. Your first meeting wasn't exactly a happy one for her."

"I realize that," Vivian snapped.

"You might drop in at Soot's General Store between eight in the morning and seven at night," the woman said. "I think you'll find her much changed, Vivian."

"Thank you, Ruth." Vivian grasped her hand in both of hers. "I mean it. Thank you. And if you ever need anything, anything at all—" She extracted her card from her reticule. But Ruth turned away, and she saw from the woman's profile that her features gathered as if she were trying to keep from crying. She put the card on the hall table.

*V*ivian returned to the hotel in the late afternoon. When she entered the lobby, there was the lull of emptiness. Many of the swells preferred to retire to their suites the few hours before dinner to rest, read, or contemplate the conversations of the day. She expected to find Larissa with her magazines and dressing gown, but when she arrived at their suite, it was empty. There was a hasty note on the table in her mother's handwriting. The Griffiths had invited her to their suite for afternoon bridge, and she would be back to dress for dinner.

Vivian opened the balcony doors and stepped out. The beach below was less crowded than in the mornings, though not deserted. She wondered whether Bertha saw the resort side of Waxwood before she died. Bertha had been the sort to delight in novelties, just as a child would. Vivian could imagine she had coaxed Ruth into taking the ferry across, just to see what it was like. And, though it was clear from the shabby house that the Rosses had been in rather dire circumstances in the last years, she knew such had not always been the case. Her grandmother's letters told of the opulence of the Ross house and their position in Waxwood. Perhaps such luxuries as the towers of The

Waxwoodian wouldn't have been such a novelty to Bertha after all.

The sea wind revived her as she felt its waving arms opening to touch her face and shoulders. The events of the past month were still on her mind, and nothing made much sense. This path, unlike the last, had many twisted trees and mirrored rocks. She closed her eyes and imagined a narrow line of red dust gravel between two walls of the wax wood trees with their monster feet hanging downward, tearing at her back each time they dipped with the wind. Little forks emerged with odd little creatures peering at her through the murky blue, their eyes wide and shining as if trying to tell her something.

And what would she say to her mother now that her path had split between this and the path to Mr. Leblanc? How much did Larissa know about what her mother had done after she left Waxwood? Vivian suspected her mother knew more than she had told. The family dream book Jake discovered and hid in the play-room cabinet did not hold all the Alderdice secrets. There were those that read like ciphers to anyone who refused to think about the past like Larissa.

She could not tell her mother anything. Not yet, at least. But she could ask more innocuous questions, and Larissa might answer without suspecting Vivian was rushing down another path to the past.

When her mother returned to the suite, Vivian was already dressed for dinner and sitting on the couch with her book in her lap.

"Mrs. Griffith said Mr. Leblanc was asking after you several times today," Larissa remarked. "She's on your side, you know."

"I didn't think the Griffiths have any side but their own." Vivian closed her book.

"They would rather see a native catch the man than an East-erner. Even Amber," her mother called to her from her room.

"You needn't put it that way, Mother," she snapped.

"Vivian—"

There was a knock on the door. When she opened it, Mr. Leblanc stood looking a little sheepish as he leaned against the door frame. He had discarded his frilly shirtwaist for the more sedate attire of a high stand collar and neat cravat befitting American men at their leisure. He looked, to Vivian, like a bare-knuckle boxer she had seen walking down Market Street, a little too dressed up for his muscular figure.

"I hoped you might take a constitution with me, Miss Alderdice," he said, somewhat slowly and formally. "It's a grand evening."

Vivian felt her mother's expectant eyes on her. "It's very thoughtful of you," she said, stalling for an excuse. She still felt the distress of Ruth's visit on her mind.

"Vivian enjoys walking immensely, don't you, dear?" Larissa smiled at the man. "Oftentimes, I can't keep her indoors, unless it's for her books."

"I'm a little tired tonight."

"You ought to get some fresh air, Vivian."

"I've been taking fresh air since we got here, Mother," said Vivian dryly. "Any more fresh air, and I might blow up like a hot-air balloon."

"You make a fiction out of everything, Miss Alderdice," Mr. Leblanc said, laughing. "Perhaps it's because you read so much."

"I don't make fictions," Vivian said. "I'm more practical than you think."

"Women are always more practical than men," he agreed. "It's what makes men need them so."

"Do take her out, Mr. Leblanc," said Larissa. "She's been rather morose all day." Her mother gave her a sidelong look that contained a dash of worry.

Vivian softened. "Perhaps a breath of air would do me good. Especially with such a soothing companion." She smiled up at him.

He took this with a grateful bow.

"I apologize if I offended you when I said you were making a fiction," he said as they strolled the boardwalk. "I find it very charming, really. I spent twenty-two years with business talk, so it's refreshing to hear something more imaginative."

"I suppose that's why you like traveling so much," Vivian said. "Always meeting new people and seeing unknown places."

This observation seemed to delight him. "There is never a dull moment wherever one is."

"I suppose you find Waxwood boring, then."

"Not in the least." He held out his arm. "But sometimes one prefers solitary companionship to the crowds, especially if that companion is very pleasant."

"You're very complimentary." Vivian smiled. "Perhaps we ought to walk in the woods again. That would give you your solitary companionship, if you're willing to risk a raised eyebrow or two at dinner, if they saw us."

He laughed. "I can stand it if you can. But I thought the woods were haunted for you."

"Not always," said Vivian. "They're lovely this time of day."

They moved away from the beach to the path that led toward the hill, and they climbed. She studied the ground for a sign of her and Jake's footsteps from the year before. The nettles looked crushed, as if more people had discovered this lonely path, but the trees and rocks gave her a comfort of home.

"You know this way very well," Mr. Leblanc remarked.

"I've taken it several times," she said.

"With that brazen young man with the figure of a poet?" His eyebrow jumped.

"What brazen young man?"

"The one with the flaxen hair," he said. "And the arrow mustache."

She laughed as she realized he was talking about David. His expression was one of jealousy. "No, not him," Vivian said. "With my brother. And once with a friend of mine." Her mind flashed to Ruth and what she had told her about the wax wood trees: *The surface softens with the sun and hardens with the moon.* "Why do you say David is brazen?" she asked absently.

"David?"

"The man with the flaxen hair."

"He has seen you twice," said Mr. Leblanc. "Once at the fish market and once at the hotel. I gathered he wasn't exactly I invited the second time."

"No," Vivian admitted. "He wasn't. And maybe I shouldn't have gone with him."

"Oh? Was he inappropriate in his manner?" There was almost something savage in his voice.

Vivian laughed. "I didn't mean him. He took me to see his aunt and — oh, it doesn't matter."

"If he bothers you again, tell me," he said. "Men know how to talk to other men."

"If I need a protector, I shall inform you of the fact, Mr. Leblanc," she said breezily.

"I meant no harm." His voice grew a little agitated.

"I'm flattered you want to protect me," she said. "But David is harmless. Actually, I was happy to meet his aunt. She knew my grandmother."

Interest replaced the stern, fatherly look. "Mrs. Griffith told me about her. She was an exceptional woman, wasn't she?"

"'A celebrated socialite and benevolent lady who will be greatly missed by all who knew her,'" Vivian quoted.

"Eh?"

"That's what they said about Grandmother in her obituary."

"I see." He was quiet for a moment. "And do you agree with that description?"

"Partly." Vivian tapped at the feathery dust on the ground with the toe of her slipper. "But she was also an artist once."

"Indeed?" His interest piqued.

"She drew fish." Vivian couldn't help but smile. "Down to the last gill."

"Perhaps the richness of your San Francisco bay inspired her," he suggested.

"She drew here," said Vivian. "In an artist's colony called Brandywine."

He nodded. "Miss Tisher told me about that place."

"You speak of David being brazen, but those girls are just as brazen," she teased.

"They're just girls." He shrugged. "Delightful, lively girls, but girls all the same."

Vivian eyed him. "And Miss Sowberry?"

"She's much more serious," he admitted. "But I don't know her very well. She asked Miss Tisher a lot of questions about Brandywine."

"She asks questions about everything," Vivian said. "I can only imagine what Fern told her. Probably that Brandywine was a place for savages with immoral purposes who called themselves artists."

He grinned. "Something like that. But I told you, I might listen to the gossip, but I don't always believe it."

"I visited it seven years ago," she said. "It was a lovely place with people who just wanted to make pictures."

"Is it anywhere near here?" he asked.

Vivian had to smile. "You're quite an adventurer, aren't you?"

"I relish hidden corners," he said.

She shook off the dust that had clung to her shoes. "Would you like to see it? It's just up the hill. I warn you, there isn't much to see," she added.

"I should love to!"

She looked at the sleepy eyes and even smile under the mustache that she still disliked because of its dragoon appearance. She felt again the serenity of his simplicity, and the way anything that cracked the shell of boredom aroused his interests.

As they climbed toward the peak of the hill, she felt apprehensive. She remembered the year before, when Harland Stevens had persuaded her to see the place again. She had responded by warning him *some things, once locked, ought to stay locked*. She had been right, for when they had reached the summit, Brandywine lay before them as a dismal, gnarled place with empty shacks and overgrown vegetation. She could not imagine what it would be like now.

"They hid themselves well, these artists," Mr. Leblanc remarked, his voice a little shallow from the climb.

"They wanted isolation," said Vivian. "People in town didn't like them."

"I gather," he said. "I've met many such gypsies in my travels."

Vivian glanced at him. "They weren't gypsies. They had a place until they were driven out."

"Driven out?"

"I told you, people here didn't like them." She could already see the peaks of the gate with the strange drawings made by those who had lived there, now faded and brushed away. She had hoped she would find new drawings of wax wood trees and poppies and faces illuminated with contemplation rather than grief. She had hoped in a year, there had been new life.

As she and Mr. Leblanc stood looking, there was only the echo of past voices, the red dirt smooth from untrodden feet, and the shacks empty. There was a strange stillness to it, the same stillness Vivian remembered once when they had stayed at a lake house in Tahoe with the Millers. The hostess had explained to them it was not a residence for many who lived there year round. "They come in the summer," she had said. "So, you might find it a little deserted now, after what you're used to in the city." The place had the same hollow silence that Vivian felt now. It took her several days to realize the silence was not of a ghost town but of an inhabitance, abandoned but intending to be sought after later. Overgrown flowers bloomed in the gardens, well-worn gates did not creak from neglect, and advertisements hung in the windows of the stores with anticipation of future sales.

Brandywine now reminded her of that summer. The shacks, though still silent and run down, looked cleaner, and some were even freshly painted. The red road was empty of dry leaves and storm debris. The building that had been the store where Verina Jones worked had shiny windows and dark curtains she didn't see the last time she had visited there.

"I wonder who's been here," she murmured.

"Eh?" Mr. Leblanc's eyes had been wandering, but now they came to rest on her.

"This place," she said. "It doesn't look so abandoned anymore."

"Your ghosts, perhaps." He smiled at her. "One can hardly be alone when one's ghosts are lurking about."

She leaned one hand against a post. "We shouldn't have come, Mr. Leblanc."

"It's my fault," he said, genuinely distressed.

"No, no," she said. "I meant *us*, my mother and I. We shouldn't have come back to Waxwood. There are reasons you don't know about."

"Your brother?" he guessed.

"My brother, yes, but there were others involved."

"I'm sorry." He held out his arm to her. "We'll go back to the hotel and have a lively dinner, eh?" He smiled.

She smiled back. "I'm being silly. Mother and I should have come. We're having a marvelous time."

As they began on the path back down, Vivian glanced over her shoulder at Brandywine. The shacks were almost watching her with their small window eyes, as if happy for the company. Then her heart quickened as something moved in the distance, toward the upright redwood trees at the end of the red road. She gave a screech, jumping away from her companion.

"Are you all right, Miss Alderdice?"

"There was something there!"

"In the woods, everything feels alive," he said in a soothing voice.

"You mean game is alive," she said. "This was no game."

"It might have been a fox or even a goat," he offered. "You would be surprised at how often goats wander into woods like this."

"No, I'm sure this was a man." Vivian's head ached as the heat closed in around her. It *had* been a man, or something that could pass for a man — dark, primitive, and savage.

"We've walked too far." Mr. Leblanc patted the hand wrapped around his arm. "That was my fault too. I can go on for miles, but I forget ladies are more delicate."

This made Vivian indignant. "I tread miles in the city, Mr. Leblanc, and up and down the San Francisco hills. I'm hardly in a delicate state." She felt ashamed of herself for having alarmed him. "I apologize for my startling behavior."

"We'll get out of these woods, then." He took larger strides with which she kept up admirably.

When they reached the incline before Brandywine disappeared altogether, Vivian glanced back again. The place was now deserted once again, its movement confined to the rustling of leaves in the early evening breeze.

~

Dinner that night was a jolly affair. She and Larissa had been fully accepted into the Tisher set, and Mrs. Tisher behaved as if she were glad of it, though Vivian felt Fern giving her a dubious look now and then across the row of tables. Afterward, they all retreated to the hotel parlor, and Cecily consented to play the piano while several of the younger ladies and gentlemen of her acquaintance moved furniture aside to make room for dancing. They waltzed and two-stepped as if the dawn would never come. As their feet thumped against the wooden floor, and their laughter filled the parlor, the older people smiled and looked on.

Several times, Vivian felt Monte Leblanc glancing in her direction, and once, when Fern, who had taken her sister's place at the piano, began a new piece, he half-lifted his arms as if inviting her to dance. But she was loath to leave the safety of the cushioned seat behind the row of people standing near the dance floor. Once or twice, her eyes caught the view outside of the waves pulling up over the sand, and she thought of the agile creature she had seen slinking in the woods.

As she undressed for bed that night, Larissa appeared in the doorway and announced, not without a note of delight, "Amber believes you've completely enchanted Mr. Leblanc."

Vivian shrugged as she avoided her mother's eyes. "Our conversations have been rather serious as of late."

"You underestimate the charms of serious talk for men like Mr. Leblanc, dear," said her mother.

"I'm really not concerned with what Amber thinks," Vivian remarked. "Nor Coleen, nor Hannah, nor any of the others. They're as bad as matchmakers."

"You needn't be so caustic," Larissa said. "They all want to see you settled." She gave her a heavy look. "I thought you were yourself."

"I suppose I am," Vivian said, slipping her nightgown over her head.

Her mother entered the bedroom and sat on the edge of the bed, smoothing down the folds of the dress Vivian had carelessly thrown down. "Mr. Leblanc thinks he upset you tonight."

"Why would he think such a thing?"

"It was obvious he was aching to dance with you, but you ignored him." Larissa said. "I understand you're not fond of dancing, Vivian, but you could have made more of an effort."

Vivian sat at the dressing table and began putting cold cream on her face. "I've had a lot on my mind today."

"I know," Larissa said. "You've been disturbed since you returned from your walk with Mr. Leblanc. I know you too well."

Vivian twisted around, feeling the chair's cold bars against her chest. "I saw a man in the woods tonight, Mother."

"Is that all?" Her mother smiled. "I'm sure you and Mr. Leblanc weren't the only ones taking a constitution before dinner. Mrs. Tisher told me those woods have become more popular."

"This place was deserted," said Vivian. "I took Mr. Leblanc to see Brandywine."

"Oh." Her mother's hand went to the skirt of the dress again.

"I'm sure I saw a man there."

"Perhaps it was a deer."

"That's what Mr. Leblanc said!" Vivian's throat felt dry. "But it wasn't, Mother."

"Well, I can't see why it would upset you so much that you would refuse to dance with Mr. Leblanc," said Larissa in a mild voice.

"You'll think I'm mad if I tell you who I think it was."

"Your specter?" Her mother frowned.

"No, someone very much alive," she said. "I thought for a moment — he was such a large, dark man, I thought for a moment it was Mr. Stevens."

"Mr. Stevens!" Her mother was alarmed. "Your imagination was running away with you, Vivian. I don't believe Mr. Stevens is even in Waxwood."

Vivian turned back to the mirror and wiped the cream off her face. "Maybe it was my imagination."

"You're just upset because you went to see the Rosses."

Vivian shot her mother a look. "I was wondering when you would get on the subject, Mother."

"And I was wondering when *you* would."

"Why should I?" Vivian looked into the mirror at her now shiny naked face. "It was only a social call."

"And how are the Rosses?" asked her mother.

Vivian turned to her. "Bertha died eight months ago."

"I'm sorry," Larissa said. "I know you liked her. But it does no good to bring back unpleasant memories."

Vivian turned the chair around so she could study her mother. "Don't you realize that what you try to drown floats back up again, like a dead body?"

"That's a rather morbid analogy." Her mother winced.

"Morbid it may be, but apt." Vivian looked down at the zigzag carpet. "I learned that lesson seven years ago. I think I just forgot what I learned for a time."

"That only happens if you let it," said Larissa. "Once you marry Mr. Leblanc, you won't have to think such morbid thoughts."

Vivian blinked at her. Larissa, ready for bed, had pulled the pins out of her hair, and it now hung in a golden mane around her shoulders, making her look twenty years younger. She turned back to the mirror and began removing the pins from her own hair. "Poor Ruth was left with nothing after her mother died. She has to teach piano to earn her living."

"I don't wish to hear about her." Larissa's voice was unnaturally severe.

Vivian rose, shaking out the dress on the bed. "Don't you want to know what we discussed?"

"What could she have told you?" This was spit out with such contempt that the dress nearly slipped from Vivian's grasp. The skin around Larissa's eyes and mouth gathered. Her mother really looked distressed.

Vivian smoothed out the lines of lemon silk before she hung the dress in the closet. "Did you know Grandmother was ill when she had you?"

Her mother's shoulders relaxed. "Why should that interest you?"

"Because Grandmother was never very sick in her life that I remember," said Vivian. "Until her deathbed."

"Well, dear, there were circumstances—"

"Yes," said Vivian, impatient. "I remember them."

Her mother stretched her feet out, exposing a little of the solid ankles underneath her long nightgown. "Is that what Miss Ross told you?"

"She was so ill, she needed to go to the mountains for her confinement," Vivian continued. "Bertha went with her."

"There's nothing unusual about your grandmother wanting a woman with her," said Larissa. "Though I think she might have chosen someone more suitable."

"Apparently Grandfather thought so too." Vivian watched her mother carefully. "He took a nurse when he and Grandmother went abroad." Her mother's features never wavered. "You know they went abroad after you were born?"

"Naturally," she said. "He wanted both of us to have the best care. He loved us."

"If he loved Grandmother so much, why did he leave her alone when they were barely married a year?"

There was silence as her mother rose and picked up the silver brush on the vanity table. "Would you like me to brush your hair, dear?"

The question took Vivian by surprise as her hand lifted the brush over her head. "You never did that before, Mother. Not even when I was a child."

Larissa smiled a little. "I do it rather well. You'll see." Her mother had a surprisingly delicate hand as she stroked the brush through Vivian's long waves.

"Do you think Grandmother was very lonely without Grandfather?" Vivian could not help but recall the echo of Bertha's words in Leona's ear: *Penelope didn't miss Malcolm in the least.*

"A young wife always misses her husband when he goes away."

Her mother sighed. "I remember how melancholy you were when Miles left for his expedition."

"Was I?" Vivian could hardly recall now those years with her husband. It was as if they had never happened. "Well, Miles was only away for six months before he was killed. How long was Grandfather away?"

"Keep your head still, dear."

"How long, and when did he go?"

"What does all that matter now?"

"It doesn't." Vivian shrugged, trying to sound resigned. "I'm only curious."

"Yes, I know how curious you are about these things," Larissa remarked. "Your great-grandfather sent him to Hamburg to establish offices there for the shipping line about a year after he and your grandmother were married."

"That would be 1854, then." Vivian felt a slight pull on the ends of her hair. "He must have come back rather quickly."

"He was there for most of the year, I believe."

"Most of that year?" Vivian glanced up at her mother.

"I don't know exactly." She handed the brush to Vivian. "Now, I hope that satisfies your curiosity?"

"For the moment."

"Clean the brush, won't you, dear? I'm sorry now we didn't bring Mollie with us."

"I thought it was decent of you to let her go back East to see her brother for the summer."

"She's a good girl, and one does not antagonize dutiful servants," said Larissa.

Vivian couldn't help but chuckle. "You always were adept with household matters, Mother."

"So will you be, when it's time." Larissa was quiet for a moment. "I trust there will be no more of this 'visiting friends' while we're here. Promise me, Vivian. For your own good and mine."

When she had left, Vivian began plucking the hair from the brush, her mind churning. How could she explain to Larissa that she had not hunted up anything, but that it had hunted her up? She couldn't. Larissa's answer would be as it always was: *It's the easiest thing in the world to put it away and forget about it.* Easy for her mother with her list of Unmentionables. But not so easy for Vivian.

CHAPTER 9

The next day, she and Larissa sat at the table alone, as the rest of the Tisher party had finished their apple pie and coffee and dispersed to various afternoon activities. Vivian had been watching the faces of other guests, and she couldn't help but reflect now on the lightheartedness in their smiles, their slacked countenance, their limbs moving so freely as they threaded around people in the crowds. She was anything but lighthearted and at ease, weighed down like a sleepwalker wandering about.

She knew Larissa noticed her contemplative silence but said nothing. She was used to Vivian's brooding, as it had always been a habit of hers as a child to take up a small corner of the room and silently watch. She remembered one particular moment when she was twelve and had frequented the parlor teas and garden parties that made up the life of a young woman preparing to be a young debutante. At a recital in Mrs. Brewster's large downstairs parlor, she and Jake, then eight, hid themselves among the silk curtains on the corner window and, although they hadn't spoken, Jake knew the music enhanced the precious solitude she found so warm after the coldness of their upbringing. Vivian suddenly realized those moments of solitude would be a luxury she could not afford once she came out at eighteen.

As they walked home that night, Vivian declared, "I don't want to be trapped in marriage, Mother."

She expected her mother to snap at her to stop "talking in circles" or, at the very least, dismiss the comment as one inspired by the melancholic violin music they had just heard. But Larissa remained silent for a time, absorbing this remark with all the seriousness of her character. Then she answered, "Every young woman feels that way at first. Until she gets used to being married."

"I don't know that I can get used to the idea," Vivian said. Her voice was unusually loud, or perhaps the street was unusually quiet. "No, I can't get used to it!"

Her mother's moment of understanding vanished as they reached the front door of Alderdice Hall. Her gloved hand grasping the knob, the key dangling from her other hand, Larissa turned to her and, with a flash of determination that frightened Vivian, said, "You will because it is your duty. To us and to *them*."

She chuckled at the memory now. Mr. Leblanc, who had left with several of the others, now returned to the dining room. She watched him making his way gingerly around the tables. His smile below the curling mustache and the lazy eyes struck Vivian as disingenuous.

"Good afternoon, Miss Alderdice." He bowed.

"Good afternoon," Vivian said, distracted.

It was clear he took her distraction personally, as he then turned to Larissa and asked, "Do you play croquet, Mrs. Alderdice?"

"I haven't played since I was a young woman," she said, blushing.

"Then you will honor me doing so now," he said. "You and Miss Alderdice, of course." He turned to give Vivian a wide smile.

"My father and I took quite a liking to the game when we were in England. I'm told there is quite a good lawn here."

"There is," said Larissa.

"My father would be most pleased if you would be his partner," he said. "I would never tell him so, but he is a little crooked with his aim."

Her mother gave a short laugh. "I've been told my aim is a little too straight, so perhaps it's just as well."

"You will come, then?"

"We would be delighted."

Vivian put her coffee cup back in the saucer. "I'm sorry, but I have other plans." She thought about what Ruth had told her regarding Verina. The path was rolling out in front of her slowly in the vision of the woman in her angelic face and braided hair.

"You always seem to have other plans," he said, a little pouty.

"Not always," she said. "Only lately." His tone annoyed her, implying, as it did, that it was impertinent of her to have plans other than those he had made for her. "I have some people I need to see." She felt her mother's cutting look.

This put him out. "You're not going back to find your savage in the woods, I hope."

"No," Vivian said. "I have no wish to see him again."

He turned to Larissa with a lively smile. "Your daughter told you of the apparition she saw yesterday near that strange, empty place?"

"It wasn't an apparition," Vivian said shortly.

"I think I have an answer to the mystery."

"Do you?" Vivian raised an eyebrow, her irritation now turning to amusement. "I'm eager to hear it."

"Mr. Tisher told me clapper rails have been sighted in the woods lately. They're said to be rare, and a bird watching society has come to see them." He looked almost triumphant. "I know such men well from my travels. They will go to any length to see a rare bird."

"This was no bird watcher," Vivian insisted. "I know who he was."

Her mother leaned forward so abruptly that she caused the coffee pot to jiggle when she pushed against the table. "You can change your plans, can't you, dear?"

"No, Mother," she said. "I'm afraid I can't."

"Maybe I'll ask Miss Tisher to join us," he said, his face a little crusty.

"Do so," said Vivian. "Though I'm afraid you'll find she's not much of a player."

"I might help her improve her game, then." After a brief silence, he gave a deep bow and withdrew.

She could tell her mother was indignant but, in her usual way, restrained. "That wasn't very courteous of you, Vivian. I'm sure he's been looking forward to that game with you all morning."

"We've been thrown together so much these past weeks," said Vivian. "I'm sure he's a little tired of me."

"No man is tired of an excellent woman's company," said her mother. "It's precisely why she needs to keep him company as much as possible."

"He's been getting all the company he can stomach with the Tisher girls." Vivian brushed the crumbs from the tablecloth. She never could stand them around her.

"He was very annoyed with you." Larissa's look was grisly.

"Because I wouldn't be at his beck and call?" Vivian snarled. "If he wants that sort of girl, he ought to marry Christina Sowberry."

"But he likes *you*," said her mother. "And I thought you liked him."

"And so, I must spend every waking moment with him?" Vivian leaned back, looking incredulously at her. "You know, Mother, I'm sure you never practiced half of what you preach to me."

"After you're married, you'll have your own interests," Larissa assured her. "But until then, you must be a little more complacent."

"Complacent!"

Larissa lingered over her coffee. "What is it you have in town that is so important?"

Vivian flinched. The last thing she intended to do was tell her mother about Verina. "Call it unfinished business."

"What unfinished business?" The cup came down in the saucer with such a clatter that the waiter who was clearing off the table next to theirs looked up with curiosity.

"You needn't worry about me, Mother." Vivian couldn't help but smile. "I won't get myself into trouble."

"I didn't think you would."

"My entire life has been as a nonentity," she said. "Nonentities hurt no one."

"You're behaving in that curious way," said Larissa.

"What curious way?"

Her mother looked straight at her. "As you did seven years ago."

Vivian looked down at the table, her eyes wavering. The waiter had set it for three, and the third setting sat untouched between them. She suddenly tore the linen napkin out of the empty glass and folded it on top of the silverware. It no longer gleamed in the insidious sunlight.

"Come with us instead," her mother was saying. "We'll play croquet and then in the evening, we're all going to a showing of Emmett Oldridge's paintings at Culver's Gallery. They say he will be the toast of San Francisco before the year is out."

Vivian stared at her. "You would go to Culver's after what that man said to Jake?"

"That has nothing to do with this," Larissa insisted. "If you don't come, I'm sure Fern and that mousy Miss Sowberry will have the best of Mr. Leblanc's attentions."

"Let them!" Vivian said, throwing her napkin on the table in a heap.

"You're being unreasonable, Vivian."

"I'm sorry, Mother," she said, rising. "But I'm late already."

"Late for what?"

"To see someone. That's what I've been telling you all this time."

"You sound like your brother when he was a child, making up those silly stories."

This made the stab in Vivian's chest pierce more. "He made up stories so he wouldn't have to hurt anyone with ugly truths."

Her mother was silent, her lip in a straight line as she struggled to regain her composure. As Vivian left the dining room, she could feel the flash of those cobalt eyes following her.

*Vivian took the ferry, greeting Mr. Blaine, who was back at the wheel, with the warmth of an old friend. He smiled but did not talk beyond asking how she was and remarking upon the harshness of the wind that morning on the bay. The people on the street as she walked to the drugstore seemed to sense her need for silence, as they passed her by without the usual smile or tipping hat, much like the rushing bodies of those she knew in the city.

She found Nettie among boxes from a shipment that had just come in, papers scattered all over the floor. The young woman was trying to sort them out.

"I don't have very much skill with bookkeeping," she remarked. "It's a wonder I haven't gone bankrupt yet."

"I don't want to disturb you." Vivian felt uncomfortable there among all the papers with the scribbled numbers.

"You're not." Nettie motioned to a chair.

Vivian toyed with the fringes on her dress. "I must go visit someone, anyway."

"One of those important appointments I hear so many of your kind talk about?" Nettie smiled.

"I wouldn't call it an appointment," said Vivian. "She has no idea I'm coming."

"And she wouldn't welcome you if she did," Nettie guessed, opening a box and extracting from it small, heart-shaped jars.

"No," Vivian said. "She wouldn't." She looked down at the shiny tops flashing a gold sticker scripted in black with *Feather's Vanishing Cream*.

Nettie paused, balancing jars in each hand with little effort. "Anyone I know?"

"Her name is Verina Jones."

"The name sounds vaguely familiar." The woman carefully placed the vanishing cream in place on the shelf.

"I met her in Brandywine about seven years ago."

"That place has been dead and buried a long time."

"Perhaps not as long as you think." The flash of dark eyes and wild-looking beard disappearing behind the redwoods made Vivian tremble.

Nettie regarded her with a tiresome gaze. "You are rather hazy sometimes, Vivian."

She couldn't help but smile. "My mother calls it circle talk." She fingered a jar in the box. "But circles end where they start, don't they?"

"They do indeed," said Nettie.

"I've been feeling just that way ever since I got here."

Nettie laid a hand on her shoulder.

"I don't know where I'll end up, but I've got to keep going." She opened the jar of cream, and a strong whiff of lilac made her feel suddenly dizzy. The next moment, she was sitting at a table near the window, the sunlight offering a warm blanket across her knees, and Nettie was holding a glass of water to her lips.

"Feeling better?" Nettie asked.

Vivian's throat felt ragged as she drank the water and rose. "The dead are dragging me down a path I don't want to go."

"Sometimes we're drawn down by fate or will," Nettie said. "My mother always said that."

Vivian smiled. "Your mother was a wise woman. Far wiser than mine."

Nettie grimaced. "And what would the Queen of Denial say?"

Vivian laughed. "She would say, 'Don't worry any more about the past.' If she knew."

"But she doesn't know," said Nettie.

Vivian picked up the last jar of cream sitting in the dusty box. "I wonder if this cream would make a specter vanish."

Her friend laughed. "It's hardly more than perfume and water."

Vivian took off her gloves, hitting them against the side of the counter to shake off the dust. The gesture somehow made her feel better, as if the heavy words of David, Mr. Henderson, and even Ruth were flying away like so many dust particles.

Nettie watched her. "You don't have to see this woman if you don't want to, you know."

"I don't know if I want to," said Vivian. "I only know I have to."

Nettie wiped her hands on her apron and then untied it, folding it neatly on the counter. "Then you don't have to go alone."

Vivian turned toward the door, suddenly ashamed of the redness in her face. She was ashamed because, for the first time, she needed someone.

"A few hours with the lock on the door won't make much difference," continued Nettie.

"I'd pay you for your time," Vivian insisted.

This made the mousy eyes flash, and the straight lips harden. "It's a gesture of friendship, Vivian."

Vivian grabbed her hand. "I'm sorry. I didn't mean that."

Nettie smiled. "I don't imagine there is much chance for gestures of friendship behind those hollow smiles in the drawing rooms of Nob Hill." She washed her hands at the sink in the corner and, over the rush of the water faucet, asked, "Are you sure you really want me to come?"

"I would be relieved if you did," said Vivian.

Nettie shut off the water and dried her hands. "I only ask because it sounds like a private matter."

"I've already broken down to you," said Vivian. "Soon, you'll know all my secrets."

"And you'll know mine." Nettie smiled, and then regarded her with a funny gaze, her hand hovering over the black hat on the peg. "You sound almost afraid to see this woman."

"We didn't part on very amiable terms the last time," said Vivian. "She accused me of trying to make my phantom hers."

Nettie led her out of the shop, closing the shutters over the windows and sealing the padlock on the door. She hung a wooden sign that said, *If you need anything, go to Washer's on Parkinson Street*. She turned to look at Vivian with narrow eyes. "And were you?"

Vivian squeezed her hands together. "Yes. Perhaps I was." For a moment, she felt a bitter tinge in her chest, as if someone had suddenly plied her with poison.

The woman shrugged and took her arm. "I take it this Verina is no longer living in Waxwood."

"She works at a store in Goldspur."

"Goldspur!" The woman grimaced. "If we're going to Goldspur, I suggest we rent a horse and buggy at Shelley's. Unless you'd like to try your hand at one of those horseless carriages." Her eyes sparkled.

"You mean the automobile?" Vivian asked. "I should think not!" Her mind flashed to the one time she had ridden in one — a boxy, silent thing that crawled like a panther on the road. The car had been as stealthy as its owner, Harland Stevens.

Nettie smiled. "I don't think Shelley would rent us one, anyway. He's the sort who believes women ought to be carried across a puddle in the street."

Nettie proved to be correct. Mr. Shelley, a gruff man, insisted on sending his elder son who worked with him in the business as their driver rather than allowing them to maneuver the horse on their own. He remembered Vivian from the previous year as "one of Mr. Stevens' guests" and was amiable, recalling with some humor how Vivian had "softened him" with her questions about the horses.

As they waited outside the stalls for the driver to arrive with the carriages, Vivian couldn't help but sweep her eyes about for any sign of the boxy automobile. But she saw nothing that resembled the Brata.

She tried to sound unintentional. "I suppose Mr. Stevens still keeps his motor car here?"

"Not for a while, miss," said Mr. Shelley, chewing the edge of a cigarette. "I haven't seen Mr. Stevens at all for months."

"Oh?"

"Decent man, he was," said Mr. Shelley. "Always kept that Brata of his in tip-top shape and he asked me all the time about the horses, too. Hope nothing's happened to him."

"I'm sure nothing has," Vivian said.

The coach came, a fancy vehicle with curved doors and scrolls, and both women settled in. As the younger Mr. Shelley drove away, carefully maneuvering the reins, Nettie glanced at Vivian. "A former beau, this Mr. Stevens you were asking about?"

Vivian chuckled. "Hardly. We disliked one another."

"Then why did you inquire after him?"

"Curiosity," Vivian said.

Nettie snorted and looked ahead.

They were silent for a time. The road was filled with pebbles so that the younger Mr. Shelley had to steer carefully, causing the coach to swing right and left. But the scenery was pleasant, with vineyards scenting the air in heady wine. Later, they came upon a grove of oranges that made Vivian think of a summer when the family had gone to the French countryside and stayed in an inn surrounded by citrus trees so orange, lemon and grapefruit awakened her in the mornings.

"I think I know now why Monte Leblanc finds travel so invigorating," she said, breathing in the air.

Nettie laughed. "The Canadian buccaneer you're trying to catch?"

"I no longer think he's a buccaneer," said Vivian. "And I wouldn't say I'm trying to 'catch' him."

"Aren't you?" Nettie glanced at her.

Vivian shrugged. "I spent the years since my husband's death with my books for company."

"I thought you wanted a husband."

"I want to fulfill my duty," Vivian said sternly. "Just as all my ancestors did."

Nettie studied her as the wagon turned onto a smoother road. "You make it sound like a death sentence."

Vivian was silent as they passed into a low area where the mountains shone yellow and gold in the distance. "I want a husband," she said. "A husband who will let me be free."

Nettie looked at her with a crooked smile. "That's not so odd."

"Mr. Leblanc — I don't think he's the sort to make me follow his path. I think as long as I fulfilled my wifely duties, he would let me do as I pleased."

"You're taking a lot for granted." Nettie folded her hands in her lap. She wore gray gloves that looked a little frayed, and Vivian made a mental note to bring her new ones the next time she came. "And what would you do with your freedom, if you had it?"

Vivian examined a circle of birch trees out of place in the

yellow landscape. It was, she almost felt, the silver question gleaming so brightly, it hurt her eyes and her heart. She turned to Nettie, meeting her challenge with, "What would *you* do with your freedom if you had it?"

"I've no wish to marry. Not now, at least."

"There are other forms of confinement." Vivian glanced at the woman, noting her black and dove gray dress. "Such as prolonged mourning."

Nettie gazed ahead at the back of Mr. Shelley's head. "I never thought of it that way."

"Six years is a terribly long time to live with the dead," Vivian said gently.

"How long have you been living with your dead?" Nettie asked. She was not agitated or angry. She sounded, in fact, almost sad.

Vivian took her arm. "Perhaps we both need to bury our dead this summer, Nettie. If nothing else."

As they entered Goldspur, Vivian perceived the town was the dismal place Marvina had described to her. Although they had veered from the main road into town to a little quieter and less shabby neighborhood, the stench of beer and cheap perfume lingered from the saloons and places of ill repute they had passed. Mr. Shelley glanced back at them with a worried look. "It ain't a place for fine ladies," he mumbled. "I'd just as soon go with you, wherever it is."

Vivian stiffened. "We can take care of ourselves, Mr. Shelley. You're welcome to treat yourself to a beer or whatever libation you prefer, and we shall meet you here in a few hours." She extracted a few dollars from her reticule. "For your trouble."

"No bother, miss," he said, his face relaxing. "'Course, if you insist—" He gingerly took the money, then helped them down from the carriage.

Nettie, Vivian had to admit, took the place much more in stride. She was unbothered by the leery glances they received from a group of men lingering outside the hardware store. Nor did she flinch when two women in rough cotton dresses, their hats hanging halfway down their heads, passed them with a sniveling look sending the message they didn't belong. Nettie merely nodded at them and took Vivian's arm, waiting for instructions.

They entered Soot's, which was dark and dusty but amply attired with the usual odds and ends of a general store. The largess of it made Vivian feel better as she looked up at the wooden stairs that led to an open second floor. Somehow, after the openness of the redwoods at Brandywine, she felt better that Verina was not, at least, stuck in some tiny corner of a musty, mouse-infested shop such as some she had seen in the undersides of Market Street.

A heavy-set man with slick hair that did not quite cover his balding head approached them with a clownish grin. "Ladies, ladies, what can I do for you?"

Vivian used all the haughty refinement she had studied in her mother and grandmother as a child. She was almost grateful for the steady ankles she inherited from Larissa and the poise befitting her square shoulders. "You have a woman employed here named Verina Jones, sir?"

"Oh, yes, miss!" The man was clearly taken aback.

"We should prefer she wait on us."

"I could do just as well, miss," he said. His tone lost some of its jubilance.

"I'm sure you could, sir," said Vivian with a gracious smile. "But Miss Jones is an old friend of ours."

A small hush came from a pair of ladies who looked a little more refined than the ones Vivian had seen on the street. She had no doubt they were the better citizens of the town. They stared at her rudely, their eyes exposing a level of dour judgment she knew from the tea parties she had attended when she mentioned her friendship with Marvina. These women clearly did not like Verina.

"I see." The man's surprise disappeared as his voice became smooth, "I shall call her immediately, then."

"You needn't worry," Nettie said. "We've come to buy."

Her naturally sneering eyes regarded him with freshness. "I have no doubt of that, miss. Miss Jones never has any visitors." He headed for the back of the store, calling over his shoulder, "If you'll wait, I shall bring her to you."

Nettie said in a low voice, "They don't care much for your friend here, do they?" She looked fully at the two women. The women looked at one another and left the store.

Vivian's hands suddenly grew damp, and she realized she had not removed her gloves. She turned away from Nettie and yanked them off. Her hands smelled of the vanishing cream she had seen at Nettie's.

She saw immediately what Ruth had meant with her warning about Verina. The cherub serenity Vivian remembered from seven years before was gone. Her features gathered into little knots, and her dark eyes regarded Vivian with intrusion. Her smile was disingenuous and uninviting. Instead of the flowing brown dress with the coral beads she had worn when Vivian first met her, she now had on a dark, plain skirt and jacket over a shirtwaist with a high collar. The thick, dark hair that had so intrigued Vivian with its wild braid hanging loose against her back was now short in the front and swept up with hard little pins that looked as if they were almost pulling her temples up.

"Good afternoon, Miss Alderdice." The tone was distant.

Vivian held out her hand. "It's been a long time, Verina. Can't you call me Vivian?"

"Under the circumstances, I prefer it this way." She glanced at the portly man who had met them at the door, pretending to be occupied with the shelves nearby.

"It's all right," said Vivian. "I've already informed Mr. Soot we're friends."

This made Verina's eyes sharpen like knives, but her tone was the same. "To what do I owe the pleasure?"

"I stopped by to say hello and to buy a few things." Vivian put her reticule over her wrist. "This is my friend, Nettie Grace."

"I've been to Miss Grace's store." Verina's voice softened. "I was very sorry to hear about your mother."

Vivian saw a pained look cross her friend's face. "Thank you," she murmured.

Her eye had caught the bolts of fabric near the back of the store, and she suddenly had an idea. "Nettie has been trying to teach me to sew," she said. "We've decided to begin with a skirt, but we haven't yet found the right pattern. I was looking for something very durable and smart."

The woman's eyes jumped toward her employer. "We've some very fine linens. If you'll follow me."

Vivian was relieved to see that, just as they started, a few men came in, obviously friends of Mr Soot, and his attention went immediately toward them. She could see the severity in Verina's face soften as they reached the bolts of fabric lying on the table in a quiet corner of the store.

Vivian tried to be cheerful as she asked, "Aren't you curious about how I found you?"

"I know you have your ways." The woman's tone did not increase in warmth in the way Vivian remembered. Nettie was looking at her, almost fierce with protectiveness.

"I went to see Ruth a few days ago."

"I'm not the only one for whom your phantoms have become a casualty." The woman began unrolling a shade of crimson linen.

"I've come as a friend, Verina," Vivian insisted. "I have no phantoms trailing me this time."

The woman studied her with enormous eyes. "I don't believe you, Miss Alderdice."

"You're frank, aren't you?" Nettie snarled.

"I'm sorry you don't," said Vivian. "I've often wondered what became of you since Brandywine disbanded."

"Oh, I rolled around here and there," said the woman. "Is this too bright a shade for you, Miss Alderdice? We've some lovely peach and blue."

"I'd like to see those too," said Vivian, fingering the crimson. "I thought you might return to San Francisco after the colony shut down."

"Return?"

"I believe you told me you and your uncle Evan were in the city for quite a while," said Vivian. "Five years, you said."

The woman was silent, heaving the peach and blue bolts on the table. As she unrolled them, she mumbled, "We were in San Francisco one year."

"You told me five years."

The woman flushed. "We were going to stay for longer, but Uncle Evan decided to go back to Brandywine."

Vivian leaned with both hands on the edge of the table. "Why?"

"I don't know. I was only a child then." She pushed another bolt toward her, and her tone was more businesslike. "This, too, might suit you."

But Vivian was not looking at the bolt of mint and cream stripe calico. "Now I'm the one who doesn't believe you, Verina."

"Please keep your voice down," hissed the woman. Vivian could see Mr. Soot, though still chatting with the men, was glancing in their direction.

She lowered her tone. "I know you and Evan were in San Francisco a year or so after my grandmother left Waxwood."

"If you went to see Ruth, I imagine you do," said Verina.

"He didn't take to the place?"

"On the contrary," said Verina. "We were living with some jolly people, and I think he caught the spirit of the city rush and bustle. He couldn't shake it off even if he had wanted to."

"Then why the sudden departure back to the woods?"

Verina shrugged, unfolding the lemon muslin she had put on the table. "Perhaps this might suit you better than the calico."

"How old were you?" Nettie asked, half sitting on the edge of the table.

"Seven, eight." The young woman lowered her voice. "Mr. Soot is looking this way again."

Vivian took some of the crimson linen in her hands and said in a clear, decisive voice, "This is very nice, don't you think, Nettie?" In a lower tone, she said to Verina. "You'll have a decent sale to make him happy, I promise you."

"It makes no difference to me," Verina said offhand. "After this week, Mr. Soot will have no claim on me."

"Oh?" She glanced at her.

"People don't like me very much here." Verina smirked. "Any more than they liked me at Brandywine."

Vivian felt a wave of sadness as she looked at the woman rolling up the calico bolt. "The offer I made seven years ago to help you still stands."

"Your friend who has connections with the shopkeepers in San Francisco." Verina narrowed her eyes. "Does she take pity on women like myself, with no husband, no family, and not even their pleasant memories to hold on to?"

Vivian looked away. Then, her Alderdice pride got the better of her, and she lifted her chin. In a loud voice, she said, "I should like this, please. And you might show us some needles and thread to match."

Verina led them into a small alcove where the front of the store was no longer visible.

"I know you came to San Francisco without your mother." Vivian looked expectedly at Verina. "I'm sorry."

"Why should you be?" Verina glared at her. "It was your grandfather who made it possible for her to live out the last of her years in comfort, wasn't it?"

Vivian held on to the wall, feeling the splintering wood. "You said you lived with some jolly people."

"Friends of Uncle Evan's," she said.

"Artist friends?" The woman did not answer. "I imagine he took advantage of the artistic community in the city while he was there."

"Why do you suppose that?" The woman gave her a piercing look.

"I recall your uncle was a friendly fellow," Vivian said. "He liked people."

"You mean unlike me?" she challenged.

"If the place was so jolly, I imagine the flat had many visitors," Vivian ventured.

Verina's face suddenly went as clammy as a fish. "You asked for needle and thread, didn't you?" She led them to the principal part of the store and extracted both. But her hands were shaking a little, and the needles and thread clattered to the floor. Nettie picked them up as Vivian studied the woman's face.

"Were there many visitors?" she repeated.

"I don't remember." Verina's face was white.

"I think you do," Vivian hissed. "I think you know to whom I'm referring."

There was silence between them. Nettie was looking from one to the other but said nothing.

Verina placed the items on top of the fabric. "You may pay at the cashier, if you please. I've work to do." She turned away.

"Wait!" Vivian grasped the edge of the linen. "Matches. I'd like some matches, please."

Verina gave her a vicious look. "You appear to burn through everyone's resistance without them, Miss Alderdice."

"Not yours, obviously," Nettie snarled back.

Vivian grabbed her wrist. "Did my grandmother come and see your uncle at the flat?"

The woman began heading toward the front of the store. "If you'll come this way."

Vivian's gut drew in as she followed Verina's stoic gait. She untangled the drawstrings of her reticule from her wrist and held out the money. "I remind you what Ruth said: You have no right to deny me what you know."

"But I don't know."

"That's exactly what Ruth said."

Verina said nothing, holding out the change.

Vivian pushed it away. "You keep it."

"You left me no choice but to accept your charity the last time," said Verina with a note of anger. "But I have a choice now."

"Then give it to anyone you wish." She gathered her packages in her arms. "You do know, Verina, and so does Ruth. But I'm facing two Sphynx. I shall have to solve the riddle on my own."

She let Nettie take a package out of her hand as they left the store, her lower lip quivering with rage.

They rode back to Waxwood in complete silence. Mr. Shelley was not intoxicated, but he was not as careful with guiding the horses as he had been. Vivian was almost grateful for the carriage's knocks and starts. The violent shakes of the wheels made the coldness that she had felt from Verina ease.

When they were back on the smoother road leading into Waxwood, Nettie finally spoke. "She oughtn't to have talked to you like that. I don't care what went on between you."

"It was my fault," said Vivian. "I made her face her specters when she wasn't ready. I do that often, I should warn you."

Nettie grinned as the carriage pulled into the blacksmith's stable. "My mother always told me there was a blue-eyed monster lurking about somewhere, and if I shut my eyes, she would go away."

"That was hardly a reassuring thing to say to a child." Vivian accepted the senior Mr. Shelley's helping hand as she climbed down from the carriage.

"She was trying to get me used to sleeping in the dark," said Nettie. "Mama — her ways weren't always conventional." The note of devastation came into Nettie's forceful tone, but it disappeared quickly. "You didn't find what you were looking for, did you?"

"I wasn't looking for anything in particular," said Vivian as they began walking back toward the drugstore. "I was hoping to *know*."

"And do you?"

"I know I must discover it on my own."

Nettie chuckled. "You need a private detective, like a Pinkerton."

"Perhaps not as sordid as that." Vivian smiled.

"What is it you wish to find?" She began walking, her arm threaded through Vivian's.

"Not what," Vivian said. "Who. Verina said she and Evan stayed with some jolly people in the city. Artists, I imagine."

"They might be dead by now," Nettie pointed out.

"Perhaps," she said. "But if these artists were friends of Evan's, they might remember something."

"Like whether your grandmother came to see this Evan?"

"Maybe," Vivian said vaguely.

Nettie shrugged. "I know of a detective who used to work for the Pinkertons."

"A private person?" Vivian asked.

Her friend nodded. "Would you consent to a woman?"

"Why wouldn't I?" Vivian asked.

"Because so many people have ideas about women who immerse themselves in the private details of people's lives," Nettie said. "But Alda Quigg is as fervent a bloodhound as the most Sherlock of Holmes."

Vivian smiled. "Then she will suit my purposes."

Nettie glanced at the bundle still in Vivian's hands. "If you give me that parcel, I shall make that skirt for you."

"That's very generous of you," Vivian mumbled.

They slipped the packages in the shop, which looked as if it had been deserted of any customer's prints in the dust outside the door. Nettie led her down the street further away from the center of town. The buildings were lower and the signs more faded. One wooden board swinging from chains read in deft script *Miss Alda Quigg, Private Investigator.*

The office was small, made smaller still by the enormous desk that took up nearly half the room. It did not have the seedy look of peeling walls, old scents of ink, and mustiness Vivian imagined it would. The room was, in fact, rather immaculate.

The woman who sat behind the desk was intimidating, in her own way. She was more matronly than Vivian had expected, adroit in her features, and as assured as any man Vivian had ever seen. A holster and pistol swung from a peg behind her, as if waiting with impatience for someone to take them up.

Miss Quigg noticed Vivian staring at the gun and leaned back in the swivel chair, her hands laced together. "That's so people are aware I know how to use it."

"I imagine your work can be dangerous," Vivian said.

"The more danger, the more pay," she said. "I'm a business-woman, Miss — Alderdice?" Vivian nodded. "Seen your name in the papers, of course."

"Really?" Vivian's eyebrows arched.

"I have occasion to read the society pages in my work." The woman chuckled.

"Alda can ferret anybody out from under any rock," Nettie insisted, sitting a little further away on the leather couch.

"Is that what you want, Miss Alderdice?" asked the woman. "Need me to find someone for you?"

"In a manner of speaking." Vivian twisted the strings of her reticule.

"Not a cheating beau, I hope." The woman chuckled again.

"No, Miss Quigg," she said.

"Call me Alda. We'll get friendly soon enough." The woman eyed her. "Who, then?"

"That's my problem," said Vivian. "I don't know."

"You don't know!"

"I'm going on a feeling." Vivian told her about her conversation with Verina.

The woman listened, twisting the cap of the ink bottle on the desk. When Vivian finished, she said, "You got the right idea, I think. Likely this man Evan Jones found these people he stayed with through one of those organizations for artists in San Francisco."

"He might have gotten some commissions through them, if his friends were helping him," Nettie offered.

"Very likely," Alda nodded, "but it's going to take time to hunt those organizations down. And no guarantee any of them have records from forty years ago."

"I realize that," Vivian said.

"Still, a challenge's a challenge and money in the bank." The woman grinned. "And I've got nothing pressing at the moment. Waxwood isn't exactly the center of crime, bless their hearts."

Vivian smiled. "You'll help me locate these men, then?"

"I won't say no," said the woman. "Where are you staying right now?"

"I'm staying at the Waxwoodian." Vivian rose. "But don't send any messages there directly. My mother — she knows nothing about this."

The woman nodded without asking questions. "When I have word, I'll give Nettie the note, and she can get it to you any way she pleases."

Vivian shook the woman's hand more firmly.

Later, as she settled herself on the ferry, the solemn feeling overtook her again as she gazed out at the bay, seeing flickers of dark fish slip through the clear blue. The water was churning just as they had seven years before.

CHAPTER 10

Vivian had little time to think of Verina in the following days, as July had come, and with it, the community picnic at the city park on the Fourth. Vivian knew from the year before that, until the resorts had established firm ground upon Waxwood's seaside, the Fourth celebrations had been modest gatherings exclusive to the residents. But the hotel proprietors came together and marched into the room at Parker's Restaurant, where the town council gathered to make their plans, and demanded their guests have the privilege of attending, as they were, like temporary citizens, and "We are all of one nation under God and ought to partake in the celebration of being so." Thus, posters declaring the event hung all over the Waxwoodian, and the *Waxwoodian Review* published one long page with the schedule of games and events, including a new bicycle race with a five-dollar first prize and two one-dollar second and third prizes.

The swells reacted to the announcements with their usual haughty temperament. At the Tisher table the night before the celebrations, Mrs. Tisher at once expounded upon the duty of "the more refined classes" to ensure the joviality and leisure of others did not get out of hand with "such vulgar nonsense of which some people are capable." Mrs. Griffith, in her usual quicksilver manner, agreed, adding, "We mustn't allow the good intentions of our forefathers to suffer from immoral behavior."

Vivian's mind was hardly on the festivities to come as the Fourth neared. Every time she entered the lobby, she looked expectedly at the desk, trying to peer over the shoulders of the clerks at the small pigeon holes of the mail cubby to see if there was any small envelope from Nettie. There was never anything but the long, starched letters her mother received from the city. She tried to remind herself that Alda had warned it could take time to find the names of artists from forty years ago. But her nerves grew more on edge with each passing day.

On the Fourth, they crossed the ferry into town and walked in a well-dressed, well-scented procession to the city park, garnishing ogling eyes and arch eyebrows from the residents. Vivian felt alive with the sight of so many smiling faces, children with their balloons and apples, young couples holding hands, and older people beaming like the sunshine. She was astounded by the collection of bicycles on the street. They threaded between wagons and carriages, cluttering up the road, their bells making high-pitched calls that drowned out impatient shouts from the other drivers.

"Even San Francisco doesn't have such a bicycle craze," Vivian remarked, her hand firmly under Mr. Leblanc's arm. He had made clear she was his companion for the day, much to the chagrin of Fern Tisher and Mrs Sowberry. Her anxiety over Verina's sincerity made her pliable to any distraction, and she had welcomed his attentions for days.

"Have you ever ridden one?" he asked.

She shook her head. "My mother believes they're too dangerous on the hills." In truth, Larissa had been horrified to see young ladies swinging their skirts between their knees as they road down Market Street, insisting it would be "the height of indecency" if Vivian should ever attempt to ride one.

"Would you try it, if there were no hills?"

Before she could answer, Amber slid up behind them, clinging to her husband's arm, who had been persuaded by means Vivian could only imagine to come down to Waxwood for the holiday. "Vivian would try anything. She has an athletic nature, don't you, dear?"

"Your opinion of me has changed." Vivian glanced ahead of her. "You used to accuse me of being bookish." She heard a gruff laugh escape the lips of George as the young woman bestowed upon Vivian her most conceited snarl.

"Well, just lately, you seem to have forsaken your literary pursuits." The ferret-like eyes slid toward Mr. Leblanc. "I suppose we have you to thank for that, Monte."

"Don't tell me you don't approve of sports for ladies?" the man joked. "I heard you talking only this morning of how you mean to finish first in the archery competition."

"Only very few of them," said Amber. "For men, it's entirely different."

"Then you agree with your brother," Vivian said.

The young woman gave her a prickly smile. To George, she said, "Jacob had an argument with Huey last summer. Huey invited him to join his football team and, somehow, Jacob found that objectionable."

"It was Huey's idiotic insinuations about why Jake refused that he found objectionable," Vivian said in an icy voice. "My brother put it rather succinctly when he said Huey's football was no better or worse than his art."

"I quite agree with you," said Mr. Leblanc. "I find gridiron football rather dull myself. But, ah, horses, hunting, boating — those are elegant and worthy exercise for a man."

"You forget, Mr. Leblanc," she said, "many young women nowadays prefer the bicycle to the scrub board."

"Oh, that's only a passing fad," he insisted.

"Are you going to turn into one of those New Women, Vivian?" Amber asked archly.

The woman made it sound so much like an insult that Vivian colored. "It would be a sight more flattering than a nagging wife," she retorted.

"Ladies, ladies, not on the Fourth, please!" George's voice quivered.

"George was on the rowing team in college, weren't you, precious?" Amber glanced at him with a possessive smile.

"Marvelous for the physique," said the man, though his seedy figure hardly looked as if it belonged to a former rowing champion.

Mr. Leblanc and George were still talking about rowing as they plodded through the grass to the area the swells had coveted as their own, complete with tables and umbrellas to block out the sun. She thought about her grandmother and the letter she had written to Great-Grandmother on this same holiday forty years ago. Then, too, there had been celebrations and fireworks and a picnic in the park. Grandmother had already broken from Bertha and Loretta and the others, living in Brandywine with the artists — and in love. And yet, she had envied the Waxwood Belles for their finery and self-assurance.

Not long afterward, Mr. Leblanc joined her, leaving George to his wife, and said to her, "Miss Alderdice, George told me there is a croquet lawn here."

"Shall we play a game, then?" She smiled, rising. She had not forgotten how she had abandoned him to Fern's wooden movements the day she had gone to see Verina.

Fern jumped up. "We shall make a foursome. It's hardly worth taking up the mallets unless there are at least four people, don't you agree, Vivian?"

"I don't," said Vivian. "I think a quiet game for two is much more interesting." She glanced at Mr. Leblanc.

He turned to Fern with a most polite bow. "Next game, perhaps."

Fern, not a little annoyed, sank down on the blanket again.

Mr. Leblanc turned into a young man again as he trotted off with Vivian through the tall grass, weaving among the families that had settled down, the children playing a circle game, and the more authoritative men who were clearly setting up a race with their chalk and markers. He led her to a place near a muddier area where the grass was shorter and cut into a definite rectangle with iron hoops already stabbed into the ground. He insisted on choosing the mallet for her, weighing each one with a critical eye before handing one to her.

"You don't give yourself much advantage, Mr. Leblanc," she said in a light voice. Just as the sunshine and the park had taken ten years off his life, she felt like a debutante again, basking in the attention of a sought-after man.

"I would be more than pleased to lose any game to you, Miss Alderdice."

Vivian gave him a sly smile. "But you don't believe you will lose the game to me. Isn't that right?" He chuckled, but did not deny it.

They played, not so much a competitive game, but a concentrated one. Vivian forgot Verina, David, Ruth, everyone who had been burdening her for the past weeks. Nothing existed but the rug-like lawn, the hoops, and the red and blue balls.

She knew Mr. Leblanc was growing impressed that she was true to her word. Despite her passion for books, she also had a certain athleticism. She knew it came as a surprise to many people, who looked at her sometimes ethereal countenance and her compact figure and guessed she was one of those who fainted easily. Croquet was one of the few games in her debutante years that young ladies could play with the men, and she had developed a strength in her arms and an astute eye that allowed her to capture two, sometimes three hoops at a time.

She won the game easily. Unlike some young men she had played with who were put out when a woman beat them, Mr. Leblanc was charmed with her victory. He extracted a thorny rose from the bush on the border of the park close to them and presented it to her. "For your crown of victory. You have an impressive skill, Miss Alderdice."

She laughed, glancing over her shoulder. "We're about to have company."

A group of young men were coming up the small incline. She placed the red mallet into the rack and, just as she turned around, the young men approached. She recognized all their faces. "Hello, gentlemen."

They stopped, blinking with bewilderment.

"Surely, you haven't forgotten me," she said. "You wouldn't forget my brother last year."

One of the young men, whose scraggy face made him look much older than the others, advanced. "Who was your brother, if we may inquire?" He was polite but guarded.

"Jake Alderdice." Her eyes shifted from one face to the other. More mature countenances and refined manners of dress and posture had replaced the slippery faces and goggling eyes of last year There was none of the slouching and sauntering she had witnessed the year before. They stood dotting the green with their shoulders back, feet a little apart, and some of them had their hands in their pockets.

They threw glances at one another, their earlier confusion replaced by something more concealed. One of them, wearing thick glasses and a hat that covered his eyebrows, held out his hand, his smile a little too horsey. "Miss Alderdice, yes! We remember your brother well."

"I'm sure you do," Vivian said. "Especially since you almost let him drown."

There was an embarrassed silence while Mr. Leblanc glared at them.

"Honest, it wasn't us, miss," said another young man. "We liked Mr. Alderdice."

Vivian sighed, feeling as if her arms were going to fall away from her shoulders. "No, it wasn't you. I'm sorry I said that."

Mr. Leblanc coughed beside her. He took her arm. "We must get back to our friends, Miss Alderdice."

"This is Mr. Leblanc," Vivian said. "I don't think I ever got your names last year."

"Ivan Morvell, miss," said one with a bow. The others introduced themselves with mumbling voices. The last, Andrew Trent, regarded Mr. Leblanc with the look of one dog surveying another.

"What about Mr. Roger Howe?" Vivian asked. "Isn't he one of your friends too?"

Norris Harrington, a young man with a whiney voice who looked younger than the others, gestured toward the open park. "He's here, miss. Just sitting with the swells — I mean — the rich people, I mean—" His lip quivered as his friends chuckled.

"I know what you mean, Mr. Harrington," said Vivian.

"And your brother," said Mr. Trent. "Where is he, if I may ask?"

"You may *not* ask," snapped Mr. Leblanc.

"Come to play a game?" Vivian asked.

"Yes, miss," said Mr. McDonaugh. "Mr. Stevens taught us last summer, and well, we sort of took a liking to it. We have a croquet team now at the university."

"I'm sure Mr. Stevens would be glad to hear it," Vivian said with a wry smile. "We shall leave you to it, won't we, Mr. Leblanc?" She settled her hand inside the crook of his arm.

"Won't you join us?" asked Mr. Williard Adams. "You and Mr. Leblanc."

Vivian glanced at her companion. "You will, won't you, Mr. Leblanc?"

"If you wish us to play," he said.

"Not me," she said. "I haven't the manly skill and precision to play on a team. But you, sir, your strokes are admirable. I'm sure you have much to teach these boys." She tried not to smile as she saw one of Mr. Trent's thick eyebrows rise to the challenge.

"But you wish to go back—"

"I need to find some friends of mine anyway," said Vivian, extracting herself from the man's grasp. "It would bore you to tears. Please, I insist. And with you in the game, it would make the two teams even, wouldn't it?" She then turned a little away from the young men, who were inspecting the mallets, and whispered to him, "I know they're arrogant, but I think if you were to show them how a gentleman plays the game, they would take heed."

The calculated response came as Mr. Leblanc's mustache twitched with the closed-mouth grin of pride, and even his chest went out a little. "I cannot deny I have taught many young men to behave like gentlemen."

"I've no doubt," Vivian said, feeling a little self-satisfied as she watched him join the college boys, his voice booming with the authority of an older man who had much to teach the younger ones.

She hurried away, glancing back only once to make sure Mr. Leblanc had kept to the field. Then she veered a little from the path they had taken away from the Waxwoodian party and went in another direction so she could survey the people seated in their little clusters.

She found whom she was looking for rather unexpectedly, as she had been prepared for the loose-limbed young man she remembered from the year before. But Roger Howe had matured as much as the rest of his friends had. While their maturity had swept aside the physical aspects of age, Mr. Howe had not only matured but aged. He looked older than a man about to finish his college education. A fuller torso now replaced the lanky build of last year, and he even had the shadow of a slight paunch around his gut. He had a mustache now, short and elegant, and the sandy hair fell across his temples and forehead as if he were trying to hide signs of premature balding. He sat with a small cluster of younger people, most of whom she didn't know, but his blanket edged a little away from them. As Vivian watched him, she noted he did more listening than talking. She fumbled through the tall grass until she reached him and, without asking, dropped to his side.

"How do you do, Mr. Howe?" she asked in a clear voice.

She expected him to be astonished, but she did not expect he would be so pleased. The one encounter she had observed between Jake and Roger had been anything but amiable. But his countenance softened, and his eyes glowed with pleasure as he grasped her hand in both of us.

"I'm delighted to see you, Miss Alderdice." His words were sincere. "Won't you call me Roger?"

"Perhaps we should be on a first name basis," Vivian said. "We were thrown together several times last year."

"That we were." The gladdened quality in his voice dropped a little. "Summer vacations are odd things. One spends one's time with people one would normally ignore or even shun during the winter. And then everyone goes back to their little world and thinks no more of it. It's only when they meet once again that they feel like old friends."

"Are we old friends, Roger?" she asked.

He looked at her warmly. "I should hope we would be, Vivian." He offered her a glass of wine from the tray sitting near them and she accepted, her throat suddenly dry. "How did you know I was here?"

"Your friends told me," she said.

Here, a little of the younger Roger appeared with the thin line of his lips and the snarl in his voice. "Yes, I should have known!"

"You don't take to them as much this year as you did last year," Vivian guessed.

"I've learned a few things in the past year," said Roger. "One is to choose my friends more cautiously." He sipped at the wine. "I go into Vanbrugh & Gunn next year."

"Really?" Vivian was impressed, as Vanbrugh & Gunn was the most prestigious architectural firm in San Francisco.

"They've offered me a position," he said. "Junior, for now, of course, but my uncle has no doubt I shall rise in the ranks quickly." He said the last with a detectable irony.

"You mean your uncle will see to it you rise in the ranks quickly," she said with a wry smile.

He laughed. "I always admired your quick-wittedness, Vivian."

"Do you still have that lovely Bible your mother gave you?"

He nodded, his eyes softening with gratitude. "It's kind of you to remember that. I do still have it. And I still use it in church every Sunday."

"And your cousin?" She gazed at him. "You haven't, I gather, persuaded him to join you?"

The mention of Harland Stevens melted the lightness from the young man's face into something that resembled a seething panther. "Harland's godlessness is none of my concern anymore."

"Oh?" She looked at him.

"I thought your brother would have told you," he said.

"Everyone thinks Jake would have told me everything," she mused. "He can be very closed-mouthed, though."

"It wasn't very pleasant, I'm afraid." Roger said. "We had a quarrel near the end of last summer. I don't think I've had a complete conversation with him since."

"I'm sorry I asked."

"We rarely see Harland anymore in the house. Sometimes, he's gone for days at a time."

"But he was so attached to that castle of his." Vivian recalled the strange trip she and Jake had taken last year to the sprawling, solitary castle, with its turrets and stone walls, sitting on the edge of a cliff.

"I don't think he ever really was," said Roger in a grave tone. "He only wanted Uncle Joseph to think so."

"What is he doing with himself, then?" She felt a tightness in her gut as she thought of the wild-eyed man she had seen at Brandywine.

Roger shrugged. "He won't tell us. He just disappears with no word or explanation, the cur!" The last came out over a wave of screeching children's voices, as a race was going on not far off.

"It's very odd," Vivian agreed.

"It was the devil of a thing," lamented the young man. "He takes his clothes and things, as if he's never coming back. But he always does."

"Just runs off into the night," Vivian murmured.

"Sometimes, we don't have the faintest idea he's gone until we find Maestro locked in the cellar," said Roger. "I suppose the mutt tries to follow him."

"Poor dog!"

"It's for my aunt, I'm worried," he said. "She's not well, you know. And his going away for days like that is shattering her nerves even more. It's a selfish thing for him to do."

"I never imagined Mr. Stevens was anything else," said Vivian wryly. She wondered if she should mention to Roger that she had seen a wild-looking thing she thought resembled his redheaded cousin, but decided against it. She was still unsure of whether it had really been Mr. Stevens, and Roger looked genuinely distressed. "What does your uncle say?" she asked instead.

"Oh, what you would expect," he snarled. "'Harland is not a child, Roger, and he may do as he likes.' Uncle Joseph has always made excuses for him."

"Why do *you* think he goes away like that, Roger?"

She watched as he pulled at the grass, his thin hands yanking the blades as if they were small knives. "The devil knows. He's been restless since he came back from Waxwood last year. When he is home, he spends most of his time wandering around the castle. And just lately, he's taken meals in his room, as if he doesn't want to see any of us."

"Perhaps it's better he stays away from people," Vivian advised. "I needn't tell you why."

"No, you needn't tell me." He smoothed down the grass. "How is Jake?"

Heat made her heart pulse, as it always did when she heard her brother's name. "He's doing well."

"I noticed he's not with you this summer."

"No, he's in Europe."

"So I heard."

Vivian suddenly did not like the way the young man's wide eyes were studying her. "He decided last year he needed more training in his art, so he went to Paris."

"I'm happy to hear it," he said. "I always thought he had talent."

She glanced at him. "I wasn't aware you saw his paintings."

The man gave a biting laugh. "He drew a rather unflattering portrait of me one evening."

"I'm sure he didn't mean to be cruel," Vivian mumbled.

"He didn't," said Roger. "It was some creature with the head of a wolf and the body of a man. Harland tried to make it mean something more than it did."

"He was rather good at that," Vivian growled.

"You seem to be good at that yourself." The young man regarded her with a keen eye. "Only because you're a woman. It's meant with good intentions rather than bad."

Vivian glanced away, seeing their party in the distance. Mr. Leblanc had returned, and his searching eyes told her he was looking for her.

She rose. "It was good of you to speak with me, Roger."

"It was my pleasure." He smiled. "You're better company than some others I know." He flicked his head toward the hill where his friends were still fumbling over the croquet game.

"May I ask you one more question before I go?"

"Of course."

She shifted her weight to one side. "You no longer hate my brother, do you?"

He blinked into the sun. "I don't think I ever did, Vivian. We were forced into hostile circumstances not of our making."

"Because of one man?" Vivian asked.

"One man they may find dead in the woods one day, for all we know." There was a note of savagery in his voice as he added, "I hope to God he will be!"

Vivian felt a shiver down her spine as she returned to her party. She looked back to see Roger was plucking at the blades of grass once more.

CHAPTER 11

For the next few days, Vivian felt as if she were standing outside of the funnel she herself had stirred up at the beginning of the summer. The talk with Roger Howe had closed a chapter for her, at least temporarily, and pursuing anything more taxing than the emotional upheavals of the heroine in the latest novel she was reading unnerved her. She was unnerved, too, by Mr. Leblanc's continued attentions. That Alda Quigg had not contacted her as she had promised she would hardly eased her nerves. It was as if she had disappeared from the folds of the Waxwood town.

She endured breakfast every morning at the center table and tried to be lively only because her mother expected it. Larissa was now the fourth Muse in the little group of society women who headed all the activities of the smart set and, as Vivian had learned last year, this required more of her presence in the activities her mother helped organize. The benefit of this was that Larissa's preoccupation with resort life prevented her from asking too many questions.

Vivian did her duty through dinner and after dinner, when everyone retired to the hotel parlor. But she still refused to engage in the sort of coquettish conversation expected of an unmarried young woman, and Mr. Leblanc appeared to prefer it that way. He no longer helped Fern or Cecily turn the pages of the sheet music as they banged away at the piano. Instead, he sat with her in the window seat at the end of the room and played card games as nearby voices floated like fog above them. They said few words to one another, and Vivian sometimes wondered whether they had inadvertently reached a silent understanding of one another.

That Saturday had been an unusually pleasant day, with a soft sprinkle of rain early in the morning that had cleared away some of the dust of the past blazing hot days. The sky had the pallor of a robin's egg, and even the wax wood trees in the distance looked more green than gray. The sea itself was a line of brilliant green, and the sun beamed off the sand in competition for the light. Everything looked as if it were a wet painting.

Vivian, in a mood for solitariness, set out for her private sanctuary on a beach where an enclosed cave shielded it from visitors. She stayed there until the light showed hues of a darker pallor. She returned to the hotel just as night bloomed in its true colors, a mere fifteen minutes before the dinner gong. She rushed into the suite, throwing her book and bathing things onto her bed, calling out, "I won't be five minutes, Mother! I have my dress already picked out."

"No rush, dear," Larissa said in a calm voice. "We're dining in tonight."

"Dining in?"

Vivian suddenly realized the parlor room had been transformed into a dining room of sorts. The couch and chairs were pushed near the door, and in their place was a large, square table and gilded chairs that had not been there before. The table shone with four place settings of crystal and chinaware.

"I've invited the Leblancs to dine with us," said Larissa with a smile.

Vivian's heart fell. "Why on earth would you do that, Mother?"

"Because," she said in a brisk voice, "I discovered the reason they and the Tishers were not at dinner yesterday was because the Tishers invited them to dine in their suite."

"Oh, Mother!" Vivian snorted. "I never thought you could play such petty games."

Her mother straightened a candle in the candelabra. "I told you when you first came out: with only one fox out, the hounds must be extra clever."

Vivian couldn't help but laugh at her mother's sincere analogy. "I think I'd rather be the fox than the hound!"

"You're now on the other side of the hunt." Her mother's voice was prickly. "Whether or not you like it, that's how it is, Vivian."

"Well, I suppose there's some satisfaction in drawing the Leblancs away from those coy Tisher girls." Vivian smiled. "I'm sure Mr. Leblanc was quite relieved when his father accepted the invitation." She headed to her room to dress.

"I've ordered foie gras and venison," said Larissa. "They say the way to a man's heart is through his stomach, you know."

Vivian emerged from her room, doing up the last of the pearl buttons on her dress. "For this fox, I fear the only way to his heart is through a map or a compass."

"Then you must be sure and ask him more about his travels at dinner," said her mother in an arch tone.

"Yes, I gathered he's eager to have a wife who will sit like a puppet with her chin in her hand, smiling daintily as she listens to him go on and on about his adventures." Vivian adjusted the pins in her hair. "I sometimes wonder whether half of them are true."

"He's keen to have a wife under any circumstances," Larissa said. "That much I gathered from his father."

"Are you sure it isn't the father who is eager?"

Her mother adjusted one of the dining room chairs. "Their

family needs heirs as much as ours, Vivian. There is a second cousin somewhere in Boulogne, but other than that, they have nothing."

"Just as we have nothing," Vivian murmured.

"We will have everything," her mother assured her, "if you continue to behave in such an engaging manner and ask all the right questions."

"I've been asking questions," Vivian insisted. "If I hear once more about the curry in India as opposed to the curry in London, I shall go mad."

Larissa glanced at her. "There is no other way for a lady to win a man's heart but to be vigilant at all times about what is coming out of her mouth."

"I'm buried in vigilance, Mother," Vivian snapped. "Do you know what happens to women who bury themselves?"

Her mother consulted the clock on the wall. "They'll be here any minute."

Vivian leaned against a chair with both hands. "You know, Mother, I've been reading a book lately—"

"Have you, how nice." Larissa was distracted by the door, expecting to open it at any moment, either to admit the Leblancs or the waiter.

"It's about a woman who engages in an affair with a younger man because her vigilance was so complete all her married life that the only way she could keep from going mad was illicit love or suicide."

"She shall choose suicide then," said her mother. "Those authors always make the heroines pay for their sins."

"A woman wrote the book!"

"All the better," her mother said. "If she is the right kind of woman, she will have a sound moral judgment she wishes to impart on her readers."

"I don't know that Kate Chopin is that kind of woman," said Vivian. "I read she wrote her book because she had a score to settle with Mr. Darwin regarding the inferiority of the female sex."

A knock on the door saved her mother from answering. Both Leblancs entered, with Emile Leblanc carrying a tray of drinks carefully with both hands, a wide grin on his face.

"Papa dismissed the waiter and insisted on bringing it to you himself," said Mr. Leblanc after he had kissed both women's hands. "He is a great believer in the American cocktail hour."

"So we've noticed," Vivian said, earning a seething glance from her mother.

"It is a charming custom," said the father. "Oh, I know, Europeans say it ruins the appetite, but for me, there is nothing like warming up the tongue before one is committed to one's dinner companions." His gaze swept to Larissa, who had put on a lavender gown that befitted her light coloring. "That is of no consequence to us tonight, as we shall dine with the two most charming ladies we have met in America."

"You are too gracious, sir," said Larissa with a maidenly blush. "I'm very glad you approve."

"One must change one's dinner companions often when one is on vacation," said Mr. Leblanc. "It's no use seeing the same faces repeatedly." Vivian suspected he was trying to send the message he had tired of the Tisher girls.

"But when one encounters such lively and delightful companions as you have, Mr. Leblanc, I suppose one doesn't mind staying in their company as long as possible," she answered as he handed her a glass.

"Ah, yes, Californians are lively." He seated her on the couch and took his place near her. His father and Larissa had wandered out to the balcony. "And they all behave as if they are young, even if they aren't."

"Maturity has its promises," Vivian pointed out.

"And its pains," he added.

"And its pains." She tried not to look at him.

"That's one reason Papa and I want to settle here." He glanced at her. "We have started looking at architects, you know."

"Yes, I heard that from Mrs. Griffith," Vivian said.

"We've already contacted several," he continued. "Naturally, the house won't be ready for a few years. But Leila has found a place on Taylor Street we can rent in the meantime."

"Then you're really coming to Nob Hill?"

"Only in the winter," said Mr. Leblanc. "When the season opens. And in the summer, perhaps we shall be here again." He smiled.

"I'm sure Mrs. Griffith will be most happy to guide you," Vivian said.

"Or maybe I will have a wife by then," he said boldly. "That would make things complete, wouldn't it? Oh, it's been so merry with you lot here!" He looked at her. "Except for you, Miss Alderdice. You've been grave these past few days." He leaned back, crossing his legs and spreading one hand over the back of the couch at a safe distance from her.

Vivian toyed with her empty cocktail glass. Mr. Leblanc jumped up, offering to refill it, but she shook her head.

"I'm sorry if I struck you that way," she said carefully.

"Maybe your interests are far too serious for a summer holiday, if I may say so," he said. "You're not much older than the Tisher girls. You ought to be as lively and carefree as they are."

She smiled. "My nature is, I hope, more substantial than theirs."

He resumed his casual position with his crossed legs and arm on the couch. "All the young ladies I've met in America have plenty of freedom." He quickly added, "I don't mean that is bad."

"Maybe that's why we're so lively and carefree," Vivian said.

"Not you. You're different from the others, Miss Alderdice."

"Because I'm grave?" she asked ironically.

"Because you would rather read books than paddle a boat or skate or dance."

She sighed, looking down. "I've been hiding from the world for the last seven years, Mr. Leblanc."

"Forgive my asking, but is that why you don't have a husband?" he ventured.

Vivian felt a breeze enter through the open balcony doors. She couldn't see her mother and Emile Leblanc behind the billowing curtains. "Maybe it is," she admitted.

"It is odd that you haven't married again."

"It's odd that *you* haven't," she countered lightly.

"Ah, but I'm a man."

"All the more reason," she said. "Men are rather bad at taking care of themselves after they've had a woman taking care of them for a time."

He laughed and bowed his head in compliance. Then his gaze became uneven. "Miss Alderdice — would you consider — if you knew—"

The thundering knock on the door saved her from answering. Two waiters came in and set the food on the table.

Dinner turned out to be a more festive affair than Vivian expected. The elder Mr. Leblanc proved an adequate storyteller and a keen observer of men, as he told tales of his days as a fur trapper. The affection between father and son was clear, as Monte Leblanc would intervene, correcting his father's sometimes exaggerated accounts, and Mr. Leblanc would scold him lightly but with grinning eyes. Vivian realized how long it had been since her mother had really laughed. Larissa's careful consideration for appearances hindered her from laughing out loud in public, and she usually condescended to give little more than a low chuckle or a smile in response to a funny story. But tonight, her entire body contracted with humor, and she sometimes held her handkerchief to her lips, which Vivian knew was a sign of her laughing hard and trying to remain within her ideas of decorum. Larissa always said, "A woman ought not to laugh too heartily in public."

Over a dessert of maple pudding chomeur, Mr. Leblanc spoke of a yacht he and his son had just purchased earlier that summer. "She rides so smoothly you'd think the bay was butter!" he said with a roar. "We're calling her *The Ava*." His tone dropped as he glanced at the younger Mr. Leblanc, then continued with the same enthusiasm. "She needs some repairs, so she's down in San Francisco at the moment, but we'll have her in a few weeks. Perhaps, Mrs. Alderdice, you and Miss Alderdice would care to join us on a run with her when she comes." His gaze, like his son's, had a sleepiness in it that widened when he was excited.

"We should like that very much," said Larissa. "Won't we, Vivian?"

"I suppose so," said Vivian, looking down at the smudge of pudding on her dessert plate. The last thing on her mind at that moment was a yachting trip.

The waiters arrived on cue to remove the dinner dishes, bringing the coffee with them. Larissa and the elder Mr. Leblanc withdrew discreetly again to the balcony, leaving Vivian and Monte Leblanc in the parlor room, still within glancing distance but concealed behind the billowing curtains.

When they had gone, Vivian broached the subject. "Who was Ava?"

"My first wife."

"I gathered as much," she sighed. "The way your father looked at you."

Mr. Leblanc smiled a little. "Papa was trying to spare me."

"But one must move on," Vivian said, leaning back. "I remember you saying that. What was she like, if it's not an impertinence to ask?"

"Not in the least." He looked far away. "She was like her name. A delicate bird. Ah, my poor Ava!"

"I'm sorry she died," she said softly.

"I was a foreman in Peterborough in the mill," he said. "Still, it was hard for her. She and my son — they weren't very strong."

"I'm sorry," she repeated.

"The boy was more like her than me." His voice broke.

"A shame for both of them," Vivian sighed.

"Marie, my second wife, was very strong," he said. "She was what they call 'strong as a horse.'"

Vivian shifted in her seat. "Did she come from Peterborough too?"

He shook his head. "Lyons. Ah, but she loved riding and boating and fishing." His eyes were narrow with reminisces. "She even went on a hunt with us. She wanted to shoot a bear once, but, naturally, I wouldn't allow it."

"Naturally," Vivian echoed.

"She was excellent with a bow and arrow," he said. "All the men in town used to be afraid of her because of that." His face dulled. "Perhaps that's why the river took her."

"She died in an accident?" Vivian asked gently.

He nodded, twirling the coffee cup inside the circle of the saucer. "It was a dreadful storm. We ought not to have gone out, but she insisted. Sometimes, a woman can have too much courage."

Vivian felt a bristle in her chest at the thought of a young, spritely Frenchwoman caught in a storm because she had "too much courage." But she lowered her tone as she said, "They were both very devoted to you, I'm sure."

"When a man is young, he wants his wife to follow him." He put the cup on the tray and Vivian, recognizing the cue, offered to pour him another cup. "He's finding his own way of doing things, you know."

"I know." Vivian thought of her grandfather.

"But when a man is older, he wants more of a companion," he continued. "He isn't looking for the blind love of his youth. A woman is different, isn't she?" He looked at her.

Vivian hid a smile. "Not always. Many of us are reasonably practical."

"Forgive me, Miss Alderdice." He bowed. "I meant only that a man my age, he has his own life, his own interests. He hardly wants a woman clinging to him."

"I should think no man, at any age, would want that," Vivian remarked.

He rose and sauntered about the room, his hands in his pockets. "My father accuses me of having too modern ideas about family."

"I respect your ideas," she said, smiling.

"I'm not so sure your mother would," he said, chuckling. "I have a notion your mother and my father are in agreement on that subject."

"Mother has certain ideas about legacies and traditions," Vivian admitted. "But I don't necessarily favor them."

He glanced at her with a sly smile. "We're of one mind, then."

"Still, I can't deny," she continued, "My family raised me to believe there is nothing more sacred than tradition. And heirs to carry on the family name."

"Papa is that way!" He said this with such force that Vivian thought she saw Emile Leblanc turn his head from the balcony door. In a lower tone, he said, "Ever since I made my fortune, I believe it's been on his mind. He was even more devastated than I when my son died. And he was disappointed that Marie—"

Vivian looked into the unlit fireplace. "Miles and I never had a chance to even discuss it," she said. "He left four months after we were married." Her throat caught as she slipped her handkerchief from her sleeve. But she was not in tears.

~

The Leblancs left soon after with promises of an invitation to the yacht when it was in the Waxwood harbor. Just as they stepped into the elevator, Vivian saw a messenger step out, his gait quickening as he walked toward them, grasping the cream-colored envelope with the Waxwoodian seal in both his gloved hands. "For Miss Vivian Alderdice," he said in a clipped voice.

"I'm Miss Vivian Alderdice." Her heart beat faster as she took the envelope from the boy, who bowed and turned on his heel to scurry back down the hall.

"What is it, dear?" Her mother stepped into the doorway of her room.

Vivian slipped the envelope in the pocket of her dress. "It's nothing, Mother."

After she had readied for bed, she picked up the envelope again. The pape was elegant, and the handwritten *Miss Vivian Alderdice* showed an elegant script. Her breath sank as she thought it may not be from Nettie.

At a soft knock on the door, Vivian hid the note under her pillow and put the cover over her. Luckily, her mother had always held on to the rule that one did not burst into a room, even if the room belonged to one's children. Larissa opened the door carefully. Vivian could see her mother in the silver light from the hallway, dressed in her nightclothes. The shadow of the darkened room hid the features of her face and figure, and she looked almost like a shy child.

"Are you awake, dear?"

"I'm exhausted, Mother," Vivian said in a heavy voice.

Larissa sat at the edge of her bed. "Monte Leblanc looked a little solemn tonight. I hope you didn't talk about unpleasant things."

"He told me about his wives."

Her mother looked disappointed. "That's a rather morbid subject, isn't it?"

"Would you rather I have read him some of the more enlightening highlights from one of my books?" Vivian snapped.

"You don't want to appear to be too intelligent, dear," said Larissa. "Not at this stage of your courtship."

"Courtship!" She sat up. "Is that what this is?"

"His father thinks so," she said. "He seemed rather nervous, thinking they were taking liberties by coming to the suite at all."

"He's learned the rules of American high society in a hurry," Vivian remarked.

"So much so he's overdoing them," her mother answered dryly.

"It's little wonder he believes his son's ideas of marriage are too modern."

"Does he?" Larissa blinked.

"You know, Mother." Vivian propped herself up on one elbow. "I understand now why Monte Leblanc is trying so hard to find a wife this summer. His father is pushing him as much as you're pushing me. And for the same reason."

"I don't see that I've pushed you into anything," her mother objected. "You're the one who insisted we come here intending to meet him, if you recall."

"We both have our expectations," Vivian said. "The stone necklace has been placed around our necks because we're the only ones left in our family."

"If that's true," said Larissa slowly, "I'm sure Monte Leblanc will do his duty by his family, just as you intend to do yours."

Vivian looked into the pattern on the blanket. "It's such a waste. A waste of two lives, and possibly three, four, even five."

"Whatever do you mean?"

"He's not looking to marry for love," Vivian said.

"Well, neither are you." Larissa patted her hand. "Love ruins a woman, dear. Trust me. I know." A shadow crossed her face, graying the pale features.

"But if there isn't love, or, at least, respect and regard," Vivian insisted, "what use is it to fulfill a duty with emptiness, simply to fulfill it?"

"I don't think you need be concerned about what Mr. Leblanc

said." Larissa rose. "He was probably trying to appeal to what he believes is *your* sense of modernity."

"I thought I was rather old-fashioned." Vivian lay on her back.

"Not in your books or the way you speak, dear," said her mother.

"Do you think he has the notion from Fern that I'm a bluestocking?"

"If he has, I'm sure you've dispelled it by now." Larissa went to the door, then added, "You're a clever girl, Vivian. Use that cleverness to your advantage." She suddenly looked over her shoulder. "Who sent you that note?"

"Nothing important," Vivian murmured. "From a friend in town."

There was silence for a moment. Then, her mother said, "I thought it might be about your brother."

Vivian felt her blood go cold. "What makes you think that?"

"You looked troubled when the boy handed it to you," said Larissa. "As if you had been expecting it."

"You told me not to contact him ever." Vivian voice was bitter. "I've never gone against your orders, have I?"

"I never gave you orders," her mother insisted. "I'm trying to do what is best for us all. We've had too much unpleasantness these past years. Now, we finally have a chance for some peace."

Vivian thought with irony of the past few days. "Yes, it would be peaceful for us both if I were to become Mrs. Monte Leblanc."

"And just what you need in your life."

A pain shot through Vivian. "What do you mean, Mother?"

"You always accuse me of ignoring the truth," said Larissa. "But you don't like it when someone else shows you the truth you've been ignoring."

Vivian turned up the gas lamp on the night table and observed her mother's face illuminated by a yellow halo. "You're a shrewd one, aren't you, Mother?"

"I'm trying to make you see!"

"See what? That I'm not getting any younger?" Vivian's eyebrows arched. "That's what you meant, isn't it? You think I ought to grab the first man who asks me, like Cousin Emma did."

"I wouldn't go so far as that." Her mother's voice was reasonable. "But twenty-six is an age where a woman can expect little out of life if she's not married."

"You make twenty-six sound like ninety-six." Vivian grumbled.

"You can do a thousand times better than your cousin." Larissa leaned forward and rested her hand on top of Vivian's. "I only want your happiness. I know you and your brother never believed that, but it's what I've always wanted."

"I know that, Mother," Vivian said, her voice softening. "The trouble is, we don't have the same definition of happiness."

"Yes, I've learned that." Her tone was thick with remorse, and Vivian knew she was thinking of Jake.

She clutched at her mother's hand. "I promise I'll try to make you happy."

"I know you will, dear." Larissa patted her head. "You're starting in the right place with Mr. Leblanc. Neither of you have illusions about one another."

Her mother looked at her for a few moments in silence. Then she did something she hadn't done in years. She kissed Vivian goodnight. As she went out of the room, Vivian realized love was one of those things her mother had regulated to the Unmentionables.

She took the envelope from under her pillow. Inside was the message she had been waiting for:

Alda found the two men — Matthew Lord and Ember Warren. Matthew Lord is dead. Ember Warren is alive.

Address:
62 Clementina Street
San Francisco
Nettie

The morning after the Leblanc dinner, Vivian rose early, feeling as if she were emerging from under the surface of the sea. It was nearing the end of July, and the sweltering heat of mid-summer had descended upon them. Its pressure bore on her head and parched her throat. She reached for the crystal pitcher and water glass on the end table, but the water was warm and bitter.

She was just in time to catch the train to San Francisco. She sat in the parlor car, gazing at the scenery as it flickered by through the small, boxed windows. The little pieces of her grandmother's past that didn't fit flew past her just as the scenery outside the window: Grandmother's confinement when she had always prided herself on her good health; the sudden trip to Europe so soon after her mother was born; Bertha's strange behavior, strange, even for Bertha; and Evan in San Francisco just when her grandfather was away. She also could not forget the evasions and the lies from Ruth and Verina. What did it all mean?

Seven years ago, her idea of who she was as an Alderdice had been altered. Now, she had the same feeling of standing over

Pandora's box of woes, even more afraid than she had been before, to lift the lid.

She tried to think of more pleasant things, and her mind wandered to Monte Leblanc. There was no question his interest was genuine and had been since the beginning of the summer. Even the Washington Street ladies observed the way the man coveted her company during their excursions and activities in the daytime and cornered her in the hotel parlor in the evenings. Their previous apprehensions about her and Larissa were waning. Her mother sat near the head of the table with Mrs. Tisher, Mrs. Griffith, and Mrs. Bilton. For the first time in a year, social duties consumed Larissa's attentions, not to mention the senior Mr. Leblanc's cordial regards as exclusive to her as his son's were to Vivian.

And yet, as the train rumbled on the tracks, she couldn't help but feel her own bones shaking with apprehension. She wondered what it would really be like to be the wife of someone like Monte Leblanc. He had already hinted he would travel for long periods of time, and she — what would she do? She wanted to do something! She wanted to be out of this idle and self-absorbed life, living, like Amber, Coreen and Hannah, in the shadow of her socialite mother, filling in the gaps left free by Larissa's neglect. She wanted to do something that was really *something* and not nothing. Something she chose from her own free will, whether any husband she took approved of it.

She gradually dozed from the passing scenery, waking up only when the conductor called the next stop San Francisco. She felt almost as if she were awakening from a dream.

Skirts brushed against hers as women passed her, and men ran toward their train, excusing themselves hastily as they did so. Taxi cabs lingered outside on the curb, the drivers hunched in their seats like jockeys, waiting for the race to begin.

She found a taxi with an older man in the seat, his blond hair and beard streaked with gray, and gave him the address for

Ember Warren. The man glanced at her tailored suit, looking concerned. "That's well in South of Market, miss."

"What of it?" Vivian challenged him.

"Well, miss, it ain't a place for a young lady if you'll pardon my saying so, to be walking about." A side of his lip curved upward.

"I won't be walking about, if that's what worries you," Vivian said. "And I imagine where I walk about is my business."

"No offense intended miss," said the man briskly. "I have two daughters of my own, that's all."

Vivian gave him a warm smile. "I didn't mean to be short with you, sir. I appreciate your concern."

The man blinked at her under heavy brows, then shrugged and cracked the whip on his horse as it trudged through the muddy street.

She had never been to South of Market before, though some of the young men on Washington Street went there for a lark, dressing in ragged clothes to blend among the "tramps and dere-licts" who trailed in the dirty streets. As the cab turned into the narrow alleyway of Minna, she felt as if the buildings and resi-dences, topped off with straight roofs and fire escapes, were closing in on her. Debris gathered at the corners of the sidewalk, waiting for someone to take it away, and she had to cover her nose and mouth with her rose-scented handkerchief, for the stench of manure, old cooking, and sewage was overwhelming. Men loitered outside, their jackets too short for them and their sleeves torn, staring grimly at the cab. Children played on the sidewalks and on the steps of the buildings, and a few hung their legs and arms through the slots of the fire escape, ogling with their dark, wide eyes at the horse that pulled the cab. She saw no women anywhere.

She was glad when the driver reached Clementina and stopped near the number sixty-two, a half-crumbled building. But she saw windows with curtains on them, as if someone had attempted to make whatever lay between its pressing walls livable.

As she paid the driver, adding a generous amount over the fare, he lingered, his hand on the head of his horse. "Don't you want me to wait, miss?" Before she could answer, he resolved. "I think I'll wait."

"I don't want to keep you from your work," she said.

"No trouble, miss, no trouble," he said. "What I'm here for, ain't it?"

"Thank you," said Vivian, feeling relieved.

Two men lingered near the entrance, their heads turning as she passed. She understood the building had probably been a warehouse now converted into residences, but there was little privacy. Each floor she passed was like one gigantic space where families had set up their abode, with sheets hanging over lines as makeshift walls. There was at least less of the stench she had experienced outside, as a potent scent of cheap soap dominated. Washing hung on lines tied between posts, swinging back and forth from the bay breeze coming through the open windows.

The women she had not seen on the streets were here, doing housework, aprons tied to their waists. Vivian was conscious of the way their eyes seethed at her. She caught sight of several smoothing down their wrinkled skirts. She wanted to reassure them she couldn't care less about how they looked, but then, a frazzled-looking old woman clomped toward her as she began walking up the stairs to the last floor. Vivian felt her gnarled fingers plucking at the hem of her skirt. She stopped and turned to see the woman's crazed eyes and smiling lips bending down toward the fabric, smoothing it in her soot-covered hands, petting it like a favorite cat. She realized the women were as little concerned for the dirt on their skirts as she was. It was only that they wished for the linen that draped her figure. She had never felt so naked in her life.

She reached the last floor, flooded with light from the glass hatches on the roof. She could hear the cawing of birds above and saw their dark bellies against the glass panels, their scurrying feet slipping from panel to panel as if looking for their nests. The tapping and cawing made her shrink away, horrified that they might not realize a hatch was open and fall in.

"Ain't nothin' to worry about, miss," a grated voice spoke from the far corner. "They won't hurt you."

She caught sight of a young man, whose coloring was so pale, his features almost disappeared in the light. He was rail thin and his arms looked like sticks as they rose toward an easel positioned under one of the open hatches. Various artistic paraphernalia filled the room, like dirty easels, canvases, paints, blocks of wood and metal. Thin mattresses made a pattern in the middle of the floor.

She came toward him. "Are you Ember Warren?"

"Lord, no, miss," said the young man. "I'm the lamb what keeps away from the lion's jaws." Two other men, one working with clay, and the other with an easel, guffawed.

"Spenlow, you fusspot, now you know we're all one happy family," said the sculptor. "Don't give the lady no bad ideas about us." He bowed to Vivian.

"Is Mr. Warren here?" she asked in a lighter tone.

The sculptor jerked his head toward the back corner of the room. "If you lookin' for a portrait, Spenlow or Jewkes here will do just as well. And be a hel—be a sight more civil about it."

Vivian gave him a gracious smile. "That's very generous of you, but it's Mr. Warren I've come to see."

He shrugged. "Suit yourself. Warren!" he bellowed over her shoulder. "Lady come to see you. And mind you be a gentleman to her." Jewkes guffawed again and Spenlow blushed.

Vivian turned around, but all she could see was a dark figure lurking in the corner where the posts looked like heavy blocks. She gingerly made her way around the place, feeling a little flustered as she caught sight of male undershirts and shaving things, some thrown on the beds, others set neatly in a row near the posts. When she reached the back of the room, the figure came into sight.

Ember Warren reminded one of a lion with his mane of light hair and his face that looked ready to pounce. His stalky figure hunched over on the bed was also like a lion's, and the bed creaked in protest to the heavy way in which he stared at Vivian. His grizzled face bore an expression of bitterness. He did not smile.

"Mr. Ember Warren?" She leaned forward but kept at a distance.

"You're looking for a portrait, are you?" His eyes suddenly became uneven, one of them milkier than the other in the light.

"I wanted to speak with you."

"Talk takes me away from my work, you understand." He rose now and nodded toward an easel that showed a thin film of dust in the sunlight.

She understood immediately. "I wouldn't want your livelihood to suffer." She took her reticule in both her hands.

He attempted a smile, but it looked more like a grim smirk. "I don't suppose you would care to sit down? I still mind my manners, see." He whipped his head toward the back of the room. "Hear that, you sod? I still know how to treat a lady," the sculptor snarled at him from afar.

"I'd rather stand, thank you," she said coolly.

He took a step closer, and she drew her hands around her reticule. "You remind me of someone I once knew."

Vivian's heart jumped. "My grandmother, Penelope Alderdice."

"Don't remember names," he said. "Not even ladies' names."

"You knew a friend of hers very well," Vivian said. "Evan Jones."

The man scoffed. "Haven't heard that name in thirty years, I guess."

"Maybe forty?" she ventured.

"Maybe forty." He nodded. "I still got a memory sharp as a tack. For those who have a generous hand." He eyed the reticule.

Vivian took out a few bills. But when his hand reached out, she held them to her chest. "My hand is generous when I get what I pay for, Mr. Warren."

Jewkes and the sculptor howled, and Warren's cloudy eye gleamed with a vicious gaze in their direction. But when he looked at Vivian again, his face had relaxed, and he managed a grin. "You're a smart chit, ain't you? Like my auntie used to be. Couldn't cheat her." A gleam of regret crossed his face. Then he continued, "What do you want to know about Evan?"

"I understand he and his niece lived with you and a Mr. Matthew Lord."

Warren threw his head back and laughed, a pleasant, deep laughter. "Don't think anyone ever called Matt 'Mr' in his life. Not a proper lady, anyway." His face became distant. "Funny to think of it. Nothing but a hollow shell, those days."

Vivian asked gently, "Do you remember exactly when Mr. Jones came to live with you?"

The man leaned one hand on the post and the other on his hip, regarding her with amusement. "Now, why would I remember that especially?"

"Because he was your friend," Vivian said briefly. "And because he had a child with him. I don't imagine you're likely to forget a man with a child."

The two artists in the corner howled again, and Warren shot them another one of his savage looks, yelling, "Haven't you sods anything better to do than listen in on a gentleman's conversation with a lady?"

"Gentleman!" The sculptor spit on the floor. "Whiskey Willie is more a gentleman than you!"

"I'll—" He advanced toward them with a brutal look on his face, making the sculptor turn back to his clay and Jewkes fumble with his easel. He returned to Vivian, his voice more amiable. "I *was* a gentleman once. You won't believe it, I'm sure. Circumstances make a man grovel like a pig!" The last was a snarl.

"I believe you, Mr. Warren," said Vivian in a kind voice.

He blinked at her. "You're a decent one, miss. I'll tell you what you want to know, as much as I can. I can't remember when Evan came, but I remember when he left. Was March right after St. Patty's Day. I'm part Irish, see, and so was Matt, and we were out — well, celebrating. We come home at dawn to an empty flat. No Evan, no little girl."

"He didn't leave a note?"

"He weren't one for writing, miss," said the man. "Except for that diary of his. And maybe a letter or two to a pretty girl." The last made him grin.

Vivian perked up. "Any woman in particular?"

"Oh, there were a few." He was again staring at the bills in her hand. She held one out to him, and he snatched it without ceremony.

"Do you remember if he ever mentioned a Penelope Alderdice?" Then she quickly added, "He may have referred to her as Grace."

He cocked his head. "What'd she look like?"

"Like me." Vivian couldn't help but blush.

The man studied her with unblinking eyes. She noticed he turned so the clear eye was facing her, as if he wanted to see her better. "I recall a redhead coming around often. Thought she was Irish at first. Imagine my surprise when she turned out to be a blue blood!" He laughed.

Vivian felt her hands grow icy, and her bag slipped to the floor. She swooped down to pick it up before Warren reached it, but he was too swift for her. She watched him examine the embroidered handbag. "Shouldn't be so careless with your money, miss." Then he handed her the bag.

"Thank you," she said.

"You didn't think I'd try to take it from you, did you?" He eyed her. "I may have fallen on hard times, but I ain't no thief."

"No, of course not," she said briskly. "How often did this redhead come?"

"That I couldn't say."

"Mr Warren." She shifted to one foot. "I must ask you a bold question."

He chuckled. "I ain't one to shy away from a bold question. Not if you have the boldness to ask it."

"Do you think there was something between this redhead and Evan?"

"You mean, were they more than friends?" He was obviously enjoying her discomfort.

"Something like that," she mumbled.

"Can't say as I know for sure," he said. "But they were — how would your kind put it — they seemed on intimate terms." He said the last word with a delicacy as if he were picking up a lady's handkerchief off the floor.

"And what do you mean by 'intimate terms'?" Vivian eyed him.

"You're forcing me to be indiscreet, miss." His good eye loitered on the reticule in her hands. "A man don't like to be indiscreet without a reason."

Vivian took out a few more bills but held on to them. "I think you'll find it worth your while to tell me what you know, Mr. Warren."

He accepted this, sitting on the bed again. "There ain't anything disgraceful in it. I just meant it was more the way they were together."

"They stood close to one another?" Vivian asked.

"That," he said. "And this redhead — now that I come to see her again in my mind, I'd say she and you were nearly the spitting image — used to come often. Nearly every day at one time."

"But she was with you and Mr. Lord too, wasn't she?" Vivian asked.

"Only when it suited her," he said. "Evan said she was trying out her wings again, so to speak. Artistically, that is."

"What did he mean by that?" Vivian asked.

"Matt and I reckoned she hadn't had much practice." He stopped and opened a wooden box near the bed, taking out a crudely etched pipe and a pouch of tobacco. "Mind if I smoke?" Vivian shook her head. He continued as he filled the pipe with the care of a man who had once been less frugal with his smoking. "Looked to us she was once keen on art and then gave it up."

"Yes, that would make sense." Vivian nodded.

"Evan was helping her get into it again," he said. Then he chuckled. "The way of most artist when they have an interest. Helping others get their start."

"So he persuaded her to take up drawing again," Vivian said.

"He did indeed," the man declared. "Matt and I couldn't keep still for too long for fear she'd order us to pose for her."

"She drew people?"

"What did you expect she drew, apples?" The man eyed her with amusement.

"No," said Vivian. "Fish." She remembered Bertha's words: *every gill, every fin, and those eyes...*

The man burst out laughing. "Wish we'd have known that. We mightn't have been so impatient, if we knew what the alternative was."

"She came alone?" Vivian asked.

"What do you mean?"

"There was no one with her on her visits to your flat?"

Again, the seething humor showed through on the dirty face. "You mean did her husband come with her?"

"I didn't say that, Mr. Warren," Vivian snapped.

"Oh, we knew she was married all right," he said. "No ring or nothing — I expect she took it off — but we knew. And so did

Evan." He cocked his head. "Now that it comes to my mind, he was away then, wasn't he? Her husband, that is."

"He may have been," said Vivian.

"I recall something about a Malcolm Alderdice being in Europe or some such place," he said. "Malcolm your grandfather?"

"Yes." Vivian's blood turned cold.

"Cat's away, mice will play. I guess that's about right, eh?" He grinned.

"I'll thank you to remember my grandmother was a lady, Mr. Warren," Vivian said in a stony voice.

"Sorry, miss," he murmured. "Never was no doubt about that. She didn't put on airs, though. She liked the flat well enough. Said it had character." Again, he spoke with delicacy.

"She would have," said Vivian with a smile.

"Mind you, we had an attractive place then. Big, with a court-yard in the back. Owner was an elderly lady who thought grass and flowers were a gift from God that we oughtn't to squander. She took care of the place right nice." His voice echoed with nostalgia.

"Was Verina ever with them?" Vivian asked.

"Who?"

"Evan's niece."

"Oh, that one," he sniffed. "Kind of standoffish, but I expect she wasn't used to the city. Sometimes the noise bothered her, you know. Went around with cotton in her ears most of the time, unless Mrs. Alderdice asked her to pose."

"My grandmother drew Verina too?"

"'Course she did," he said. "Mrs. Alderdice drew anyone that would pose for her."

And Verina had told her she didn't know if her grandmother had ever visited the flat!

"Do you have any drawings of hers?" she asked. "Ones that she did of the flat, for example?"

"Not a one, miss," he said. "If I did, I'd give 'em to you, and that's the God's truth. I ain't one to keep what rightfully belongs to someone else." His fierce sincerity touched Vivian.

"Did she give them to Evan?"

"Not so's I remember."

"Then they might be somewhere in the house," Vivian lamented.

"Ain't likely she'd throw 'em away, husband or no husband." Then the man chewed on his pipe with some thoughtfulness. "Was your grandfather a tall man with a walking stick?"

Vivian fumbled with the strings of her pouch. "How did you know?"

"Matt and I went out carousing one night and got back at eleven or so," he said. "And just as we was coming up the stairs, a man like that was coming down. It was our floor, and there weren't no one there except us, so we knew he must've been to see Evan. Didn't speak, of course. Turned his back as if we were dirt."

"When did this happen?"

"Oh, few days before Evan run out on us," he said. "A week, maybe."

Her head reeled, and she looked up, waiting for the air to come out of the open hatch. She saw peering at her two black heads with black eyes of the birds, their cocking beaks making her feel suddenly sickened by the entire place.

She took out a few more bills and handed them to Warren. "I'm much obliged, Mr. Warren."

"It ain't nothing, miss." His good eye shone brightly as he counted the bills. "Look, if you're really wanting to know all about the redhead, ask her chittering friend."

"Friend?" She glanced at him.

"It suddenly come to me. Your grandmother didn't come to the flat with a man, but she visited with a lady. Little thing, round as a top, she was. She only came a few times. Didn't think she liked our place." He chuckled. "Heard her say once we were too 'naughty' for her."

"She had dark hair and a sweet face?"

"Something like that."

"Bertha," Vivian murmured.

"Reckon that was her name," he said. "Now, I've told you all I remember, miss."

"You remembered quite a lot, Mr. Warren," Vivian remarked.

His face looked almost young, with the marks of age removed from it at that moment. "When a man's better days are behind him, he remembers every detail, don't he?"

"Yes," said Vivian with a brief smile. "A woman does too." She turned toward the stairs, then turned back and held out her hand. She expected him to shake it, but he bent down and kissed it with unexpected chivalry. This earned a scoff from the other corner of the room.

Vivian approached the three artists and dug into her reticule, removing more coins and bills. She turned to Spenlow. "I think I can trust you, Mr. Spenlow."

The young man threw down his brush and gave her his attention, his mild face widening. "To the death, miss."

"I don't think we need go as far as that," she said, smiling. "Will you see that every artist who lives here gets a share of this?" She handed him the handful of money.

All three men eyed the gleaming coins and crisp bills lying in both Spenlow's cupped hands.

"Oh, miss!" the young man said. "You're too generous."

"Please take it," she said. "Consider it faith in your work." She glanced at the easels and clay behind them. "Not charity."

"We'd hardly care if it were charity," said the sculptor. "Some of 'em, they ain't seen a decent piece of meat in—"

"Quiet, Wallace!" The hiss came from Jewkes. In a more even tone, he said, "We're all much obliged, miss. You're a good sort. Ain't got no airs."

"I don't have airs, like she didn't have airs." She tried to give them a bright smile. "Good day, gentlemen."

She started for the stairs, but felt a soft grasp on her arm. She turned and looked into the bright eyes of Spenlow. They almost popped out of his head, his features were so thin. "Miss, I wanted to ask — would you — would you sit for me sometime?"

The man's eagerness touched her. "Maybe someday," she said.

"Someday," he repeated. He glanced down at the floor at his pointed feet which, attached to his thin legs, looked like a puppet's.

She felt the tears rising in her eyes and escaped down the stairs.

~

When the cab driver asked her where she wanted to go, she gave him the address of Alderdice Hall.

To call Alderdice Hall a "home" was an exaggeration, as, for Vivian, it had never been much of one. Rooms fed into other rooms and hallways led straight through to the garden with no turns or crevices. She had often been told how lucky she was to live in such a place. But the museum atmosphere had intimidated her as a child and now, as she let herself in with her key, she realized it still did.

She expected to see Basset, their butler, gliding out from some hidden corner of the house, his statuesque countenance showing no surprise at her being there alone. But for once the house was silent. They had left the servants to care for Alderdice Hall, and her mother, with her excellent powers of observation, had chosen the most devoted. Thus, as Vivian went down the hall peering into the parlor, dining room, and study, everything looked as dustless and tidy as if they had not been away for more than a month.

She went immediately to the room her grandmother had

occupied before her death. The oval windows looked at her like wide eyes, and everything was as it had been when she last entered it. Even the edge of the bedspread she had wrinkled with her hand was now smoothed down. Yet, the room still had the foreboding of one who had recently died.

Vivian searched in the drawers of the bureau and the large cupboard against the wall. She felt like a child again, the inquisitive little girl whose eyes were everywhere. She remembered once, just before Jake was born, she had wandered into her grandmother's room and had begun, with little thought, to open the chest at the end of her bed. The lid was so heavy that she had to grasp it in both her hands. Just as she pried it open, she felt a pair of eyes watching her and whirled around to see her grandmother standing in the doorway. A chill went through her, but Grandmother was almost pleased, smiling that serene smile of hers. She said, "It's good for a child to be curious." She put a light hand on Vivian's head. "Be as curious as you like, darling." Then she had walked out of the room.

There was nothing anywhere that resembled anything related to drawing, and certainly no drawings. Vivian left the room, closing the door carefully behind her as silently as she could in case a maid was lurking about.

Then it struck her. The room wasn't really Grandmother's. When her illness began, she had been moved there under the doctor's orders because by then, her legs were weak, and a room on the first floor had become necessary. Vivian remembered the day two vigorous men had carried down the stretcher, Grandmother drowsy under the influence of sleeping powders. Then Annie packed some necessary things in Grandmother's suitcase and took them down to her. Surely, Annie wouldn't know to take Grandmother's drawings down to her.

This was where she needed to go — to Grandmother's old room.

Just as she climbed the first flight of stairs, a door opened, and

Basset emerged. He showed no surprise or any other emotion upon seeing her.

"Have you come back already, miss?" The glassy eyes never left her.

"I'm only in the city for the day," she said. "I found myself short of money for the train, so I came here to get some."

"Yes, miss." He bowed.

"Don't let me disturb you in your work, Basset." She started up the stairs.

"Shall I have Anthony prepare the carriage?" he asked without turning toward her.

She looked at him over her shoulder. "Whatever for?"

"To take you to the station, miss." He said this with a little tone of surprise.

Vivian's shoulders relaxed. "Oh, yes, naturally. I won't be long. Thank you, Basset."

He bowed again, and turning on his heel, went down the stairs.

Vivian hurried first to her mother's room, where Larissa kept a silver box with cash, in case anyone should need it, and took only a few dollars. Then she crossed the stairwell into the left wing and went to her grandmother's old room.

Here, too, nothing had changed. She marveled at how different this room was. The modest surroundings of the downstairs gave way to a lush carpet of tulips running in stripes up and down the entire room. She entered the front Grandmother had once called "my little playroom" with its rounded, puffy chairs where one could sit comfortably and read for hours, and the fireplace and bookshelf. Curtained doors led into the bedroom and the four-poster bed draped in pink and white tulle. The windows here were not watchful eyes but pleasant squares that let in light and did not compromise privacy.

Vivian felt tears well up as she thought of how she used to rush into the room before bedtime as a child, when her grandmother retired after she had had enough of the upstairs parlor with Grandfather and Larissa. Grandmother would sit on a chair facing the fire, a book in her lap or her knitting beside her. But she would always put aside whatever she was doing and take Vivian to her lap. Usually, they would open the curtains of the two largest windows and look out at the stars. The room had a view of the bay in the daytime, but at night, the blue-black sky absorbed the bay, and the stars came down to earth, dancing on the edge of the water. Her grandmother had tried to teach Vivian about them, but something in Vivian's mind could not grasp these cosmic pieces of light, though Jake took to it quickly.

Vivian broke into a sob. She wished she had been more attentive to Grandmother's creamy voice telling her about the North Star and the Big Dog, while she had only squinted at the carpet of black, thinking all the stars looked the same. She knew now when Grandmother was at Brandywine, she and Evan had looked at the stars together.

She began searching in the closet, still hung with some dresses her grandmother had worn as a young woman, with the full crinolines. She fingered one in pink tulle, recognizing it as the dress Grandmother had worn to her own debutante ball and in which she shone, as bright as a diamond, posing with her pink handkerchief for the portrait by Willis Cox. She let the sleeve lie in her hand, remembering how Grandmother had not wanted her to wear them for her own debutante ball because "dresses have unhappy memories too."

Finding nothing else of interest in the closet, she looked in every drawer, corner, and alcove she could find. But it was barren, as if so many things that had been a part of Grandmother had disappeared, perhaps floated into heaven with her. As Vivian sat on the bed, feeling sad and dejected, she realized so much of what she had known of her grandmother had been a part of the persona that was Penelope Alderdice, "celebrated socialite and benevolent lady." The modest jewels, epistolary paraphernalia, appointment books, all those things she thought of when she thought of Grandmother, had not belonged to Grace Carlyle, the woman she discovered years ago.

The thought made her feel less weighed down by a sense of loss, and she rose, making her way toward the door. Just as she passed the fireplace, she faced the corner near the closet that was closed off by a curtain. It was odd, that curtain, and she let her fingers flutter against it, feeling the grittiness of the dust. She thought with amusement of how Annie, who kept the room in order, had neglected that space.

There was another slim door behind the curtain that led into a cabinet on the wall. With little thought, she flung it open. Three small shelves stood with tiny china knick-knacks, now pushed back to reveal a space in the wall. Reaching her hand in, she pulled out a carved wooden box.

The box held a sapphire necklace and a string of pink pearls Vivian recognized as the ones in Cox's painting of her grandmother as a debutante. Both were as pristine as if the maid had polished them only that morning. A sapphire lotus blossom with spiky petals protruded from the setting. Her hands trembled as she turned the necklace over in her hands. *For better or worse, expectations hang around our necks like a stone necklace,* Grandmother had written Great-Grandmother Joanna when she was a young woman.

She dropped the necklace in the box, feeling the burn of its icy stones. As she slipped it back in the hiding place, her fingers rubbed against rough pages. She reached both hands in and pulled them out. They were her grandmother's drawings all right, ones she did not burn, as her mother insisted seven years ago.

The first pages were not what she expected. Instead of black lines, she faced a portrait of her grandmother looking young. She remembered the letter Grandmother had written on Christmas of 1852 about the portrait she received from Evan Jones. A shiver ran down her spine when she realized she was looking at the face of a woman twice dead, first in body at fifty-nine, and again, as a young, spirited woman who had taken the name Grace for a summer.

She felt indebted to the man she had never met for capturing her grandmother just when the light had blazed around her as one saw the light around the heads of angels in Renaissance paintings. Evan Jones had captured her "untarnished loveliness," as Bertha's mother had described it. And yet, she could also see the darkness and the angular coldness in the face and posture, and she understood why her grandmother had written in the letter that there had been also mendacity in the expression.

Vivian carefully set the portrait aside and picked up what was now a slightly frayed sketchbook. It bore no title, and the cover was bare. It felt heavy, possessed with the markings of the woman who had dared to veer from her path of expectations. And yet, like Pandora's box of woes, Vivian was afraid suddenly to open it. But then, she remembered she had not chosen to take the path this time. She had allowed chance to pique her curiosity, but others out of the past were steering.

She pulled back the first page. The startled face of a man with square cheekbones and large, dark eyes gazing up at her. She knew from having seen portraits of Evan Jones that this was the man her grandmother once loved. Though the drawing couldn't have been made more than a year after the others she had seen seven years before, the countenance had transformed. Those portraits had been of a man with the face of a boy. This one was of someone who had absorbed enough pain to turn those boyish cheeks into hollows. Vivian understood she was looking at the face of a man who, within a year, had lost his sister, his lover, and his home.

Wind rattled against the windows. She thought she heard Basset calling her, though she knew it was only the echo of voices left behind in such a large house as Alderdice Hall. She went through the sketchbook a little quicker, her eyes lingering on faces she recognized. She saw a few sketches of Ember Warren as a young man and was stunned to see joviality and affection shone through his bright face. Another man appeared in the sketches, this one with hair over his forehead and a devilish smile. Vivian judged him to be Matthew Lord. Both men were more like practice portraits, drawn from every angle in small size, as if her grandmother had been trying to get the feel of the features.

Drawings of Evan filled the last pages. These were more matured, the faces fleshed out and the backgrounds more concrete. She could see the furniture in the background of what looked like a charming, though scantly furnished, flat. She understood Warren's nostalgia. It did look as if it had a coziness Vivian would hardly have thought possible from three bachelors.

She closed the sketchbook, and, as she turned it over to return it to the space, she saw her grandmother had drawn on the back. There was no mistake in the figure of a little girl, her eyes haunting and her hair tumbling across her shoulders. Vivian felt her head swim with anger. Verina had lied to her, just as she had seven years ago. She held the sketchbook to her, although it was dusty, and she knew it would leave marks on her clothes. Here was something so precious that, like a dying bird, its heart would stop beating if she let it go.

She took the sketchbook with her. As she passed Basset while he held the front door open for her to descend into the waiting carriage, she could feel his impassive eyes on it, as if he knew what she had taken, but he remained his usual silent self.

CHAPTER 13

The train reached Waxwood in the early evening. As she stood on the platform, she faced the stretch of bay alongside the train station and the back of the hills. She could almost see shining eyes peering at her between the glossy leaves furled together, wide eyes regarding her with worry and curiosity, as if to say, "What have you now? What do you intend to do?"

She stumbled a little, feeling a hand catch her arm. "Everything all right, miss?" The station master was peering at her.

Her Alderdice demeanor took over, and she straightened, pinning her shoulders back. "Yes, thank you."

"Wind's a bit railing this evening, miss." He pulled up his collar. "Best get home before the rain begins to pour."

"Home." Her lip quivered as she thought about the giant house sitting on top of Nob Hill that was Alderdice Hall. "Home." She repeated the word to the man's empty gaze, feeling her composure once more. "Yes. I'll go home."

She moved toward the main road, catching sight of the ferry waiting at the pier, but she continued down the street, passing the shops, the more plebeian hotels, and the restaurants, many of which were closing for the night. She turned at the park and walked into Nettie's.

She immediately felt the cheerful glow of the gaslights Nettie had lit, realizing for the first time how many of them there were. Then she realized there were, in fact, few, but light carried from candles spread all around the store: sitting on the counters, on boxes, in bowls and plates and even a few in candelabras. The light sent milky shadows bobbing across the ceiling and walls in unidentifiable shapes, though Vivian could see, as she unwrapped the coat around her shoulders and hung it on the rack, they were figures of women. There were, in fact, three women seated at the soda fountain, and they had all turned on their stools to examine the newcomer when the bell hanging above the door rang as Vivian entered.

All three wore identical starched cotton shirtwaists, dark skirts and no jackets. All three had hair in the pompadour style, but the pins sagged a little. All three looked tired but cheerful. Vivian recognized them as working women like the ones she saw dragging about down Market Street with their worn boots and impassive faces.

As with the women in the South of Market warehouse, Vivian felt self-conscious in her unwrinkled suit and considered putting her coat back over her shoulders as she neared the soda fountain. But two of the ladies smiled and saluted her as if she were an old friend.

Nettie, who had been arranging sandwiches on plates for the trio, set them down and, wiping her hands on her apron, motioned for Vivian to follow her to the back of the store. Vivian could see her brows furrowing toward the bridge of her nose and her straight lips etched with worry.

"You look the worse for wear," she said in a low voice.

"I'm all right." Vivian brushed her forehead with her hand. She realized she had not taken off her gloves. "I went digging for old relics."

"So I gathered." Her friend took out a handkerchief, coarse but clean, and began brushing Vivian's skirt. Vivian looked down and realized with dust from the cabinet in the wall of her grandmother's room had left patches on it.

"I didn't even notice," she said absently. "Is that why they were so amiable?"

"Who?"

"Those women out there," said Vivian. "They think I'm one of them. Dust on my clothes, my hair untidy." She was aware the pins holding up her own pompadour had also slackened. "I wish I were." Her voice suddenly boomed through the little room. "God, I wish I were!" The tears standing in her eyes finally broke through, and she covered her face with her hands.

She felt herself being almost lifted across the floor and led to a quiet space, seated on a hard chair. A door closed beside her. She let the sobs come, filling her hands as when she was a child and would rush to the stream in the woods, gliding her hands across the surface of the water to gather the lilies floating above. But they always ran away from her, and one day, she fell to the ground, digging her hands into the mud. When her tantrum subsided, she saw her grandfather was standing there. He had been, in her six-year-old eyes, like a Cyclops, rarely smiling, never affectionate, and disappointed his first grandchild was a girl. But at that moment, he stood in the sunlight, his flaxen hair beginning to show gray streaks, his hands in his pockets, grinning. The grin was genuine, as if they shared a joke. He bent down and helped her up, brushing away the muddy leaves that had stuck to her knees and dress. Then he said, "Don't let what you want get away. You can't stop, not even for despair."

His words stayed with her like the song of the birds in the trees on that day. It was the first time her grandfather had spoken to her seriously, as if she were a person rather than merely a girl whom everyone must tolerate until the coveted heir to the family arrived, which he had in the form of Jake only two years prior.

As she sat in the wooden chair, her gloved hands still covering her face, but her tears gone, she saw why Grandfather had spoken to her like that on that day. Jake was born a sickly child and outgrew his sickliness only when he reached school age. He had been puny for his age, and the doctors were always warning Larissa to take him out into the sunshine. The excursion in the woods had been for his benefit. She knew her grandfather had been worried about what the years would make of his pale and placid grandson. He had seen in Vivian that day a semblance of what he called "the Alderdice spirit," wasted, perhaps, on a girl child, but still present.

She took her hands away from her face, feeling more composed. She was in a tiny room piled with boxes and a small window on the opposite wall. Nettie had dropped a damp towel on one of the empty crates, and she dabbed at her face and eyes, welcoming the coolness. She also wiped off her skirt and used the small round mirror hanging on the door to set the pins in her hair. She looked presentable as she slid the door open and ventured into the store.

Nettie had been chatting with the young ladies, but now she darted toward her, a smile on her lips. "The imp went back into his cave?" she asked. Vivian blinked, and the woman laughed. "My mother used to say that after a good crying spell."

"I'm sorry." It was all she could manage.

Nettie took her hand and squeezed it. "I used to do that nearly every day for two years after Mama died."

"That's why you were prepared," Vivian said, managing a smile as she thought about the wet towel and mirror.

Nettie nodded, taking her arm. "Have a bite to eat?"

"I ought to go," said Vivian. "I don't know why I came, anyway."

"It doesn't matter why," said the woman. "The point is, you came."

"Perhaps I wanted to avoid returning to the hotel," Vivian said with a sigh. "I dread going back now to the mundane gossip. I hardly know how to make myself agreeable."

"To a certain party?" Nettie asked slyly.

"*That* party at least might agree if I were to keep my lips sealed and only nod behind my fan." Vivian gave her a wary look. "It's the others I'm worried about. Especially my mother."

"Stay in town, then," said Nettie.

"Is there room at one of the hotels on the main street?"

"You wouldn't need one," said her friend in a firm voice. "I'll give you my bed."

Vivian was so touched that she almost felt the tears well in her eyes again. "I couldn't think of it."

"You didn't," Nettie said. "I did."

"But your own bed—"

"I have a large couch I slept in when Mama was alive," she said. "It became like an old friend to me when she was ill." This last made a flash of the lost look appear in her eyes.

Vivian grasped her hand. "I don't think I've ever known anyone as generous as you, Nettie."

"When one holds out one's hand to someone else, one forgets about one's own troubles," she said softly. Then her voice became bright. "Come, I'll teach you how to work the soda fountain, and you can make those crows a milkshake. You ought to learn a new skill." She winked.

She let the woman lead her to the trio engaged in a lively discussion.

"And where do you think those women will go if they don't have money for bread and milk for their children?" One of them, whose hair was as fiery red as her green eyes were ablaze, challenged the other two. "The streets, that's where!"

"Must you be so vile, Odele?" the young woman sitting at the end answered. Her hair, a little too bleached for Vivian's taste, outlined her sallow skin. "We know what you mean."

"Then you ought to know it's a crime to waste your time on

union meetings when you could be with me at the YWCA picketing the city hall so those partridge men will give more to these women," the one named Odele declared.

"I don't think Sue is wrong in that," said the third young lady, a quiet-spoken woman of indiscriminate countenance. "Factory girls need as much aid as widows."

"But they've no children to care for!" Odele screeched.

"My dear, you mustn't scare the mice away with that siren of yours," said Nettie in a wary voice. "Chocolate or strawberry?"

"I've no stomach for it," the woman muttered.

"Oh, yes you do," said the blond, laughing. "You need a bit of sugar to sweeten your tongue, Odele."

The woman considered this. Keeping her eyes on them, she said, "Chocolate, I suppose."

There was quiet for a time as Nettie showed Vivian how to shake up the milk, cream, and syrup. Vivian's hand was adept at using the cocktail shaker and, as she placed the drink in front of Sue, the blond. The girl smiled. "Are you Nettie's new helper?"

Vivian shrank back. "Just a friend."

"So are we all," said the third woman. She held out her hand across the counter. "Lena Hill. Pleased to make your acquaintance." She then introduced Sue Bagstock and Odele Redfern. The last gave Vivian a critical eye from head to toe. Vivian almost wished she had kept the dust and wild hair.

"What do you think ought to be done about the widows?" she shot out.

"I beg your pardon?" Vivian was suddenly feeling a little hazy, and she realized she had not eaten since breakfast. When she gave Nettie a helpless look, her friend, as if reading her mind, sat her down on a stool and began making her a sandwich.

"Are you one of the Tea Cake Sistren?" asked the woman in a sly voice.

The other two burst out laughing. Nettie, however, did not laugh. "Odele is rather harsh on ladies who use their wealth to help their more unfortunate sisters," she explained. "Like the Bay Area Women's Social and Political Rights League."

Vivian thought about the meeting she had attended with Marvina the year before. She could not deny it *had* looked more like a tea party than a suffragist meeting. "I'm not one of the League," she muttered.

"You may be interested to know, Odele, that, regarding the widows, Vivian happens to be one."

"I'm not talking about *that* kind of widow," the redhead sniffed. "I'm referring to the work widows, the women left with no coin because the crass giants of industry won't pay compensation when one of their machines eats a husband's arm or leg. The widows left without a penny and three or four mouths to feed."

"I feel sorry for them, naturally."

"Naturally," the woman mocked. "And *that* is precisely the problem."

"I thought that YWCA of yours was doing wonders with legislation," said Miss Hill, stirring the straw in her vanilla milkshake.

"We do what we can, pet," said Miss Redfern. "But the supply cannot meet the demand."

"You sound like one of those crass giants of industry you described." Vivian eyed her.

"And you look like the daughter of one." The woman eyed her back.

Vivian looked down at her now empty plate, the crumbs scattered across the wilted lettuce Nettie had placed for garnish. "You're mistaken."

"Oh?" The shape of the woman's mouth was more oval than round.

"I'm the granddaughter of one," she said.

"Well, at least you admit it," snapped the redhead. But though she was disgusted, the other two young women nodded with approval.

"You can't fault the BAWSPR." Nettie leaned both arms on the counter. "We're doing what we can for the widows. We just sent a truck loaded with vegetables and fruit from Greer's, and I contributed blankets—"

"Fruit! Blankets!" Miss Redfern nearly spit the words out.

"A contribution is a contribution, Odele," Miss Bagstock reminded her.

"What about Greer buying tomatoes and herbs in the settlement house gardens from the ladies? What about you selling the knitted blankets they make in your store?" Her face was now as fiery as her hair.

"I don't understand," Vivian said, accepting the coffee Nettie put in front of her.

"When one gives charity to a woman, it ends there," Miss Redfern said. "But when one lets a woman earn her own bread, she may have a lifetime of earnings and the will to give her children more than just bread besides." Miss Redfern cocked her head, regarding Vivian with molded eyes.

Vivian couldn't help but admire this wiry woman whom, she could now see, was not as young as she first thought. Freckles hid the lines on her skin and around her mouth and jaw. The brightness of her eyes showed the years of struggle and forbearing. "I see what you mean."

"Do you?" Her brow jumped.

"You're a contradiction, Odele," said Miss Hill. "You rage against charity, and yet, you tell Sue she's wasting her time with the union when it is just that sort of do-for-oneself the union is for."

"It's a matter of priority, pet," said the woman. "The widows need more now than the working girls with their call for ten-hour days and thirty cents more a week. The starving children need food now. Food, not books." She gave Nettie a meaningful look.

"But what Nettie wants is precisely what you want," Miss Bagstock argued. "Books educate one to work, don't they?"

"Oh, how naïve you are, pet!" Miss Redfern exhaled with her exasperation and began slipping her gloves on her hands.

"I don't think it's naïve," Miss Hill said, adjusting her hat. "All women, widow or factory girl or otherwise, can benefit from reading books. And the reading room would probably be the smallest bit of solitude most women will ever have. Especially the widows, who always have their children clinging to their skirts."

Miss Redfern rose, looking at Nettie. "I don't question your intentions, pet. You, more than anybody I've met, have the right spirit. I only think it rips a page out of those Tea Cake Sistren's book. Cultivate a lady's refinement, and the rest will follow." She said the last with such a nasal haughtiness that even Vivian had to laugh, as it was close to how Larissa sounded.

The trio left, tossing their coins on the counter with the nonchalance of a wealth they did not possess and waving with warmest regards. When she and Nettie were alone, she turned to her. "Your friend has a rather narrow view of what you do."

"Odele's a good sort," said Nettie. "She's a woman with ideas."

"A woman with ideas is generally open to other ideas," Vivian remarked.

"She's had a hard life, Vivian," she said. "Came from Ireland during the famine. Few were kind to the Irish then, nor are they very kind now."

"I don't begrudge her the right to be angry," Vivian said. "I envy her, in a way. She's doing something. They're all doing something."

Nettie glanced over her shoulder at Vivian with a smile. "They do something all right. They spend every free moment showing women how to earn their own bread."

A wind blew in, patting Vivian on the back, and she turned around to find the door the ladies had shut behind them was now open. Her arms instantly went to her chest, feeling protective of her breath and space. Standing in the doorway was a tall, sturdy man with wild hair and clothes reeking of damp leaves.

The face was the same one she had seen that day at Brandywine.

She could make out two dark eyes fixed on Nettie, who had come out from behind the soda fountain, her face showing the impassiveness and caution of a store proprietor. Vivian doubted the man even saw her. Underneath the overgrown hair, his forehead wrinkled, and his entire face looked as if it were lit by agitation.

"Have you some witch hazel?"

Vivian had been unsure of the blurred figure she saw at Brandywine, going only by the feeling that had washed over her. But there was no mistaking the voice.

"To what purpose?" Nettie asked with some trepidation.

"A man's had an accident in the woods."

"What is the cause?"

"What does it matter?" The man's voice shook with annoyance. "Do you have it or don't you?"

"I may have some in the back," she said. "It's not the sort of thing I keep out on display."

His voice became less pointed and more cultured. "Will you please be so good—"

"Good evening, Mr. Stevens." Vivian chose that time to speak.

Harland Stevens looked at her with the full force of the dark eyes. His ginger-headed mane no longer offered the tin shade she remembered from the year before, nor was his pleasant countenance and amiable smile conveyed with the charm she had begrudgingly admitted he possessed. Here was a man who had aged, his color darkened, and his face worn by the elements. It was as if he were half-savage.

"Good evening, Miss Alderdice." He spoke in the mild-mannered voice she remembered, the only thing that remained of the old Harland Stevens. "I'm surprised to see you here again."

"I'm sure you are." Vivian glared at him.

He looked around, but Nettie had disappeared. "Is there any reason I shouldn't be?"

"You can ask that?"

"You're looking very well," he said. "Time has been good to you."

She cocked her head. "It hasn't been as good to you."

He laughed the deep laugh Vivian remembered that had a way of sweeping joy out of everyone else. But she felt anything but joyous.

"Perhaps you're right," he said. "Time does not welcome some of us with such open arms as it has you."

"One's deeds tell on the face," she said. "Have you ever read Mr. Oscar Wilde's novel?"

"I have gotten out of the habit of reading these days." His eyes anxiously pointed toward the back of the store.

She leaned against the counter. "Mr. Wilde wrote about a man named Dorian Gray. He was a wealthy young man with goodness in his heart. But an older man whose cynicism and self-destruction tainted everything he said and did led Mr. Gray astray."

His dark eyes arched with pain and anger. "I suppose you consider that an apt allegory of my friendship with your brother."

"The years passed as Mr. Gray sank further into sin and vice," she went on. "But time was good to Mr. Gray. He remained a beautiful youth, but there was no hiding from the ravages of his shame because a portrait of him hung in a secret place grew as devilish outwardly as he grew inwardly."

"I see." Mr. Stevens was now more interested. "I suppose you're going to tell me the young man came to a terrible end."

"He did indeed," said Vivian. "Only because he tried to kill the portrait. One cannot kill the ravages of time, can one?"

"No, they are as clear as any heartbeat," said Mr. Stevens. "So, we are two sides of this Mr. Gray. I am the portrait, and you are the young man. But is not one the mirror image of the other?" He looked at her with a keen eye.

She felt the rage swarm inside her like a hive of bees and turned away from him, staring down at the marble counter. The swirling patterns kept her occupied until Nettie emerged from the back with a bottle. "I imagine you will need cotton."

"Yes, miss," he said.

She brought the cotton balls and put the items near the cash register.

Here, Mr. Stevens' head bent like a little boy caught stealing candy. "I'm afraid I have no money."

"No money!" Vivian scoffed.

"If you give me what I need, I shall return any time you say and work for you until I pay them off."

"Don't believe him, Nettie," Vivian said in a hard voice. "Mr. Stevens is wealthy. He even lives in a castle."

"The ointment is for a young man your brother knew and liked," he said patiently. "I'm sure you wouldn't want him to suffer because of your hard-heartedness."

Vivian felt the shame burning her cheeks, as if someone had struck a match to them. "I'm sorry."

He looked at her for a silent moment, then turned to Nettie. "The boy was exposed to hogweed. He's very uncomfortable at the moment."

"I imagine he is." Nettie removed her apron. "I've taken care of quite a few illnesses in my time, sir. I would be happy to accompany you—"

"No!" The word came with such violence, it almost shook the walls of the small store. In a more measured tone, Mr. Stevens added, "That is very thoughtful of you, but I have quite a skill for such things myself."

"You protest rather suddenly, Mr. Stevens," Vivian remarked.

"I wouldn't want to put the lady out," he said. "I'm sure she has better things to do than nurse a panicking boy."

"Very well," Nettie said. "However, there is no need for you to come back and work off the payment." She put the items in a paper bag.

"No, miss." His voice gained a confident ease. "I can't accept those terms."

"I insist," her friend was just as firm. "Take them with my blessing and Godspeed to the boy."

But Stevens remained with his hands at his side. "Please, miss. It's a point of honor with me."

"Honor!" Vivian snarled under her breath.

She knew Mr. Stevens had heard her, as the muscles of his neck strained. But his voice was as mild as ever as he continued, "Perhaps we can make a bargain. When does your next stock arrive?"

"Thursday morning."

"I shall be here early Thursday morning," he said with a bow. "I imagine I could do the work of a day for you in a few hours."

"I imagine you could," said Nettie, returning the smile.

He took the bag with words of endearing gratitude. Nodding at Vivian, he turned on his heel and started toward the door.

She called out, "Mr. Stevens!" The man turned around. "You haven't asked how Jake is." He looked stunned for a moment and she couldn't help but add, a little viciously, "Don't you want to know how your protégé is doing?"

"I hope he is doing well," he said in a quiet voice.

"If you were to ask my mother — you remember my mother, don't you?" He nodded silently. "If you were to ask Mother, she would tell you Jake is doing splendidly. She tells people he decided he needed more artistic training and went to Paris to study with a master recommended by an old friend of hers."

The words had their effect on Mr. Stevens. The man's dark eyes dampened, and the hard lines in his forehead sagged. He clutched the bag in his hands as if it were a child. "Perhaps it's better that way, Miss Alderdice."

"Much better to lie than to tell the truth, you mean?" Vivian asked. "For you, I'm sure it is. After all, the truth, the real truth, is so sordid." She felt almost triumphant as she saw the bag slipping from his hands. But he caught it in time.

He spoke in a soft tone, "I've always admired your courage, Miss Alderdice." He turned to the door again.

"I spoke to your cousin Roger the other day," she continued.

She heard Nettie say in a low voice, "Vivian, stop."

"He and I had a long chat," she said. "He doesn't care what you do, of course."

"I'm very much aware of that." Mr. Stevens' voice was hard.

"But he told me your mother is rather worried about you."

This put the final clutch on the man. His entire figure stooped, and he held on to the doorknob as if trying to regain his balance. Vivian felt a rush of remorse, realizing her lashing tongue had gone too far.

"Perhaps I shouldn't have said anything," she said apologetically.

"No, Miss Alderdice," he snapped. "You shouldn't have." He glanced back at her, his eyes blinking as if fighting tears, then pulled the door open and walked out. Vivian felt her hands trembling as she closed it after him, the scent of fresh pine and mud falling behind him.

"You weren't generous, Vivian." Nettie's voice was firm. "He was trying to help this boy."

"I know how Mr. Stevens helps young men," said Vivian. "He tried to help my brother last year." She whirled around, confronting her friend. "I never told you where Jake is, did I?"

"I don't ask questions." Nettie went to pull down the shades of the shop.

"I don't mind telling you," Vivian said. "My brother is in jail. Mr. Stevens as good as put him there."

Nettie didn't say a word. She merely locked the door, hung the CLOSED sign, and then returned to Vivian, where she put her hands on her shoulders. They felt warm and strong.

CHAPTER 14

It was the first time Vivian had spent the night on the other side of the Waxwood bay. Unlike her room at the Waxwoodian, there was no sign of pomp in Nettie's small flat. Its thin curtains whipped out from the breeze of the open windows as if they would tear away at any moment. The floor was bare wooden panels except for a smattering of small rugs that looked as if they were made some time ago. The scents of past dinners lingered in the single room in which Nettie slept on the couch to give Vivian the bed, and Vivian's eyes nearly watered from past vaporous odors of onion and garlic. And, yet, she felt more comfort here than she ever had in any of the lavishly furnished rooms of Alderdice Hall or any of the elegant hotels or pensions they had stayed at. Here, invisible warm arms embraced her, holding in all the confusion that cluttered her mind. Here she was safe.

Because of this, she slept well, even with the occasional jolt of a howling dog on the street or the tin sound of footsteps on the sidewalk. She did not wake up at five o'clock in the morning when, as Nettie had warned her, the truck for the produce stand roared down the street. When she did finally wake up, she felt a weight had been lifted in the arms of the nightmare phantom, the bright sun streaming through the windows and the scent of eggs and bacon softening the onion and garlic. Nettie had lent her a nightgown and, as the former wearer had been taller and stockier than Vivian, she sat up and felt one side peeling away from her shoulder. The wind increased, and goosebumps appeared on her arm.

"Here." Nettie tossed her a knitted shawl. "I ought to have told you the bay sometimes accosts us with an icy breeze here in the mornings."

"I've been waking up to the sea for over a month now," Vivian reminded her, wrapping the knit around her. It was warm and soft.

Nettie grinned. "The difference between the bay and the sea wind is like that of Nob Hill and South of Market," she said. "They may linger in the same place, but one has the refinement the other lacks."

"Yes, so I've seen," Vivian said, thinking of her visit to Mr. Warren and the ladies she had passed on her way.

Nettie turned over the bacon strips with a fork. "I suppose you won't sniff at a cracked sink for your morning wash?"

As Vivian played with pins for her hair, Nettie glanced at her and said, "The cupboard is full of them if you need more."

Vivian saw a low cupboard with several drawers. She bent down and opened the cabinet doors. The hollow space was immaculate and nearly empty, except for a small structure that looked like a doll's house. There lay two faded photographs. One was of a woman, which looked to be from forty or fifty years ago, and the other with the same woman, a little older, and a child. Several trinkets, of high quality but as faded with use as the cupboard, were arranged on the structure floor with impeccable care. In the center was a small candle and a wooden cross.

As Vivian looked at them, she felt like she had intruded upon a private moment. She realized who the woman in the photographs was and what the structure was for.

Behind her, Nettie's damp voice said, "The pins are in the drawers."

Vivian rose. "I'm sorry," she said. "I didn't mean—"

"It doesn't matter," said the woman briskly. She opened the drawer and put the pins in Vivian's hand.

"Nettie," she ventured, "don't you think—"

"I don't think," interrupted her friend, her voice more sad than angry. "Not yet, anyway." She trailed back to the kitchen.

Vivian returned to the mirror and put up her hair so her face looked clear and ready. But the sadness of Nettie's voice had crept into her veins.

The table was already set with what looked like a costly set of china, though when she sat down, she saw it was shabby and well used, as if it had come down through the generations. "May I help?" she asked.

Nettie nodded toward the table. "You can cut the tomatoes. Mama always insisted on them with the morning meal. She said they were like plump, smiling children sitting at the table."

Vivian laughed and sliced them carefully into round disks. She was conscious of Nettie watching her.

"You know, Vivian, I give you credit for having more spark than most of those sugar-water friends of yours," she finally said.

Vivian shrugged. "They're not my friends, really. Not genuine friends. They're merely girls I grew up with."

"Yes, it's a very different thing, isn't it?" Nettie observed.

"Those women I met yesterday," Vivian said. "They're your friends or just women you grew up with?"

"I consider them friends." Nettie let the bacon tumble onto two plates and brought them to the table. "Perhaps not devoted friends, but women who would help me if I needed it."

"Miss Redfern has a quick-wittedness about her," Vivian remarked as she watched Nettie bring the coffeepot to the table.

Everything was made of white ceramic, except for the coffee things, which were delicate china, much worn and chipped, with bluebells painted on them.

Nettie laughed, laying a napkin in her lap with care. The crooked placement of it showed Vivian she didn't do this often, and the way the woman was trying to behave in a refined way for her sake touched her.

"Odele drives an ambulance for the Goldspur Hospital," she said. "She's used to picking up the rough ways of questionable men injured under questionable circumstances."

"You don't take offense to what she said last night, then?" Vivian picked at the eggs and bacon. They were greasy and unadorned by sauces, unlike the breakfast she was used to at the Waxwoodian. But they were cooked with the same care with which Nettie had set the table and laid out her napkin on her lap.

Nettie glanced at her, amused. "Odele has been foaming at the mouth about my library since I told her about the idea."

"How long have you had the idea?"

Nettie glanced down at her plate. "Since Mama died."

"Such things make you take stock of your own life," Vivian murmured, thinking of her own journey after her grandmother died.

"It wasn't that so much," she said. "Well, perhaps it was. Mama died of exhaustion and overwork. She didn't know how to read or write, except her own name. Her father didn't believe women should be educated, as it was a sin against God to let them." A seething look appeared in her eyes. "He died in an accident one day on his boat with a shark. They discovered the shark was female. Poetic justice, I call it."

"And the shrine?" Vivian gestured toward the cupboard. "One can honor the dead just so much, Nettie." The woman pressed her lips together in a thin, hard line. Vivian changed the subject. "What is this library, then?"

Nettie's eyes became bright. "Nowadays, even a girl working

in a factory must have some education, certainly one working in an office. And where does a woman who has hardly money for herself and perhaps her children get it? From books!"

"I couldn't agree more," said Vivian, smiling. "But I didn't get the impression Miss Redfern thought so."

Nettie smirked. "I tried to get her to read 'The Merry Wives of Windsor' once, and she threw it in my face," she said. "Odele isn't one for books. She has more revolutionary ideas."

"So I gathered," Vivian said, spearing a tomato. She was now thankful for the fruit, as it lightened the load of the heavy breakfast.

"It isn't just the books, though." Nettie leaned back with her coffee cup in her hand, her eyes half closed dreamily. "There is no use giving a woman a book if she has no place to read it."

"I don't imagine Odele would have a quiet corner with good lighting to read," Vivian agreed.

"That's just what I want to do," said Nettie. "Give them the books and the quiet corner with the good lighting with which to read it." Her eyes narrowed with determination. "And I shall. Someday."

"I will be there when you do," Vivian said, raising her cup.

"Lady Benevolence, holding out her heart in her hands to the masses?" Nettie eyed her, but she was smiling. "I might ask you to hold out your hand rather than your heart. I'm not too proud."

Vivian felt her cheeks grow hot. "I would, if I had money of my own," she said in a low voice. "I would do more, too."

"I know you would," said her friend, pressing her hand. She rose and began collecting the dishes. "You'll want to catch the early ferry if you're to be back in time for whatever silliness the swells have planned for today."

"I'm not going back yet," said Vivian. Nettie glanced at her. "There's someone I need to see first."

"Not that insulting woman again?" Nettie put the dishes in the wash bin and began pouring the water out.

Vivian joined her, taking the towel in her hands. "No, I won't be seeing Verina again," she said. "I know now the truth will never come from her."

"She's a cautious one," Nettie agreed.

"I can't blame her," said Vivian. "I forced her to face the truth once, and I think it ruined her somehow." Her brother's shadow appeared then, the words floating through the air: *Sometimes, Vivian, you harm others with your dagger.*

"You're going to see someone who will give you the truth?"

Vivian made long circles on the back of the china plate in her hands with the towel. "There's a chance she will tell me more of what she knows, just a chance. I know she knows more than she told me the first time."

"The first time?"

"I went to see her a few weeks ago," said Vivian.

Nettie put the sponge down. "Has this anything to do with your visit to Ember Warren?"

"In a way." Vivian felt her hands shaking and set the plate down as carefully as she could.

Nettie turned off the water and covered her hand. "There's little use in a friend if you can't confide in her."

"I've never done so before." Vivian's voice was thick. "The only one I ever had was Jake, and now he's—" She pressed her lips and her eyes together.

Nettie sat her down in the chair that had the most cushions in the living room. "What is this truth you're searching for, Vivian?"

Vivian did not answer right away, feeling that the storm was lingering inside of her, too heavy to let her speak. Her own battle with herself in the Alderdice spirit allowed it to subside after a time, and she could answer Nettie. "I want to know what happened with my grandmother after she left Waxwood in 1853."

"Why should anything have happened?" Nettie asked.

"I don't know," said Vivian. "But I feel it did. I feel something about me has changed, and I don't know what it is."

Nettie nodded. "I can understand that. And you think this woman you want to see holds the key?"

"Her mother held the key," said Vivian. "Seven years ago, I felt she held the key and she did. Now she's dead, but I know she still holds the key." She grabbed Nettie's wrist. "I wish I could live without it, but I can't. I must follow this path."

"Paths can sometimes lead to dead ends," her friend reminded her.

Vivian rose and picked up the towel again. "If that turns out to be true, I'll marry Monte Leblanc with a clear conscience. I'll even live in a square mansion on Washington Street and give myself over to the life of a socialite, just as my grandmother did."

"Was her conscience clear?" Nettie looked at her.

Vivian did not answer, circling the rim of the coffee cup in her hands with the same orderly strokes as she had before.

Nettie watched her, then wiped her hands and put her arm around Vivian's shoulders, giving them a squeeze. "You know you've only to come here to unburden your heart."

Vivian smiled, feeling the comfort of the pressing grip on her shoulders.

~

When Vivian arrived at the Ross house, it appeared deserted. Only a few birds lingering in the rickety tree from the neighbor's garden were alive, grumbling in the harsh morning light. She knocked on the door, but there was no answer. She then remembered the little garden she had seen out back. She found Ruth bent over a plot of sea breeze flowers, the lines on her face even more severe with concentration under the enormous hat.

"You're a gardener too?" Vivian asked.

Ruth whirled around. The harsh flare of her eyes told Vivian she was less than glad to see her. Nevertheless, she attempted to smile. "I wasn't much of one until Mama died."

"Doing something with one's hands is the best healing," Vivian said wistfully.

"Oh, it wasn't that," said the woman. "Mama always loved flowers and trees, but she couldn't tend to them herself."

Vivian nodded, remembering her first glimpse of Bertha Ross crouched in a wheelchair in the Alderdice Hall chapel at her grandmother's funeral service.

Ruth wiped her brow with a linen handkerchief and peeled off the thick gloves. "Poor Mama fell off a horse and broke her spine. Her legs were useless after that."

"I'm sorry," said Vivian.

Ruth let out a dry chuckle. "She rode that horse to please my father. He was a winsome man but not very considerate. My grandfather put his business in his hands, and he ran it to the ground." She glanced down at her plain gingham dress. "I suppose you didn't know Mama was one of the belles of Waxwood society when she was a young woman."

"She told me that herself at my grandmother's funeral," Vivian reminded her.

"She did, didn't she?" Ruth drew out a wicker chair from the patio and gestured toward it. "You have a good memory of that day, don't you?"

"I liked your mother very much," Vivian said. "I would have come to the funeral, had I known about it."

Ruth was silent for a moment. "I have lemonade in the icebox, if you'd care for some."

"Please," said Vivian.

Ruth returned with the drink and a plate of gingersnaps. "Very simple fare, I'm afraid. But I haven't known you so far to turn your nose up at the simplicity of others."

"Thank you, Ruth," said Vivian. "I know from you, that is quite a compliment."

"Perhaps I've softened my opinions of people in the past years," said the woman. "When one realizes how alone one is in the world, one becomes more tolerant of human nature."

"Your mother accepted people as they were," Vivian reminded her. "Even those of us who pry open Pandora's box of woes."

"Haven't you had enough already?" The woman looked at her sharply.

"You've been lying to me, haven't you, Ruth?"

"I haven't!"

Vivian stiffened, preparing for battle. "I can understand Verina not telling me what she knows. But I expected more from you."

"Maybe we've been trying to spare you," said Ruth softly.

Vivian gave her legs a little push from under the table, exposing her firm ankles. "I didn't ask anyone to spare me, did I?"

"You know, Vivian, not all of us can pry open Pandora's box," said Ruth. "Not all of us desire to know what ought to stay buried. Not all of us are that brave."

"I lay no claim to bravery," said Vivian. "I don't even have much backbone."

Ruth gave her a smile. "I think you have more backbone than you realize."

Vivian glanced at the hedge in front of her. "Two compliments from you in one day. You can't despise me so much, Ruth."

"I never said I despised you." Ruth put her hands in her lap. "All right. I won't tell you any more lies. What do you want to know?"

"You insisted Bertha didn't know Evan was in San Francisco while my grandfather was away," Vivian began. "She and my grandmother visited him in a flat where he and Verina were living at the time with friends. You knew that."

"May I ask how you found out?"

Vivian sipped at the lemonade, which had a bitter flavor that matched the scent of the tree in the yard. "A friend of Evan's told me."

She saw Ruth's face change from acquiescence to caution. "You don't need me to tell you anything, then, do you?"

"Is that why your mother was upset when she came back to Waxwood for Loretta's funeral?" Vivian asked. "Because she knew my grandmother had been seeing Evan in the city. Because she — suspected — my grandmother had renewed her close relationship with Evan?"

Ruth brushed her napkin against the dripping pitcher and poured herself more lemonade. She leaned back and played with a gingersnap. Her eyes were half-closed, avoiding Vivian's gaze. "I don't know that Mother would have suspected anything. And she was upset because she loved Loretta."

Vivian reached into the bag she had brought with her and took out the sketchbook. She held it out to Ruth. "My grandmother drew these the year Grandfather was away. I think you'll recognize some faces."

She sipped at the lemonade, which had become lukewarm, peering at Ruth's face. She noticed now how Ruth's skin had become as leathery as Bertha's had been and how, beyond the hard quartz, a shadow of Bertha's dancing eyes were also in hers. But her countenance remained impassive as she looked through the sketchbook. She laid it down on the table.

"There's no date on any of those drawings," Ruth pointed out. "They could have been done at any time. Your grandmother could have drawn them here in Waxwood."

"A man named Ember Warren told me about them." She turned to the profile drawings. "This is him."

"He may have been lying," Ruth insisted.

"I paid him well not to lie," Vivian said with a wry smile.

"He was a friend of Mr. Jones', you say?"

Vivian nodded. "He remembered your mother. He called her my grandmother's 'chattery friend.'"

Ruth sighed. "Mama complained once of how they always had to go to that 'dank little flat' on Darby Street whenever they set out on one of their excursions in the city."

"Then you knew about Evan."

Ruth began folding her napkin, smoothing down the edges. "Yes, I knew he was there. Mama wasn't one for hiding things."

"No, she was far too gullible for that." Vivian leaned forward. "But was she gullible enough to believe there was nothing between Evan and my grandmother?"

The garden became still. Even the pair of birds settled in the crown of a tree were waiting.

"What makes you think there was something between them?" Ruth asked.

"I knew a long time ago my grandmother never loved my grandfather," Vivian said. "Although he was always trying to make her love him." Through the glint of sunlight rolling into her eyes, she saw the evenings in the parlor, her grandfather with his pipe, watching Grandmother. Never speaking, but watching her with his eyes. She had thought the gaze prying at the time, but now Vivian realized it was begging. Begging her to let him in.

Ruth replied with a snarl, "I imagine he asked for it."

"Yes," Vivian admitted. "He did in a way."

The other woman's hand lay on the table near Vivian's, though she did not touch her. "I had no right to say such a nasty thing." She took up a thin shawl draped over the bannister. "The wind is picking up, isn't it?"

"Yes," said Vivian. "Leaping off the bay, as my brother used to say." She rose and joined Ruth. "Bertha wasn't gullible, was she? Not about that."

"I don't think Mama knew," said Ruth. "All she said was that they seemed to be as close as they were in Brandywine." Her voice rocked with hesitation as she held on to the bannister.

The air escaped from her chest. "There was something else she said, wasn't there?"

"Penelope asked Mama not to mention Mr. Jones to Malcolm when he came back to the city." Ruth gazed at the garden with hard eyes.

Vivian's heart sank. "She didn't want to upset him."

"Do you really think Penelope much cared whether Malcolm was upset?" Ruth asked.

"What do you mean?"

"I got the impression from Mama that your grandparents weren't getting along in quite the way a young couple ought."

Vivian stared. "Is that what Bertha said?"

The woman shrugged. "Mama was too gullible for that. She mentioned 'that strange bed in the study.'"

Vivian gasped but caught herself quickly, and, trying to sound reasonable, remarked, "My grandfather was working long hours then to build up the business. He didn't want to disturb my grandmother when he came home so late."

"You expect me to tell you the truth, and then you try to explain it away." The quiver in Ruth's voice made the accusation sting.

They both stood silently for a time, staring at a bee that had found its way into one of the upright roses.

"My mother said the same thing to me recently." She glanced at the sea breeze plants, their centers like yellow eyes staring through the blaze of purple petals. "You're both right. If you have the courage to tell me, I must have the courage to accept it."

Ruth hunched her shoulders, pulling the shawl closer to her. "All right. My mother was, as you said, not as gullible as people thought she was. She noticed the things people ignore, and what she noticed about Penelope during that trip worried her."

Vivian felt her hands suddenly grow cold inside her gloves.

"That was the word she used," Ruth said. "'It was worrisome, Ruthie, dear, very worrisome,' she used to say, shaking her head."

"What was?"

"To begin with, she said your grandmother had become one of those society ladies who 'clutched at her smelling salts.'"

Vivian nodded. "You told me last time she thought Grandmother wasn't actually ill."

"Feigning delicacy, she called it."

"But what made her think Grandmother wasn't ill?" Vivian's hands flew to her face, waving them about.

Ruth led her back to the table. "I should have cut those roses a long time ago. But Mama always loved them, and I don't have the heart."

"Ruth." Vivian clutched at her arm. "Why did Bertha think my grandmother was feigning delicacy?"

"When they were in Lico," said Ruth, "Malcolm was in Santa Barbara most days, as he had to continue to work."

Vivian eyed her. "I'm sure that's why Grandmother asked Bertha to be with her."

"Mama told me," Ruth continued, "that when Malcolm was home, Penelope stayed in bed, and when she joined them in the parlor or dining room, she always had some spell to drive her back to her room. When he left, it was as if she came alive. She was the spirited woman everyone had loved in Waxwood."

"I see," Vivian murmured.

"She dragged Mama out walking. And she was drawing." Ruth leaned against the bannister, looking at her. "When Malcolm came home, she was back in bed."

"You mean your mother thought she was trying to convince Grandfather she was ill?"

"Not exactly," said Ruth slowly. "Mama thought it was like a game they were playing. A game of Penelope being sickly when she wasn't."

They remained silent for a time. Vivian looked at the roses. They were a deep red, almost violet, and deceptively strong. But their petals were dry from the sun and waved precariously in the wind, their stalks swinging back and forth like whips when the breeze passed through them.

She rose and gathered her things. "Thank you, Ruth. Truly, I thank you."

"Vivian." Ruth looked at her. "Your brother must know all this. Or some of it, anyway. Why don't you ask him?"

Vivian stopped slipping on her left glove. "Why do you think Jake knows?"

"Because he paid Mama a visit last summer."

The gloves dropped to the floor. Ruth bent down to pick them up, dusting them off before she handed them back. "I'm sorry. I had the impression you and he were very close."

"Yes," Vivian said, trying to keep her voice from breaking. "We were."

Ruth took the tray as Vivian followed her to the kitchen. "I see now. You haven't been to see him — in that place."

Vivian blinked into the glaring sunlight from the window that made a cross on the kitchen table. Her eyes burned. "He asked us not to," she said in a thick voice.

"Mama always thought he was a sweet young man," said Ruth kindly.

"Yes, he was — is — very sweet," Vivian whispered. She felt for a moment as if she were going to faint. But she regained her composure like a cat that could always land on her feet. When she spoke next, she felt more upright. "What did they talk about?"

"I don't know," said Ruth. "He asked to speak to her alone. And Mama never told me."

"I thought your mother told you everything," Vivian snapped.

"I thought your brother told you everything," the woman retorted, placing the glasses on a towel to dry.

Vivian ran her finger against the bottom of the glass, feeling its smoothness. "He couldn't tell me this."

"Perhaps he chose not to," said Ruth, turning off the faucet and drying her hands.

"You mean he wanted to spare me too?" Vivian asked warily.

"Perhaps." The woman was looking closely at her with a glint of compassion. She took Vivian's arm. "Maybe he would tell you now, if he knew you had already opened Pandora's box."

"Yes, maybe he would." Vivian could catch her breath again. "Maybe he would now."

She felt as if an iron shield was wrapped around her. She knew the sign of her own stubbornness.

~

Vivian trudged up the incline away from Ruth's house, ignoring the heaving breath and the dampness on her forehead. She reached the city park and flew across the street without noticing a man driving a cart was just about to pass. He grumbled at her and his horse neighed in protest. Vivian kept going, ignoring people glancing at her as if they never expected a lady like her to be running.

When she reached Nettie's, her breath was coming out in gasps, and she knew she must look a sight. Pins had flown out of her hair, releasing the bun from underneath the hat, and the shorter coils in the front were wet from the dampness of her forehead. Nettie poured a glass of ice water and forced her to sit down on a stool.

"You look as if you've been chased by a panther," she remarked.

"Nettie," she grasped her elbow. "Will Alda be in now?"

Her friend nodded. "I suppose, unless she's gone out to lunch. I thought you finished with her."

"I need her again," said Vivian.

Nettie pulled off her jacket and hat from the peg nearby. "Then we must see her, won't we?"

"You needn't come with me." Vivian glanced at the door

where a few young people were lingering, eyeing the soda fountain.

Nettie shooed them away. "I won't let you go alone in the state you're in."

"I'm in no state!" Vivian insisted with all her Alderdice pride. "I have urgent business to discuss with her."

"Just as a runaway horse has business with the whipping master," said Nettie with a smile. "Come along now."

Vivian felt the tears stand in her eyes, but she couldn't express her gratitude just then.

Alda Quigg was in. The massive desk was cleared of every bit of paper, and her lunch was spread out in front of her. Vivian held back a smile as she glanced at the woman's lavish table. But for someone with the ample figure so pleasantly fit in the brown suit and blouse, Alda only pecked at her food.

"I'm sorry to disturb your lunch," Vivian mumbled, suddenly feeling ill at ease.

"Not the first a client has spoiled," the woman remarked. "What can I do for you now, Miss Alderdice?"

"I'd like to hire you to find someone else for me."

Alda regarded her with a wry smile. "I take it you know who you're looking for this time?"

"Yes," said Vivian. "My brother."

She heard Nettie draw in a breath. The woman blinked and put down her fork and knife. "Is he lost?"

"Not exactly."

The hard-bitten eyes regarded her directly. "Does he want to see you?"

Vivian fiddled with the edge of her skirt. "I don't know."

"Then—"

"I must see him!" She sprang forward. "It's about a family matter. A grave matter."

"You make it sound fatal," mumbled Alda.

Vivian's tone was curt. "A matter only he and I would understand."

"I see." Alda picked up her knife and fork again, picking at the stew and mashed potatoes. Their heady scents filled the silence left by the quiet voices. Then, she laid the utensils down again and sipped at her beer. "If he expressed a desire not to see you—"

"I never said that!"

"He did, though, didn't he?"

Vivian looked down at her lap. "Not in so many words."

"But now this grave family matter has come up, and you must see him."

"I don't believe he meant it!" Vivian said in a savage voice. "He was thinking of my mother — of our social position—"

Alda picked up her fork and knife once more and attacked her lunch with a little more vigor. Vivian realized the woman had been deliberately pecking at her food to give her time to think. She waited impatiently, counting her fingers. Thumb, one, two, two, three, four, up to the pinkie, then back down again, repeatedly, like a ladder.

The woman finally dabbed at her mouth with her napkin, signaling she had finished her lunch. Leaning back, she said, "Understand, Miss Alderdice, I don't make a habit of finding people who don't want to be found."

"He's hardly in hiding," Vivian said. "He's in prison."

She heard Nettie's intake of breath again. Alda regarded her with more interest. "Then you don't need me, do you?" she asked. "You need only know what state he's in and check with his lawyer."

"He refused a lawyer," said Vivian.

"Not a very judicious young man, is he?" Alda's voice was wary.

"On the contrary," Vivian regarded her with a steel gaze. "He was judicious enough to turn himself in."

"And what did he do?"

Vivian looked into the brightness of the window. "I'm not at liberty to reveal that."

"No, and it hardly matters anyway." Alda pushed her plate away. "It's not just that you want me to find him. You want something else of me."

A shudder rang through Vivian's bones. "I want you to speak to him, so he'll agree to see me."

"I would need to know a little more about this grave family matter," the woman said.

"I believe he has information I need to complete this path I've been following the past few months," Vivian said, impatient. "At the moment, I don't know who I am. And this concerns who he is too."

Alda gave her the hard-bitten look again. "And what do you intend to do with this information once you have it?"

Vivian sat in silence for a moment, her fingers counting up the ladder. "I suppose what I did the last time."

"Which was?" Now Alda sounded amused at Vivian's shilly-shallying.

"Speak to my mother about it," she mumbled.

"You mean confront her." Alda eyed her. "Do you think that would be wise?"

Vivian grimaced. "You don't know my mother."

"And beyond that?"

"I don't know," said Vivian. "I don't know right now."

"And if he refuses to see you?" Alda stared at her. "Will you set up camp outside the prison gate until he does?"

Vivian gave her an equally steady look. "I might."

Alda looked at her, a closed-mouth smile on her lips. Then she laughed, slapping the table. "Well, you got the gumption for it! Yes, you got the gumption." She became serious. "All right. I'll take the case."

Vivian felt her body collapse like a rag. "Thank you."

"On one condition." The woman leaned forward. "If your brother refuses to see you, you drop the matter."

"Yes, I'll do that," Vivian said. "I promise."

Alda rose and put out her hand. "I know you won't break that promise."

"No," said Vivian. "I don't break my promises."

CHAPTER 15

When Vivian returned that evening, she encountered not only the storm brewing on her mother's stoic face, but her ragged voice spearing words as edgy as the blue shade of her eyes.

"You were gone two days. *Two days!*"

"I'm aware of that." Vivian tried to sound breezy. "I needed a rest. I've done nothing to be ashamed of."

"Going off without a word is shameful enough!" Her mother's lips were trembling.

"I'm a grown woman, Mother." Vivian's hands curled with stubbornness. "Why shouldn't I go where I please and do what I please?"

"Because women in your position don't!"

"My position?" Vivian asked. "Which position do you mean? An unmarried lady on the verge of spinsterhood? An heiress-to-be? Or an Alderdice?"

Larissa grabbed the back of the stuffed chair, as if needing support. "Did it ever occur to you I might worry about you?"

Vivian peered at her from the couch. "Worried that Mr. Leblanc and his father might think me a tart?"

"Vivian!"

"It's true, isn't it?" Vivian flashed. "Your concern for social rectitude usually outweighs your maternal instincts."

She could see her mother's chest release under the corset. She sank into the chair. "I *was* worried about you, Vivian. Truly worried."

Vivian felt her own anger sinking. She covered her mother's hand with her own. "I ought to have sent word, but it never occurred to me."

"You've never stayed out like that before," Larissa said. "I don't think you realized the effect it would have on me, nor how disgraceful it would look."

"I told you." Vivian sat up as erect as her mother. "I did nothing to be ashamed of."

"What did you do, then?"

"I stayed with a friend in town."

"Not Miss Ross?"

"No, not Miss Ross." Vivian couldn't help but smile. "A woman named Nettie Grace. I met her at the suffragist meeting I went to last year with Marvina. She's a perfectly respectable woman, Mother. She owns a drugstore in town."

"At least you weren't gallivanting all over the city all night," her mother snapped.

Vivian glared at her. "Did you think I would be?"

Larissa considered this, then she sank back with a sigh. "You're right, dear. I thought nothing of the kind."

"So, am I forgiven?" Vivian asked.

"Not quite." Her mother sat up, her full height emerging from the sunken cushions. "You're not a child, Vivian. You're a woman with responsibilities now."

"I thought I was responsible," Vivian remarked.

"This is no joking matter," said her mother.

Vivian sighed, crushed by the weight of the last several days. "All right, Mother, what reprimand have you for me now?"

"Not reprimands, dear, merely advice."

Vivian chuckled. "How judicious you are! All right, what is your advice?" She said the last word with mock delicacy.

"I think you ought to stay close to the hotel for the next three or four days at least."

"Why?"

"Mrs. Tisher and her daughters have organized a little theater performance in the city park on Saturday," she said. "It's all everyone has been talking about. Not that you would have noticed." She shot her a look.

"No, I hadn't noticed," Vivian said.

"I obtained a part for you, but only with the most delicate arrangements," said Larissa. "Monte Leblanc has a part in it as well. He's very excited about the entire thing."

"Is he really?" Vivian looked up. "I would have thought the theater would bore him."

"I told you he's a very cultured man," her mother snapped. "I'm disappointed you haven't discovered that."

"It's no trick for a man to attend the theater when he's traveling in high society," Vivian remarked. "I've seen how those wild men listen carefully to their European betters and mimic their language and tastes."

"You're being unjust toward the Leblancs," Larissa insisted. "They are *not* wild men. They have a special affection for the theater. In fact, Monte Leblanc suggested the play."

"Which one?"

"*Margaret Fleming*," said her mother.

Vivian snorted. "I'm surprised Mr. Leblanc would know such a risqué piece."

"I'm surprised *you* are," Larissa said shortly.

"I've only read about it," said Vivian. "Who am I to be?"

Her mother grimaced. "A young immigrant named Lena. That ought to appeal to your sense of modernity."

"More so than if I had to play Hedda Gabler," Vivian answered dryly.

"I thought you found Hedda refreshing," Larissa said, equally dryly.

"Her fate wasn't very refreshing." Vivian rose and stretched.

"Vivian." Her mother took her arm. "We haven't much time left here. Monte Leblanc is very excited about this play and very keen on having you be a part of it. He wanted you to have the lead, but Mrs. Tisher overruled him."

"In favor of Fern, no doubt," Vivian muttered.

"But doesn't that tell you something about his feelings for you?"

Vivian looked into her mother's eyes. Their shocking blue faded like the sea on a gray day. She patted her arm. "I can't vouch for my acting, Mother. But I shall try."

~

The days that followed were almost like a dream to Vivian. Her mother was right. There was a commotion among their set about the play, and their excitement infected the rest of the hotel, even the other resorts. Every time she went down to the lobby or out to the courtyard, she felt the bouncing air of people chattering more than usual. The Tisher girls abandoned their glaring games with her, pulling her with them after breakfast almost every day. Amber joined them, but she was snippy because she had wanted to play the part of Lena, until Mr. Leblanc convinced Mrs. Tisher that Vivian's serious countenance would suit the part better.

There was plenty to occupy her, with the rehearsals and the costume fittings, more elaborate than what they had been in 1890 when the play debuted. Vivian thought she looked more like a scruffy debutante than an immigrant woman. She saw Monte Leblanc often. He was to play the part of Doctor Larkin, and though they had no scenes together, he somehow was in the Tisher suite, one of largest in the hotel, on the days she was.

She would have liked to at least receive a note from Nettie about the progress Alda Quigg was making. But despite her promise to stay near the hotel, she sensed Larissa didn't completely trust her. Her mother accompanied her everywhere, and after dinner, when Vivian was exhausted from the play and wanted only to go to bed, she went up to the suite with her.

On Saturday morning, there were decorations all around the hotel and a banner strung up on the windows proclaiming the Theater in the Park that evening. Breakfast was a rushed affair, for Mrs. Tisher had made a thundering appearance in the hotel parlor the day before, ordering everyone to be on the ferry by ten o'clock. Monte Leblanc chatted away about the play more than he ate his breakfast.

"I was a little hesitant to suggest *Margaret Fleming*," he admitted. "I had heard the play didn't go well in the East."

Amber intervened with, "That was only because the actress who played Margaret began nursing a baby right on the stage!"

"I read some critics didn't appreciate its realism," Vivian agreed, helping herself to another muffin.

"Realism?" Mr. Leblanc's sleepy eyes narrowed.

"Showing things as they really are in art," said Vivian. "A woman would nurse a baby in real life, wouldn't she?"

"Not in public!" Amber declared.

"I don't see why she shouldn't," Vivian said with amusement. "I think it's one of the most beautiful things in the world."

"It's very noble," said Mr. Leblanc. "But I agree with Amber. Such things ought to remain private."

"You can't pretend something doesn't exist because you don't wish to see it, Mr. Leblanc," said Vivian softly.

"But some things are better unseen," the man argued. "Even if they aren't skeletons in the closet."

Vivian tried not to think of Alda Quigg and what she had

asked of her, nor where it might lead if she found Jake, let alone convinced him to see her.

The party boarded the ferry while a boat Mrs. Tisher had hired trailed after them with costumes and props. When they reached the park, it amazed Vivian to see how the place had been transformed. An ample wooden stage with velvet curtains blocked out the largest green space, as expertly built as in any outdoor theater. Chairs were unfolded on the lawn as if waiting for five o'clock to arrive with impatience.

"Your mother is taking all this very seriously," Vivian couldn't help but remark to Bethel, who was standing next to her.

The girl's head flounced, absorbed in more a caricature of her sisters' arrogance than her own possession of it. "Mother wants it to be the resort event of the season. If such a thing is even possible in this boorish place." Her lip curled.

Her sister Cecily added, "Mother even told the town council they ought to put up posters for the people to come and watch us. So it will be an actual performance in front of a large audi-ence." Her usual wayward tone was breathless with self-consciousness, as she had the role of a maid in the play.

"I don't think those chairs will accommodate so many people," Vivian said.

"Oh, they're not for *them!*" Bethel said. "They're for us. The grass is good enough for *them.*"

"Yes, I imagine it is," Vivian said dryly. "And much more comfortable than those wooden chairs."

Both girls' hawk-like eyes lingered, as if trying to understand her gist. Then, they looked at one another with a shrug and went off arm in arm.

Mrs. Tisher, whom, Vivian found out later, had some vague aspirations for the theater in her girlhood, insisted they rehearse behind the curtain rather than in front of it. The wind kept shaking it so its snapping sound roared above the relatively hushed voices, as Mrs. Tisher had also insisted they keep as quiet as possible so as not to spoil the surprise of the performance later on. Once, as Fern was attempting to balance a rag baby wrapped in a blanket, the curtain suddenly rose in waves, looking like sails in a high wind, and her sister Bethel darted past her so quickly, the toy fell from her arms. Everyone laughed good-naturedly, and Mrs. Tisher could barely hide her smile behind the stern scolding. Vivian imagined it would be awhile before Fern spoke to her younger sister in a civil tone again.

Evening came sooner than Vivian expected. The sun turned orange and violet among the clouds, and the hills above the bay were a reposing sight. She sat on the grassy incline with her knees up, watching it.

"It would have made a marvelous painting," she said.

"For your brother, you mean?" This came from Mr. Leblanc, who stood leaning on his stick beside her. The grass, he insisted, was too damp for his taste.

"He would have liked it," Vivian said. "Yes, I think he would have."

"Was he a landscape painter?"

"Oh, mostly. He loved trees and woods." She looked down at the now fading grass.

"Diana in the woods," he recalled with a smile. "He learned on his own?"

"My grandmother taught him."

"And you, you have no interest in such things?"

"I enjoy the beauty of them," said Vivian. "But I have no talents for it. I'm not talented in anything, really." This came out in a tone of regret. "I suppose if I had, it would have been better. Or maybe it would have been worse."

"Eh?" The man looked at her with his squinting eyes.

"Women who have a talent always suffer," Vivian sighed. "But at least they're doing something."

"Don't women in your society do things?" Mr. Leblanc asked, amused.

Vivian blushed, looking down at the grass. "Not worthy things."

"And what do you consider worthy, Miss Alderdice?"

"I don't know," she admitted.

"You'll find out one day, I expect," he said with a smile.

"Yes, I'm pragmatic that way," she said.

"Pragmatic?" He said the word as if it were in French.

"I've always considered the practical side of things," said Vivian.

"And yet, you enjoy the beauty of the scenery as no one else here has."

"One must have both," Vivian said. "The practicality to live, and the love of beauty to enjoy it."

He bowed. "You always say things admirably, Miss Alderdice."

"I steal them from the books I read," Vivian said. "Maybe that's my one talent."

He laughed and reached his hand down to help her up from the grass.

The park filled up with resort guests, many of whom wore lavish, sometimes gaudy, attire, as if they were going to an opening night at the Grand Opera House. They took up the wooden chairs, some adjusting their rather unwieldy figures in the narrow seats. The chairs quickly filled up, and a few of the more enterprising young men ran into town and produced stools and crates, helped by some local proprietors who wanted to be a part of the ceremony. Later, the locals arrived, finding places in the surrounding area, lugging blankets, pillows, and bags of straw. May brought jugs and bottles of wine with them, and bread, meat, and cheese. The swells, many of whom had dined early, looked at their more philistine neighbors with an archness showing disgust in the way they treated this exclusive performance like a picnic.

Vivian almost envied these people, many of whom were delighted with the excitement of breaking the dullness of their

Saturday evening and curious to see what these blue bloods would produce. She glimpsed at a group of women, all in colorful cotton dresses and embellished hats, crossing the street, many of them with their beaus. She watched them turning their heads, nodding and laughing with careless ease. She recognized Miss Hill, Miss Bagstock, and Miss Redfern among them. Even Miss Redfern's face relaxed, the fierce freckles displaying a pale prettiness as she waved her hand wildly to the young man whose arm she held.

Shielding herself from the storm of emotions that made her feel like a ghost wandering through a family reunion, Vivian concentrated on the play. She appeared in the first act and did well, despite being intimidated by the jewel lights, the swinging curtain, and the crowd of blank faces. Her words were wooden at first, but then, she envisioned herself as Lena, the immigrant factory worker, in the company of such young ladies as Miss Redfern, and her voice gained more confidence. As the curtains closed, congratulatory nods and smiles from the other players surrounded her, even from Fern, whose starring role made her critical of everyone else, whether they had the misfortune to play opposite her or not.

Vivian did not appear in the second act, but she stayed backstage, listening to the action out front. Monte Leblanc had a role in that act, so she listened to his careful voice mimic the words of the play, leaning against a pole that held up the stage. Suddenly, she felt a tug on the pinched sleeve of her costume jacket and jerked her head around. She was surprised to see the grooved face of Ruth Ross peering up at her from the wooden staircase.

"I need to see you," she whispered. "Is this a good time?" She glanced nervously at the velvet curtain.

Vivian nodded. She followed Ruth down the stairs. That Ruth had come to the play already told of the seriousness of her intent, as Vivian imagined she had kept away from community events since her mother died.

They found a quiet place a little distance from the stage. A cluster of trees shielded much of the light, so she could not see Ruth's face very well. But her voice came through like a wire thread, cutting into the thick, dark air. Their voices hushed underneath the calling tones from the stage.

"I went to see Verina after we spoke," she said. "I wanted to see if she was all right."

"And was she?" Vivian asked.

Ruth nodded. "Rather angry at you. But I'm sure you expected that."

"Anything having to do with her uncle brings back painful memories for her," Vivian said. "I regret having done that."

"We had a little wine," she said. "A treat for women like us."

"I imagine," Vivian murmured.

"We spoke of you," said Ruth. "And she told me your brother came to see her too."

Vivian gazed out into the veil of black. A sudden explosion of laughter from the audience shot out, striking her as vaguely odd, as the play was a serious one. But her mind was hardly on *Margaret Fleming*.

"Soon after he came to see me," the woman continued. "The same day, I believe."

Vivian's throat grew narrow. "Why did he see her?"

"That she didn't say," said Ruth. "And I was loath to press her."

"Naturally," said Vivian. "You're very considerate, Ruth."

"Perhaps I didn't want to know," said the woman. "But after you left me, I realized your way is better."

"I'm glad you see things differently, Ruth."

"Evan kept a diary," the woman said.

"Yes, Mr. Warren told me that."

"I'm sure he didn't tell you Evan left it to Verina along with everything else he owned, what precious little there was," said the woman. "It was my impression Verina no longer has that diary."

"Oh?" Vivian peered into what she thought was Ruth's face, but it was impossible to decipher the grooves in the darkness.

"I think she gave it to your brother."

"Why do you think that?"

"She said, 'Miss Alderdice has one piece of my uncle, so I thought Mr. Alderdice may as well take the other, for I have nothing left of him, anyway.'"

Vivian shut her eyes, tears welling up at how her dagger had twisted into Verina.

Just then, the actors who had been in front of the stage filed to the back. Vivian realized there was a roar of applause, signaling the end of the second act.

"I must get back," she said.

"I'm sorry to have kept you." They moved toward the stage, where the gaslights were now strong, and she could see Ruth now.

Vivian grasped her hands. "Thank you, Ruth. I know this wasn't easy for you."

"I only stand by what I said seven years ago," she said. "Now that I know, you've a right to know too."

Larissa had been standing not far off with Mrs. Tisher and Mrs. Griffith and a few of the other ladies, but now she broke away. Her gait was swift, her head and shoulders pinned back. She took Vivian's hand. "Come, dear, Mr. Leblanc has been asking about you."

"Mother, you remember Ruth, don't you?"

"I'm not likely to forget her," said her mother in an even tone.

"Nor am I likely to forget you, Mrs. Alderdice."

Vivian glanced from one to the other. They were both tall women and both with their own brand of haughtiness, so they stood on equal footing. Larissa's expression was patiently tolerant, as when she faced someone she disliked at a party. Ruth's countenance had less subtlety. She looked, in fact, as if she were working up a rage.

But her mother was, as always, cordial. "You're looking well, Miss Ross."

"Thank you for saying so," said Ruth. "But I would rather you tell me how my mother's death has worn on me than be polite and lie."

Larissa hissed, "I see your manners have not improved over the years."

"One can hardly be civil to a woman who refused to attend her mother's funeral!"

Vivian scowled at Larissa. "You knew Bertha died?"

For the first time in a long time, Vivian saw her mother was genuinely embarrassed.

"I see your mother neglected to inform you that I wrote inviting you to the funeral," said Ruth. "I know how much Mama appreciated your hospitality in letting us come to Penelope's funeral. She would have been very gratified to know that you came to hers."

"Mother!" Vivian's anger rose like a whirlwind. "That was indecent of you!"

"May I extend my condolences now?" Larissa held out her hand. Ruth was taken aback, but she accepted the hand with what Vivian detected was perhaps too firm a grip for her mother's sense of propriety. "Vivian, we really must go." She took her arm.

"Ruth and I were just talking," Vivian blurted out.

"For the third time this summer."

"I beg your pardon?" Larissa glanced at her

"I said," the woman repeated, "for the third time this summer."

Vivian's nerves became a little taunt. "I wanted to know more about Bertha."

"Vivian has a rather apt metaphor for it," Ruth said. "She calls it 'opening Pandora's box of woes.'"

"Yes." Larissa's voice was crisp. "I'm aware of it."

"I told her some of us prefer not to know things," said Ruth. "We are not bulls, you see. We are birds. Rather than charge forward with our horns poised, ready for battle, we fly away with our hearts beating in our chests."

"I agree." Larissa regarded her with an icy smile. "Some of us prefer to stay out of trouble. Good evening." She punctuated this with a nod of dismissal.

This made Ruth's rage storm. Her pale face flushed, the bones filling in with anger. "It seems both your children are more willing to engage in what you call 'trouble' than you, Mrs. Alderdice."

Here, Larissa froze. "What do you mean, both my children?"

"I suppose Vivian didn't tell you that your son Jake came to see Mama and me before he went to that place." Ruth's voice was loud and piercing. "Oh, he told Mama all about it. I suppose he was looking for maternal sympathy. He apparently did not receive it from you."

Vivian had never seen her mother so mortified. Her face turned a pallor of yellow, and her eyelids wavered, as if she were about to faint. She yanked Vivian away, her tread smooth in the thick grass, and nearly plucked her in front of the waiting Mr. Leblanc, who held two glasses of punch. Vivian did not have a chance to look for Ruth until it was time for her to mount the stage again, and when she did, Ruth was gone.

CHAPTER 16

Although the sun had set long ago, the city park was lit with so many kerosene and gas lamps and candles that it looked as if a wave of fireflies had descended upon the grass. The townspeople had gone home, and most of the resort guests from other hotels, even the Waxwoodian, had taken the ferry back. The only people who remained were the players and their supporters. Mrs. Tisher had cajoled as many as she could into helping to dismantle the stage and arrange the props and costumes so they could go back on the boat she had hired.

She asked Larissa and Vivian to help fold the costumes so she could return them to the shop from where she had rented them. So, Vivian found herself alone with her mother in a quiet corner of the park where only a few kerosene lamps illuminated the costumes which had been thrown in a heap. Mrs. Tisher had recruited the Leblancs to help with disassembling the stage, as Mrs. Tisher needed strong men for that job.

She reflected how strange it was she should suddenly feel so nervous with Larissa. They had been alone for the past year, and conversation came easily, if not always pleasantly. And yet, tonight there was a heavy air between them, penetrating her lungs so that each breath came out with a struggle. There was wind, and yet no rustling of it in the leaves of the trees or the costume skirts.

Vivian sat on the grass, picking out the suit she recognized as belonging to Doctor Larkin. "Mr. Leblanc did well," she remarked. "I didn't think artistic endeavor would suit him, but he's a competent enough actor."

Her mother did not answer.

"He might have been an admirable actor," Vivian continued, "had his circumstances been different."

Her mother cleared her throat, making Vivian tense her muscles. "You shouldn't have invited that woman here tonight."

"You mean Ruth?"

"You know very well who I mean!"

"I didn't invite her, Mother." Vivian folded the jacket Mr. Leblanc had worn. "She came on her own. Mrs. Tisher was generous enough to invite the philistines of Waxwood to this play, remember?"

"She did not come to see the play," her mother insisted. "She came to see *you*."

"I'm sorry she was rude," said Vivian. "But you weren't exactly an angel yourself."

"You heard her insinuation about me — about your brother —" Here, her mother's voice broke.

"Well," Vivian peered up at her, "you haven't exactly been the most affectionate of mothers."

She could hardly see her mother's silhouette in the muted light, but she heard a gasp that sounded almost as if Larissa were trying to choke back a sob. Alarmed, Vivian rose and reached out, touching the lace sleeves capping her mother's thin shoulders. "Mother, are you all right?"

"I tried my best." The tone was listless.

Vivian realized then how much Ruth had hurt her mother.

She lamented, "She only made that remark to hurt you, Mother. She didn't mean it. And it isn't true."

"Thank you for saying so, dear." Now Larissa's face was more in the light, and Vivian could see the features were even again, with only a slight curve in the corner of her mouth to show her earlier devastation.

"I wish you would have told me Ruth wrote you when Bertha died," Vivian said.

"I thought she was trying to mock us," said her mother. "And we were both still recovering from our own tragedies."

"Still, you ought to have at least told me," said Vivian. "It was a cruel thing to do. Cruel and inconsiderate." She felt tears stinging her eyes. "I would like to have gone to Bertha's funeral. To say goodbye."

"I keep telling you, she was not our friend." Larissa's voice was gentle. "She wasn't even really your grandmother's friend."

"She was not 'one of us,' you mean." Vivian sniffed. "Tell me, Mother, if Bertha had kept the social wealth and position of her girlhood, would you have welcomed her into the chapel that day of Grandmother's funeral? Or would the fact that she was the belle of Waxwood society not have been enough for you?"

"We're not talking about Bertha Ross!" The words vibrated through the night air in a way that startled Vivian. It was a rare thing that her mother raised her voice in a public place. "We're talking about her daughter." She bent down to the costumes. "If nothing else, that woman's insolence must have made it clearer to you why we must keep away from your brother from now on."

Vivian sat down on the grass again and folded a dress Fern had worn in the play. "And how do you come to that conclusion?"

"Vivian." Her mother's voice was low. "If she knows where your brother really is—"

Vivian stared at her, then burst out laughing. "You mean you think she's going to babble to everyone she meets that Jake is in jail?"

"Not so loud!"

"I doubt Ruth has any connections with the Tishers or the Griffiths or even the Biltons, Mother," Vivian said. "You needn't worry about it getting to 'the right people.' And as for the 'wrong people' — I hardly think you would care."

"That's not the point." Larissa lowered her voice further. "If someone like her knows, how long do you think it will be before others we care about know?"

"They all suspect something, anyway."

"But they don't *know!*"

Vivian peered up at her mother. "You've always cared more about what people think than anything else, haven't you, Mother?"

They were both silent for a while, the swishing sound of the costumes between them as they folded them into the chest a workman had set down for them. Then Larissa's voice rose in the warm night. "I could never make you understand."

"Try." Vivian grabbed her mother's hand. "Try now."

She could see Larissa's face sagging under the light, its tautness gone, the hollows of her cheeks gaunter than ever. She leaned against a tree. "You know your grandfather came from Flesa." Vivian nodded. "It was a town so thick with soot and smoke and people who rarely had two dimes to rub together that it was like the pit of hell."

"Grandfather's description, I take it," Vivian said.

"When he came to San Francisco, it was as if the world had opened up for him," said her mother. "And you remember how your grandfather was a determined man."

Vivian gave a slight smile. "I suppose that quality carried him through life."

"That, and his sense of duty," said Larissa. "He married your grandmother because he loved her—"

"He married her because he knew she would give him a place in San Francisco society," Vivian insisted. "Just as Monte Leblanc knows if he married me, he will assure his place in society. At least we have *that* to our credit."

"Exactly." Her mother let go of the tree. "And we have it because of your grandfather's courage and faith in himself as a businessman and a man of substance."

"I thought we have all that because of Grandmother," Vivian said dryly.

But Larissa was not listening. "Your grandfather had no illusions. He knew there would always be the stench of soot and smoke about him in the eyes of the social set, even as they smiled at him from their dining room tables and ballroom dances."

Vivian couldn't help but recall the remarks made by the Washington Street swells during her grandmother's funeral service. The muffled dome of the Alderdice Hall chapel could hardly suppress the words under their breath: *who can say how far the buccaneer will go to make himself one of us?*

"He knew they never full accepted him, but he hoped his grandchildren would be," said her mother. "That's why I've put my faith and energy into making us a part of Washington Street society. For your sake, for your children's sake, and for their children's sake." She knelt on the grass beside Vivian and took her hands. "Any hint of scandal would ruin us socially. The Alderdice family would fall, and we would have nothing to catch us. Nothing."

Vivian tried to see Larissa's face, but one of the kerosene lamps had gone out, and there was even more of a black shroud around them. Her mother's voice sounded tired and put-upon, as if she were dragging an iron ball around her neck.

Her mother rose. "Vivian, don't see that woman again, please. She'll only bring you sadness. Both of us have had sadness enough to last us a lifetime."

Vivian felt a substantial weight on her shoulders, and she leaned against the tree her mother had just abandoned. The splintered wood pinched her hand. It was not the soft bark of the wax wood trees.

As they were folding up the last of the costumes, a figure came toward them. At first, Vivian thought it was Mrs. Tisher, who had taken her supervising of the folding up of the play a little too wholeheartedly. But when the figure came into the circle of light, Vivian saw Nettie's face between the folds of a shawl she had put over her head. The woman's expression was grave and serious.

"Mother," Vivian came forward, "this is Nettie Grace."

"Anette Grace, ma'am," said the woman, holding out her hand, which Larissa took with her usual curt shake.

She hated the way her mother's eyes swept over her friend, taking in the simple skirt, the ruffled shirtwaist underneath the cotton jacket, and the shawl around her head. But Nettie was anything but intimidated. Vivian could see the shadows of her features looking more amused than anything else.

Larissa began folding up the last dress on the grass. "It's rather late to be calling, isn't it?"

"I came to deliver a message."

Vivian, realizing it could only be about Jake, sprang to her feet. "I'll be back in a moment, Mother." She pulled Nettie to the gazebo, which was far enough away for Larissa not to see her. "A message from Alda?"

Nettie nodded. "She wants you to come and see her as soon as you can. She's sitting in my flat right now."

"Has she found Jake?" Vivian felt as if her heart was going to beat out of the silk dress she had put on after the play.

"She knew you were here in the park, so she sent me to tell you to come," said Nettie. "That's all I know."

"Nettie!" Vivian suddenly felt dizzy and clasped her friend's arm.

"Don't worry, I'll be there," said Nettie in a gentle voice.

"That's a great comfort." She smiled. "Now, to get away from Mother—"

"I imagine the only way would be to do just that," said Nettie. "Get away without a word. You're not a child."

"No," Vivian said. "I'm not a child." She had regained her composure. "But I won't run away from her either. Wait here and I'll be back in a few moments."

She found Larissa putting the last of the costumes in the chest. "Mother, I'm going with Nettie for a little while. I'll see you back at the hotel."

Her mother gave her a severe look.

"I'll be back later tonight," Vivian promised. She seized her mother's wrist. "You know I would never disgrace you, Mother."

"What is this all about?" Her mother eyed her.

Vivian blinked at her. "Pandora's box of woes."

"Vivian, for God's sake, this is not the time of night for nonsense!" Larissa's voice shook in the standing air.

"Make my excuses to Mr. Leblanc," said Vivian. "Tell him I had to help a friend."

She suddenly had the mad urge to kiss her mother's cheek. But as she leaned forward, Larissa drew back, her eyes unfolding like two glittering moons.

~

The store looked almost haunting with all the lights out and the wares sitting quietly on their shelves waiting for all human steps to cease before coming to life. Nettie led her upstairs to the small room where Vivian had slept. At the narrow table, Alda was sitting with a bowl of oranges Vivian guessed she had brought herself. She sat with her feet propped up on a chair, peeling an orange.

"You made a convincing working girl," she remarked with her clownish grin.

"I'm glad you thought so." Vivian lowered herself into a chair.

"I saw it from my office window." She deposited half the skin of the orange on the table.

"Did you find out where my brother is?"

Alda smiled. She peeled a layer of the pith, which she had left generously on the orange, and nibbled on it. "Are you still determined to see him, no matter what the cost may be to his peace of mind and yours?"

"I take it you found him, then." Vivian sank into the chair, now feeling its wooden seat for the first time. She caught Nettie's eye as she stood over the pot making a fragrant, flowery tea, its scent merging with the strong citrus from the peeled orange. The woman's unruffled smile reassured her.

"Answer my question first," ordered the woman.

Vivian's eyes fell on a glass globe sitting on the table. The minimized reflection of her face resembled her mother's only a little while ago — gaunt, gray, pleading.

She moved it to hide the reflection from view. "I have no intention of sacrificing anyone's peace of mind, but, yes, I'm still determined."

"I found him," Alda confirmed. "It would hardly have been a credit to my profession if I hadn't, seeing as he's in a place he can't get out of."

Vivian winced. "Must you put it like that?"

"He's in jail, my dear, and he shall stay there for another year, maybe more," said the detective in a firm voice. "He's accepted that, and I think you ought to. I've found when people accept the wrongdoings of their family members—"

"It was not wrongdoing!" Vivian snapped. "It was — it wasn't his burden alone to bear." She was quiet for a moment, seething like a volcano in her whole being at the memory of Harland Stevens. She said in a softer tone, "You saw Jake, then."

"Yes," said Alda. "Had a time of it too, with a story about being sent by his lawyer and all. He didn't believe a word of it, but he agreed to see me. Your brother is rather shrewd."

"His are the still waters that run deep," Vivian said with a faint smile. "Does he want to see me?"

Here, the woman paused, allowing Nettie to pour her a cup of tea. She reached the last of the pith and chucked the small piece on the table along with the pile of carved peel. But the orange itself interested her very little, and she tore it into sections, then pushed it toward Vivian. "You ought to eat something. Steady your nerves."

"Does he want to see me?" Vivian's patience had worn thin, with the events of the day and the fatigue of the play now catching up with her.

Alda looked at her for a moment and then answered, "He's agreed to see you."

Vivian's eyes became blurry as she felt firm fingers pushing her up in the seat and the hot rim of the teacup held to her lips. Nettie gave her a small smile and went to the stove where she was heating something that smelled of onion, carrot, and broth.

"I will repeat," Alda said. "I advise against it."

"But if he wants see me—"

"I didn't say that," said the woman. "I said he's *agreed* to see you. I didn't say he wanted to see you."

"I don't understand." Vivian put her hand on her forehead.

"I gather he would never refuse you anything," said Alda. "I think if you visit him, it would take an unfair advantage of him."

Vivian sat up. "What do you mean?"

Alda gave her a crooked smile. "Most inmates avoid subjecting their loved ones to such a place, if they can help it."

"He knows I don't care about that!"

"But *he* does," she said. "And there are other considerations. Your mother, for one."

"My mother has nothing to do with this," Vivian snapped.

"Nevertheless," she said, "he guessed you weren't telling her you went searching for him."

Vivian looked away. "Whether I did or didn't is my business."

"I didn't say it wasn't," said Alda. "But he's trying to spare you."

Vivian gave a disdainful laugh. "Everyone has been trying so hard to spare me."

"Of what?" Alda seemed interested.

Vivian looked down into the teacup that was now empty, though she had no recollection of drinking it. The pattern of the leaves and water left at the bottom looked like a fox with pointed ears and nose. A fox with one eye, staring up at her menacingly. "I don't know."

"Leave her alone, Alda." Nettie turned from the stove. "Don't press her."

The detective shrugged. "It's your business, I suppose. But you might find yourself skating on thin ice."

"Please tell me where my brother is."

Alda rose, placing all the orange peel in an empty paper bag on the table. "Sitwell Prison."

Vivian felt her stomach churn. "Where's that?"

"Sitwell County," said the woman. "Out past Monterey. I've made an appointment for you for seven o'clock tomorrow morning. Mr. Shelley's son will drive you in one of their wagons."

Trying to ignore the dizziness that made her forehead ache, she asked, "Is it a very terrible place?"

Alda shrugged. She moved toward the door. "Warden Jenkins believes in prison reform, luckily." The last word left a mark in the warm air. Alda suddenly gave Vivian a pitying look. "I wish you luck, my dear." Without waiting for an answer, she left the flat.

Vivian rose, stumbling to the window. She threw it open, and at once, she felt the cool air skimming her cheeks. She closed her eyes and thought of the playroom at Alderdice Hall where she and Jake had spent their days, like children in a self-imposed prison. It had been like a prison with its dark walls and sailboat windows. But there had been toys and games and the glass circus in the cupboard. There had been the make-believe world her brother had painted, and stories they made up filled with sympathetic friends. Who was helping Jake to make up stories now?

She opened her eyes, and her head felt clear, her stomach soothed. She returned to the table where Nettie had put some pretty place settings, complete with linen napkins. A bowl of stew sat waiting for her and slabs of thick, dark bread and butter sat in the middle of the table alongside Alda's oranges.

"I told Mother I would come back tonight," Vivian lamented.

"I don't think you'd better," Nettie said.

"If I had to face her now—" She felt dizzy again.

"You wouldn't be able to keep up the charade," Nettie finished, pouring her a glass of cold water. "Drink this." Vivian obeyed in silence. "You're always welcome here, you know that."

"Thank you, Nettie."

"Would you like me to come with you tomorrow?"

Vivian stretched her feet under the table. She suddenly glimpsed at them peeking out from under her skirt. The boots were still shiny, though they had been plodding through grass, and the hem lifted a little to show their tops, which covered her ankles. The steady Alderdice ankles. Somehow, the glimpse of them gave her courage.

"I don't mind coming."

"You heard what Alda said." Vivian laid her hand on Nettie's. "It's not a place anyone visits if they can help it."

"Vivian, do you think you ought to go?"

Vivian couldn't help but smile. "I grew up in a fancy prison. I hardly think Sitwell will be much different."

"I didn't mean that," said Nettie. "I meant — well, he didn't *ask* to see you."

"I know my brother," said Vivian. "He'll be glad once he sees me."

"But he asked you to stay away, didn't he?"

Vivian leaned back, her eyes burning from the dust that had flown in from the window. "I know what you think. I know what Alda thinks. I'm being selfish, insensitive. I ought not to go where angels fear to tread." She sighed, thinking of Jake's words: *Walking into other people's dark rooms.* "But, Nettie, I miss him." Her eyes finally filled with tears she couldn't stop rolling down her cheeks. "We were once one another's only companion. Even with other people, we understood one another as no one understood us. You can't know what it's like to lose that."

"I think I do," said the woman softly.

Nettie said grace over the stew, and just as they both unfold their napkins, a scrape came from the other side of the room. Vivian jumped, thinking it might be a mouse or even a rat, though the small room was immaculate. Nettie's countenance remained even as she rose and pulled out an iron ring hanging on the wall that Vivian had not seen before. The wall suddenly opened out to a door.

A woman was standing there, the shadows around her hiding her features. Her pale peach dress was an ancient style, and it was dirty, as if she had rolled around in the dust: the ribbons were untied, the square skirt mashed, and the lace collar frayed around the neck. Her hair was arranged in a high net piled on her head, but Vivian could see the peeks of false hair and wires, as if the elegant style had gone awry.

"Good evening, Olivia." Nettie's voice was light, as if the woman appeared every time the sun went down. "You're just in time for dinner."

"Dinner?" the woman asked.

"How long as it been since you've eaten?" Nettie led the woman to the table.

The woman did not answer. Her eyes immediately fell on Vivian. She leaned forward, studying her with perplexity, as a doctor did a patient. She was close enough for Vivian to see her face showed the first signs of middle age, and her eyes were a clear honey shade. "Who is this?" she asked.

"My name is Vivian Alderdice," she said, as Nettie went to the stove for another bowl of stew.

The woman took her hand as if to shake it, but held it in a claw-like grasp. "You look woefully engaged, my child," she breathed.

"Perhaps I have been." Vivian thought of the chaotic summer months she had endured.

"I have been as well." She leaned forward and whispered, "They are going to kill me, you see. I've been trying to escape."

Vivian then noticed the woman's face sagged with liquor and grief. The scent of wine made Vivian sick, as it was so heady in the small, dark room. The woman wobbled and grabbed Vivian's arm.

"But they can't, you see." Olivia gave her a vague smile. "Because I've been dead for some time."

Nettie placed the food in front of her and asked in a gentle voice, "Who are you today, Olivia?"

"Antoinette," she muttered.

"Marie Antoinette," Nettie mouthed to Vivian.

"They will not take the child, will they?" She clawed at Vivian's arm. "Surely, they wouldn't hurt innocent children."

"No, of course they wouldn't," Vivian said.

"They may send me to the guillotine if they wish." Olivia sat up with a stern dignity. "I have made all the little ones suffer, with my extravagances and my jewels. But the child — the child is innocent! Olivia is innocent."

"You mustn't let your dinner get cold, dear," Nettie said. She gently released the woman's hand from Vivian's arm.

Olivia looked down into the bowl as if it were a crystal ball. "Shall it be the last?"

"No, dear," said Nettie. "Not yet."

The woman turned to Vivian. "I was rich once. They took

everything away from me. I had nothing to do with the diamond necklace affair, but they never believed me." She looked at Vivian with terrified eyes. "Don't let them hurt the child!"

Vivian's gaze met Nettie's. Something in them told her not to break this woman's spell, that, should there be any glimmer of the light of reality, the woman would never survive it. So she guided Olivia's fork to her dinner. But the woman threw it down.

"I have already eaten the poison!" she shouted. "The poison of the hard life they never prepared me for. Those gold-faced people, my mother and father, they objected to my going out into the world." She leaned toward Vivian, grasping her wrist again. "I only wanted to be a doctor and perhaps of some use to someone in the world. The gold-faced people said a woman like me, it isn't done, it just isn't done."

"It isn't done," Vivian repeated.

"Bread, at least," Nettie said. "Take some bread."

"No, no!" the woman cried. "There are little knives in it, I know.!"

"An orange, then." Vivian picked one up from the bowl. "They can't put anything in an orange."

"No, they can't, can they?" Her eyes became wide and bright. "And I am so hungry, oh, so hungry!" Her countenance became that of an old woman's.

Olivia let Vivian peel the orange for her and ate two more with relish. She could barely rise, her limbs spilling on all sides. It amazed Vivian that she could walk at all. She and Nettie helped the woman into bed.

"We ought to let her sleep," said Nettie in a soft voice. "She'll be gone before daylight. She always is."

"Where did she come from?" Vivian looked down at the peaceable face that showed its prettiness in the stillness of sleep.

"Oh, some forgotten alleyway at the edge of town, I expect," said Nettie with a sigh. "She's right, you know. She used to be like you. Lived in a big house, the biggest in the county. She left, and they cut her off. And now, she's like most of them."

"Most of them?"

"Women who have lost everything," she said. "Their families, mostly. They never even had a chance because the foundation was never there. They're like those porcelain eggs, glorious on the outside but hollow on the inside."

"Surely we can do something for them," Vivian said.

"There are differing opinions about that, Vivian. You heard Odele." She started for the door. "I've a mattress in the storeroom downstairs that you can sleep on. It's a bit lumpy, but it's clean. Unless you prefer the luxury of your hotel bed." She glanced back at her.

"I'll stay here," said Vivian in a firm voice.

When she left, Vivian found her reticule and extracted all the money she could find in it. She had seen Olivia come in with a pouch tied to her belt, and she uncovered the woman and found it spilling over the side of the bed. She gently placed the money inside.

The figure stirred, and she heard the bird-like voice moaning, "Yes, yes, everything disappears in sleep."

Vivian reached up and put her hand on the woman's head. Olivia opened her eyes, peering softly at Vivian, but Vivian knew she wasn't seeing her. She said, "Go back, go back. Oh, how I wish I could go back!"

Fear rocked Vivian's entire body. Those had been her grandfather's dying words: *Go back, go back*. For her grandfather, going back had been Waxwood. But for Olivia, there was nothing to go back to.

hen Vivian awakened early the next morning while the gaslight outside the window was still flashing through the dark, the bed was empty, just as Nettie had promised. It looked as if a different person had slept in it, one who had the wherewithal to recognize a moment of hospitality. The blanket was neatly tucked inside the sides of the mattress. The area was tidy and swept. And, to Vivian's dismay, all the money she had put in the woman's pouch the night before lay neatly on the bed, the coins lined up one next to the other and the bills unfolded and smoothed down, as if Olivia had wanted to show her it was all there.

Nettie smiled at Vivian. "Don't take it to heart, dear. When Olivia is herself, she's proud."

Vivian grimaced as she put the money back in her reticule. "Miss Redfern wouldn't have approved."

"Perhaps not," said Nettie. "But sometimes practicality must come before ideals."

"And we women are so practical," Vivian mocked.

"Sometimes we must be. What does one care for books when one has washing to do and a house to clean? What use is counting when one has dinner to prepare before the husband and sons come home, or there will be trouble? But knowing how to read and write well — that's an entirely different thing."

"So you want your library to teach women how to read and write well," Vivian murmured.

Nettie couldn't help but smile. "I want to give them the opportunity. The library would be a place where they needn't be ashamed of stumbling over words."

Vivian put her elbows on the table. "I'm sure if you explain it to Miss Redfern like that, she would help you."

"Odele has her own ways," said Nettie. "She believes we ought to give women a vocation, not books."

"But one feeds into the other," Vivian argued.

Nettie laughed and rose, collecting the plates. "I have faith she will see that one day. The humbling experience will do her good."

Vivian almost wished she had gone back to the hotel, at least to choose a more becoming dress. The mauve satin she had put on after the play looked a little sallow in the worn mirror hanging from Nettie's wall. But she realized it wasn't the dress that was pale, but her own face. It looked as if a layer of white dust had settled on it.

The younger Mr. Shelley was waiting for her outside the stable with the same carriage she had taken to Goldspur.

"Alda — Miss Quigg — mentioned a wagon?" Vivian asked.

"I know, miss," he said. "But seeing it was you, I knew you'd want something finer."

Vivian glanced at the lavish scrolls. "Please get me the wagon Miss Quigg hired," she said. "I would prefer it." She flinched at the thought of pulling up at the prison gate in the elegant gig.

"But, miss, a wagon ain't fitting for a lady."

"The wagon, Mr. Shelley." Vivian gave him a meaningful look.

The man slunk out of the carriage seat. "Yes, miss."

He returned with a flat-bed wagon, the wooden panes carved with figure eights, so it was clearly the sort of wagon used for

Sunday church. But Vivian did not argue as he helped her up to the front seat.

"Afraid you must sit with me, miss, unless you prefer to ride on the bed." His mouth twisted with disapproval.

"This is just fine," she said as she settled the reticule and her grandmother's sketchbook in her lap. "Did Miss Quigg tell you where to take me?"

"No'm, she left that to you."

Vivian's posture shot up, a lesson her mother had taught her when she was about to face an uncomfortable situation: *Sit tall, and never allow them to see you nervous.* "We're going to Sitwell."

"Miss?" His eyes widened.

"We're going—" She had to catch her breath, "—to Sitwell Prison."

The man's face never slacked from its impassive state. "Are you sure that's where you want to go, miss?"

"Perfectly sure." She leaned back in the narrow seat, looking straight ahead.

"Sure you won't want the carriage?" he asked. "Sitwell's a mighty long way, and it ain't so comfortable in the wagon."

She gave him a pointed look. "I'm not so spoiled as you might believe, Mr. Shelley."

"I wasn't thinking of that, miss, honest."

She smiled wanly. "That's all right, sir. To Sitwell."

Mr. Shelley was right in that the ride was "a mighty long way," and the wooden seat bounced with every rock on the gravel road. But Vivian welcomed the bumps and shifts, as they interrupted the running throughs in her mind and lulled the anxieties that went with them. Mr. Shelley was blissfully silent and skilled at directing the horses.

She knew immediately when they reached Sitwell, though there was no sign to proclaim the city's population. It was hardly much of a city, merely a few dotted structures that sold provisions, along with a post office. There were no houses or farms through the stretch of swampy land they passed between the buildings and the prison. The wagon went slowly, as the mud was thick on the road, and Mr. Shelley had to steer the horses with care. Vivian imagined there were hardly visitors to the prison, and the provision wagons came infrequently.

She saw the barbed wire fence around a field of dry grass even though there was not a building in sight. It was at the bottom of a small incline, and once Mr. Shelley mounted it, she saw the prison. She had to force herself to look at the red bricks surrounded with several layers of barbed wire.

"It doesn't look so bad, no, it doesn't," she said to herself.

But Mr. Shelley heard her words, and answered in perhaps a too proud voice, "I wouldn't know, miss."

"No, I'm sure you wouldn't," Vivian snapped, feeling her anger swarm. Even a simple man like Mr. Shelley considered himself above anyone who might fall into the bounds of those barbed wire fences.

She steeled herself for grim countenances and curt manners, but the guard at the gate was mild-mannered. He indicated that she was expected and directed Mr Shelley to a gravel area under a shade of oak trees where he could park the wagon.

As Mr. Shelley helped her down, he said, "I'd just as soon come with you, miss."

"That won't be necessary." Vivian felt more assured now that they were inside. The front entrance to the prison looked more like a well-protected house.

"I really think I ought to."

"I appreciate your concern, Mr. Shelley," she said firmly. "But this really doesn't concern anyone but me."

"I reckon you aim to see a friend?" he ventured

"Yes," she mumbled.

"Well, miss, it might be in the visiting room." He shifted a little. "I ain't never been but A man who worked in a prison hired me once, and he told me about them places. They ain't exactly cheering."

Vivian squared her shoulders. "If I need you, I promise I will send for you."

"Fair enough, miss." He brought her to the door, then pausing, he remarked, not without a little admiration, "My but young ladies is fearless nowadays."

"And foolhardy at times," Vivian said with a wry smile. "But we learn from our foolishness, Mr. Shelley. Everyone does."

He gave a tip of his hat and returned to the wagon.

The moment she opened the door, a heavy-set man strode forward with his hand out. "Miss Alderdice? I'm Thurman Jenkins, warden here." His grasp was firm and warm. "We're informal, as you'll see. You needn't concern yourself." His swift eye caught her jerking head.

"What you meant to say, I'm sure, is that I needn't be frightened," Vivian said evenly.

He smiled. "I can see you're a clever woman. More's the better. Now that Jake has consented to tell us a little about his family—"

"He didn't tell you about us?"

"Well, no, miss. Fact is, he tried to deny he had any family when he first came." His voice was as mild as the guard's had been. "He would have denied his last name even, but that was on the record."

"Yes," Vivian murmured. "Yes, he would do that." She fought the hurt that threatened to beat down her courage.

"It's nothing new to us," Warden Jenkins reassured her. "Many men who come in here try to give us a false name and deny their family. They've honorable reasons, and we respect that."

"I'm glad," she said.

"I'm sure you're impatient to see your brother." He led her down a hallway which, she was glad to see, had no bars and no evidence of anything but what she might find in an office building on Market Street. The room they entered was almost like a study, though its furnishings were shabbier. But there was a masculine coziness to it. She guessed it was the warden's office, as he adjusted himself comfortably behind the wide desk.

The moment he had seated himself, she looked squarely at him. "Do I need to prepare myself for the worst, Mr. Jenkins?"

She could see he knew what she meant. His face became thoughtful for a moment, the eyes weighing, as if he were picturing Jake in his mind and surveying him from her point of view. He answered carefully, "I think you'll find him in good physical condition."

"And his state of mind?"

"That you must determine for yourself," he said. "Jake isn't an easy young man to reach. Oh, he's pleasant enough, mind you. He doesn't stir up trouble. But, well,—"

"I think I know what you mean," Vivian said. "He gets along, but he doesn't communicate." She looked away. "That's for my mother's sake."

"He's shown an aptitude for organization," said the warden. "So, we opted to put him in the prison library rather than out with the rest of the men in hard labor. His character was more suited to the job."

"I see." Vivian closed her eyes for a moment, willing the fuzzy line that had flashed in front of her to go away. She opened them and said in a business-like tone, "I understand you are a believer in prison reform, sir."

"Absolutely." His tone became stronger. "I've been here less than two years, but I assure you, there are none of the more pervasive means of discipline you will find in other prisons."

"I don't know what I would find in other prisons," Vivian said.

"I shall not enlighten you," he said. "You come from a distinguished family, and such things aren't in the way of virtuous young ladies."

"Virtuous or not," Vivian said, her voice amplified in the small room, "I want to know. Tell me."

He stalled for time as he adjusted the ink wells on his desk, checked the tips of the fountain pens in the holder, moved the small paperweight around. Then he said, "The whip is the preferred choice of punishment in most prisons, Miss Alderdice. That and the hole."

"The hole?"

"A small cell where a prisoner is given only bread and water and no light." Shame lingered in his voice, followed by anger. "They ought not to allow it!"

Vivian bowed her head. "I'm grateful you don't allow it."

He leaned forward. "Your brother would never have been subjected to such things even if he were in San Quintin. He has been very complacent."

"A model prisoner," she lamented. "Yes, Jake would do that. Guilt and shame would make him numb."

"That is the reason I am allowing this visit," Mr. Jenkins continued. "I believe in prisoners seeing their loved ones if they have earned the privilege."

Vivian rose. "You may take me to the visitors' room now, sir."

"I've arranged for you to see Jake here."

"In your office?"

"There will be a guard," he said. "As a regulation, of course. I have no fear of either you or Jake doing anything unorthodox. I thought it would be much more pleasant for you if you were to see him here and not in the visitor's chamber."

Vivian turned away so he wouldn't see her tears. "That was very good of you."

"I will put you on your honor that you have nothing to give him." His eyes lingered on the sketchbook. "Jake is fond of drawing, as the chaplain will tell you."

Vivian glanced down at the book, realizing the warden had

misunderstood its intentions. But she gripped it in her hands. "I'd like to see my brother now."

"Forgive me for taking up so much of your time." The man shook her hand. "I shall tell the guard to bring him to you." He lingered for a moment at the door. "I believe you'll find his countenance not much changed. We don't insist on striped uniforms here."

It felt as if hours passed as she waited alone in the room. Vivian noticed the windows in the room were not unpleasant, as there were two large ones that let in the light. She could see a faint outline of the bars on the outside. She had never seen the sky so vivid blue, glaring in her eyes against the line of yellow grass further away, distorted somewhat by the barbed wire fence. She wondered whether the prison library had windows where Jake could see the sky. She fumbled for her handkerchief, for she suddenly felt the tears coming. Jake, who had languished always in nature, loved the woods as if they were a second home to him, and now had to fight for a view of the sky.

For a moment, she wanted to turn and run out of the building. She imagined Jake's pained face when she showed him the sketchbook and demanded to see the diary Verina had left with him. Perhaps Alda was right about her taking unfair advantage of Jake's tender feelings toward her. Had she the right to walk into his dark room, and seek whatever she might find there that would alter the lives of both of them?

Footsteps clanged against the floor of the prison. They were far away at first, then came closer, their echo clear. With each step, Vivian clutched her hands in her lap. The sketchbook fell to the floor, and she bent down to retrieve it. As she did so, the footsteps stopped.

She straightened, keeping her gaze straight at the wall opposite where there were several paintings of birds with the detail an ornithologist would appreciate. How ironic Mr. Jenkins should have so many birds on his walls! Birds painted with such find detail that they looked as if they could leap off the canvas at any moment and fly out the tall windows. She saw she and Jake had been all these years like those painted birds, looking for an opportunity to fly away.

A throat cleared, and the warden approached her. "I'll leave you now. Mr. Thomson will be in the room if you need anything. Good luck." With the last words, he took hold of her gloved hand, clutching it.

She swallowed, her gaze still on the birds. She heard his heavy tread out the door, followed by a moment of silence. Then, a different tread came into the room, but only a few steps, as if the person had come just beyond the door. Then silence again.

She rose and turned around. The first glimpse was of the guard in his uniform standing in the corner near the door with his hands behind his back, as immobile as a toy soldier. Then she saw Jake. She took in his tall figure and blond hair and found warmth in his eyes, and in a moment, she was in his arms. They held one another in silence. She felt the roughness of the shirt he wore, a scratchy cotton that had no resemblance to the finer textures she associated with his old style of dress.

She held herself away so she could really look at him. She saw what the warden had meant. Outwardly, her brother had not really changed. He still had the same lanky figure, still the pale skin and the green eyes. But the dash of sparkle in them had gone. The face stood with more rigidity and a refined dignity he had never possessed before. He looked, she realized, just like her grandfather.

"You look well, Jake," she said.

He offered a fragile smile. "Did you think I would be emaciated and pasty?"

"Frankly, yes," she said. They both chuckled. A cough escaped from the corner where Mr. Thomson stood, and Vivian led her brother to the table in the office.

"Viv, why did you come?" He spoke in almost a whisper, and

Vivian wondered if this was what he had learned in prison to keep the guards from hearing conversations.

"To see you, naturally." She hesitated, glancing at the man in the corner, but saw he was deliberately looking at the birds on the wall. She reached over and put her hand on Jake's.

His face was grave. "If Mother knew—"

"What makes you think she doesn't?" she asked quickly.

He grimaced. "Because I know you, and I know Mother."

"I thought — I hoped — after a year—" She suddenly found her tongue wooden.

"I told you to forget about me," he said. "It's best that way."

"I had to see you," she said.

"Why?" The question shot out at her like a bullet from a gun in a voice that was unusually gravel and curt.

"You even sound like Grandfather." Her brows arching.

"Perhaps I do," he said. "He didn't mince words, did he?"

"Then I won't either."

"Dagger Girl." His tone was almost affectionate. "I gathered it was something like that when Miss Quigg came to see me."

"Mother and I are in Waxwood again, Jake."

"Miss Quigg told me," he said. "I didn't think Mother would ever want to see that place again."

"It's a long story," she sighed. "But a less important one."

"What is the important one, then?"

"I've walked into another dark room, Jake," she said. "Only you can help me get out of it."

He was silent for a moment, his feet tapping, his knees jiggling. Even as a boy, he had had a hard time keeping still. "You can escape it, Viv. Just walk out."

"I can't," she said. "The walls are closing in on me." She leaned forward, catching his gaze. "You walked into that room too, didn't you, Jake?"

He glanced at the birds on the wall. "The only dark room I've walked into this last year is a cell."

She felt herself almost gag. "I know you went to see Bertha before you went to the police. And you saw Verina Jones too."

He cupped his hands. "Bertha told you that?"

"No, dear," said Vivian. "Bertha has been dead for eight months."

His head dropped. "I'm sorry. I liked her."

"So did I," said Vivian. "She was our guide out of the forest. *Dans le fond des forêts votre image me suit.*"

"There is no shadow that follows us anymore," he insisted in the same gravel voice.

"I didn't think so either," she said. "Until I met David Potter on the train coming to Waxwood."

"I don't know who he is, and I don't much care." He gave her a thorny look.

"Am I talking in circles again?" she asked with a shrill laugh. "And I promised I wouldn't mince words. All right. I know you talked to Bertha, but Ruth couldn't tell me what she told you. I've come to find out."

"I won't tell you either!" This came with an almost vicious denial that had belonged to their grandfather.

"I think I can guess." She drew out the sketchbook and pushed it toward him. Mr. Thomson took a few steps forward. But when he saw what it was, he returned to his discreet corner.

Jake looked at the cover for a long time before he opened it. He went through the pages slowly, his eyes lingering without expression. But Vivian saw from the way his forehead wrinkled and his mouth puckered that he was trying to keep from crying because he knew to whom the sketchbook belonged.

At last, he closed it carefully and laid it on the table between them. "So, you know Evan was in San Francisco."

"It's more than that, and you know it!" Vivian's voice rose for a moment, and the guard glanced at her. "It was the year Grandfather went to Germany."

"What of it?" he asked. "Grandmother and Evan were friends."

"Grandfather made Evan promise never to see Grandmother again once she left Waxwood," said Vivian. "That was in the letters."

"I didn't read those damn letters," he hissed.

"No," she said. "But you read Evan's diary."

The tapping feet began again, and his eyes grew bleary. She took his hand in hers. "I don't want to upset you, dear."

"I don't want to upset *you*."

"You know I always want the truth," she said.

"Yes," he said. "Evan and Grandmother saw one another for some months. That's what Bertha told me." He looked at her. "But it ended when Grandfather came back to San Francisco. Evan went back to Brandywine."

"What ended?" Vivian asked. Her brother didn't answer, only looked at the birds. "What ended, Jake?"

"Does it matter?"

"It matters!"

Her brother shifted in the chair, crossing his long legs. "Their friendship, naturally."

"Naturally," said Vivian, her anger emerging. "And what else besides friendship?"

"Don't push me, Viv." He glanced at the guard in the corner. "I can ask the guard to take me back to my cell."

Her hands returned to her lap. "You never used to threaten. That's Grandfather too."

"Maybe I've learned at last to be a man of the world," he said shortly.

She leaned toward him. "I gather Bertha also told you she was with Grandmother in a town called Lico when their friend Loretta Potter died in September 1855."

"Potter?" he muttered.

"David Potter's aunt," she said. "The man I spoke to on the train."

"Well?"

"Grandmother didn't attend the funeral because she was going to have a baby," said Vivian.

"Well, Mother was born in November," Jake pointed out.

"Grandfather wrote the Potters a letter explaining that Grandmother was too ill to attend the funeral." Vivian traced her finger on the smooth surface of the table. "He said they were going abroad. Jake, how come Grandmother couldn't travel to Waxwood, but she could go abroad?"

He blinked at the windows that suddenly shone in the brilliance of the morning sun. He did not answer.

"And I learned from Leona — Loretta's sister — that Bertha was behaving oddly. When she returned to Waxwood, she was distressed, as if something wasn't right."

"Bertha was confused," Jake mumbled. "I told you that years ago."

"She was not confused!" Vivian admonished. The guard shot them a look. "She told Ruth she thought Grandmother wasn't ill at all."

"Wasn't ill?" He sat up.

"She was pretending to be in her confinement," said Vivian. "Bertha told Leona she would go walking and drawing the moment Grandfather left for the Carlyle Shipping offices in Santa Barbara." She tilted her head so she could look at him. "Grandfather made her give it up after they married, but she was drawing again."

"That was Evan's influence," said Jake.

"You know that from the diary, don't you?"

He dipped his head. "Viv, where is all this leading?"

Vivian placed her hands flat on the table. "Jake, has it ever occurred to you we might not be Alderdices at all?"

She did not dare look at her brother's face. The air was heavy with suspension, and she could almost feel it descending around them like a cape. There was a sudden cackling of birds from outside.

"If we aren't Alderdices," he said slowly, "then we would be free, wouldn't we?"

She gazed at the face that had lost its lines and now softened in the way she remembered. His eyes were like green gauze, and his lips quivered. "Are we free, Jake? Are we?"

The stone face returned. "You ask too much, Viv."

"I want to see Evan's diary."

His eyes shifted from one side of the room to the other, resting on the bird paintings. "I don't have it."

"You've never lied to me, Jake." He had wounded her now, and there was no hiding it. "Don't lie to me now. I know Verina gave it to you."

He looked at his feet. "Did she tell you that?"

"No," she said. "Verina buries her sorrows in a void existence."

"Maybe she has the right idea," he said. "When one lives for nothing but the moment, one is happy. I've learned that here. Oh, can't you leave well enough alone?" he cried out.

"Put it away and don't think about it?" she shot back. "I see you're still under Mother's influence."

"I have my own philosophies now," he said. "They may not be the right ones, but they're mine."

"You've read the diary," she declared. "Now I want to read it."

He did not answer, crossing his arms over his chest. Vivian recognized the gesture from when he was a boy and their grandfather would interrogate him about his schoolwork. It was not a gesture of defiance, but of shielding.

"You read it, and you were free." She continued watching him. "You may resemble Grandfather now, but you've come into your own differently."

"You may call it that," he said.

The guard in the corner cleared his throat. When Vivian glanced at him, he held up five fingers. Vivian knew they had five more minutes.

"Please let me see it." She grasped his hand. "I've come this far. I must go all the way."

"The dagger girl must twist and twist the knife, mustn't she?" His eyes flashed a jade green.

"Would you rather I asked Mother about it?"

He half-jumped out of his chair. "Don't ask Mother anything! I have harmed her enough."

"Wounded?" The rage wailed in her. "She ought to be here, and she isn't. Doesn't that make her the instrument of pain rather than the recipient?"

"Don't, Viv." He sagged in the chair.

Her eyes filled with tears. "I didn't want to go down this path. You must believe me, Jake."

He studied her face, hard edges forming around his lips. "I believe you."

"But now I must follow it wherever it leads," she said. "Down a dark path, there is eventually light."

They were silent for a moment. Then he rose. "The diary is with the chaplain. I gave it to him to keep safe. I suppose I knew one day you would come."

Vivian leapt up and threw her arms around her brother's neck. This time she cried, letting the tears spill down her face and onto his shoulder. He held her for a few moments. She saw the guard was standing near the door. Panic grew as she saw a ring of keys swinging from his hand.

"You'll let me come see you again?"

He turned to face her with an expression she had never seen. It was not of the boy she had known who was thoughtful and dreamy. This was a man whose will was as cutting as iron spikes. "If you come here again, I'll refuse to see you."

She gave a small cry, her hands trembling. The icy countenance melted, and the boy she knew gave way. "I don't want to hurt you or Mother ever again. I asked you to pretend I'm dead. It's better that way."

Her voice was murky now, drowning in tears. "Won't you let me write to you at least?"

"If you do," he said. "I won't write back. You understand that."

She nodded. He watched her for a moment. Then, his hand floated upward like Grandfather's had in his last days, as if reaching for something that was not there. But just as she neared, he stepped away. In a moment, he had vanished down the hallway, the clicking steps punctuated by the clanging of the guard's keys.

She stumbled to the window, feeling the harsh sun on her face. Her sobs grew louder, and she felt herself gasping for a breath. She tried to drown the noise by burying her face in her handkerchief, but the flimsy satin only sagged against the flow of tears. She stayed that way for a while, bawling as she had never done even as a child.

But gradually, the silence between sobs grew, and the gasps became breaths. Her handkerchief was soaked, but there were no more tears for it to absorb. She felt wobbly, holding on to the back of a chair. She turned around, and she looked into the face of Mr. Jenkins. She wondered how long he had been standing there.

He said in his gentle voice, "It isn't easy, seeing them, is it?"

"You've been terribly decent." Vivian was aware of her tear-stained face. "My brother told me I could see the chaplain about some things he wants me to take home."

"Of course." He leaned out to the corridor and summoned a guard standing at the end, whispering instructions to him. The man disappeared, and Mr. Jenkins opened a narrow door which led into a small room with a washbasin, towel and mirror. "I don't always get home in the evenings," he said, almost self-consciously. "My wife insisted I have this. You're welcome to freshen up." He disappeared down the hall, leaving Vivian alone.

She washed her face with the fragrant soap, scrubbing away the remnants of tears. She pulled out all the pins in her hair and redid it, making sure the pompadour looked presentable peeking out from under the rim of the hat. She took a few breaths, feeling more like herself. The aches from her sobbing had subsided, and she could walk with ease again, feeling the rigidity of those inherited ankles guiding her with poise and grace.

When she emerged from the small closet, the chaplain was standing with his hands folded in front of him, the warden behind him.

"Father Gonzalez, Miss Alderdice," said Mr. Jenkins.

The man was elderly and small in stature, but there was something peaceable about him that made Vivian immediately feel his presence. He bowed, his robes dipping. "At your service, my child."

"Thank you, Father," she said. "My brother has given me permission to take some of his things with me. He said they're in your possession."

"We shall go to the chapel," he said, swinging toward the door.

The warden grasped Vivian's hand warmly. "I hope I shall see you again someday, Miss Alderdice." The hesitant words told Vivian he guessed at the result of her visit with Jake, perhaps by her tears.

"Thank you for all you've done for my brother," she said. "I hope you succeed with your reforms."

"They will come," he said, squaring his shoulders. "Despite all the obstacles, they will come someday."

"Yes," she repeated. "They will come."

She walked alongside Father Gonzalez. They went outside the building to a more congenial yard where there were even lemon trees giving off a fragrant scent. He saw Vivian looking at them and smiled a rather waxy smile, like a doll. "In the summer, we give prisoners lemonade with their meals," he said. "Mr. Jenkins won't allow the fruit to go to waste."

"He's very humane," Vivian said.

"He understands when one is in confinement, minor pleasures make one more responsible and answerable for one's deeds," he said with a dip of his head. "One feels less the hand of God has forsaken him."

"Yes," Vivian agreed. "One is apt to be more amiable when one has modest comforts."

"You understand well." The chaplain paused in front of the wooden door to a small stone structure.

"I know what it's like to be in prison, Father," she said grimly. "Even if it's one without bars."

He looked at her for a few silent moments. He had small eyes, very dark and very round, like a badger she had seen once near a river. The animal had frozen halfway through a plot of foliage and had stood looking at her without motion, as if he were also studying her. It had made her shiver and retreat to the group of young people with whom she had gone on the excursion. Now the gaze of the badger Father Gonzalez possessed made her shiver again.

He seemed to notice and, as they entered the chapel, said apologetically, "It can get chilly here, even in the summer."

"I'm all right," she said in a brisk voice. "I'd just like to get my brother's things."

"Assuredly." He led her down the aisle where narrow wooden pews stood in rows waiting for Sunday services. Her heels echoed on the stone ground. She looked up at the room with its wooden beams running across, higher than Vivian had imagined they could be in such a small place.

The chaplain led her to the back corner where a door opened into a small office. The room was like none she had ever seen. Apothecary cabinets in different styles and different shapes took up every available wall space, some stacked one on top of the other. There was little else in the room except for a desk and a few chairs. Vivian was glad to see there were no bars on this window.

Father Gonzalez smiled. "Sometimes people think of me as

one of the never satisfied." He chuckled. "They do not understand the drawers are filled with other men's possessions, not mine."

"You mean, you keep their things here when they enter the prison?" Vivian accepted the chair he offered her.

"Not all of them," he said. "There are the mundane objects the guards keep. But those that are the most priceless to them — that they would not trust to anyone but God or His disciples — they give to me."

Vivian couldn't help but notice the drawers looked as if they had been opened many times, and none had locks. "Aren't you — and they — afraid of thieves?" She felt her face grow red.

He shook his head. "There are no thieves in Canaan."

Vivian gave him a wary look. "You are an optimist, Father."

"I am hopeful, my child." He took out a drawer from a cabinet and brought it to the desk.

"You looked as if you chose my brother's drawer with divine guidance," Vivian remarked. Then, realizing she may have offended the chaplain, she said, "I didn't mean—"

But he laughed, a light, almost teasing laughter that surprised her. "I claim no such divinity, Miss Alderdice. I am more familiar with his possessions because he comes to see me often to look at them."

"My brother comes to see you?"

"That surprises you," he said. "He has perhaps acquired a faith in God he did not have before he came here. Many men discover a more divine light when they are in the most darkness."

"I should think the opposite was true," Vivian admitted. "Where there is more darkness, there is more despair."

"But many are here for a long time," said the chaplain. "Some for life, and some will go to the hangman. They seek to grasp *something* that will guide them through their despair. Something or someone."

"I appreciate that, Father," Vivian stiffened, "but I am not here to discuss theological conceptions with you."

"No, indeed," he said. "And I am not here to give you counsel, though I am always happy to offer it, if you need it."

"Thank you," she breathed.

He pushed the drawer toward her. "You may take what you like. Your brother has no secrets from you, I know."

She stared at him. "How do you know?"

"Oh, he has spoken to me many times of his family."

This warmed Vivian's heart, and she held her handkerchief to her lips, willing the tears not to flood again. "Mr. Jenkins said many men deny their families when they are in prison."

"He has to others," he said. "He goes by the name of Jack Albright here."

Vivian tried not to cry out, pressing the handkerchief again to her lips, so hard this time that she felt the sting on the skin of her upper lip.

Father Gonzalez saw her despair, for he added, "To the other men and the guards only. The warden knows his true identity, and he speaks of it freely to me."

Vivian wanted to ask what it was Jake spoke of about her and Larissa, but she realized it would be selfish. It hardly mattered anyway.

The chaplain had taken the drawer from one of the larger cabinets, so it was longer and shallower than many of the rest. It had ample space, as Jake had hardly much to fill it. There was a small leather book tied with a strap, which Vivian guessed was Evan's diary. There were also some thin sheets of paper gathered in a portfolio sealed with string.

Vivian took the book. "I believe this is what I want." Something about its worn cover and the tie that bound it almost prettily told her it had belonged to Evan.

"The thoughts of a man he never knew," said Father Gonzalez wistfully. "That was what Jacob told me."

"Jake never knew him," Vivian said. "I know him." It was an odd thing to say about a man who had died thirty or so years ago.

But she felt as if she knew Evan Jones from her grandmother's letters.

The chaplain was watching her, his hands in his lap. "One need not meet a person to know them."

She glanced at him, suddenly feeling those badger eyes haunting her. She rose. "I must go."

"You have no interest in your brother's drawings?"

She gazed at the portfolio. Then, setting the diary on top of her grandmother's sketchbook, she carefully opened it. The pages had a slightly rough surface.

Father Gonzalez smiled. "Rag paper. We use it for church documents."

"Very good of you to give it to him," she said.

"It was the least I could do when he showed an interest in drawing," he said. "There is only the prison letter paper for inmates, and it's quite impossible to use for his purposes."

Vivian studied the drawings. She expected the prison materials would make for a cruder style, but the drawings were actually more delicate than the ones he had done the year before. The first showed a man and woman standing at the rim of a lake while a girl and boy played in the grass beside them. Shades of restrained green, red, and brown added blandness to the scene. The other paintings had a similar air of quietude in matching color palettes.

A stinging pain ran down her spine as she realized, scrutinizing the faces, that the woman resembled Larissa, the boy Jake, and the girl herself, though he had drawn them all rather generally, as figures in an advertisement. The man's face was unfamiliar to her and almost like a caricature in its exaggerated handsomeness, but Vivian knew Jake was trying to draw his father.

"There is a lake visible from the library window," Father Gonzalez spoke. "Jacob is quite fond of it."

Vivian remained silent as she continued to study the pictures. Inside, a hurricane of emotions whirled.

"He told me he draws from memory," the chaplain continued.

Vivian threw the drawings on the floor. "If he is drawing from memory, then memory paints a pretty picture!"

"I don't think your brother has any illusions about that," said the man in a quiet voice.

"These are not memories, Father." Her voice was bruised. "Jake never even knew his father, just like I never knew mine. My mother was widowed twice, you see."

"I see." The man nodded.

"These are delusions," she said in a grim voice. "Jake has always wanted what was never there."

"Is that so wrong?"

"Wrong!" Her voice filled the small room. The chaos of the hurricane inside her exploded. "When one is a child, one dreams. And there are always those who will take the dreams away and replace them with their own. After all, children are there to mold, aren't they?"

"Don't be angry, my child."

"I'm not angry at my brother. He's not to blame." She wandered to the window. "But I am angry at others. You're right, Father."

"What others?"

"The pillars of Far Western society," she said, "whose tidy rules and proprieties have killed any character my family ever had." Her throat was scratchy, making her voice come out ragged. "The docile clanswomen and the cowardly clansmen of Ancestor Hall who don't even belong to us."

"I don't understand you, my child," said the man gently.

She went on, hardly hearing him. "And, perhaps, someone I can't see." Her hands trembled as she returned to the chair. "There are peering eyes all around me. There always has been."

"The eyes of God?" he asked. "You feel as if God has forsaken you."

"Not God, no," said Vivian in a hard voice. "Only my family. My legacy."

"You share many of the same feelings the men do here," said the chaplain.

"And what counsel do you give the men?" Vivian looked at him.

"I counsel forgiveness."

"Forgiveness!" She looked away.

"'Do not judge, and you will not be judged. Do not condemn, and you will not be condemned. Forgive, and you will be forgiven,'" Father Gonzalez quoted.

All at once, the hurricane subsided, and the blood running through her veins warmed again. She felt ashamed at her wretched behavior, humbled in the face of this amicable man. She retrieved the drawings, placing them neatly inside the drawer.

"Wouldn't you like to take them?" he ventured.

"I don't think so," she said. "I couldn't bear it —" She hid her eyes behind her handkerchief.

"I understand," he said. "You prefer to look at the lake as it is, not as you would wish it to be."

"I only wish for peace of mind," she said in a throaty voice.

He rose and held out his hand. His gasp was gentle as his voice. "I hope you will find it, my child. But look for it with kindness in your heart. Not with bitterness and malice."

"I'll try to remember that, Father." She sighed.

He saw her to the wagon where Mr. Shelley was already waiting. Vivian turned to the chaplain. "Take care of Jake, won't you, Father?"

"He can take care of himself perfectly well," the man remarked. "He is not a little boy, Miss Alderdice."

"No," she said, staring into the dust. "He isn't. Not anymore."

As Mr. Shelley maneuvered the wagon silently back onto the muddy road, and they bounced and rambled, Vivian grasped the diary and the sketchbook as if they were children about ready to fall to the ground. It occurred to her Jake had asked nothing about their mother. Larissa was as dead to him as he was to her.

CHAPTER 18

By the time they pulled into the blacksmith's stable in Waxwood, it was late afternoon. The main road buzzed with the activity of merchants and shoppers, people of all classes mingling on the street. Vivian stared idly at the women, some in gingham dresses, while others were in more lavish materials, their skirts swinging behind them as they walked. Most of the men were in work clothes, though there were some who wore clean jackets and hats to signal the significance of their positions.

She climbed down from the wagon before Mr. Shelley could reach her and, staring at the people passing by, she murmured, "It's all as usual. Just as usual."

"Miss?" The driver peered at her.

Vivian peeked at him and then smiled. "I often talk to myself. Don't pay any attention, sir." She took out her reticule and shoved several bills in his hands, which he tried to protest, but she shrugged off.

She walked away from the pier where the ferry was waiting and went to Nettie's, feeling more temperate as she became one of the crowd. Her fine silk skirt was a little frayed from the dust of the ride, and her hair already escaped the little pins under her hat. She glimpsed at herself in the mirror. The reflection dulled the materials she wore, but she knew she looked like any other working girl. She looked like Miss Redfern. It made her feel prouder and more stable.

She reached the store where Nettie was helping two older ladies, explaining the contents of a few bottles on the counter. She glanced at Vivian over their shoulders as Vivian sat down at the soda fountain. Her scrutinizing eyes took in Vivian's anguish, and she quickly finished with the women. When they left, she shut and locked the door and turned the OPEN sign to its CLOSED side.

Without a word, she filled a glass with water and ice and pushed it in front of Vivian. Vivian drank as if she had not seen water in days, the iciness of its temperature burning her throat, making her choke. Then she held her handkerchief to her lips until the coughing subsided.

"Thank you," she said in a meek voice. "I was parched."

"You've had nothing since breakfast this morning, I take it?"

"We just came back."

Nettie led her to the flat above. "You'll stay right here, and I'll make you some food. Then you'll rest."

Vivian closed her eyes. She felt suddenly as if the world were caving in on her, and the only thing she could do was lie still and wait for it to fall.

She heard the pleasant sounds of meal preparations — the clang of spoons in pots, the rubbing of glass against wood, silverware being sorted. Nettie had opened the window all the way, and the bay lifted its pleasant afternoon breeze into the room, floating like cool waves against Vivian's face. She could take a few breaths and feel the light scent of the sea fill her chest. The dry, yellow grass and the mud piles of Sitwell faded out of her mind.

She must have fallen asleep, as Nettie was gently shaking her awake. They sat down to a light lunch of cold cuts, cheese slices, salad and coffee. The pleasant temperature of the room and the food slackened Vivian's reserve, and she told Nettie about her visit with Jake.

When she finished, her friend was looking at her with her exacting eyes. "And you're surprised he hardly mentioned your mother?"

A fist formed in Vivian's gut. "No, not surprised. Not that he doesn't care about her. It's that he's always been afraid of her."

"It sounds as if he's had a rough time," said Nettie. "And your needling him with this Pandora's box of yours didn't make it easier."

"I realize that." Vivian dawdled over her coffee.

"Did you really expect him to tell you what you wanted to know?" The lips formed a seething grin. "In some ways, you're rather naïve, Vivian."

"We once told one another everything," Vivian said sadly.

"Some secrets are best kept buried with the treasures," Nettie said.

"That's what Jake always used to say," she said. "'Leave well enough alone.'"

"But it isn't well enough for you," said her friend. "And now you'll find all the buried secrets in that book he gave you."

"I don't know how I shall hide it from Mother." Vivian sighed.

"You could stay here another night," Nettie suggested. "Read it here, and let me keep it for you, if you wish."

Vivian glanced at her, smiling. "I don't want to make you my refuge from the storm."

"Why not?" Nettie leaned back. "We must all have some refuge. And I would appreciate your company tonight of all nights."

"Why tonight of all nights?" Vivian asked.

"Because, my pet, the BAWSPR are holding a meeting," she said. "And it should be quite a celebration. Miss Albina Fowler has been making her way down the coast, and she's going to speak tonight."

Despite the deflation she still felt from her visit to Sitwell, Vivian felt a pang of excitement. "I've heard so many things about her."

"Marvina and the others are quite enamored with her philosophies," said Nettie. "She's a celebrity amongst the San Francisco suffragists because she comes from the city. I shouldn't wonder if all that glitters will be on display in Mrs. Elfrieda Adler's ballroom this evening."

"Who is she?"

"Oh, the bluest of the Waxwood blue bloods." Her friend's eyes sparkled. "Loftier than your Nob Hill folks, I'm sure."

Vivian gazed out the window, feeling the sky blur. "I don't know if I'm up to seeing people."

Nettie reached for her hand. "It will take your mind off your troubles."

Vivian glanced at her with a grimace. "You don't know us on Washington Street. Our entire lives are made up of distractions."

"This would be a different distraction," Nettie said. "A worthy distraction thinking about others besides yourself."

Vivian smiled and squeezed her hand. "I should like to hear Miss Fowler speak. Marvina has told me so much about her."

"Then it's settled." Her friend rose, collecting the dishes. "You'll rest until then. In the meantime, take off that skirt and blouse. They're rather filthy. I don't mind, but Mrs. Adler and her sort might take you for one of Odele's comrades if you show up like that."

Vivian smiled and began unbuttoning her skirt.

The fine breeze in the small flat did not kick up into a harsher wind as it usually did in the evenings by the bay. It remained sedate and numb. As the air lent itself to so fine an evening, Nettie suggested they walk to Mrs. Adler's house, though it was some distance, since they needed to cross the main artery of town into the hillier area toward Ruth Ross' house. After the barbed wire fences, the towers with the men with guns, and the confinement she had endured that day, Vivian felt nothing would please her more than a long walk.

They set out in the early evening. Nettie had washed Vivian's clothes and hung them over the window and chairs to dry and had lent her a robin's blue suit and blouse, simple but clean, like the ones Miss Redfern and her fellow working girls wore. Nettie herself had changed into what Vivian guessed was her Sunday best. The dress was still black, but it was in the half-mourning style, with a pleasant plum trim and gold buttons. The small bit of color lent a flush to her skin that was becoming and made the mousiness of her hair and eyes less noticeable.

Vivian took Nettie's arm as they started out. "The suit fits me fine," she said, smiling.

"I would give it to you, if I didn't know you had much finer ones," said her friend.

"I wouldn't take it," Vivian said. "Not because it isn't as grand as anything I have, but because you shall wear it again one day soon."

Nettie glanced at her. "You don't think black is becoming to me?"

"I think life is becoming to you," Vivian said.

"You sound like my mother." Her friend's steps dragged a little as they took the bend near the city park. "She used to say, 'Don't always look for the cracks in the china.'" She was silent for a while as the breeze brought out the scent of geranium bushes near the park. "I suppose that's what made her death so painful to me. She gave up on life."

Vivian said softly. "It's hard to fight the duel of death, even if one has lived."

"She was facing the duel too soon," said Nettie. "She was only fifty-two." Her voice grew loud. "She worked hard all her life. My father left when I was only a few years old. Said he had the chance for a rare game that would make his fortune on some riverboat in the East. He was a card player and heaven knows what else."

"But he lost?"

"We never knew." Nettie's voice was bitter and her smile seething. "He took what little money we had and went off. We never heard a word from him again. All he left behind were his promises." Nettie sighed. "It's of no importance now. Mama and I fended for ourselves like many women do. It wasn't easy, but we managed. Until it broke Mama down like a horse in harness."

"It must have been difficult to nurse her," Vivian ventured.

"The doctor said it was mostly a matter of rest and will. I could give her the rest. I insisted on it. I just opened the drugstore, so she no longer would have had to work."

"I always thought the drugstore was your father's," Vivian said.

Nettie grimaced. "He never did work that required honest energy for honest pay in his life. He was always trying to get something grand from nothing."

They walked down the road that turned into smaller streets with more run-down homes and passed by the turn into Ruth's house. Vivian couldn't see the crooked house from the road, and she was grateful. She had little desire to encounter Ruth just then.

"How did you get the drugstore, if you don't mind my asking?"

Nettie grinned. "What you really want to know is, how did I get the money?" She looked ahead. "It was an inheritance of sorts. Not from Mama, of course. Poor Mama, she had nothing to leave me but some moth-eaten clothes and old furniture and the rather pathetic set of china you've already seen."

"Who then?"

"I had an aunt. A great-aunt, really. Her name was Queenie Ellis, and she was a truth seeker like you, in her own way."

"I shouldn't wonder, with a name like that." Vivian smiled.

Nettie laughed, pressing the short cape around her shoulders. "She was always looking for something, you see. And when she couldn't find it, she tried to give it to me."

"She sounds like an admirable woman."

"She was, in some ways. In many others, she was frivolous." Nettie took a deep breath as they started up a steep hill. "Queenie taught me a lesson: One must judge no one by appearances, for there may lie wisdom or foolishness underneath."

Vivian nodded, pulling her jacket around her shoulders. She could not help but think of Father Gonzalez' words that morning: *Do not judge, and you will not be judged.*

"She had a rather airy way to her, like someone whose head is vacant of ideas," her friend continued. "But she wasn't vacant in the least. She had seen the world, and she talked about the lives of other people, especially other women. She had insights about them."

"Such as?" Vivian leaned toward her, feeling her interest rise.

"She spoke of the women in Egypt, and their infinite patience, despite the way they were treated like chattel," said Nettie. "And Russian peasant women who worked harder than their husbands. She used to say, 'A woman's silence can speak louder than her words.'"

"So, she encouraged you to speak with your silence." Vivian smiled. "Now I know why you're sometimes a woman of few words."

"I wasn't aware that I was." Nettie smiled back.

"How did you end up taking care of her?" Vivian asked gently.

The hill caught a sweeping, stiff wind that made them retreat to an abandoned shack half-eaten by termites but sheltering enough from the icy breeze.

"She came back from India, or some such place, and caught an exotic bug," said Nettie. "She sent a cable asking me to come."

"She was not in California?"

Nettie shook her head. "Maine. Some little cottage by the sea.

It was the first time I had ever been out of Waxwood." Her friend sounded ashamed.

"It was generous of you to go," said Vivian. "I'm sure your mother needed you."

Nettie glanced at her as they began walking up the hill again. "Queen was dying. I couldn't leave her to die alone." Nettie's face was a little pale now. "It was a ghastly illness. It took all the life out of Queenie. I think that was her greatest punishment. Not that she lived for life, but that she died without it."

"She left you an inheritance because of it," Vivian guessed. "She wanted you to have the life she could no longer live."

"In her will, she wrote that I was to have the money — ten thousand dollars — to run any business I chose, and I was to run it myself."

"Those are strange conditions," Vivian remarked.

"Not really," said Nettie. "I remember exactly what she wrote: 'My great-niece, Annette Grace, must not be, as I have been, a parasite in life. A woman who sacrifices her dignity to allow others to care for her is a poor wretch.'" Nettie smiled, her eyes a little glossy.

The hill had grown steeper. Vivian glanced ahead and saw a forlorn-looking house at the very top of the hill on the dead-end street. "Why a drugstore?" she asked. "You could have bought your library and reading room then."

Nettie looked down. "Mama was ill, and I had to be practical. I wanted something so she would never have to work again."

Vivian pressed her hand, feeling a glow of admiration for her friend.

Nettie stopped in front of the forlorn house. Despite its dark coloring, it was so overgrown with elegance that it looked like its owner had been trying to outdo the Nob Hill mansions portrayed in the tourist postcards. Gables and turrets soared up to the sky with more haughtiness than a socialite's chin when passing a poor woman on the street. Their footsteps echoed up the long stairs that led to the front entrance.

A butler escorted them through a maze of hallways with high ceilings to a pair of high, oak doors that opened up into an enormous room with long windows and velvet curtains, all of them drawn. Vivian felt the slickness of the floor under her heels, as the ballroom had been turned into a lecture hall, with wooden chairs and a desk in front in the front. Several flags and banners proclaiming the BAWSPR were placed at the front in a triumphant arc. Vivian glanced at the words sewn into the banner below the organization's initials: *Civility in all things, aid to those in need, a voice for all women.*

Nettie led her to one side of the room. Vivian noticed many women dressed in evening clothes, but even as the silk swayed across the marble floor, the women kept their voices in check, their hands folded in front of them as they made conversation, waiting patiently for the star of the evening.

A pair of hands covered her shoulders. She turned to meet Marvina Moore's somewhat cocky gaze. Looking at the familiar face made the strain of the morning ease, and the smile, with just a little of its usual irony, was like a tonic. Without thinking, she threw her arms around her friend.

"Well, dearest, that's the warmest welcome I've had in a long time." Marvina laughed. "I'm happy to know You've missed me."

"It's been—" Vivian gulped for air. "Difficult."

"What, this summer?"

She could only nod, digging into her bag for her handkerchief.

"Now, now," Marvina soothed. "It can't be so difficult to resist your mother's little maneuvering with that insignificant bit of Canadian logger cousin of Mrs. Griffith, can it?" The bright eyes gave her a wicked gaze. "Oh, I've been keeping tabs on you."

"Through whom?" Vivian asked.

"That's my little secret," she said. "From what I've been told, that Monte Le Blank is about as appealing as an old shoe."

"Leblanc," Vivian said, laughing. "He's not so bad, really."

"Suddenly you're partial to the idea?" Marvina raised her eyebrows. "I recall a time when you were more interested in Miss Brontë's Rochester than in any young men buzzing around you."

"Much has changed since last spring," Vivian mumbled.

"Yes, it has." Here, Marvina took her hand. "Nettie, dear, we must see that our Vivian doesn't end up a jewel presented for the inspection of that Canadian logger."

"I imagine Vivian can decide for herself whether she wants to be a jewel," Nettie insisted.

"I'm glad to see you've taken to one another." Marvina led them to a few empty chairs near the stage. "I thought you would when I introduced you last summer."

"Nettie has been a tower of strength." Vivian smiled at the mousy woman.

"She always is," said Marvina. "But a tower of strength is apt to topple when she has no one to lean on herself."

Nettie's eyes cast downward at the black boots she had polished carefully before they left.

"Have you ever met Albina?" Marvina glanced around the room.

"No, I haven't," said Vivian.

"No, of course you haven't." Marvina gave her a sly smile. "Your mother would hardly have let you out of your room if you had."

Vivian hid a smile. "I would like to."

"We've become good friends in the last year — ah!" She raised her hand with a smile at a small crowd of women, their heads slightly bent toward another woman with a very tall hat and spectacles. The woman in the center stepped forward while the crowd parted from her and, giving Marvina a controlled smile, approached them.

Vivian had heard Albina Fowler was a tall and muscular woman with features that stood out as strong as her position among the suffragists, and with a voice that could rise and fall like a preacher's. The woman Marvina introduced to her had solid features and spoke with a forceful tone. But her figure was slender, even a little angular. Her mannerisms were a little cool, though not cruelly. She made Vivian feel as if she were being assessed, as a farmer would look at a bull he was about to purchase.

"Call me Albina," she said right away. "Marvina told me about you. I'm glad to see you've stepped forward to support us at last."

"I'm afraid my mother is a little hesitant about the suffragists," Vivian said with a nervous smile.

"I met Mrs. Alderdice a long time ago." The woman peered at Vivian. "We both came out the same year in San Francisco."

Vivian was a little shocked this woman who held the reins of such a progressive movement was so blasé about the fact that she had been a debutante.

"Perhaps you can report back to her we're not as dangerous as everyone believes." Albina gave her a bare smile.

"Mother doesn't think that," Vivian objected. "She has no objections to the independence of women, really she doesn't. She is one herself."

"Oh?" Albina removed the spectacles. "I haven't been in Nob Hill society much since I started my lecture tours."

"She insisted my brother and I return to her maiden name rather than take the name of our fathers when they died," Vivian lamented.

"Very sensible of her," said Albina. "Sometimes women do better alone, if they can afford to do so. And the Alderdice name carries weight in San Francisco."

"Yes, I know," Vivian said.

Albina's eyes slid away from her for a moment. Vivian realized she was looking at Nettie, who returned the woman's gaze, her brown eyes the hue of jasper. They held a combination of interest, amusement, and defiance.

Vivian cleared her throat. "This is Nettie Grace."

"Yes, we've met," said Albina, not without a little animosity. "The convention last year, I believe."

"Yes, we did," Nettie answered. "It's an honor to have you in our humble little town, Miss Fowler."

"Every town with women fighting for our rights is important to me." The woman's tone was serious and cool. "I do not, perhaps, have the following of Miss Stone Blackwell or Mrs. Chapman Catt, but my passion about the issues we face is as warm as theirs."

"I'll look forward to hearing you expound on those issues tonight," Nettie said.

Albina looked at her for a moment with narrow eyes, as if trying to decipher some message that lay behind the innocuous words. Then she turned to Vivian again with a congenial smile. "It's been good meeting you, Miss Alderdice. I hope we shall see you at our meetings from now on." She turned on her heels, the edge of her skirt sweeping back, and returned to the crowd of admirers.

Marvina glanced at Nettie. "I take it you and she had some words at that convention last year? I wasn't there."

"Let us say we had differing opinions about Lyman House," Nettie said.

"The settlement house in Goldspur?"

Nettie nodded. "It shut down this spring. Irreconcilable differences amongst some of us working girls and our hostess for the evening."

"I see," said Marvina. Vivian glanced at her friend, who was looking at Nettie with a chilly gaze, uncharacteristic of her usual warmth.

There was a general bustling of skirts, and women went silent as they took their places. Albina Fowler had mounted the stage.

Vivian's head ached a little from the bright lights, but she soon found herself mesmerized by Albina's weaving words and oratory elegance. She did not speak in the way of a minister on the pulpit, raising and lowering her voice for effect. She spoke with a direct but amiable manner, trusting her listeners' intelligence without having to resort to artificial manipulation. Vivian could see why she had earned the respect of the movement.

Albina turned to the subject of factory conditions for working women. She approached the topic from the perspective of a storyteller, relating anecdotes of women she had met on her rounds in the factories, making the women in the room gasp. "I know of one German lady," Albina told, "who begged the foreman for an advance of just three pennies to buy milk and bread for her children." She held up three elegant fingers. "Three pennies to feed them. He refused. The other ladies had to scrape from their own pockets, although it meant their own babes would go without dinner that night."

Albina then spoke of "an uneven distribution." "On the one hand, we are elevated as angels, delicate guardians of home and hearth. On the other, our elevation comes from the power of a society of men where the only position a woman has is on a pedestal."

"I don't suppose I ever thought of myself as being on a pedestal," Nettie muttered in her ear. "Unless one may count my step ladder as a pedestal, though it raises me more to the level of a stock clerk than an angel." Vivian could barely hide her smile. Marvina, who had heard the sarcastic remark, shot Nettie a look of disapproval.

"Our aim in this organization at the moment is to campaign in Sacramento for higher wages for our working sisters so they may not need to beg for a few pennies for their infants' milk or their children's bread," Albina continued. "So they may hire other women to watch over their babes as they work, and their children do not end up in the streets because there is no one to care for them while their mothers are out making a living. So they can do virtuous work and not be lured into immorality and vice by the clinking of coins in a scoundrel's pocket." This last earned the wave of nods from the crowd.

"Miss Redfern and Albina have the same idea," Vivian whispered to Nettie, thinking of the argument at the drugstore weeks before.

"The same idea, perhaps, but their conclusions are different," Nettie said.

"I hope," Albina said, "that you will join me in the fight to free our working sisters. Perhaps they cannot be freed from the shackles of their unfortunate circumstances, but we may at least fight to provide them with the minimum wage they need to care for themselves and their children." She took a few steps back from the podium and bowed her head, signaling the end of the lecture.

There was thundering applause, and women whose refinement Vivian would have put in any parlor on Washington Street stood and cheered, and some even whistled. Albina Fowler shook hands with several ladies seated near the stage and glanced at the crowd, a humble smile adorning her lips.

"She looks rather like Hera," Nettie whispered. She again incurred Marvina's disapproving glance.

During the talk, servants had noiselessly arranged a buffet table at the other end of the room. Vivian detected scents of smoked meats and fruit and even confections. The room filled with the clattering of china and voices bouncing off the marble floor and high ceiling. The pressure in her head return. She took Nettie's arm. "Let's wait until it's cleared a bit," she suggested.

Nettie nodded and sat down again.

"Do you want me to get you something, dear?" Marvina asked.

"A sherry, perhaps?" Nettie suggested.

"I've had a very trying day." Her eyes met Marvina's. "I saw Jake."

The woman's face showed sympathy as she patted her hand. "I think Nettie's right. A sherry is just what you need, dearest. I will fight the throng for you. I've no sword to guide me, but perhaps a well-placed hat pin would do." She gaily removed a pin from her hat and held it in her fist like a sword.

"Thank you, Marvina." Vivian smiled as her friend saluted and disappeared in the crowd.

Just as Marvina folded into the veil of women, Albina Fowler and another woman appeared.

"Did you enjoy the lecture, Miss Alderdice?" Albina inquired.

"It was very enlightening," Vivian said.

"Albina is always so enlightening!" breathed the woman beside her, her matronly bosom heaving and falling with each word.

"May I present Mrs. Adler?" Albina said. "She is one of our greatest supporters. We welcome all supporters, you see." Her eyes slid toward Nettie.

"I do hope you will join our little group in the city when you return," the woman continued.

"I should like to," Vivian said with all sincerity.

"We will need every young lady we can get in the next several months," said Albina. "We will have letters prepared for the raising of factory wages, and we need every able-bodied woman to work miracles with her friends and acquaintances."

"Why not go to the streets?" Nettie asked.

Albina, whose spectacles were in her hand, now placed them at the edge of her nose. "I beg your pardon?"

"You may have all the signatures you like if you go into the street and ask for them." Nettie leaned against a chair. "Plenty of women are interested in this issue."

"But, my dear," said Mrs. Adler in a spidery way, "we don't want merely signatures. They must be the *right* signatures."

"The right signatures?" Nettie asked, but Vivian could see her lips curved at one edge and knew perfectly well what Mrs. Adler meant.

"People of influence," the woman declared. "Otherwise, they are hardly worth the ink used to sign them."

"But who better to tell the governor they want higher wages than the women who work for those wages?" Nettie asked. "I'm sure *you* never had to work in a factory in your life."

"Certainly not!" Mrs. Adler's face turned red.

"Then it's ridiculous for you and others like you to be the only names on letters asking for higher wages on work you've never done." Nettie's eyes were growing narrow, and her lips curved into that seething smile.

"We have our own way of doing things, Miss Grace." This came in an icy tone from Albina just as Marvina returned with two sherry glasses, handing one each to Vivian and Nettie.

"I haven't been a member of the BAWSPR for nine years without knowing that, Miss Fowler," Nettie said, just as icy.

"Frankly, Miss Grace, I'm surprised you joined at all." The woman's long eyelashes swept up. She took a plate of food someone gave her without taking her eyes off Nettie. "You seem to have such differing opinions about everything we do."

"As you say, you have your own way of doing things. I have mine too," Nettie said.

"We are all fighting for the same thing, aren't we?" Marvina's voice was oddly uneven. "Surely, we can agree on that."

"Do you approve of petitions, Miss Grace?" Albina's voice was very arch.

Nettie eyed her. "For the factory workers, you mean?"

"For any worthy cause."

Nettie tipped back her head and drank down the sherry in one breath, then said, "Not really."

This bald answer silenced the room. A large group had formed around Albina, and these women held their breaths.

"May I ask why not?" Mrs. Adler questioned in a rough voice.

"Surely you agree our government must know these poor girls are not getting the wages they deserve."

"Of that, there is no dispute," said Nettie. "But I have a fresh approach."

"Do you?" Albina asked. "I'm sure we would all like to hear it."

"I'm sure Nettie doesn't mean—" Marvina glanced around the room.

"I have no objection to telling you," Nettie said. "I think you may find it rather bold."

"I entirely approve of bold moves," Albina said, "though I cannot sanction the use of violence."

"It's vulgarity, pure and simple," Mrs. Adler declared.

"My suggestion isn't vulgar, Mrs. Adler," said Nettie. "I merely say it's bold because it suggests that, rather than bestow benevolence toward the women who need higher wages, I propose we get them out of the factories entirely."

Albina's lips formed into a grimace. "And what do you propose we do with them? Send them back to Europe in steerage the way they came?"

Nettie stood very straight, her eyes blazing. "Not at all, Miss Fowler. We need those women, and there are many of us who want them here."

"I believe Nettie means get them out of the factories by educating them for better jobs," Vivian said. Her friend gave her a grateful smile.

"Is that what you mean, Miss Grace?"

"Vivian has put it succinctly," said Nettie. "Precisely because she has had a fine education."

"You forget," Mrs. Adler said stiffly, "most of those women work fourteen-hour days, Saturdays included. That hardly gives them time to open a book."

"Have you ever spoken to these women, Mrs. Adler?" Nettie turned to her.

"Well, no, not personally." The woman shifted in her tightly corseted dress.

"I have," said Nettie. "They are eager to learn, and they have dreams of their own beyond the factory whistle. When one has a dream, one finds the time to fulfill it."

"Very true, Miss Grace," Albina said. "However, I think we must consider the position of these women *at this moment*. And at the moment, they *are* in the factories, and in the factories they will stay."

"Until someone gives them the resources to broaden their knowledge and skills, they shall stay in the factories," Nettie agreed. "And perhaps it is just what many of the ladies signing those petitions want, seeing that many of their husbands own those factories."

A buzzing anger filled the room, though there were no real responses. Even Albina had lost her tongue. Marvina fumbled for her handkerchief, dropped it, and looked down at it, unsure of how to retrieve it with discretion and elegance. Vivian looked at Nettie, standing very erect, her lip wavering. She could feel the fury rippling under her friend's skin.

"There is always at least a little self-interest in every altruistic deed, isn't there?" she mused gently. "But if the deed benefits others, does that really matter?"

Albina turned her eye on Vivian with a spark of condensation. "Perhaps you have a point, Miss Alderdice, though such is not the case in this instance."

"Feeling better, dearest?" Marvina asked.

"A little," Vivian said. "But I'm exhausted. Do you mind if we go home, Nettie?"

Her friend took her arm. "I believe I'm finished here. Aren't I?" She glowered at Albina Fowler.

"Yes, Miss Grace," said the woman. "I believe you are." Without ceremony, she turned her back to Nettie and attended to the food on her plate.

he moment they were out on the street, now dark with only glowing gaslights to guide them, Vivian unleaded her own anger. "What a narrow-minded shrew she is!"

"Now, don't take it so hard." Nettie wrapped her cape around her shoulders.

"She practically threw you out!"

"She's too tactful for that," she said. "She would have left it to Mrs. Adler." Vivian couldn't help but laugh. "You saved her the trouble with your own tact," Nettie added.

"I don't know why Marvina was so silent," Vivian panted. "She's always so outspoken. She's never afraid to tell the blue bloods what she thinks, and she thinks plenty about them."

"I know why she was silent," said Nettie. "She has to live with them. She already has so many marks against her."

Vivian nodded. "I know that well enough."

"She hasn't an influential name like Alderdice to fall back on like your mother," Nettie added. "I imagine she often has to take the crumbs offered."

Vivian could see her features sliding in and out of lightness as they passed under the gaslights. "You're not angry anymore."

"This was a long time coming," said her friend. "I never belonged there. They knew it, and I knew it. They were only trying to practice what they preached by letting me in."

"There are no other organizations?" Vivian asked.

Nettie shook her head. "I wanted desperately to become involved, and this was the only way."

"It's because of Queenie you became interested in suffragism, isn't it?" Vivian asked.

"It was providence," said Nettie. "A clashing of events. I discovered the group soon after she died, and I thought it was the place she would have wanted me to be. Now I see she would have spit in their faces." She smiled.

"And you?" Vivian asked. "Now that you've spit in their faces, will you give up the fight?"

"What do you mean?" Her friend glanced at her.

"Perhaps this was the push you needed," said Vivian gently. "For your library and reading room."

Nettie's forehead wrinkled. "That takes planning, Vivian. And money."

"If they can float their petitions, I'm sure you could scratch up a few pennies from the working girls and anyone else who cares to contribute," Vivian pointed out.

"It's a big undertaking."

"Why not start small, then?" Vivian took her arm. "Even if only with a few books and an invitation to your flat." She stopped and grasped her shoulders. "Queenie was a pathfinder, wasn't she? Don't you think you could be one too?"

They had stopped under a gaslight. She could see Nettie's face melting under the yellow glow, her face softening. She looked as pretty and innocent as any debutante.

CHAPTER 19

She awakened the next morning to find Nettie wrapped up in a scratchy blanket on the sofa, her breathing light. She washed her face, and, finding one of Nettie's many shawls in the closet, wrapped it around her shoulders to keep out the chill. Then she sat down on the bed and opened the diary.

Evan's handwriting was neater than she would have expected of the jerky, free-spirited young man she had met through her grandmother's letters. The voice speaking from the pages was, in fact, the voice of a young man who had aged in mind rather than matured in years.

The diary began in February on a sad note, alluding to Ebba's unfortunate fate: "My sister has gone to Glockpool at last. Perhaps it is better this way." He spoke of Verina, a child of seven, and her stony silence regarding her mother's going away: "How much does she even comprehend? Is she afraid she may show signs of the madness herself when she is older?" Vivian thought of the Verina she knew, whose stony silence came from a sense of loss rather than fear of madness.

Entries followed that were short and more cheerful about the decision to leave Brandywine for San Francisco ("I must give the child a new life away from the memories,") the trip to the city jumping trains and hitching rides ("Verina was content to ride in back of the farmer's truck and tend to his chicks!") and settling in with Ember Warren and Matthew Lord ("They are pleasant, good-natured fellows.") Vivian skimmed through the diary until she found an entry for March 3, 1855:

I broke my promise to Malcolm. I couldn't help it. It was seeing her one day passing out of the Occidental Hotel with Bertha Ross; her face still lovely and lively, her air that of a woman settled in marriage, her mannerisms and dress finer than they had been in Brandywine. It was then I realized what I had asked her to sacrifice last year. I was almost glad she had not done so, though I could see from her somewhat sagging features that she was not happy. No, I don't think she's happy.

Evan did not expound on how he "broke his promise" to Grandfather, but Vivian guessed he had stopped Grandmother on the street, making known to her he was in the city. The following entries included jangled words about "my Grace." Vivian realized her grandmother had wasted no time renewing her acquaintance with Evan. She quickly became a part of his world with frequent visits to the flat, bringing little gifts for Verina. Vivian came to the entry she had been looking for and, she realized, she had been fearing:

April 12, 1854

I begged Grace not to return to her parents' cold, dull house last night. She has been so wretched there. She says it belongs to Malcolm now, not her. Her father has been under his spell, but she has resisted, made herself as separate from him as her bedroom is from his. She stayed.

Vivian's hands dropped the diary on the bed, and the poor springs underneath groaned in protest. Nettie shifted on the couch but did not wake up.

She looked a while out the window at the thin blue line of the bay distorted under the murky morning sky. Though this was what she had suspected, and what both Jake and Ruth had denied so fervently as to confirm her suspicions, she felt a great sense of sorrow. She was not angry at Evan or her grandmother. They had loved one another once and had even been engaged. Nothing could have been more natural for them. But the tone of the diary, though joyous, foreshadowed hopelessness and doom.

The entries for the rest of that year told of "Grace" coming nearly every day to the flat and drawing: "At last, she is beginning to forget her little Tiresias and sketching human subjects." Bertha sometimes came with her, though "Ember says the little woman's face always reminds him of a crushed banana, the disapproval is so lingering on it!"

On January 7, 1855, Evan wrote the following: "Malcolm returns today. Grace feigned a headache to keep from meeting him at the boat and came here instead. She darts about the flat, upsetting the canvases Matt had so carefully arranged for his exhibition next week. I have tried to tell her she need never go back to that house, but she keeps telling me, 'There is little else I can do.' That man is insufferable, the way he treats her like a pretty little canary he can coax to sing for him whenever he pleases!"

Vivian tried to picture her grandmother as she looked in her wedding portrait, with her silk wedding dress and the veil flowing to the floor, pink roses pinned to her hair. She tried to picture that same woman with her face contorted in anxiety. The pictures did not fit.

The entries after that were routine, with one exception. There was no mention of "Grace." A few scattered references to "she has not written me today" attested to Evan's growing angst, but nothing that pointed toward any assignations between them. Vivian felt almost relieved.

She then reached an entry that surprised her. It was dated March 16, 1855:

One senses when the devil will appear, and such was true when I came home this evening and found Malcolm Alderdice waiting for me in the front room. Heaven knows how he got in, with Matt and Ember away and Verina with Mrs. Venable. But he has his ways.

He has not changed at all, except his countenance is more alert and his gaze harder. The countenance of a successful businessman. He was dressed as if on his way to an important meeting, no doubt to intimidate me. But I was not intimidated.

I do not know how he found out about Grace and me. But his manner was one of such self-assurance that it made me want to bash the towering figure to pieces.

He asked me if I had heard of "our good fortune" (meaning his and Grace's coming child). I said I had read about it in the papers (in truth, I had not — Ember told me of it.) Malcolm crossed his long legs and said, "Now that we are to have a family, I'm sure you will understand you must take yourself out of our lives for good." I could feel my anger rising at this pompous reference to "our lives." As if I might have anything to do with him but to carve a knife in his heart, if I had the courage!

I told him the choice would be Grace's. I did not mince words. I said, "Perhaps Grace would prefer to bring up her child in its father's world." This grated Malcolm, as I saw the tower show its crumbling edges. "The child is already in its father's world and shall remain there." "Indeed?" I asked. "It is rather a trick to conceive when a man has been away for a year and takes his sleeping quarters in the study, isn't it?"

This was ungentlemanly of me, but it achieved my goal. The tower crumbled, and Malcolm leapt out of his chair. I felt his hands upon my throat. They were powerful hands. I always thought the namby-pamby clerk had barely the strength to hold a pencil. But he proved a formidable opponent, but I managed to unpin the devil from my throat.

Through heavy breaths, Malcolm said, "So she told you that, did she?"

"She told me everything."

The tower returned, as granite as ever, but his voice was still shaking when he said, "I warn you, Jones. Return to Waxwood or go wherever you like. But never see Penelope again. Keep your promise this time, or I won't be responsible for the consequences." He then pulled out a handful of bills from his pocket, which he threw on the table. "That should be enough for your travel and perhaps a little to start besides. For the sake of your niece. You do her no favors by making her a party to your wayward ways."

"I will accept your money, but not for myself," I said between breaths. "For Verina. As for Grace, it will be up to her if she prefers my waywardness or your prison."

This made Malcolm burst out laughing with the arrogant assurance of a man who was sure of his course in life. "You will be sorely disappointed, sir. My wife has more sound judgment and foresight than you credit her."

"But there is one thing she does not have, and that is love for you." It was my turn to be arrogant and self-assured. "She does not love you and never has. We both know it."

His face flashed like lightning across a stormy sky, but he was not allowing himself to lose control again. He merely sniffed and left.

I wait to hear from Grace herself. I know she will write me now. She must.

Vivian's hands trembled as she lay down the diary. She thought again of how her grandfather had looked at her grandmother in the upstairs parlor, those evenings after dinner, silently watching her read or try to teach Vivian how to play the piano. She had seen the intensity of those blue eyes, clear like blue ice. She had realized long ago he was trying to read her grandmother's mind, but she had never known why. Now she knew. He was trying to figure out how to make her love him, knowing all the time he was fighting a losing battle.

Her head was spinning. That her grandfather had come to Evan with such self-righteousness was no surprise to her. It was that audacity that put him at the top of his game in business, and he saw no boundaries between his personal or public life in that regard — both must always be within his grasp. But had Evan not fought against this? Had he again left her grandmother with nothing? She struggled to believe this.

And yet, the answers to her questions were in the following entry and proved even more surprising. It was dated a week after the previous one:

I am in despair. That Malcolm should be right about Grace... It cannot be! And yet, I hold the note in her own handwriting. It is a steady hand, a determined hand. And the message? "Do not try to see me. Forget about me and become the great artist you were meant to be. I am fulfilling my duties. You cannot change them. All my love. G." I have half a mind to knock down that damned guarded gate and sweep her away in some absurd way. But she has made her choice. Malcolm was right. I shall never look upon anyone again with complete trust.

It was an almost ludicrous ending to the drama, and Vivian nearly laughed out loud. Nettie stirred on the sofa.

There was only one entry left in the diary. It was a strange, half-hearted one, written on September 9, 1855, some five months after the last one. It was clear from the contents Evan had returned to Brandywine. It was also clear that he was unhappy. They were hardly etching out a living with drawings he did of the summer people on the pier, he said, but the people of Brandywine did what they could for them. He vowed to continue Verina's education, so she at least attended the school in Waxwood and was doing well with her studies. The entry's ending caught her attention:

Yesterday was Loretta Potter's funeral. As she was a friend of Grace's, and Grace would surely be there, I thought it best not to attend. It would have cut open fresh wounds. But Sterling and Markum and a few of the others to whom Miss Potter had been kind went and were, if not exactly welcomed by the family, not asked to leave. They returned earlier this evening. Markum told me Grace had not attended. He also said Miss Ross had been in a strange mood, speaking quickly and fluttering about as if she were a bird whose wings had been cut off. I reminded him Miss Ross had always been rather nervous. But he insisted she was odd about the entire affair. He stood just behind her during the funeral and heard her mumbling, "The child is coming, too soon, too soon!" He knew from my tales from the city she was referring to Grace. She turned around, and, staring at him fully in the face, said, "She oughtn't to go out into the woods in her condition, oughtn't she?" Markum answered her, with delicacy (as he thought she must be distraught from the death of her friend) that no, she oughtn't to be. Then Miss Ross said, "Grace's baby shall be big. It's wrong, it's all wrong!" Markum asked me if I would care for him to go down into town and ask Miss Ross what she meant. I told him it was unnecessary, as Miss Ross probably wouldn't remember what she said, let alone what she meant. Grace is in another world, detached from me now. I must leave her to her own will.

Vivian closed the diary softly. She felt herself empty, as if all inside her had disintegrated, and she was left with only a hollow shell of flesh. She rose, her legs weak, wanting to go to the mirror to look at herself. But she suddenly had a terror of seeing a smooth face with no features. Somehow, she knew, there would be no auburn hair, no blue eyes, no inherited jaw and cheekbones. There would be nothing.

Nettie stirred and sat up slowly, her hair tumbling into her eyes.

"I woke you," Vivian said. "I'm sorry." She bent down to retrieve the diary where it had fallen on the floor and gently closed and locked it before putting it in her reticule.

"You look as if you're going to faint." Nettie blinked into the light.

Vivian leaned against the bedpost. "I must go back this morning. I must face my mother."

"You needn't yet if you don't wish to." Nettie stretched her arms above her head. "It might do her ladyship some good to worry about you a little."

"Mother doesn't worry." Vivian laid out her dress and underclothes on the bed with shaking hands. "She seethes. She's probably sitting at the breakfast table at this moment, silently seething."

"Let me get you something." Nettie cringed a little at the coldness of the boards under her bare feet. "You really look like you're about to faint, you know."

"I don't want anything." Vivian grasped her friend's hand. "I've never had anyone I could rely on, not really. I can hardly repay you."

"One doesn't repay a friend," said the woman. "One returns the favor."

"Then I shall one day," Vivian said.

Nettie insisted on walking her to the ferry and seeing she was settled in with a blanket on her knees. By then, Vivian was feeling a little stronger, with the sun coming out from behind the thin veil of clouds. Mr. Blaine was at the wheel of the ferry, finishing his cigarette, when she boarded. He did not hide his delight at seeing her again. "Been a long time, miss," he said.

"Yes." Vivian looked vaguely at the row of hotels in the distance. "It's been a lifetime."

"Ah, only them that are old may say that, miss." He laughed. "You young 'uns, you have all the time in the world." He steered the ferry toward the hotels.

"But it isn't the years we have left, Mr. Blaine," she said. "It's what we make of them."

"True, true," he lamented. "But that's the trouble, miss. Seems like every young 'un's got to be at the helm more than they ought these days. Now, folks like me, we're simple people. Life sweeps us along like these here waters, and we just go with 'em. And she's always steering us right 'cause we don't try to get the best o'her. Suppose I'm sounding like a preacher stuck for a sermon." He grinned.

"No, sir," she said. "You're making a lot of sense. Perhaps we're even trying to go against our own nature."

"Eh, that's so, miss," he said. "Can't let people tell you what to do all your life, can you?"

A couple came up to the wheel with a small boy, and Mr.

Blaine chatted with them the rest of the way about the temperament of the wheel and the waves of the bay. Vivian was silent, listening to the lapping water underneath the flat belly of the ferry.

She had hoped to find Larissa still in the dining room, though the breakfast hour had passed, and there were few stranglers lingering over their coffee. But their table had already been cleared, the chairs pushed in as if no one had pulled them out. As she passed the desk, the clerk motioned to her. "Miss Alderdice?" She nodded. "Mrs. Alderdice left you a note, miss." He handed her the sealed envelope with the Waxwoodian crest.

The muscles in her chest tightened as she withdrew to one of the stuffed chairs and carefully opened the envelope. Her mother's handwriting was more jagged than usual, but the message was in her formal tone:

There is a small sailboat waiting for you on the west end of the pier. It will take you to Mr. Leblanc's yacht. I hope you haven't forgotten. Mother.

Vivian blinked into the sunlight streaming into the lobby. She had forgotten they had set the yacht trip with the Leblancs for today. She suddenly burst out laughing. The last forty-eight hours she felt as if she were emerging from a grave, and now her mother wanted her to go yachting!

But suddenly she felt helpless, a puppet whose strings had been detached from her body. She recalled Mr. Blaine's words: *Life sweeps us along like these here waters and we just go with 'em.* What was there for her to do now but let herself become swept by the waters until her thoughts were less jumbled, and she could sort them out — until she could talk to Larissa alone? Now, it all came down to her mother, just as it had seven years before.

She went up to the suite and bathed, changing into clothes more suitable for sailing. A glance at the mirror struck her as ironic. She looked for all the world like a carefree, well-to-do young lady, past her debutante prime, perhaps, but unencumbered by the battering of life and eager to follow the path laid out for her since birth.

She found the sailboat with a rather hefty sailor who was polite and soft-spoken just where Larissa said it would be. She was on the water again, only this time, heading in a different direction. She could see the yacht halfway there, with its trapezoid and triangular sails flapping in the wind, looking like a dominating monster with the long hull sliding quietly on the shiny water.

They were all waiting for her. Her mother stood near the railing. She was glad to see the Leblancs were preoccupied as she scrambled up the ladder.

"This is inexcusable, Vivian!" her mother hissed. "I've told them you stayed the night with friends."

"Mother, I need to speak to you."

"Not now." Larissa glanced at the two men. "Tonight, perhaps." The Leblancs were advancing, and she said in a louder and more artificial tone, "You had a pleasant visit with your friends, dear?"

"I had an interesting visit," Vivian said. "A very interesting visit."

Her mother was startled for a moment. Then she turned to the elder Mr. Leblanc, holding down her hat from the wind by the knot of the scarf she had tied around it. "Mr. Leblanc was just telling me some seals were spotted off the rocks there."

"You're late, Miss Alderdice." Monte Leblanc sidled up to her.

"I apologize," Vivian mumbled.

"We were afraid you would forget us and remain with your friends."

"I did forget," said Vivian honestly.

Mr. Leblanc laughed. "It took us time to get the boat here, or we would have taken you and your mother out much sooner."

"Show Miss Alderdice around the yacht, Monte," his father

said, his voice rivaling the vibrations of the wind. "Breakfast will be ready soon."

"Breakfast?" Vivian stammered. "That's right, I haven't eaten." But the thought of food made her stomach queasy.

Larissa and Mr. Leblanc senior remained at the bow while Monte Leblanc offered her his arm and began leading her toward the back of the yacht. It was clear from his distracted manner and the way he threw out his hand as he pointed toward this or that feature of the yacht, he was anything but interested in showing her around. She was equally uninterested in the bobbing boat.

When they reached the stern, Mr. Leblanc gave up all pretense and motioned for her to sit on the cushioned bench. Her skirt whipped against her ankles as the wind came up from behind her. But it felt good to her, something she could fight against. After days of rambling on a path where unpleasant faces appeared and disappeared at every turn, it made her feel stronger to have something she could push against.

"I've wanted very much to speak with you for days," the man began.

"I'm sorry I was gone."

"I have never met a woman like you, Miss Alderdice." He peered at her. "You are free and, yet, you understand your duties better than most."

"Am I free?" Vivian gave him a wan smile. "Perhaps I only appear that way. I've been on my own since I was a child, Mr. Leblanc. One is forced to find one's own way when left alone."

"I don't object to it," he said. "I rather prefer a woman independent in mind and spirit."

She tried not to grimace, remembering the conversation they had had about his former wives and their reassuring complacency. "You're very forward-thinking, then."

He cleared his throat and went on, "I told you, my father and I are eager to move to Nob Hill. Our cousin has been very generous with her introductions. But she's made it quite clear that, if we wish to establish ourselves in your society, we must have a capable woman who belongs to that society and knows it well."

"And knows all its tricks," Vivian added. "I quite understand, Mr. Leblanc."

"Won't you call me Monte now?" His mustache quivered.

Her heart beat quickly. "Is there any reason I should?"

"Miss Alderdice!" The man's strong features contorted with corpse-like paleness. "Vivian!" She glanced out at the bay. "I'm going about this poorly, aren't I?"

"Perhaps if you said what you mean," Vivian remarked. "I never imagined you to beat around the bush, Mr. Leblanc."

"Monte, please!"

"Monte," she said with a terse smile. "If you prefer."

"You want me to put it bluntly, then." He was not at all pleased at this prospect.

"We've been together for most of the summer," she said. "I would imagine you know by now I'm not some coy maiden."

His manner became more congenial as he sat down beside her, taking her hands. "It's one of your many higher qualities. I have no use for a coy maiden."

Vivian couldn't help but smile.

"If you would consent—" He cleared his throat. "If you would do me the honor—"

"Yes?" Vivian breathed.

"—to be my wife."

The sun sparkled on the peaks of the bay's rough surface, making them flash like diamonds. In the past weeks, she had thought often about what she would do when this moment came, even considered discussing it with her mother in the way daughters and mothers discussed impending marriage proposals. Now that it had come, it was a like an absurd joke. In the shadow of what she knew, from the guides in the path she had chosen through the murky woods of the past, what could it be but a joke?

She burst out in a hysterical laughter that floated over the rough ocean which the waters absorbed like a handkerchief, kicking back a flurry of damp wind in her face.

Monte continued in a loud, fast way, "Neither of us have grand ideas about marriage, do we? And that makes us start out with fewer barriers for happiness than most, I should think."

"Mr. Leblanc—"

"Monte, please!"

"Monte," she said carefully, "I cannot thank you for the honor you've done me. But I can't marry you."

"Oh, I know your objections," he said. "Your independent spirit. That I'm a stranger to your set—"

"That would hardly matter to me," she said savagely. "Especially now."

"Why especially now?" He blinked.

She looked out to the sea again. "I'm not who you think I am."

"You're very confusing, Vivian." He sighed.

"I don't mean to be." She pressed his hands. "We spoke once of skeletons in the closet. Let's leave it at that."

"That hardly matters," he insisted. "Not for us. We're both outsiders, in a way." He gave her a meaningful look. "As an alliance, we shall become a part of something."

"But do we want to be a part of it?" Vivian asked slowly.

He blinked at her. "I should think anyone living in San Francisco would!"

Vivian surveyed the peaked waters again. "That's the trouble. Everyone thinks there is only one path to Paradise, but really, there are so many."

He went on hurriedly. "Your mother and my father have already consented to our marriage."

"Have they?" Vivian said sharply. "How dreadfully Medieval of them."

The man's whole being sagged against the small bench. "I only wanted to assure you that nothing prevents us from marrying as soon as you wish."

Compassion returned in her as she laid her hands in her lap. "I know that's what you meant. But there are things my mother doesn't know yet. Things I need to speak with her about."

"What has that to do with our getting married?"

She said softly, "You can do much better, Monte."

"You are lovely and intelligent," he insisted. "And you have your own interests, just as I have mine. We would never get in one another's way."

"As long as we keep up appearances in society?" Vivian eyed him.

"Only for the season," he said.

"How comforting!" She couldn't keep the archness out of her voice.

His voice became a little less appeasing and a little firmer. "If we've already agreed to be blunt, I may point out neither of us is twenty."

"No, we're not, are we?"

"Your mother told me you turned twenty-six in February. I will be forty-eight in a few months."

"And that's as good as old for both of us where marriage is concerned," Vivian finished with a little irony.

"Time is running out."

"Yes, I know," she said in a steely voice. "Your father and my mother. They have the same aim in mind."

He winced. "I wish you wouldn't put it that way."

"We're determined to be blunt with one another, aren't we?" She looked at him. "I told you before I couldn't marry you. Bu there's another reason, Monte. I don't *want* to marry you."

"But I thought—"

"I thought so too," said Vivian. "But I realize now my path lies elsewhere." She looked at the sea again, the diamond peaks flashing like knowing eyes.

"This young man with the mustache — is he the reason?"

"No," she said. "There's no other man. There's only me."

He sprang up and kissed both her hands. "If there is no other man, then won't you at least reconsider it? We can make arrangements, Papa and I, to go to Egypt. Papa has an old school chum there on a dig who invited us. We can leave tomorrow morning and be back in San Francisco in the spring. That's enough time, isn't it?"

"Go to Egypt if you wish, but there is no use in coming back here for my answer." Vivian rose. "It will be the same." She took his hands. "You're a good man, and I know you will find the right woman for you. But I'm not the one."

He was completely bewildered, the sudden rush of wind swaying his military figure like the leaves of a weeping willow tree.

"I know you would be generous and give me freedom." She peered anxiously at him. "But I don't wish for anyone to give me freedom. I want to take it in my own way."

His eyes narrowed. "So you refuse to marry me?"

"I refuse to marry anyone," she insisted. "I have only a vague idea of what I want, Monte. But I know what I don't want. I don't want to be the wife of a wealthy man, the mother of heirs to a family legacy, and a socialite who spends her days on frivolous activities."

The anger that had been gathering in his brows eased, and his countenance grew more even. "I think I see. I don't understand it, but I see now."

"I'm still trying to understand it myself," said Vivian.

He nodded, his gaze a little stronger. "And you won't at least give yourself some time?"

Vivian shook her head. "I don't change my mind once I've

made it up." She grimaced. "I inherited a rather fine obstinacy, you see."

"Oh?"

"From my grandmother," she said. "Everyone thought she was a remarkable woman. She would have been, if she weren't weighed down by the stone necklace of expectations. I mustn't be like her, you see."

They both sat back on the bench and looked out to the bay for a long time in silence. The yacht had sailed closer to the hill opposite the one with the wax wood trees. Several cottages stood on the haunches, and a thin line signaling a road curled its way up to the bridge, linking the two hills. There were no wax wood trees there.

Monte spoke then, "I don't think we ought to tell them, at least not until Papa and I leave."

"I think that's wise."

He rose and held out his arm to her. She could see his mild nature had returned, and he was not bitter or angry. It was the countenance of a man not disappointed by love because there had been no love to disappoint him. He had merely taken a fancy to an idea that had not been reciprocated.

As they walked around the other side of the yacht, Vivian said, "You know who you ought to marry, Monte?"

"Eh?" He glanced at her.

"Christina Sowberry."

He laughed. "You're now a matchmaker?"

"No, it just occurred to me," she said. "She's a lovely young lady, and she's — she's more suited for you." She did not say Miss Sowberry might prove as agreeable as his first two wives.

"Ah, but that mother of hers—"

"I'm sure Mrs. Sowberry will settle down once her daughter does," Vivian said. "Mothers are often a little much during the courting, but when their daughters become wives, they ease off."

They began talking of Mrs. Sowberry's obnoxious mannerisms and were laughing over them when the senior Mr. Leblanc and Larissa appeared from below deck. A sailor came and said that breakfast was ready. Vivian knew her mother was trying to catch her eye with a questioning gaze, but she kept up the conversation with Monte. They were as gay and bright as magpies, and Vivian almost felt as if they were sharing a certain satisfaction in deceiving the two anxious parents.

CHAPTER 20

hapter 20

The rest of the morning and afternoon were spent trying to catch sight of the promised seals, but the animals eluded them. Vivian's mood was temporarily light-hearted. She felt as if a great weight had been lifted off her shoulders.

But when they returned to the hotel only half an hour before dinner, her morose and nervousness returned. She and Larissa dressed hurriedly and without conversation, appearing fifteen minutes late and very much flushed to the lavish send-off dinner Mrs. Tisher and Mrs. Griffith had organized for the Leblancs. Though other diners knew nothing about the reason for the party, they were swept up in its joviality, filling the dining room with such noise that the waiters had to bend down low in order to hear. Afterward, there was a dance in the hotel ballroom, where the ladies swirled in the arms of the men with enthusiasm, their dresses making swishing sounds against the usually silent marble floor, and their heels clicking with the rhythm dictated by the small orchestra.

This joyful pandemonium gave color to the celebration, surely the last of the summer season, as August was drawing to a close. Vivian felt Larissa was watching her constantly. Monte remained attentive throughout the evening, but with the unassuming ease of a friend. She reciprocated, feeling her gestures too jerky and her voice too ragged with agitation. They both managed to have pleasant conversation, but there was no more laughing between them.

The dancing ended at two o'clock in the morning when everyone made their way to their suites. Larissa's mood had changed. She was subdued, her eyes staring ahead. The silence that followed their climb into the elevator to their suite, the walk down the hallway, and the opening door with the sliding key mocked Vivian in its sustained breath, like the calm before the storm.

She expected her mother to accost her with questions the moment they entered the suite, but Larissa was silent. She sighed, dropping her fan and wrap on the couch in an uncharacteristically sloppy way. Then she did something Vivian had never seen her do — she went over to the bar and poured herself a drink. It was a whiskey and soda, too, which Larissa considered a "man's drink" and one no woman with delicacy should go near. She poured two of them and handed one to Vivian. "I think we both need this."

Vivian stared down at the glass. "I didn't even know you knew how to make a whiskey and soda."

Her mother gave her a sardonic smile. "There are many things you don't know about me, dear."

Vivian watched her down the drink in a hearty, almost cheap way. She looked at the perfectly pinned hair with the sheen of velvet blond, the detached countenance, the blue eyes. She suddenly saw they were not exactly the color Grandfather's had been. They were more aqua, with a hint of green. How had she not noticed before?

"You're staring at me as if you're seeing me for the first time." This came with a note of alarm as Larissa set the glass down.

Vivian sat on the couch. "I have to speak with you, Mother. I've been trying to all day."

"And I have to speak to *you*." The eyes regarded her like spears. "I know all about you and Monte Leblanc."

Vivian's hands felt weak. She let them drop to her sides.

"His father told me all about it." The voice that spoke was low but angry. "He told me you refused his son's proposal." Vivian nodded. "You led me to expect —"

"That's the trouble, Mother." Vivian looked down at her knees. They were narrow and muscular under the sheath skirt. "We've been led to expect all our lives."

"One cannot live without expectations." Larissa's voice was gentle. "I've tried to teach you that."

"Yes, you have," said Vivian. "You and Grandmother. Perhaps my inherited obstinacy prevented me from understanding. Or perhaps obstinacy had nothing to do with it."

Her mother leaned her head back. "I heard from Mrs. Griffith that Christina Sowberry and her mother will be spending time in London before the hunting season opens because the Leblancs will be going there when they return from Egypt." Her mother began to take off her gloves. "I think it prudent that we book a passage on the *Continental* to Glasgow."

"You can't be serious!"

"I don't mean we ought to chase after him," said her mother. "But a matter of coincidences —"

"Coincidences!" Vivian rose and threw open the balcony doors. A breeze rolled into the room.

Her mother's eyes narrowed with incredulousness. "Vivian, you were the one determined to finally do your duty."

She looked out to the dark sky. "Things have changed, Mother."

"I don't see that they have," Larissa protested.

"Sometimes it happens," Vivian said. "Things change in a day, even an hour. One is no longer on the sure footing one once was." She glanced over her shoulder. "I suppose it makes no difference to you that I never loved him, and he never loved me."

"Oh, for God's sake!" The voice rose with a shrill note. "I told you before, love isn't necessary. It's much better to have mutual regard and respect, and you can't tell me Monte Leblanc doesn't have both for you."

"How unromantic you are." Vivian let out a short laugh. "You're full of contradictions. You have some of the most conventional ideas I've ever known, and yet, in some ways, you're rather unconventional."

"We're not talking about me now." Larissa's voice was steel.

"But that's exactly what we are talking about, isn't it?" She returned the steely look. "In a roundabout way."

"You know what we've been through!" her mother flared. "This was to be a new start for us, for the future generation of Alderdices."

"One must do what one feels is right," Vivian declared.

"One doesn't have to *feel* something is right for it to *be* right," her mother insisted. "There are many moments in life when you simply must go with what's being done."

"Even when one is living a lie?" She looked her mother in the eye. "That's what our lives have been, Mother. A web of lies since the day *you* were born."

Larissa closed her eyes. "I can't understand why you rejected the proposal, Vivian. It was right in your lap."

"I rejected him," said Vivian in a quiet voice, "because he would have been marrying someone who had no right to be his wife."

Larissa's eyes flew open. "What are you talking about?"

"Monte Leblanc came here intending to marry into Washington Street society." Vivian's voice shook. "His interest in me was because he thought he would be marrying the granddaughter of the Alderdice shipping tycoon. But he wouldn't have been."

Her mother's face froze like ice. "I don't —"

"He would have been marrying the granddaughter of a poor artist!"

The words fell like blows of an ax. She watched her mother sink down into the chair, her pointed bones growing even sharper. Her shoulders looked as if they would pierce the cushions. "You're talking nonsense, Vivian."

"Is it nonsense?" She strolled into her room and emerged with the diary, throwing it on the table. "Evan's diary, Mother."

Larissa's eyes showed horror as she glanced at the small leather book. "Where did you get that?"

"Does it matter?"

"I've told you not to chase specters," said Larissa. "Why can't you leave it alone!" Her voice rang with agitation.

"You don't want to read the words of your own father?"

The ax lowered again and her mother looked suddenly frail.

"Read the diary, Mother."

"I have no need to read it." She rose, completely composed, completely impartial. "You've heard what your grandfather always said. I was more Alderdice than he."

"Now I know why he would say it," said Vivian. "He was trying to reassure himself the lie was the truth."

"You're my daughter," Larissa said slowly. "That makes you an Alderdice."

"I'm a Jones, just as you are a Jones."

"No!" Larissa's voice tore through the room. "I have your grandfather's name, just as you have mine."

"It wasn't yours to begin with, was it?"

It was strange how the lull entered the room just as the wind swept out of it, leaving behind a stale air. The stars reached into the room like glowing fingers, and Vivian could almost feel their silvery touch. She closed the balcony doors.

In a quiet voice, Larissa said, "Whoever gave that to you — it was a cruel thing to do."

"My brother gave it to me."

A small, frightened gasp escaped her mother's lips.

"I saw him yesterday," Vivian continued.

Larissa turned her head away, but Vivian could see from her trembling lips. "In that place?"

"I could hardly see him anywhere else, could I?" she said with a piercing laugh.

"If someone finds out —"

Vivian sat on the arm of the couch. "Mother, when were you born? Really, when were you born?"

Larissa didn't answer right away. The edge of her lip quivered. "You know when I was born."

"I know what we've always been told," said Vivian. "November seventeenth. The day Mr. Livingstone set eyes on Africa. But it's a lie."

"How —" Her mother's voice grew weak.

"It was September," said Vivian. "That's why Bertha thought Grandmother was feigning illness. It was all a ruse so that her going away to have you would hide the fact that you weren't born in November!"

"Vivian, this is ridiculous!"

"And if you were born in September, Grandfather could hardly be your father. He was just back from Germany and sleeping in his study."

"Vivian!" The name tore out of a savage voice.

She was silent, then asked in a half-whisper, "How long have you known?"

"There is nothing to know!"

"To think we were sold a lie!" Something ripped inside Vivian. "A lie about who we were from the day we were born. And you went along with it!"

"There is no lie." Her voice was firm. "Our name is Alderdice. Do you understand? Our name is Alderdice, not Jones."

Vivian studied the stone pallor of her mother's face. The eyes were set, the lips narrow.

"Is that why you never married again?" she asked quietly. "Because you were afraid it might come out?"

"I never married again because I had no opportunity," said Larissa. "You, on the other hand, have a golden opportunity, and I won't let you spoil it. That's why we're going to Glasgow."

Vivian eyed her. "Doesn't it bother you at all that you almost sacrificed Jake and me for your absurd desire to be the belle of San Francisco society?"

Larissa gave her a severe look. "I saved the both of you."

"Because you insisted that we take your name instead of our own fathers'?" Vivian couldn't help but laugh. "And everyone thought you were being so sensible!"

"I was thinking of your future and your brother's," her mother insisted. "Your brother disappointed me, disappointed us both. But you still have a chance."

Vivian rose. "You're right, Mother. I still have a chance. Which is why I'm not going to Glasgow."

"Vivian, please!"

"I can't follow someone else's path anymore," said Vivian. "Not yours, not Grandmothers. I must forge my own, wherever it is."

"It's too late for circle talk tonight." Her mother rose. "I will burn that." She glared down at the diary. "It doesn't belong here."

"On the contrary," Vivian said. "I'm leaving it for you as a keepsake." She picked up her wrap and bag.

"Leaving it?"

"Yes, Mother," she said. "I'm going away."

"Going away?" The clouded eyes regarded her with confusion. "Where?"

"To find my own path, of course." In a softer voice, she added, "It might not be forever."

"Vivian, dear, you can't mean it!"

"I'm free, you see," she said. "I'm no longer an Alderdice, so Washington Street can't burden me with its stone necklaces anymore." Her brother's words echoed in the silent room: *If we aren't Alderdices, we would be free.*

Larissa was silent for a while. Then her voice came out meek and resigned. "Where will you go?"

"Nettie Grace," she said. "She's my friend."

Her mother put her hands on her forehead. "This is too much, Vivian."

She suddenly felt tears in her eyes. She put her hand on her mother's arm. "I don't want to hurt you. But there's nothing left of what little there was. This path of my life leads to a dead end."

Larissa gripped her hand. "It needn't, if we go to Glasgow."

Now the ax fell on Vivian like a heavy blade across her back, trying to sink her into the ground and split her open. She found herself swaying, but she didn't fall. "It would be all wrong, Mother." She put her wrap around her shoulders. "I'd like —" her breath caught, "I'd like to write to you."

Larissa was standing now at the closed balcony doors, looking through the glass. The line of black sky merged with the dark sea. "If you do," she said without turning around, "I won't send them back to you unopened."

Vivian felt her entire body sagging with relief, her throat closing with the tears that gathered in her eyes. She quickly left the suite, leaving the leather book on the table.

~~~~~

She took the stairs, as the thought of meeting even an elevator boy's eyes was too much for her just then. She reached the lobby, nearly empty at that late hour, and found the clerk at the desk speaking on the telephone in a coveted way. She opened the glass doors and let the lukewarm wind sweep dry her tears. At the edge of the pier, the ferry stood as if waiting for her.

The drugstore was closed but Vivian had, by now, seen the rickety wooden stairs on the side of the building that led up to Nettie's flat. Her friend let her in, blinking a little at the glaring
~~~~~

light hanging over the door. Vivian put her reticule down on the bed and examined the couch.

"I imagine it's quite comfortable when one gets use to it," she said.

Nettie did not answer, but smiled, as if she had expected it.

"I want to help you, Nettie," said Vivian. "I don't care how."

"It would mean hard work. A lot of hard work."

"I realize that," she said. "I'm not afraid of hard work."

Nettie smiled. "I know you're not. You're the Dagger Girl, aren't you?" She reached for her hand and squeezed it.

"I will do all I can to help you," Vivian continued. "But you must do something for me." She went to the cupboard and opened the doors. The tiny shrine was gleaming of silver and wax. Nettie's eyes fell, her hands clasping together.

"Tonight, I buried my dead," said Vivian. "I shall never see the specter again. But neither of us can follow a new path if we don't both bury the specters that have been holding us in the past."

Nettie looked at her, the seething eyes wide and frightened. Then she shut the cupboard doors and locked them. She threw the key out the window.

They stepped out to the stairwell where the night spilled around them, neither of them speaking. Vivian felt as if the breath she had been holding for most of that day, most of her life, really, were exhaling into a veil of velvet darkness. A scent of lavender rose from a field of wild grass nearby, and the heady perfume filled her with a sense of belonging.

~~~~~

Author's Note

Thank you for reading *Pathfinding Women*! I hope you enjoyed the mystery Vivian had to solve to find herself and her place in the world. I don't think there is anyone who hasn't taken a new
~~~~~

direction in their lives at some point and knows how rewarding and challenging that journey can be.

*I*n this book, I really wanted to give Vivian a friend — someone she could rely on who was totally out of her social set. Since I knew when I was writing the book that Vivian's journey was going to end with her stepping away from her mother's aristocratic expectations and into a totally new (if less financially stable) life, I knew she needed someone who was going to guide and support her along the way (just like a bestie should). We all need a little help from our friends (cue Beatles song here).

*Y*ou might note Vivian doesn't really have a friend among the Washington Street set other than Marvina Moore (who is older and more like an aunt than a friend). Why? We have to remember Vivian comes from what we would call today a "dysfunctional" family. Kids from such families are often isolated and feel different from other kids who come from loving, supportive families. The Alderdices are pretty exclusive and Larissa, as we've seen, kept a tight leash on her children growing up. So it's no wonder neither Vivian or Jake were able to really make any close friends on Washington Street.

*N*ettie is one of my favorite characters because, well, she has guts. What you see is hat you get with her, and that takes courage. She's a working girl who believes in women's rights but also knows the limitations of the Gilded Age suffragist movement (exclusion of different classes as well as different races). She has a vision for what she wants to achieve in life and her heart and mind are both open.

· · ·

Book 4 might surprise you because it hails the return of an unlikely character from Book 2: Harland Stevens. Turn the page to read an excerpt from the book!

Happy reading!
Tam

Waxwood, 1900: For Vivian Alderdice, the twentieth century begins with a new start. Now a working woman and progressive reformer, she's forsaken Nob Hill for the more modest Waxwood. She's laid Penelope Alderdice's specter to rest at last. Granted, her life isn't the one she was born into. Instead of a Nob Hill socialite, she sells strawberry sodas at her friend's drugstore and helps working-class women improve their education. But she has no complaints about the calmness and predictability of her days.

Vivian's peaceful existence is thrown into turmoil when the man who ruined her brother's life appears like another specter she must exorcise.

At first, Vivian hates him with a passion. But when she sees how his own undiscovered past has destroyed him, leaving him helpless in the hands of a cousin who hates him worse than she does, she finds herself feeling compassion for him.

Is it his journey Vivian will discover in the dark forest of guilt and betrayal or her own?

"This one was a page-turner!"
    Read on for an excerpt from this book!

"*Is* he mad, Roger?" She looked fully at him.

The young man rose and wandered over to the French windows. He leaned against the frame, looking out. "They say he must be, but I don't believe it."

He spoke with more emotion than she thought him capable of, and she could not see his face in the parting of a shadow. She poured a fresh cup of tea and held it out to him. "You might feel better drinking this. Or would you like a brandy?"

"Tea will do." Roger took the cup with steady hands. "I hardly know where to begin."

"Why not with this grave matter you referred to in your note?" she suggested.

He took his place in the chair again. "My uncle died in January. Harland hasn't spoken a word since."

"Hasn't spoken or won't speak?"

"I don't know," Roger said. "And it isn't just his speech. He barely moves unless you move him, and even then, he stays in that position until he's moved again. Do you know chess?" he suddenly asked.

"I never learned the game," she answered.

"Harland is like the pawn on a chessboard," said Roger. "One can move him forward but no more, and he can't move himself anywhere at all."

"He has no will of his own," Vivian ventured.

"An apt punishment," Roger said with a little snicker. "You and I know about his past puppet-mastering. Now he himself is the puppet."

"And you're his puppet master," Vivian said, looking hard at him.

He looked at the spot on the coffee table again. "What would you have me do, leave him to rot alone in the castle? We are, after all, family."

"I wasn't criticizing you, Roger," she said. "I think it's admirable."

He grimaced. "Don't make a martyr out of me, Vivian. I'm paying back a debt I owe to Uncle Joseph. He took me in when my mother died and my father couldn't care for me, and he did it willingly. I couldn't hardly abandon his son in this state, can I?"

"No, you couldn't," she agreed.

"I thought maybe I could help him," he said. "A familiar face, you know. But he won't respond to me." He peered at her. "You're the only one he's responded to so far."

"I would hardly call recognizing a fable in a book a response," she remarked.

"The specialist we went saw in the city before you met us said any spontaneous response is a hopeful sign." He leaned forward and took her hand. "You see now why I say you're our last hope."

Will Vivian agree to help Harland Stevens a dark shadow from her past? You can find out by purchasing a copy of *Dandelions* at your favorite online bookstore at this link: https://tammayauthor.com/books-2/waxwood-series/ dandelionswaxwood-series-book-4.

How about that cool freebie I promised you? If you're into

historical cozy mysteries featuring strong women who don't let society's rules about female behavior stop them from doing what they want, I urge you to check out the Adele Gossling Mysteries! Read on for how to get hold of the series' free novella, *The Missing Ruby Necklace*.

When a jewel and a girl go missing on New Year's Eve...

Eleanor McCarthy, a lovely though somewhat flighty debutante, has graced the tiny town of Arrojo, California, with her presence. One of Arrojo's prominent ladies throws a New Year's Eve shindig to introduce her to Arrojo's high society — whatever little of it there is. Naturally, the daughter and son of one of San

Francisco's influential lawyers, Adele and Jackson Gossling, are invited.

But screams replace popping champagne corks when Eleanor's priceless ruby necklace is discovered missing. And soon, so is Eleanor!

In this historical cozy mystery set in the early 20th century, follow Adele Gossling, stationary store owner and amateur sleuth, and her clairvoyant sidekick Nin Branch as they search for a ruby necklace that may or may not have been stolen and a young woman who may or may not have run away.

Want to read an excerpt from this book? I got you covered! Turn the page.

"Coffee!" Miss McCarthy laughed. "Heavens, no! I haven't had my first taste of champagne yet." She flung her hand out to her brother. "Bring me a bottle of champagne, my good man."

"I don't mind," he said.

Before he could saunter out the door, Mrs. Abberton jumped up. "I'll get it."

"I really think we ought to get coffee," Mr. Abberton mumbled.

"She wants champagne," Mrs. Abberton was almost stern. "It's a celebration, after all!" She practically fled from the room.

Adele followed her and caught her arm. She spoke in a soft tone. "Mrs. Abberton, why did Miss McCarthy faint?"

"She just told you, didn't she?" The woman gave a shrill laugh. "Albert said we ought to open some windows, but it was such a windy night, I —"

"It wasn't the windows," said Adele. "Or the corset."

"Of course it was!" The woman examined some bottles on the floor. "I never could read these labels."

"You were staring at Miss McCarthy as if something that wasn't there."

"What an imagination you have, dear." The woman said.

"Miss McCarthy had her hands on her throat when she fell," Adele continued. "You kept looking at her throat."

"Nonsense," the woman hissed.

"Miss McCarthy wasn't wearing her ruby necklace," Adele declared.

Mrs. Abberton tore through a row of bottles lying on a table. One rolled onto the floor with a crack and the bubbly drink spilled across the marble. She sunk into one of the chairs. "You're too observant, Miss Gossling."

"You saw it too."

"Just before the lights went out," she said. "But Eleanor is one of those girls who gets easily flustered with her jewelry. She says it weighs her down."

"If that's true, why were you so alarmed just now?" Adele said.

"I wasn't," the woman insisted. "She locks that necklace in a box. Albert tried to persuade her to put it in our safe at the finance company, but she refused."

"That's rather unusual," Adele said.

"Eleanor's a lovely girl, but rather flighty," The woman said in a harsh tone. "I expect Celestine spoils her."

"If the necklace is missing, there might be a theft involved," Adele suggested.

Jewelry goes missing all the time. But does that mean theft? And why is Mrs. Abberton so nervous?

How can you get your hands on a copy of *The Missing Ruby Necklace*, not available in any bookstore? Simple. Go to this link: https://landing.mailerlite.com/webforms/landing/ 12u0c3. What else will you get when you get this novella? How about fun facts about women in history and true crime classic mysteries, which are just as fascinating, if not more so, as contemporary true crimes?

Writing has been Tam May's voice since the age of fourteen. She writes stories about powerful women set in the past. Her fiction gives readers a sense of justice for women, both the living and the dead. Tam's stories are set mostly around the Bay Area because she adores sourdough bread, Ghirardelli chocolate, and San Francisco history.

Tam is the author of the Adele Gossling Mysteries which take place in the early 20th century and features sassy suffragist and epistolary expert Adele Gossling whose talent for solving crimes doesn't sit well with the ideas of some people around her about women's place. Tam has also written historical fiction about women breaking loose from the confinements of their era.

Although Tam left her heart in San Francisco, she lives in the Midwest because it's cheaper. When she's not writing, she's devouring everything classic (books, films, art, music) and concocting yummy vegan dishes.

Tam May can be reached at:
WEBSITE: http://tammayauthor.com/
EMAIL: tammay70@tammayauthor.com
FACEBOOK: https://www.facebook.com/tammayauthor
INSTAGRAM: https://www.instagram.com/tammayauthor/
PINTEREST: https://www.pinterest.com/tammayauthor/

www.ingramcontent.com/pod-product-compliance
Lightning Source LLC
Chambersburg PA
CBHW021719110726

47902CB00005B/1254